Banning Santa

Mikael Carlson

WARRINGTON
PUBLISHING

DANBURY, CONNECTICUT

Banning Santa
Copyright © 2023 Warrington Publishing

WARRINGTON

Printed in the United States of America
First Edition
ISBN: 978-1-944972-33-2 (paperback)
        978-1-944972-32-5 (ebook)
        978-1-944972-34-9 (hardcover)

Book cover designed by JD&J
Edited by Mike Waitz at Sticks & Stones

Novels by Mikael Carlson:

– The Michael Bennit Series –
The iCandidate
The iCongressman
The iSpeaker
The iAmerican

– Tierra Campos Thrillers –
Justifiable Deceit
Devious Measures
Vital Targets
Revealed Secrets
Decisive Endgame

– Tierra Campos Thrillers Prequels –
Narrow Escape: The Summerville Massacre

– Watchtower Thrillers –
The Eyes of Others
The Eyes of Innocents
The Eyes of Victims
The Eyes of Addicts

– America, Inc. Saga –
The Black Swan Event
Bounded Rationality
Boiling the Ocean

– The Santa Trilogy –
Banning Santa

– The Dancing Trilogy –
The Dancing Life

For everyone who embraces the spirit and magic of Christmas

Chapter One

REPRESENTATIVE CAMILLA GUZMAN

It's beginning to look a lot like Christmas. That isn't unexpected on Black Friday. Unfortunately, it's looked like Christmas in this mall since early October. Retailers looking to get a jump on the holidays seem to start earlier and earlier. It's a shame. By the time shoppers get to December 25th, they're already tired of being merry. All the joy of the holiday has been sucked out.

Camilla strolls past the storefronts and reads the signs promising massive deals ahead of the holiday. This mall is a great place to find anything you need outside of the lumber needed to build a deck. For that, there is a pair of big box building supply stores a half mile away. Here, you get trendy boutiques, gourmet ice cream, Frappuccinos, and acres of walkable area in a climate-controlled environment. There are nearby malls for a good day of retail therapy throughout Los Angeles County. She prefers the ones in her district for obvious reasons.

The first-term congresswoman isn't shopping for Christmas yet. She isn't much of a gift-giver and always waits until a couple of weeks before the twenty-fifth to begin. The holiday was a big thing in the Guzman house while she was growing up, but gift-giving wasn't. Her parents were not anti-Christmas by any stretch of the imagination. It's that they couldn't afford it.

Camilla isn't sure how modern families manage without maxing out credit cards. With inflation rising and the costs of housing, gasoline, and medical treatments hitting all-time highs because of money-grubbing corporations, there's not much room left for buying gifts. No wonder people are miserable during the holidays. It's an unnecessary burden and unwanted pressure.

And then there's the nauseating commercialization. America has already had to deal with decorations since well before Halloween. Some stores kicked off their holiday promotions back in mid-September. There is an eagerness to celebrate, and then there is this. Businesses turning a special holiday meant for families and faith into a vehicle for financial gain makes her want to vomit.

Case in point, Santa's Village has been set up in the center mall area for a month. It's another venture that's designed to get parents to open their wallets and purses. Families pay almost fifty bucks to get a shot of their children mugging for the camera with Santa. The concept is almost as ridiculous as the long line queuing at the entrance. Santa is absent from his red velvet chair, likely getting coffee during his break. Camilla recognizes the need to do the same.

She gets her pumpkin spice latte with extra whip and mills around the mall's center court area. How anyone can stomach drinking black coffee is a mystery to her. The caffeine content of espresso makes it a glorious drink, but the taste is unbearable without added ingredients.

Camilla hoped window shopping would take her mind off things. It hasn't. It isn't an election year, but talk about next year's midterms has already begun in political circles. As a first-term congresswoman, she has no name recognition. Washed-up D-list celebrities get more written about them than she does. That dynamic has to change if she doesn't want to spend only two years in Washington.

Nothing of note is happening in any of her committees. The subcommittee she chairs was given to her as a political favor and has no real responsibilities or worthwhile mission. She is getting no recognition for the dozens of bills she has co-sponsored. Not that Americans pay any attention to that. They like drama and intrigue, which is why political scandals get so much airtime. The more a politician acts like a reality television star, the more name recognition they have. It doesn't usually matter whether it's good or bad. That's the nature of the game.

She needs to make a splash. For months, Camilla and her chief of staff have been chewing on what to do. Marcia Konstantinos has a brilliant strategic mind and is an idea factory, but it shouldn't fall solely on her to figure out a plan.

The loop of the center court area is complete, and Camilla spots Santa returning to the village to the sound of cheering children. All the kids point as they ohh and ah. The parents are pointing as well for a far different reason. Santa is staggering a little, and his iconic "ho-ho-ho" sounds a little slurred.

Camilla pulls out her phone, points it at the debacle, and presses record. Several parents do the same. It's the Internet Age, and this will be all over social media in under an hour. It looks like Santa has been hitting the bottle.

"Hey, Santa! What happened? Did you swap milk and cookies for beer and Cheetos?" a teenager sings out. "Look! Santa's hammered!"

"I'm Santa Claus!" the man slurs, staggering two steps to his right when he almost loses his balance. It sounded more like "I-ym Shanta Clos."

"Santa's an alcoholic!" the kid shouts, laughing with his friends.

Concerned parents begin to look warily at each other. It's not so much that they care, but the kids do. A couple of parents grip their children a little tighter. One father puts his daughter on his shoulders and bolts from the line. A mother does the same with a firm grasp on her toddler's hand. They're the smart ones.

"You! You're on my naughty list," Santa counters, pointing a gloved finger at the teen.

"Oh, yeah? What's my name? Could you even write it down in your condition?"

Santa has had enough. He staggers over to the teenager, pulls up, and punches the insolent kid in the face. It is an impressively well-aimed punch, considering his inebriation. The boy staggers, but drunken Santa is a far cry from Mike Tyson in his prime. His second swing misses by a country mile, causing the jolly old fat man to twist his legs into a pretzel and collapse.

The shock of watching a belligerent Santa accost a kid is wearing off. A couple of parents intervene, getting between St. Nick and his foe. That only gives the intoxicated Santa more targets. He climbs back to his feet and shoves one of the parents. His arms flail in bad karate maneuvers as two more move in.

The police rush in from both sides to assess the situation. It doesn't take them long to respond once they see what's happening. One of the cops charges from behind and tackles Santa to the ground. He jumps on the big man's back and wrenches his arms behind him. Then the cuffs come out.

The teen seems okay. He's only suffering from a red mark on his cheek and a bruised ego from being decked by an inebriated Kris Kringle. Santa doesn't appear to have any physical injuries, either. The public shaming will do him in when this incident hits news broadcasts nationwide. The lasting damage will be from the trauma the children in line experienced. Santa Claus is revered, and the spectacle of him being handcuffed and quickly led away will leave scars that may never fully heal.

"It's okay, it's okay," a harried mall manager says, arriving at the scene to reassure the crying children. "That wasn't the real Santa Claus. He was an imposter pretending to be Santa. I promise the real one is in his sleigh and on his way down from the North Pole. He should be here soon."

How the mall is planning to make that happen is anyone's guess. Maybe Santa's relief is already getting suited up. Maybe they have one on standby. Who knows? But that's hardly the problem.

Children are naïve, but they aren't stupid. They know what they saw. One of the police officers is talking to the children, confirming the manager's story and stating that they're certain that the real Santa would not approve of people behaving in this way. The real Santa will still be delivering their gifts on Christmas Day.

Lies, upon lies, all to support a lie. Maybe that's the tragedy here as Camilla ends the recording and tucks her phone into her pocket. The other problem is the one thing that isn't happening; nobody is approaching her. Not one adult has stormed over to appeal to their elected representative in Congress to take action. Nobody knows who she is. Despite all her campaigning, interviews, and press conferences, she's anonymous in her own district. That's about to change.

Camilla pulls out her cell phone and selects a number from a list of contacts. She waits as it rings once, twice, three times. Then, the call connects.

"Hello?" the frantic voice on the other end of the line asks.

"Hey, Marcia. It's me. I'm sorry to interrupt your family time."

"It's okay. We just finished dinner, and I'm trying to compel my children to do the dishes. I didn't hear the phone ringing until the last second. What can I do for you, Congresswoman?"

"I know you memorized my upcoming calendar. Please tell me we don't have any important agenda items on the subcommittee schedule."

"It's the holidays, ma'am. You know better than I that Congress isn't doing anything important for the next month. That includes your subcommittee. We don't even have a meeting scheduled."

She does know that. Americans have exceptionally short attention spans over the holidays. It's why Congress uses lame-duck sessions to pass controversial bills after their biannual elections. Few people outside the Beltway media are paying attention.

The slow news coming out of the nation's capital creates an opportunity. They will cover any story that captures attention and has a gripping storyline. Camilla thinks she has the perfect thing.

"That's about to change. I just saw something...I think I know how we can become the talk of the country. We'll discuss it when we return to D.C."

"Okay," Marcia says in an upbeat tone. "Can you at least give me a preview?"

Camilla grins. "We're going to create a Christmas miracle that guarantees my reelection."

"How?"

Camilla watches the distraught parents, police, confused mall employees, an anxious manager, and crying children huddled around Center Court. It's the perfect moment to illustrate Christmas in modern America.

"We're going to ban Santa Claus."

Chapter Two

WYATT HUFFMAN

Wyatt slows to a trot from his canter and then brings the horse to a stop. This is his favorite part of their expansive ranch. Northcentral Montana is where high plains meet the mountains, and this part of his family's property provides a beautiful view with the sun only now peeking over the trees in the east.

The morning temperature is brisk but not frigid, at least not by Big Sky standards. Despite Montana's enormous size, November is cold everywhere in the state. The average is about forty-three degrees, and it's expected only to be a shade north of that today. He's dressed for the temperature. Cold air makes him feel alive.

This is what he misses most about not being home – on a horse in the middle of a wide-open field with no one around. He can feel the horse's strength and sheer power in its movement. There is something liberating about galloping at nearly thirty miles per hour while mounted on a twelve-hundred-pound animal. Horses feel what a person feels, creating a real connection that words fail to adequately describe. For Wyatt, riding is like spending time with a best friend.

After watching the sunrise, he returns the horse to the stable, removes his saddle, and cleans him up. He earned his breakfast this morning. So did Wyatt. His stomach rumbles as he enters the two-story home he grew up in with his older brother and sister. It's already been mostly decorated for Christmas. His mama doesn't waste time.

Two inevitable things happen in the house once the Thanksgiving dishes are washed. The Huffman Ranch gets decked out in lights and garland, and his father begins his semiannual crusade against Wyatt's career choice. He doesn't look up this time as his youngest son enters the kitchen.

"I can't believe you remember how to ride," his father grumbles from the breakfast table.

"You've had me riding since the time I could walk. What makes you think I would forget?"

"They don't have no horses in Washington. Only horses' asses."

"No argument from me there," Wyatt says, pouring a cup of fresh-brewed coffee before kissing his mother on the cheek. "Good morning, Mama."

"Are you hungry?" she asks.

"Famished."

Wyatt takes a sip of the coffee. He likes it black as tar. Sugar and cream are almost anti-American. They're definitely anti-Montanan. Here, if you can't drink black coffee, you shouldn't be drinking coffee at all.

"I don't know how you deal with it, Wyatt. You ran off, got a fancy degree, and moved to Washington to hobnob with the rich and powerful. I didn't think I raised my son that way."

"Bill, stop it," his mother snaps.

"Stop what? He should be married, here working the ranch, and I should already have grandchildren. It's bad enough that his brother and sister are taking their sweet time, but at least they have real responsibilities."

Wyatt takes another long sip from his mug. This chess match has been played since he left for college. This is the now famous "grandchildren" opening. It's easy enough to defend against but dangerous in the midgame.

"Bill, you can't force your son to fall in love."

"No, I can't force him to do anything, apparently. I'm just sayin' that I'd like to see one grandchild before I die. Instead, he's in Washington pretending he's a big shot while he ruins people's lives."

The grace period Wyatt established to avoid unnecessary confrontation with his father expires. "Do you really want to do this now, Dad?"

"Nope," he says, wiping his mouth with a paper napkin. "I have to go into town. There's nothing I'm going to say that's gonna change your mind. You've made that clear enough."

His father doesn't quite storm out, but the gruff exit didn't lack drama either. It's just another stormy chapter being written about their relationship. The two men have never seen eye-to-eye and probably never will. Wyatt has seen Democrats and Republicans on the hill with warmer relationships than he shares with his father.

"He didn't mean that, Wyatt."

"You say that every time I'm home. Mama. You've been our referee since I was ten. He meant every word of it, and you know it."

She sighs. "Your father is a simple man. Montanan values."

"I'm well aware. He reminds me of it whenever we're in the same room."

"He does have a point," Wyatt's mother sings out as she clears the table.

"Please, tell me you aren't taking his side."

"Wyatt Huffman! You know better. I'm not taking anyone's side. It's just I would like to see you find a nice ladyfriend. You're not getting any younger. I was married and had you, your brother, and your sister by the time I was your age. Your brother and sister have already married and settled down. I'm just sayin'."

Twenty-six may not be old for marriage by modern standards, but in this household, it's ancient. Wyatt's older brother married last year, and his sister the prior year. Both were considered late bloomers. Bill Huffman married Bridget Kenneth when they were only nineteen. High school sweethearts getting married is not just commonplace in central Montana, but it's part of the region's DNA. Or, at least, it used to be.

"It's not like going to the market for milk, Mama. Having a meaningful relationship is easier said than done these days."

"Oh, not so hard. Boy meets girl…boy likes girl…boy dates girl….boy marries girl."

Wyatt scoffs. "It's a lot different than that. Women have changed. Relationships have changed. Everything has changed."

"It can't be *that* bad."

Wyatt raises an eyebrow as he brings the mug of java to his lips. "Trust me. It is."

"Well, I'll let it go. For now. I'm glad you made it home for Thanksgiving. I wish we could see you more often."

He wishes the same. His work is on Capitol Hill, and the cross-country flight takes around six hours, depending on the layover. And there is always a layover. Nobody flies directly to Montana from the other side of the country. Besides, the more often he's home, the more snarky comments he hears from his father. So, there's that.

"Me, too, Mom. I'll be back home for Christmas. Promise."

"I know how much you love the holidays. That hasn't changed, has it?"

"That will never change," Wyatt says as he hugs her. "At least, not for me."

His mother is a saint. She also knows how to give a proper hug. It ranks somewhere between being suffocated by a bear and squeezed by a boa constrictor. What it really means is that she loves him and will miss him when he goes.

"When do you leave?"

"In a couple of hours. I need to get back before Congress comes back into session on Tuesday."

"Make sure you catch up with your brother and sister before you leave. They should be back at any time."

"I will."

Wyatt heads upstairs to pack his things. Thanksgiving wasn't as dramatic as he feared. He is looking forward to returning to work, though. At this point in the year, there isn't much going on. Despite how Americans think about them, politicians are people, too. They want time off to enjoy the holidays. Wyatt is looking forward to a few drama-free weeks before he needs to go another five rounds with his father.

Chapter Three

STOWE BESSETTE

The sun's rays pour through the window and land on her face like they were aimed there on purpose. Stowe's eyes begin to open, and she shields them against the bright sunlight that interrupted her dream. She half rolls over and checks the time on the small digital alarm clock perched on her nightstand. Nine a.m. She rolls over and buries her head in the pillow.

Stowe was hoping to sleep in a little longer. She's a natural morning person, but not having to jump out of bed and get on with the day's activities is a rare treat. That's her thinking, and her grandparents don't share it. If she stays in bed any longer, they will call fire rescue to come to the cabin and check if she's still alive. Is that necessary? No. Is it overboard? Yes. Would they do it to humiliate her for sleeping in? Absolutely.

Opting not to see burly firefighters filing into her bedroom while she's dressed in pajamas, Stowe climbs out of bed and looks in the long floor mirror in the corner of her bedroom. If "hot mess" needed a picture next to the definition, this would fit. She toys with the mop of raven-black hair on her head. She's a complete train wreck.

She ties the stringy mop into a ponytail, brushes her teeth, and changes into a sweatshirt and yoga pants. She will fix the mess before heading to the airport for her evening flight to Washington. Until then, she'd like to enjoy the last vestiges of this holiday break from the Beltway rat race.

Stowe has a death grip on the rail as she heads downstairs for coffee. Her grandparents make the best brew in all of Vermont. It's so good, they should open a shop and share it with the world. Cream and sugar were once required additives for her iced coffees. After college, because of her grandparents' brew, she developed a taste for it the way it should be drunk – steaming hot and jet black.

"Good morning, Nana, PopPop."

"There is our beautiful granddaughter," her grandmother announces from the table.

Stowe is beginning to think Nana may be going blind.

"We were wondering if you sleepwalked out the front door and froze to death in the mountains last night," her grandfather says, staring over his reading glasses after breaking away from his most recent paperback novel.

That would be tragic. Part of the Appalachian Mountain chain, the Green Mountains extend north to south for two hundred fifty miles through the center of Vermont. Their scenic beauty led to the construction of ski resorts and compelled

Stowe's grandparents to build this cabin. Despite their majestic views and wonderous nature, they can be deadly. Getting lost among the peaks is a death sentence, especially in November when temperatures average in the forties during the day. It's much colder at night.

"No, I was taking one of the five days I can manage per year to sleep past eight in the morning." Stowe thinks about that for a fleeting moment. "Or seven. Or six."

"You work too hard," her grandfather grumbles.

"You know, that may be the first time in recorded history anyone from your generation said that to someone from mine."

PopPop lets out a sharp laugh. "True dat."

"True dat? Really, PopPop?"

"What? Isn't that what the kids say these days?"

Stowe shakes her head as her grandmother rolls her eyes. Her grandparents have the ultimate love story. It wasn't the mushy love at first sight kind in romance novels, but they built a relationship that has endured for decades. There were good times and bad, like the cold, snowy night when her parents were killed. But they place their love of each other before all else, and it's inspiring. It's also not realistic in today's culture.

"We worry about you, sweetheart," Nana sings out from the kitchen. "All you do is work. You don't have any fun."

"You don't have a boyfriend, either."

"PopPop! Behave yourself," her grandmother scolds, giving him a nasty look.

"What? It's true."

"What your grandfather is trying to say is that we want you to find someone you can share your life with."

"I do have someone. The two of you."

The truth is that Stowe couldn't imagine life without them. They are all she has known for the majority of her life. Dying is inevitable. She realizes that. But it's not something she is remotely willing to deal with and hopes not to for a long time.

"Honey, we're not immortal. We won't be here forever."

"Speak for yourself," PopPop says. "I plan on living forever."

"Coming from the man who can't remember what he just had for breakfast."

"It was eggs, bacon, and pancakes," he mumbles.

Nana smirks before turning to Stowe. "We just want you to be happy, dear."

"I am happy."

She takes her granddaughter's face in her hands. "Are you? When was the last time you had a serious relationship?"

"Nana, men...they aren't like PopPop. Or my father. They're different now."

"Are they? Or are you not looking in the right places?"

Stowe sips her coffee in silence. Part of it is her reflecting on what her grandmother said. A bigger part is her trying to disengage from the conversation because she doesn't want to discuss her love life. Or, more specifically, her lack of one. Growing quiet when she no longer wants to talk about a topic is something Stowe has done since she was a child. That's how Nana quickly picks up on the signal. Grandparents know everything.

"I don't mean to be pushy."

"Yes, she does," PopPop says, turning in his chair. "I speak from experience."

"Stowe, just promise me you won't sacrifice a chance for love because of your career. And never lose faith that you will find *your* person. You'll miss your chance when it arrives."

There is nothing wiser than the advice of a grandparent. Even though they were her guardians as Stowe grew up, they always presented options and never forced decisions on her. She got to make the choices but was also forced to face the consequences. It made her an independent young woman and showed her the value of being open-minded. About most things, at least. Dating isn't one of them.

"Yeah, why give up on the chance to nag someone for fifty years," PopPop adds.

"Be quiet and clean your breakfast plate," Nana orders him. "This isn't a B & B."

"See? Nagging."

Her grandmother hugs her. "We're going to miss you."

"I'll miss you, too, but I'll see you in a few weeks during the holiday recess."

"I know. And we'll make sure the cabin is fully decorated when you come back."

They have always done the holidays right. Halloween isn't a big thing here. Trick-or-treaters won't shlep up their long, steep driveway for a bite-sized Snickers bar. However, from Thanksgiving through New Year's, it's game on. Nana will drive PopPop to the edge of insanity as he moves all the boxes of ornaments, garland, lights, and décor up from storage. And there are *a lot* of boxes.

"Thank you. There's nothing like Christmas in Vermont. I love you."

"I love you, too. Now, what do you want for breakfast?"

Stowe looks around the kitchen. "Eggs, bacon, and pancakes sounds nice. That way, you can reuse the pans."

"Not really," Nana says with a devilish smile. "Mr. Immortal over there had blueberry muffins, not pancakes."

Chapter Four

REPRESENTATIVE JOHN KNUTSON

One of the best pieces of advice in the history of man is that one should stop and appreciate the moment. John Knutson stops in front of the Longworth House Office Building to do precisely that. It's not that the building itself is extraordinary. The structure features a neoclassical revival architectural style popular in 20th-century Washington. The white marble façade rests on a pink granite base, and the five porticoes of ionic columns wrap around the building's exterior. The principal portico faces the Capitol Building and is topped by a large pediment, much like the one on the north side of the White House.

No, the magic isn't the building itself – it's that he works in it. People decry politicians all the time. Americans making jokes at the expense of their elected leaders is ingrained in the national DNA. But despite being hated by two thirds of the country, there is no honor that John can imagine greater than representing the people of his district in the U.S. House of Representatives. In a town filled with opportunists and power-thirsty bureaucrats, he still believes in the miracle that is the United States of America. That's especially true as Christmas approaches, which is his absolute favorite time of the year.

John makes his way into the building and heads upstairs to his office. Each suite in the building has three rooms to accommodate elected representatives and their staff. He takes a moment to walk through the office, saying hello to everyone. Most of his people returned yesterday to prepare for the final sessions before Christmas, and apparently, begin spread a little Christmas cheer.

"Good morning, Congressman," his chief of staff says, greeting him in the outer office.

"Good morning, Cam. How was your Thanksgiving?"

"Fantastic. My mother overcooked the turkey, the stuffing was dry enough to soak up the Atlantic Ocean, and my nieces are little terrors. I'm actually happy to be back at work in D.C. Yours?"

"Better than that, apparently. I see everyone has been busy."

The office elves have been hard at work. Knutson made a sizable investment in high-end office decorations after he was elected to Congress. They pack them well and store them in a climate-controlled storage space in the city. He takes pride in decorating his office for the holidays, and few peers match his love of Christmas decorations.

Representative Angela Pratt came closest last year and promised to up her game to overtake him this Christmas. John isn't about to let that happen.

"They brought the boxes up to Capitol Hill yesterday and got to it this morning. Your love of Christmas is infectious. I didn't even have to ask them."

Cameron Alcott is the only staff member who isn't a native Montanan. He was born and raised in Chicago's South Side, managed to graduate from the University of Chicago, and didn't know a thing about the state until passing through it on a post-graduation road trip. After a week, he was hooked and immediately moved to Helena to work at the state house. That's where John found him toiling away and invited him to join the staff.

That was six years ago. Since then, Cam has risen through the ranks to become his chief of staff. He's an excellent manager, has a brilliant political mind, and excels at developing legislative and political strategies. It's rare to find someone with all three of those skill sets.

"Oh, Wyatt from legislative affairs asked me to give you this. It's the upcoming Cultural Commerce Subcommittee calendar. You should check out the events planned for next week."

John scans the sheet of paper. It doesn't take him long to find what Cam pointed out. His brow furrows as he digests the information.

"Hearings? This late in the year? Has Camilla Guzman taken leave of her senses?"

"The timing is more appropriate than you think, sir. Keep reading."

John has a sudden urge to sit down. "A resolution to ban depictions of Santa Claus in public spaces? Is she serious about this?"

"She's introducing the bill this morning and already convinced the speaker to immediately refer it to the subcommittee."

"I wonder what she promised in return," the congressman moans.

"A vote on something, no doubt."

Horse-trading is how Washington works. There is little compromise on bills without it. Votes are the currency of this realm, and trading support for something a colleague wants is the easiest way to procure support for something you want. If Americans knew how Congress really operates, they would be perpetually nauseated. The days of high-minded ideals and rational debate are long over.

John sits at his desk and rereads what little information is on the proposal. "I can't believe she wants to ban Santa Claus. The people in this country have collectively lost their minds."

"It gets worse. Camilla already put together an impressive list of co-sponsors. She must have worked the phones all weekend and called her staff into the office early to draft it."

John leans back in his chair. "This has to do with that viral Black Friday video, right? The one with the drunk Santa smacking around a teenager before getting leveled by police?"

"Safe bet. Rumor has it that Guzman was standing twenty feet away."

The congressman rubs his chin. "Thoughts?"

"Well, it could be Guzman overreacting, and it will likely amount to nothing. She could be pushing the bill and having hearings to show the people Congress is doing something. If Americans don't care, it will get ignored by the media."

"Or?"

"Or, a media starving for stories will make it one to boost their ratings and clickthrough rate. Social media could latch on and amplify the message, causing the hearings to get traction. The viral sharing combined with a mainstream media circus would be a disaster just in time for the eggnog."

The congressman sighs. "Is anyone on the hill taking this seriously?"

"Not yet. Guzman scheduled a press conference for later today. The media reaction will tell the tale. The pundits will either laugh at her, support her, or question her sanity."

Whether an issue, initiative, or policy action makes it to the American consciousness is a crap shoot. It can depend on the mood of the country, the desperation of the media, or just plain dumb luck. It could also be a combination of those three things. The media likes a spectacle because Americans crave drama despite pleading otherwise. This may fit the bill, especially in December.

"Quietly reach out to our party members on the committee. Find out what their thoughts are. When Blackburn calls, take his temperature about how he wants to play this. Send Wyatt over to the Ford Building and have him ask around. I want to see if the committee staff knows anything about this."

"Okay, I'll make it happen," Cam confirms. "What are you going to do?"

The congressman checks his watch. "My job, and then I'm going to look for allies."

"Do you really think we'll need them?"

"You know, I've been in politics since I was student body president in college. Over that time, I've learned that it's better to plan for the worst and be pleasantly surprised than hope for the best and be wrong."

He nods. "I'll let you know what I find."

Cam exits the office, leaving the congressman to mull over this latest development. He has to get to the House floor, but it doesn't sound like this session will be business as usual. He was looking forward to a light schedule that's now poised to get far busier.

"An assault on Christmas before the holidays," John mumbles as he stares at the paper. "No wonder everyone in this country is miserable. We suck the fun out of everything."

Chapter Five

REPRESENTATIVE CAMILLA GUZMAN

All laws begin as simple ideas. From there, it's far more complicated than School House Rock's "I'm Just a Bill" song makes it out to be. Camilla has already laid the groundwork for the hearings. A lot of things had to happen fast, including bringing her legislative team in to draft the text over the weekend. It was a rush job, but the hard work will be done in the full committee anyway.

Now, it falls on her. Any member of the House of Representatives may introduce a bill at any time while in session. After signing it and finding co-sponsors, she starts the process by placing the bill in a hopper in the House chamber. The clerk will assign the measure a legislative number, and the speaker will refer it to the appropriate committee for study and referral. In this case, it will go to the Energy and Commerce Committee and be referred to her subcommittee.

Most Americans don't know that the action taken by committees is the most important phase of the legislative process. They provide consideration to proposed legislation, and their hearings typically offer the best opportunity to be heard. Bills are referred to the committee with jurisdiction over the affected area, and it took little effort to convince the speaker that this measure belonged in her subcommittee.

"You've been busy, Camilla," Representative Aymos Blackburn says after he comes up alongside her outside the chamber.

The subcommittee minority leader rarely speaks to her outside of their sessions. Night and day have more in common than these two elected representatives do. There is very little reason for them to ever have a conversation.

"Are you about to chide me about the hearings?"

"I was a little surprised at them," Blackburn admits, acting like a typical politician by not answering the question.

"I don't need a lecture from your pulpit about Santa Claus."

"You aren't going to get one. I'm here to offer my help."

That stops the congresswoman cold. Aymos Blackburn was a notorious preacher in Alabama before running for Congress. Guzman doesn't characterize herself as overly religious. That's one of their *many* differences. An offer of help from him on anything is unprecedented.

"Say that again. I don't think I heard you right."

"To say we have our differences is an exercise in understatement, Camilla. But we may have found something we actually agree on."

"Wait. Since when does a religious man come out against Christmas?"

"I'm not. I'm against the commercialization of Christmas. And that commercialization is driven by jolly ol' Saint Nick. He's not the embodiment of the holiday. He's a false idol that's usurped the miracle of December 25th. Everybody thinks Christmas is about gifts. Nobody celebrates the birth of Jesus Christ."

"You know that I'm not religious."

"I'm not asking you to be. I'm saying that we share the same goal, even if it's for different reasons."

This could be a setup. Blackburn is nothing if not ambitious, even for a man who purports to represent his constituents, this country, and God, not necessarily in that order. Feigning support for something like this would be a shrewd political tactic. Unless it isn't a feint. She has heard his speeches about the wasteland secular America has become as more and more people eschew the word of God. This may be something he can get behind.

"People are going to think this bill is a publicity stunt."

"Good. That means they'll tune in. If we can capture the public's attention, we can convince people we're right. If public support builds, we can refer this to the committee for their consideration."

The congresswoman's eyes narrow. "You're serious about this."

"I know you haven't been here long, Camilla. If our roles were reversed, I would be equally skeptical. Political cooperation with the opposition has the modern relevance of horse-drawn carriages and the milkman. But you know me. I don't mince words."

"That's true."

"If we do this right, we can garner the needed attention. If we do it together, it may bring lasting change to the country."

"And if it goes wrong?"

"We started a national conversation. It's a win-win."

Camilla presses her lips together. She never thought about it in those terms. As much as she believes in the potential result, at its core, it is a stunt to garner name recognition. It could be much more with a prominent man like Aymos on her team.

"I'm assuming you have some thoughts on people to testify at the hearings?"

He withdraws a tri-folded piece of paper from his pocket and hands it to her.

"Just a few. These people will testify from a religious and cultural perspective. We can pare it down and add the ones you're thinking about to attack from a socioeconomic and psychological angle."

Camilla looks down at the paper, expecting it to be a Who's Who of crazy nutjobs. It isn't. The names she recognizes are well-respected theologians, sociologists, and anthropology experts. This isn't a joke. Their bona fides would be difficult to dispute. Aymos put some thought into creating this list.

"I'm holding a press conference this afternoon," she says, tucking the paper into her leather portfolio.

"I saw it on the schedule. I would be honored to stand next to you, provided you pledge to keep the message and the hearings' goal aligned with what you proposed in the bill."

Camilla nods. "We should coordinate beforehand."

"I will free up whatever time you need."

"Very well. My staff will be in touch. Until then, Congressman."

"Ma'am," Blackburn says, nodding.

He moves off and joins his chief of staff, who is waiting a respectful distance away. There is no deception in the man's body language. If this is a political trap, it's a good one. There is only one way to find out. It's damn the torpedoes, full speed ahead. If it blows up in her face, at least it will get reported by the pundits. That's better than being ignored.

Chapter Six

WYATT HUFFMAN

The press conference was the usual affair on Capitol Hill. There are several a day, and most don't get much attention. Usually, something controversial or a response to a significant event like a mass shooting or a looming government shutdown earns the coverage. It takes a lot to capture American attention in the Information Age. There's too much competition and indifference. People have their own problems. They don't obsess over what happens in Washington.

That makes politicians more desperate to get in front of cameras. The most efficient way to do that is to be controversial or inflammatory. The politicians who are household names on both sides of the aisle have mastered that craft. Guzman and Blackburn are trying to reach that elite level.

The press conference was held in the Energy and Commerce Committee room in the Rayburn House Office Building. The subcommittee typically meets in a different chamber, but the publicity this will likely garner may see it move here. At least, that's what Wyatt is guessing Representatives Guzman and Blackburn are hoping for.

Reporters flock to the exits once the press conference concludes. They have dates with their laptops to write articles, and cameramen have videos to submit. Wyatt needs to get back to the office to report to the congressman. He will want the highlights – not of the conference itself as he can see it on C-SPAN, but of the reporters' personal reactions to the announcement.

The building's corridors are wide, and even the crush of people leaving doesn't make them feel cramped or crowded. Wyatt stops dead when a reporter, rushing back to his cubicle, cuts in front of him. Typical.

Someone crashes into Wyatt from behind, knocking him off-balance. He grabs the wall to steady himself before turning to see who rammed into him. The crash took the woman by surprise as well. Papers scatter, and her bag spills as she crashes to the ground. When she looks up, he recognizes her almost immediately.

Stowe Bessette is Representative Angela Pratt's legislative aide. She's a beautiful woman with the personality of a rattlesnake. He had hoped the last time they interacted was the last. Wyatt can't remember doing anything to offend her other than being a member of the opposing party. That wouldn't have been enough to warrant getting treated with disdain twenty years ago. Oh, how times have changed.

"Watch where you're going, you imbecile!" she shrieks from the ground.

Wyatt frowns. First, getting rear-ended in a car is the fault of the trail driver. This is the equivalent of getting yelled at by someone who slammed into you at a red light. Second, calling him names just brought this to a new level. Times may have changed, but Stowe's personality hasn't. That's too bad.

"Uh, you ran into me," he says, offering her a hand.

"I don't need your help."

Stowe climbs to her feet, which is no easy feat to do gracefully in three-inch high heels and a skirt.

"Are you okay?"

"I'm fine," she snaps, brushing herself off.

Wyatt scoffs and starts to help collect her papers and the other items that spilled out of her bag.

"I said I don't need your help! I'm more than capable of picking this up myself."

"I'm not helping because I think you're incapable. I'm helping because—"

"Oh, how chivalrous. My white knight has arrived!"

"It's called courtesy. You know, the polite behavior people are supposed to exhibit with each other in a civilized society."

Stowe rolls her eyes. "I'm sorry, while you were busy mansplaining the definition of courtesy, I was trying to figure out how you thought I cared for an explanation."

Wyatt actually likes sarcasm. He grew up on a ranch in Montana. Survival meant growing a thick skin and learning to take it before you could dish it out. His skin is as tough as leather, but this woman has gotten under it.

"Okay. Please cancel my subscription because I don't need your issues. I'm only trying to be polite."

Stowe stops and stares up at him. "A polite man wouldn't have knocked me over in the first place. Unless you have an invisible friend you plan on blaming, which wouldn't surprise me."

"Again, you ran into me," Wyatt says, turning his head to talk to nobody standing beside him. "What's that? Oh, yeah. My invisible friend thinks you desperately need to see a therapist."

"If you're going to be an ass, at least you could go around with Juan Valdez delivering sacks of coffee to people."

Wyatt can't help but smirk. That was actually clever. Stowe may be a manhater, but she's a witty one.

"It's okay if you don't like me. Not everyone has good taste."

Stowe scoffs. "Are you kidding? You're my favorite person…besides every other person I've ever met. I'm thrilled to hear you aren't ashamed of who you are. I guess that's your parents' job."

Wyatt laughs. The comment hits closer to home than this Karen will ever know. If she wants to take the gloves off, she won't like what happens next. Courtesy and politeness only go so far.

"What's so funny?"

"Nothing. I only envy the people who have never met you."

Stowe crosses her arms and glares at Wyatt. "Is that so?"

"Absolutely. I mean, you're beautiful…so long as someone puts a paper bag over your personality."

"Oh, you think you're *so* clever."

"Sarcasm is my natural defense against stupidity."

She sneers. "Oh, so now I'm stupid?"

"Nah. I'm sure you're very bright. Unfortunately, you'd fail a personality test."

"Very clever, Mr. Huffman. I'm sure that witty humor helped you go far. Too bad you didn't stay there."

"And miss this charming interaction? There's no place I'd rather be."

Stowe collects the remainder of her things and clutches them in her arms. If looks could kill, his boss would be making his funeral arrangements. This woman is *pissed*. Time for one last jab.

"It's been lovely seeing you again, Stowe."

"I never forget a face, Wyatt," she says with a fake smile plastered on her face. "I'll gladly make an exception in your case."

She storms off after firing the parting shot. Wyatt is tempted to call out after her with a final insult but lets it go. Plenty of reporters are still around, and the last thing he needs is an insult he hurls at a woman going viral on YouTube. It doesn't matter how contemptible that woman is. Nobody ever asks what transpired before the cameras came out and started recording.

"Well, that was fun," he mumbles, thrilled that he doesn't have to work with her. A prison sentence would be more fun.

Chapter Seven

STOWE BESSETTE

Stowe returns to the office and slams her portfolio down on her desk. She collapses into her chair. It's a dramatic entrance, and most other staffers look warily past their computer screens before averting their eyes. They've seen her like this before and know to steer clear.

Stowe is normally quiet and reserved. That behavior doesn't apply when she's angry. When someone gets under her skin, she wears her heart on her sleeve and does nothing to mask her emotions. That typically means everyone in the office gives her space to collect her thoughts and simmer down. Well, almost everyone. One person can be counted on to charge into the lioness's den.

"Well, this can't be good," Mandy says, noticing the violent outburst and deciding to sit on the desk's corner. "What gives?"

"I just got back from Guzman's press conference," Stowe says, practically spitting.

It wasn't a press conference. It was a declaration of war against Stowe's favorite holiday and everything that makes it special. Santa Claus is more than a jolly man in a red suit delivering gifts. He's emblematic of a point on the calendar where everyone is a little more joyous and polite to each other. Or, at least, they are in her idyllic world.

"Ah, the announcement that Santa Claus is evil and belongs next to the swastika and Confederate flag in the pantheon of hate symbols."

"The battle flag of the Army of Northern Virginia, but whatever. Yes, that press conference."

"I can see why a woman who binge-watches Hallmark Christmas movies and sings carols in the office before Thanksgiving would have a problem with that."

"Fair warning, it's not the only reason I'm pissed," Stowe advises, knowing her friend will eventually drag the truth out of her. "I ran into that jackass again."

"Oh, this sounds like a good piece of Capitol Hill gossip. Who was it? Ryan? Blake? No, wait, you think they're idiots. Then again, you think most men are idiots, and they don't get you flustered like this. That means...it has to be Wyatt Huffman from Knutson's staff."

Stowe gives her an incredulous look and shakes her head. "You're a little creepy."

"I knew it!" Mandy says, slapping her knee. "Ohh, that man is a tall drink of water."

Amanda Derringer is from a wealthy Greenwich, Connecticut family. Despite endless partying, she somehow graduated college and found work in political circles. Stowe has no idea how Mandy ended up in Vermont or why the debutante has a low-paying job on the congresswoman's staff, considering her family's wealth. But she's here and is very good at her job.

They started working for Congresswoman Pratt around the same time and became fast friends. In many respects, they are complete opposites. Stowe likes to read and is content being alone with a bottle of wine and a good book. Mandy is a social butterfly who is at her best in a party dress with a drink in her hand. She's also the Capitol Hill queen of gossip. She knows more about the people in Congress and their staff than the FBI does.

"What would your girlfriend say if she heard you talk like that?"

"Psssh. She'd probably agree."

"You're weird."

Mandy waves a dismissive hand. "Hey, just because I don't climb mountains doesn't mean I can't stand back and admire their beauty."

"Whatever."

"Oh, come on. You may despise Wyatt, but there's no denying he's gorgeous…and rugged. I've always thought he has a little crush on you."

"No."

"Honey, you need to open yourself up to possibilities."

Stowe rolls her eyes. "You're starting to sound like my grandparents."

"Maybe they have a point," Mandy argues.

"No, they don't have a point. None at all. When I ever open up to dating anyone in this town, I promise it won't be someone like Wyatt Huffman. He's completely insufferable."

Mandy has made it her mission to find Stowe a husband. She's even more persistent than her grandparents, even though she has a far better understanding of how shallow the dating pool is. That's why she jumped out of the water a long time ago.

"Well, in that case, you can always come and play for our team."

"I would, but the only thing more annoying than the thought of dating a man is dating another woman. No offense."

"None taken. Bitches be crazy," Mandy says with a playful laugh.

"Stowe?" one of the guys in the office gingerly says, getting her attention as he cocks a thumb over his shoulder. "The congresswoman would like to see you about the press conference."

"Okay. Thanks."

"You have work, so let me leave you with this. Maybe you find Wyatt annoying because he's the male version of you."

"Charming and intelligent?"

"I was thinking stubborn and unrelenting."

Stowe frowns. "Why am I friends with you again?"

Mandy smiles before patting her friend on the shoulder. "Because I tell it like it is, honey. Finding someone who speaks the truth in this town is like catching Santa Claus delivering your gifts on Christmas Eve. No matter how hard you try, it never happens."

Chapter Eight

REPRESENTATIVE JOHN KNUTSON

There are many misconceptions the American people have about Congress. They may only work fewer than half of the days in any given year, but those only account for "legislative days" when the House or Senate is in session. The "do-nothing Congress" can be a jab at the inability of lawmakers to reach a consensus on legislation, but it also can reference how little they are perceived to work. With a base salary just south of two hundred thousand dollars, there is a natural demand for Congress to show something for the money.

People often discount the work with constituents, fundraising, events, and meetings with colleagues. A legislative day in the U.S. House of Representatives can span more than twenty-four hours and only ends when a session is adjourned. A recess marks a temporary break in proceedings. They can be within the same day, overnight, for a weekend, or for several days. Recesses are often used instead of an adjournment, which is a more formal close of proceedings.

The legislative days will become shorter the closer the country gets to Christmas. With today's session already in recess, John decides to drop in on an old adversary. Or frenemy. Or occasional ally. Most of all, she's a friend.

Angela Pratt has an office in the same building, and he has visited here countless times before. Her staff may not be warm and friendly to him, but they are far less hostile than they usually are to a member of the opposite party. Such is the state of politics in modern America.

"Why are you here arguing with my staff, John?" Angela asks, stepping out of her office to interrupt a quick debate with her chief of staff. "Come argue with me instead."

It was more of an order that was barked than a genteel request. Angela gestures him into her inner office and shuts the door. She turns and smiles.

"I think you enjoy badgering my staff."

"I'm just keeping up the illusion. We're supposed to hate each other, remember?"

In public, that's the perception. Even the trusted members of their respective staffs don't know the depth of their friendship. They have to keep it that way. The ideological divide has become that deep and that inflexible.

Angela smiles. "How was your Thanksgiving?"

"Peaceful. Yours?"

"Mountainesque. Lots of fun with family, a nice fire in the fire pit, and then I came back to this," the congresswoman says, holding up the subcommittee hearing schedule.

"Then you know why I'm here making your staff cry using logic and facts. Has your party lost its mind?"

"Guzman may be auditioning for a role as the Grinch, but she wasn't standing alone on that podium."

"Aymos Blackburn," John says with a sigh.

"I seriously didn't expect a reverend to come out against Christmas. Does hypocrisy come naturally in your party, or do you all attend a seminar?"

John and Angela are the Romeo and Juliet of the U.S. House of Representatives, although not in a romantic way. They are star-crossed friends. The two parties have been warped and jaded by decades of partisan politics, and congenial friendships between party members on opposite sides of the divide have been snuffed out by leadership.

The playful banter between them has always been just that. They may not agree on policy issues, but they genuinely like each other as people and don't buy into the narrative that people who disagree with you are enemies who need to be defeated.

"I wish I could blame it on hypocrisy. Aymos makes Jonathan Edwards look like a heathen. In his mind, Santa Claus gets in the way of worshiping Jesus Christ. He hates the Easter Bunny, too."

Edwards is one of the most recognized participants and defenders of the First Great Awakening. He has an astonishing literary output spanning seventy-three volumes in Yale's online collection, professing a God-centered worldview that has shaped the American pursuit of God's glory for centuries.

"It sounds almost like you're defending him."

"No. I just understand Aymos. I'm also from Montana, and my constituents will run me out of Congress if a committee I sit on advances a resolution to ban depictions of Santa Claus in public spaces."

"How do you think I feel? I'm a black woman representing a district in the third whitest state in America. I've lost count of how many Hallmark Christmas movies are set in Vermont. My constituents don't just celebrate Christmas – they're fanatical about it. I can't let this move forward on my watch."

"Good. Then, we're in agreement?"

She cocks her head. "You want to combine forces to fight this?"

"Guzman and Blackburn have their alliance. We need to form ours. That bill can't make it out of the subcommittee. We need to draw a line in the sand."

Angela nods. "Okay. Don't think for a moment that I don't feel dirty doing this. It's awkward on so many levels."

"You don't need to tell me. I abhor the idea of not pretending I hate your guts," John says with a smile. "Let's get our staff together tomorrow and sort this out."

"Bring bandages. They're liable to try to kill each other if we're late and they get there before we do."

Chapter Nine

REPRESENTATIVE CAMILLA GUZMAN

Media exposure is gold in political circles. Those who get it want more, and those who don't get reporters' attention crave it like a heroin addict looking for a fix. Camilla didn't expect her press conference to do more than raise eyebrows. If she was lucky, she thought a mention or two on the cable news channels and a short write-up in *The New York Times* or *The Washington Post* was possible.

She got more than she bargained for. A prime-time cable news show booker called the office and requested a live interview. Camilla decided to double down and asked if they wanted Aymos Blackburn to join her. Then, the salivating began.

Bipartisanship is as good as dead in America. It doesn't matter when that trend started. Regardless of who was in charge of Congress or sitting at the Resolute Desk in the Oval Office, the desire to work with the opposition waned until it became extinct. Thus, the appeal. Camilla doing an interview alongside Aymos Blackburn is a ratings boon.

"We're going live in fifteen seconds," a floor producer announces.

The anchor is a few hundred miles away from Washington. Since Congress is in session, neither Camilla nor Aymos could make the trip for the interview. Instead, they will be interviewed remotely in the network's Washington studio.

"There was a surprising development on Capitol Hill today when a bill was introduced by Congresswoman Camilla Guzman to ban public depictions of Santa Claus in public spaces, calling it a mental health hazard. The proposed legislation was met with consternation from both major political parties, but the congresswoman seems to have some bipartisan support. One of the bill's co-sponsors and key supporters is Congressman Aymos Blackburn, who has raised eyebrows even within his own party.

"To discuss the bill and the hearings scheduled in the Cultural Commerce Subcommittee next week, we are joined by Representatives Camilla Guzman and Aymos Blackburn from our Washington studio. Good evening to both of you."

"Good evening."

"Thank you for having us, Walt."

"We should probably start with the million-dollar question: What did Santa Claus ever do to you to deserve this?"

"Nothing," Camilla deadpans.

"Nothing?"

"The true story of Santa Claus begins with Nicholas, who was born during the third century in Asia Minor —now modern-day Turkey. He secretly did many kind and generous deeds, expecting nothing in return. That's not the problem. It's what we've turned him into."

"By that, you mean a symbol of commercialism?"

"*Rampant* commercialism. It's not about the spirit of giving that Santa embodies. Now it's about the gift. There is a cost to that, and it's more than many can bear."

"Congressman Blackburn, I understand your colleague's perspective, but why did you sign onto this? It can't be because you object to the commercialism of Christmas?"

"That is part of it, yes. Congresswoman Guzman brings up a fair point worthy of further discussion. As a reverend, my objections are more religious in nature. Christmas is a holiday that celebrates the birth of Jesus Christ. We are losing sight of that in this country."

"You disagree with the notion that Christmas is a secular holiday?"

"I believe any devout Christian would be horribly offended by that question. Evangelicals in my district have complained for decades that our increasingly secular society has become anti-Christian. Santa Claus is a manifestation of that."

"Santa is anti-Christian?" the anchor asks, cocking his head theatrically.

"He is when he's more valued than Christ himself."

"So, you teamed up with Congresswoman Guzman to introduce legislation that bans public displays of Santa? Many of our viewers will wonder how that falls under the federal government's purview."

Aymos looks at Camilla. "I can make a strong argument about the Interstate Commerce Clause, but more importantly, the Cultural Commerce Subcommittee exists to discuss topics just like this. We are empowered to make recommendations on legislation that economically impacts the culture. We have focused on social media and sports monopolies in the past, but this sort of discussion is what the subcommittee is designed for."

"You understand that this could affect an entire generation of children?"

Aymos Blackburn smiles. "A point that I'm sure will be made during the hearings. You should tune in to find out how that question is answered."

Camilla would be dancing a jig if she weren't seated at a desk on camera in front of a national audience. Aymos may be a man of God, but he knows a thing or two about marketing. That one comment will garner national media attention for the hearings. Everyone will want to hear the answer.

"We will have to leave it there. Congressman Blackburn…Congresswoman Guzman…thank you for joining us this evening."

"We're out!" the producer announces after they thank the anchor for his time.

Technicians materialize from behind the cameras to remove their microphones. Camilla can barely contain her excitement. For Blackburn, this interview was just another day in the nation's capital. The only thing that betrays his stoic demeanor is the toothy grin splashed across his face.

"Aymos, you look like a kid on Christmas morning."

The smile turns into a sly grin. "I don't know about you, Camilla, but I can't wait for next week."

Chapter Ten

WYATT HUFFMAN

The meeting room deep in the bowels of the Longworth House Office Building is tense but not hostile. The staff from both sides are here, each occupying one side of the table. This looks more like a Cold War summit than a collaboration. There were perfunctory greetings as everyone arrived. Outside of that, there was no conversation. Everyone has their phones out like teenagers checking Instagram before class.

It's better than the alternative. Congresswoman Pratt and Congressman Knutson fight for different sides in the war that has become American governance. The staff members are their loyal foot soldiers in that conflict. Banter about policy issues of days past would likely only lead to raised voices and hurt feelings. It's been a long year, and there is no constructive reason to rehash successes and failures.

Stowe won't even look at Wyatt. She's still sore about their encounter and refuses to acknowledge his existence. That's okay with him. The less she talks to him, the lower his blood pressure.

The two members of Congress arrive together and scan the room. They smirk as they scan the faces gathered around the table. They take their seats in the middle, opposite each other. Knutson nods at his colleague.

"You all know why you're here," Congresswoman Pratt opens. "This may be a set of innocuous hearings in an obscure subcommittee, but the congressman and I are taking them very seriously. Instead of fighting the battles separately, we want to combine our forces into a united front. That begins and ends with you. We ask you to set aside your differences and work together to help us combat this insanity."

"What are the odds anyone considers this more than a ploy for attention?" one of Wyatt's colleagues asks.

"Not great," Pratt concedes.

"Then why are we bothering with this?" one of her staffers asks.

"Because while Congressman Knutson and I disagree on a myriad of political matters, Christmas isn't one of them. Neither of us is interested in dropping the ball on this one. We would rather plan for the worst-case scenario."

"And there is good reason to," Wyatt's boss adds. "The subcommittee is fairly evenly split right now. Considering we're discussing Christmas, I had hoped the balance was tipped in our favor. Unfortunately, politics is being played, and several committee members may vote whichever way the wind is blowing. We need to make sure it's in our direction."

"Does it matter if this passes out of the subcommittee? It will never make it out of the full committee, and even if it does, it will never get a floor vote," Cam argues.

Knutson's chief of staff is cautious by nature. His job is to run the staff and use them to position the congressman in the best possible light. It's the mandate of all chiefs of staff in Congress. That means advising against wandering too deep into the political quicksand, which is what he sees this as.

"What would it say about us if we let it get that far without a fight?" the congressman asks.

"That we're using our resources and time on more important business for the American people."

"My own right-hand man advised me the same way, Mr. Alcott. I will tell you what I told him. Right here, right now, what's more important to the American people than Christmas?"

"Ma'am, with all due respect, I could think of a dozen things."

The congresswoman nods slowly. "A dozen things that they won't tune in for and won't really give a damn about. They will for this. It will get media attention – and I mean more than a thirty-second sound bite on the six o'clock news. They will run with this. Commentaries will be all over YouTube. People will talk about it, and as word spreads, it may take on a life of its own."

There are nods around the table. The American people are indifferent to most happenings in Congress unless the stakes are extremely high. Government shutdowns are the types of drama that dominate headlines and capture attention. This isn't that, but it is a sexy story from a media perspective. Some outlets have already latched onto it following Guzman's presser.

"We devised a game plan of how we want to tackle this. Let's take some time to review it."

The next half-hour is spent reading the bill Guzman proposed and flipping through the printout of the plan created for the hearings. Both sides like the approach, with staffers weighing in on elements of it. Stowe leads the charge from Pratt's team while Cam offers his advice. The two elected representatives listen and take notes. When they finish, John leans back in his chair.

"Wyatt, you've been uncharacteristically quiet," the congressman observes.

"Maybe he doesn't care about Christmas," Stowe says, leaning deeper into her chair as she folds her hands across her chest. "It gets in the way of hockey season."

"I think this is a great defense," Wyatt says, flipping back to the front page.

"Well, that's good to hear."

"It's missing something, though."

"It's not missing—"

The congresswoman silences her legislative assistant with a raised hand. "What is it missing?"

"Spectacle."

"What do you mean?" Knutson asks.

Wyatt looks around the table. "I mean that we're tackling this logically. That's fine, but people don't want to hear about the economics of Christmas. Nobody hangs decorations out to make their homes more energy-efficient. We don't guzzle eggnog because it's a health food."

"Unfortunately," Stowe mutters.

"Look at that. We found something we agree on," Wyatt says, causing her to roll her eyes. "This holiday is about feeling. We need to make people *feel*."

"Okay," the congresswoman says. "How do you think we should do that?"

Wyatt leans back. "Guzman and Blackburn want to put Santa Claus on trial. Fine. We should arrange for the accused to face his accusers."

There are murmurs around the table. Most are exasperated reactions to an insane proposal. Everyone thinks the same thing except one person. Wyatt sees Stowe perk up across the table from him.

"Wyatt…are you suggesting we get jolly ol' Saint Nick to testify at the hearing?"

"That's precisely what I'm suggesting, Congressman."

"Uh…I hate to point out the obvious," Cam interjects, "but Santa Claus doesn't exist."

"Are you sure about that?" Stowe blurts out, challenging the assumption.

"Fairly."

"Then why are we going through this exercise?" she asks. "Why spend time defending an illusion? Or maybe Santa Claus is alive, if not in body, then in the hearts and minds of everyone who cherishes Christmas."

"So, what's your plan? Get Santa to land his sleigh on the National Mall and let kids feed his reindeer while he testifies? Please."

"We find a Santa willing to plead his case. They want to make a spectacle by banning Santa. We should do the same by offering the man a chance to appear before the subcommittee and spread his message."

Everyone around the table goes quiet. Angela and John glance at each other, but neither looks like they think it's a horrible idea. Wyatt is well aware of what it might have sounded like.

"Okay," John says, breaking the silence. "We'll get busy executing our plan. We need to conduct some background research on the witnesses Guzman and Blackburn are calling. We can't hand the Santa haters any easy wins. My team can focus on the economic impact if yours takes on the cultural ramifications."

Angela nods.

"Wyatt, since it was your idea, it's your job to find Santa Claus."

He nods apprehensively. "Okay, but that's a big task to tackle alone."

"You won't be alone," the congresswoman says. "Stowe is going to help you."

"Wait, what?"

"Sounds fair to me," Knutson says. "We should check in with our progress before the weekend recess."

"Agreed. I will have my staff make the arrangements," Pratt says, nodding at her chief of staff.

"Let's get to work, everybody. We have Christmas to save."

Knutson and Pratt file out, each with other duties to attend to. The staff follows, smirking at each other and at Stowe and Wyatt as they do. While they may not think it's the worst idea, each seems thrilled that they weren't given the impossible task.

Wyatt collects his things before noticing Stowe staring at him across the table. Actually, glaring would be a better description. It's the look a patient gives a doctor after he orders a rectal exam.

"The idea of working with me must be like a nightmare for you."

"One that I plan on waking up from shortly," Stowe says, collecting her own things before stomping out of the conference room.

Wyatt shakes his head. Teaming up with her is never going to work. He'll likely be working alone on this, and it will be up to him to figure out how to find Santa. He frowns. This day is getting better and better.

Chapter Eleven

STOWE BESSETTE

Stowe doesn't take the direct route to the office. She is emotional, and unhinged arguments, while compelling, are often easy to counter. They may work when appealing to the masses, but playing on heartstrings or sensitivities won't work here. Angela Pratt isn't the most hardboiled politician on Capitol Hill, but she's no pushover. She worked hard to get elected, even in a district where she was slightly favored to win. Politics is a contact sport. Like football players, you had better know how to take a hit.

But Angela is also reasonable, and that's the key. Stowe needs to make an argument about why she isn't suited for this assignment that doesn't include disliking Wyatt. The congresswoman won't understand that. Stowe can't be certain she understands it herself. She only knows she doesn't want to work with the man.

By the time she reaches the office, her argument is figured out. Angela is in the outer office talking to her chief of staff. Stowe waits for a break in the dialogue before interrupting.

"Congresswoman? Can we speak in private?"

"Sure. Come into my office."

Stowe enters behind her boss and closes the door. She's been in this room a thousand times but suddenly feels self-conscious. The congresswoman sits behind her desk and dons reading glasses as she looks at several printouts. Stowe is left standing in front of her. Angela isn't purposely being rude. Representatives have busy schedules and are often forced to multitask.

"What's on your mind, Stowe?"

"I'm requesting to work on a different part of the preparation work for the subcommittee."

The congresswoman looks over her reading glasses at her young staffer. "Why?"

"I know how much is at stake with these hearings and why they're important to you. I have an equally vested interest in the result. I also want you to pick the right person for that important task, and I don't believe I'm the one."

"Stowe, you have more Christmas spirit in your pinky finger than most people in this office have in their whole bodies."

"Yes, ma'am. I couldn't agree more. That's why I'm more suited for the cultural research assignment."

"That's a well-reasoned argument," the congresswoman says, folding her hands on the desk and nodding. "I'll change your assignment once you tell me why you don't want to work with Wyatt Huffman."

"Ma'am?"

"That's what this is really about, right?"

"No, ma'am," Stowe says, getting over the shock of being called out by uttering a denial that was weak, at best.

"I think it is. I'm fairly certain you two never dated, so it's not about Wyatt being an ex. You've never filed any complaints of sexual harassment against him or anyone else, for that matter. So, that isn't it. And, from what I understand, Wyatt is a perfect gentleman who treats everyone respectfully. Do you disagree with any of that?"

"No, Congresswoman."

"I didn't think so. Then what's the problem?"

Stowe clenches her jaw. That approach went out the window fast. Now, she's going to have to switch tactics to one less savory. And more honest.

"I'm not comfortable around him."

"I see. Is that because of who Wyatt works for and what he believes? Stowe, sometimes we have to work with people we don't like or agree with. That's part of governing, even if it isn't a popular notion these days."

"I understand that."

"Do you?" the congresswoman asks, removing her glasses. "Finding the right Santa Claus to testify may be the most important part of these hearings. That's why I put my best staffer on it. It's why Congressman Knutson did the same. The two of you need to find a way to make this work. We're counting on you."

"Yes, but—"

"Thank you for sharing your concerns, Stowe. Let me know if anything about your situation with Wyatt changes."

There is no further use of conversation. The decision has been made, and that's the end of it. That is Angela's polite code for "you're dismissed." Continuing to plead her case will only result in Stowe getting the unpolite version.

"Thank you, ma'am."

Stowe ducks out of the office with her tail between her legs and makes a beeline over to her workspace. She sits in her chair and rubs her temples. There was a chance she wouldn't get her way. At no point did she imagine that the argument would be that disastrous.

"No luck getting out of working with Rugged McDreamy, eh?" Mandy asks, posting herself in the usual spot on the corner of Stowe's desk.

"Ford had better luck with the Edsel. How did you know that's what I was doing?"

"Oh, honey, I saw the look on your face in the conference room. I think you should give Wyatt a chance. I don't really think he's that bad."

"Since you like him so much, why didn't you volunteer?"

"Have you met me? I don't volunteer as a matter of principle. I do the work I'm assigned. Stowe, you don't have to marry the guy. You only have to work with him for a week. Besides, I think it will be good for you."

Stowe raises an eyebrow. "How?"

"Just a feeling. I actually think you'll make a fantastic team and will deliver the results Angela needs."

"I'm glad you're optimistic."

"I am. Do you want to know why? You both love Christmas too much not to."

It's more sage advice from her friend. Not that Stowe wants to hear it. Wyatt infuriates her, and the thought of having to work with the man will make next week a long one. All she can do is hope to solve this problem quickly so they don't need to spend much time together. That means clearing her mind and getting to work. With a little luck, she won't need Wyatt Huffman at all.

Chapter Twelve

WYATT HUFFMAN

Politicians in D.C. are fueled by scotch and bourbon. The specter of elected representatives and lobbyists swirling glasses of Bowmore Mizunara Cask Finish while striking deals on pending legislation may be a more accurate stereotype than Americans might imagine. But that's only half the story.

While the politicians attend their fundraisers and cocktail parties, the rank and file of the bureaucracy keep the city's coffee shops in business. With long hours and sleep optional, coffee isn't a morning beverage so much as an hourly requirement for Capitol Hill staffers. They are the doers. Politicians may cast the votes, but the bills are drafted, edited, and rewritten dozens of times by the army of staff that supports them. That requires long hours and a constant supply of caffeine.

The legislative day is long over, but there is still plenty of work to do before Wyatt's head hits a pillow. Much of it can wait until after this meeting. Content to take a few moments for himself, he sips a warm brew at the corner table of this coffeehouse with an open paperback novel in front of him. A lot of people use e-readers. There's nothing wrong with them, but Wyatt is still a traditionalist who likes the smell and texture of paper and the idea of turning pages.

Stowe blows in like an energetic whirlwind and bypasses the counter. She may already be hopped up on espresso. The woman knows how to make an entrance, even when she isn't trying to attract attention. Nearly every pair of eyes tracks her every move. She slides into the seat across from him without even breaking stride. It was a smooth, likely well-practiced move.

"I found our guy," she says without preamble. "He's perfect."

"Good evening to you, too, Stowe."

She rolls her eyes and pulls a manila folder out of her portfolio. She slides it across the table to Wyatt and impatiently gestures to him to open it when he takes too long. Amused, he puts down the political thriller and opens the folder.

"I thought we were supposed to collaborate on this."

Stowe smirks. "I can't help it if you can't keep up."

"All right," Wyatt says.

He lets the slight slide. There is no point in getting into a confrontation with Stowe. For whatever reason, she doesn't like him. While he may not know why, it's really not important. This assignment should only last a week.

That doesn't mean he can't torture her a little. He reads the contents of the file *very* slowly. Kris Kringle may not be the man's given name, but he had it legally changed a few years ago. He looks the part, not needing a fake beard or pillow tucked under his red jacket to complete the image. There are no obvious red flags in his background. By all accounts, he's a method actor who takes his role seriously.

"My God! The Senate moves faster than you read."

Wyatt ignores the interruption other than holding a finger up as he continues digesting the biography. He stops reading but stares at the paper for another long minute as Stowe fidgets in her seat. Wyatt closes the folder when he finishes and stares at her.

"What do you think?" Stowe presses.

"He looks good on paper. What's the next step?"

"We meet with him."

"I'm assuming you don't mean we're traveling to Decatur, Illinois."

"Of course not," Stowe says with a heavy sigh. "We'll hold a virtual meeting. Once we get a feel for Kris Kringle here, we can order a background check and fly him to D.C. for testimony prep."

Wyatt nods. She has this all figured out. There's nothing for him to add.

"Okay. It sounds like a plan. Have a nice evening."

Wyatt leans back and picks up the paperback resting on the table. He set it face down so he didn't lose his page. He begins reading, content to ignore Stowe, who hasn't yet blown out of the shop with the same vigor with which she entered. She finally stands and turns to look at the exit before sitting back down.

"That's it?"

Wyatt looks at her, confused. "Was there more?"

"No…I just thought you'd be pissed that I did all this."

"Why would you think that?"

"You said it yourself. We're supposed to be collaborating. I figured you would want the credit."

Wyatt shakes his head. "Nope. If he works out, you get all the glory. Nice job, and congratulations."

"What's the catch?"

It's not the most insane question to ask in this town. Everything that happens here is designed to get an angle or find an advantage. That's the political game. Americans are disgusted when they see it play out on their televisions or when it affects their daily lives. Fortunately, they aren't privy to ninety-nine percent of the shenanigans happening in the marbled halls of the Capitol complex.

"There is no catch," Wyatt states plainly.

"And if he doesn't work out? Are you going to turn around and blame me?"

"Blame you for what? If he doesn't work out, for whatever reason, then we keep looking. Or you keep looking."

"Oh, so you're pawning this off on me now?" Stowe asks, throwing her hands in the air.

Wyatt frowns. This woman is impossible.

"Not at all. I was the one who suggested that we meet here to collaborate. You were the one who wanted to do it yourself."

"Look, Huffman, I don't know what game you're playing—"

"I'm not playing a game," Wyatt says, starting to get annoyed.

"You clearly are."

"Are you always this neurotic?"

Stowe crosses her arms. "You seem to bring it out of me."

"Hmm. That must be why you're so eager for us to work together."

Stowe narrows her eyes at the sarcasm. "Collaboration doesn't mean we have to be in the same room. You do your thing, and I'll do mine."

"I think you should look up the definition of *collaboration*, Stowe," Wyatt says with a smile. "'You do your thing, and I'll do mine,' ain't it. Which explains why you did both of our things."

"It's easier that way...that's it! That's your plan! You're going to sabotage the interview to make me look bad."

Wyatt shakes his head slowly. "Why would I do that? Our bosses think we're working together. Wouldn't that make me look bad as well?"

Stowe starts to respond but stops. Her mouth moves, but words fail to escape it. She can't fault that logic despite looking like she's about to have a stroke. Finally, she clenches her jaw in frustration.

"Whatever. I'll email you the details of the meeting."

With that, she flees the coffee shop without so much as an infuriated glance back. Wyatt sips his coffee and turns his attention back to the paperback. It's not the best interaction he's had during his tenure on Capitol Hill, but it isn't the worst, either. Whatever Stowe's problem with him is, it's her problem. There's no reason for him to be bothered by it. This will all be over soon enough.

Chapter Thirteen

REPRESENTATIVE JOHN KNUTSON

The pair sets up a monthly meeting not long after being introduced to each other. Technically speaking, "meeting" isn't the right word because there's no agenda, debate on issues, or political maneuvering. It's just two people spending time together as friends in one of the most politically unforgiving cities in the country. Even their close work on the upcoming subcommittee hearings hasn't changed their dinner plans in a quiet Georgetown bistro.

If the Washington political paparazzi knew, they would snap and publish photos to create marital discord with their spouses. Not that it would work. Angela's husband and John's wife know about and support these friendly dinners. It helps that they've even joined in on several occasions when both have been in town.

Despite the transparency, there is little gained by courting disaster. As a result, John and Angela meet off the beaten path in a part of the city packed with college kids, most of whom don't have a clue who they are. They want it that way. There is a time and a place for publicity, and this is neither.

"Has anyone on your staff figured out we have these dinners?" Angela asks after their food arrives.

"I doubt it," John says before taking a healthy bite of his bacon cheeseburger.

That's the beauty of eating at a place like this. As nice as it is, the middle American cuisine and lack of fancy décor all but ensure no other politician or lobbyist would dine at a place like this. John is somewhat surprised that a member of either of their staff hasn't wandered in by happenstance. A few of them live in the Georgetown area.

"Mine neither. What do you think our staffers would say if they knew? We've been doing this for, what, three years now?"

"In this political environment? They would think we either hit our heads or are sleeping together."

Angela laughs as she grabs a trio of fries. "At least they aren't at each other's throats working on the hearings. It's easy to get caught up in the animosity and hatred this city fosters."

"I warned my people to be on their best behavior."

"I did, too, but let's hope they keep playing nice in the sandbox. There's too much at stake to let our staffs bicker over political issues."

"Agreed. Do you really think these hearings are going to be that bad?"

It's an innocent question, but the look on Angela's face betrays her misinterpretation.

"Having second thoughts, John?"

"No. I'm just looking for your take on it. Sometimes, the response to a problem makes it bigger and more visible. How many overreactions have led to people learning about something when they otherwise wouldn't have?"

"Fair point," Angela admits. "But I don't think we are overreacting. We didn't run and hold a presser of our own. I think we're being prudent. If there's one thing I've learned, it's to never try predicting what will and will not capture the nation's attention."

That's actually a smart lesson learned. People know when some things will go viral. When Bernie Sanders wore mittens at Joe Biden's inauguration ceremony, there was little doubt that the image would be meme-worthy for years. Many other things are unpredictable. What captures attention and what doesn't is often at the mercy of a fickle population prone to mood swings.

"Why did you assign Stowe to work with Wyatt?" John asks, curious and content to change the subject.

Angela wipes her mouth with her napkin and shrugs. "Why wouldn't I?"

"I get the suspicion they don't like each other much."

"Stowe is the most ardently pro-Christmas person on my staff. She's a hard worker and an excellent judge of character. That makes her the best person for that assignment."

"I'm sure. I was just wondering, given her apprehension about working with Wyatt. I'm surprised she didn't try to get out of it."

"Oh, she did," Angela says, almost gleefully.

"Really?"

"Yep. Stowe marched into my office five minutes after I returned from the meeting with a well-constructed song and dance about how she was better suited to work on the cultural component."

"I'm assuming you didn't let her off the hook."

"No, I deconstructed her argument. I asked her if there were any harassment issues or previous history between them, which there wasn't. So, that was that. I don't know Wyatt Huffman well, but he doesn't seem like a scumbag."

"He isn't. In fact, he's one of the most genuine people you'll find on Capitol Hill."

"That's what I thought. I don't know what Stowe's problem is, but that's something for her to work through."

"Are we asking them to do too much? I mean, finding a Santa Claus willing to testify before a Congressional subcommittee on short notice isn't a small ask."

"I know. If anyone can pull it off, it's Stowe, especially with Wyatt's help."

"Even if they're at each other's throats?"

Angela has to think about that one for a moment. "Hopefully, they can find common ground."

It's not the vote of confidence John was hoping for, but it's all he gets. Having to deal with these hearings is bad enough. He doesn't want personal drama adding to the angst. And that's only part of the problem.

"What's bothering you? I mean, other than my staffer complaining that your staffer pulled her hair during recess or something."

"I don't know. It feels like this whole exercise is a colossal waste of time. Why is Santa Claus even a focus considering all this country's issues?"

"Some will say it's meant to be a distraction," Angela admits. "Others will argue it's a publicity stunt. More will profess that it's another sterling example of government overreach into people's lives. Whatever the reason, we can't ignore it's a compelling drama that Americans will eat up with a soup ladle."

"If it gets traction," John argues.

Angela frowns as she pushes her plate away.

"I suspect Guzman and Blackburn will ensure it does."

Chapter Fourteen

REPRESENTATIVE CAMILLA GUZMAN

Camilla thinks she knows what this is about and plans her tactics as she walks from the Cannon House Office Building to the Capitol. Elected by the entire House of Representatives, the speaker is the chamber's presiding officer and administrative head. He or she is also the majority party's leader and is second in the line of succession to the presidency, coming only after the vice president. Needless to say, playing politics is as natural as breathing to the person in that position.

In addition to public areas like the Rotunda, National Statuary Hall, and the Old Senate Chamber, the second floor of the United States Capitol Building holds the House of Representatives in the south wing and the Senate in the north wing. It also is home to the formal offices of congressional leadership.

Getting summoned here by the speaker is a big deal. Camilla also knows that it's not for a good reason. That feeling is confirmed when she's shown into an ornate conference room filled with all the power players in her party. Harlan McCormack, the majority leader representing the party on the House floor, is the first to greet her. The handshake is followed by the party whip, who organizes legislation and secures votes; the conference chairman, who heads the organization of all party members in the House; and the policy committee chairman. The last to arrive is the speaker himself. He greets her warmly, flashing a toothy smile that is the hallmark of this career politician.

"Have a seat, Camilla," Speaker Hoskins says, gesturing to a seat at the table. "I'm sure you're wondering why you're here."

"No, sir, I'm not wondering that at all. You permitted me to hold hearings in my subcommittee because I've been a loyal vote for you and the party. And I still am. But then I held a press conference, and the prospective hearings on my legislation are garnering more attention than you thought they would. The other side is billing this as an assault on Christmas, and the negative publicity is making you nervous about possible lingering effects on next year's midterm elections. How close am I?"

The speaker shifts uncomfortably. Ryan Hoskins is the seven-term congressman from Missouri. His district in St. Louis reliably votes for their party, making his seat one of the safest in the country. He can be vocal without fear of voter retribution, allowing him to raise his profile high enough to ascend to this position when their party won back the House.

"Astute analysis, but not entirely correct. Let's start with the obvious. You must agree that holding hearings attacking Christmas isn't a winner at Christmastime."

"Yes, except that is a mischaracterization by the media and our detractors. I'm not attacking Christmas."

"Your bill is about banning Santa Claus," Harlan interjects. "Politics is perception, no matter how much we wish it wasn't. Santa Claus is *associated* with Christmas."

Camilla nods. "And now you see the problem."

"And now you need to recognize the problem we have. The midterms are less than a year away. People *will* remember this."

"I sincerely hope so. You're worried this will damage our chances of keeping control of the House. I argue that this will help us in the midterm election."

Hoskins smirks. "How so?"

"Watch the hearings and find out," Camilla says, the corner of her mouth curling.

The statement was meant to be a tantalizing preview of what's to come, but it wasn't interpreted that way. There are no smiles or nods around the table. These men care about political power, and a misstep that jeopardizes their control would be considered a national tragedy.

"Why did you include Aymos Blackburn at your press conference?" Harlan asks, going back on the offensive.

"Because it turns out that he supports the goal of the hearings. I was as shocked as you are."

"He's not a member of our party."

"I'm well aware of that, Harlan. It's all the more reason to include him. The American people love bipartisanship."

"Not the ones who vote. Camilla, other members are getting calls. Our biggest supporters and contributors feel you're selling out the party by working with him."

Harlan McCormack is a political pit bull. His job is to keep people in the party toeing the line. Leaders make the rules in modern politics, and the rest of the representatives are expected to support them without dissent. To ensure that's the case, Harlan plays hardball.

"That's an interesting take. Of course, I could argue that I'm bringing more people to our side."

"You need to cancel the hearings," Speaker Hoskins says, having heard enough.

Camilla leans back in her chair slightly. It's the moment of truth. Hoskins can destroy her political career. Beyond handing out committee assignments, he also controls the purse strings. The party has a fund to help its members get re-elected, and anyone who falls out of favor with him could end up without a dime for their war chest. Currency is the lifeblood of campaigns. Without that money, she will be renting moving vans this time next year. Now that he's played his cards, it's her turn.

"No."

"What?"

"I will not cancel the hearings, Mr. Speaker."

Hoskins smiles. "I know you're new here, Camilla, so maybe you don't know how things work. I lead the party in—"

"I don't need a civics lesson, Mr. Speaker. I need your full-throated support. And I will get it."

Camilla may never find out which was worse, the interruption or the demand. The looks on the faces of the leadership range from horror to confusion to sympathy. They know what's going to happen next.

"Can you excuse us, please?" the speaker commands, his eyes never peeling away from Camilla.

The leadership files out. Harlan grins at her as he leaves. Depending on the circumstances, any representative in the House can be called his best friend or worst enemy. There is no question about which side of that line she's on. Hoskin hears the door close and then makes her wait a couple of extra beats to build up the tension.

"I'm not sure who you think you are or what game you think you're playing, but I don't like being embarrassed in front of the leadership."

"And I don't like being patronized and marginalized. You could rely on my vote and count on my loyalty since I've been here. I respectfully approached you with this idea, and we struck a deal. I expect you to honor it."

"Or else what?" Hoskins asks, getting noticeably more agitated. "I'm the speaker of the U.S. House of Representatives. You're a first-term representative from California who I could have replaced in ten seconds flat."

"You don't get it. You don't see what your constituents see."

"How so?"

"You thump your chest because you think people perceive you as a political mastermind who's third in line for the presidency. They really see a white boy from St. Louis who rode a wave of black and brown support to get into office. What will your constituents do when they hear you're a racist who only thinks people of color deserve a seat at the table when it benefits *you*?"

"Really? Playing the race card against someone in your own party is a bold move, don't you think?"

"Do you think I like this, Mr. Speaker? Are you under the impression I came into this office looking for a fight? I don't want to play the race game, but I will if I have to. Once it starts, who do you think will win, me or you?"

Hoskins lowers his eyes. It's not a sign of defeat so much as a tactical retreat to find a better position to reengage from. This man never backs down. If she wins this battle of wills, there will be consequences. Those will need to be managed later. Without this hearing, she likely won't survive the next election anyway.

"I'm not asking anything from you, Mr. Speaker. I don't expect you to be a co-sponsor or order the majority whip to circle the wagons. I don't expect you to lift a finger for this legislation. What I do expect is your support in holding these hearings."

"In the interest of?"

"The American people."

"Or maybe just yours because you don't seem to care that this could hurt the party next November."

"I care that not allowing me to have these hearings or stripping my chairmanship away will absolutely hurt the party next November. I will make certain of it."

Hoskins doesn't like threats. Anyone who knows the man will offer that piece of sage advice. It's one of the worst tactics to take with him. As a result, it's unexpected. He wasn't prepared for her to outflank him.

"Very well. Hold your hearings as planned."

"Thank you. Mr. Speaker."

There is an adage in sales: When you get the answer you want, stop listening and leave. There is nothing to be gained by further conversation. With that in mind, the congresswoman rises and heads for the door.

"Camilla? I won't forget this conversation."

Guzman stops and looks over her shoulder at the leader of the House. "Good. I'll be disappointed if I ever have to repeat myself."

She passes the party leadership, all of whom are waiting patiently outside the conference room door. She nods and smiles, giving them a clear indication of who was victorious in this battle. Politics is such a fun game to play. It helps when societal sensibilities have provided her a few extra cards in the deck. It shouldn't have to come to that, but she didn't make the rules. Now, she needs to get to work making good on her promise.

Chapter Fifteen

STOWE BESSETTE

Wyatt is already typing on his laptop in the conference room when Stowe swings open the door and strides in. Neither of their offices made sense to hold this call, so she secured the same space where the combined staff previously met. Wyatt looks up and nods as Stowe takes her seat beside him.

"I'm surprised you wanted to meet in person for this. You could have just conferenced me in."

"Yeah, well, I thought this would be better," Stowe argues. "Is there a problem?"

He shakes his head. "None at all."

She opens her laptop and launches the videoconference program while he surfs to the man's website and professional resume. They sit in silence for three minutes until the computer's speakers chime to announce the incoming video call. She accepts, and the video of a man dressed in plaid with a snow-white beard, bushy eyebrows, and rosy cheeks fills the screen.

"Ho, ho, ho! Merry Christmas!"

"Merry Christmas, Mr. Kringle," Stowe says in a high voice that confirms her excitement. "How are you?"

"Very busy. So much to do before Christmas Eve."

"Thank you for taking the time to meet with us," she says, glancing over at Wyatt, who approves of the man's look.

He may not be wearing the iconic red suit, but his clothing, body language, movement, and mannerisms all exude Santa Claus. Kriss Kringle looks the part. All that's left to determine is how well he acts the part.

"Of course," Kriss says with a bright smile. "Your email mentioned there is some sort of legislative problem you need assistance with."

Stowe launches into an explanation about what is happening with the hearings. Kriss nods understanding and asks a couple of intelligent questions. He has a clear understanding of governmental processes and the ramifications of what these hearings could mean. She glances at Wyatt, eliciting a nod. Even he's happy with the exchange.

"Of course, I'm happy to help," Kriss confirms.

"Excellent. Let's start with some basic background questions. You obviously don't live at the North Pole. Is your home in Decatur, Illinois?"

"Yes, born and raised."

"And you legally changed your name five years ago?" Stowe asks.

"That's correct. I was born Harvey Rishmill, but I have always been Kriss Kringle in my heart. It just made sense to legally make the name match."

"Understood. How much do you know about Christmas?"

"Ho, ho ho!" Kriss bellows. "I know everything about it. I'm St. Nicholas. For example, did you know that the tradition of Christmas trees dates back to the ancient Egyptians and Romans? It's true. They decorated evergreens during the winter solstice to signify that spring would soon return. Do you know the song 'Jingle Bells?'"

"Of course," Stowe confirms. "It's one of my favorites to sing."

"Most people would agree with you. The song used to be called 'One Horse Open Sleigh' and was written for a church's Thanksgiving concert in the mid-19th century."

Stowe leans forward after sneaking a glance at an amused Wyatt. "I didn't know that."

"Then this will blow your mind," Kriss says, leaning closer to the camera. "Mistletoe is an aphrodisiac. It's also an ancient symbol of fertility and virility. So, the next time you have to kiss someone under it, consider yourself warned, ho, ho, ho."

Wyatt nods when Stowe looks over at him.

"I have some experience with mistletoe. My grandmother is a big fan of it. Mr. Kringle, we think you'll be perfect for the job. I'm hoping you're willing to come to Washington for some intense preparation before testifying before the subcommittee."

"Of course. I'd be honored. I can't tell you how much this will help my cause."

"Your cause?" Stowe asks, crinkling her brow as she cocks her head. "What cause is that?"

"My emancipation from America."

Wyatt's head shoots around to stare at the screen. Stowe looks stunned, taking several seconds to recover. He didn't just say that, did he?

"I'm sorry, Mr. Kringle, but I'm afraid I'm not following."

"Oh, I thought you knew, your being with the government and all. I've been fighting with the City of Decatur and state officials to declare that my home is not a part of the United States."

"Why would you do that?"

"Because I'm Santa Claus. I'm not American – I'm a citizen of the world."

"But you live in Decatur."

Wyatt immediately goes to work on his laptop, typing furiously in a search engine. He frowns at the search results and clicks on the first hyperlink. He reads the headline and spins the computer so Stowe can see it.

It's a local news article about a man calling himself Kriss Kringle, who doesn't want to pay taxes and has taken on Santa Claus's persona to avoid paying them. As of the article's date, he owes tens of thousands of dollars in back property taxes and has several liens on his home. It's likely more now.

"That shouldn't matter. I am Kriss Kringle. The city shouldn't force Santa Claus to pay taxes on his home. The federal government shouldn't make me pay an income tax, either. Maybe I can talk about that with your committee."

"We'll see what we can do, Mr. Kringle. Let me talk to my peers, and I'll get back to you."

"Sounds good. I look forward to hearing back from you. This is going to be very beneficial for all of us. Until then," Kriss says with a wave.

Stowe closes the video chat before slamming her laptop shut. She anchors her elbows to the table and closes her eyes as she rubs her temples. Wyatt runs his hand through his hair but doesn't speak.

"Say it."

"Say what?"

"Don't play games, Wyatt. I know you're dying to rub it in my face about missing that."

He shakes his head. "No, I'm not. I don't think there is a reasonable expectation of you finding out Kriss Kringle is a glorified tax cheat without knowing his real name. I had to get very specific in my search to find that article."

"You're being kind."

"No, I'm being honest."

She would almost feel better if he were taking her to task. The interview was an epic miss. Had Kriss not said anything, he could have ended up before the subcommittee. Someone would have found that information, leading to a complete disaster. The whole testimony wouldn't have been fun facts about Christmas. It would be about how Santa Claus is trying to defraud the government.

"Well, for obvious reasons, Mr. Kringle isn't going to work out."

"It kinda would have been entertaining to watch the committee dismantle him."

"You think this is funny?"

"It will be someday. Look, Stowe, it's better to learn that now rather than later. That was the whole point in vetting him. Stop beating yourself up for doing the proper due diligence."

"Yeah, I guess," Stowe says, unconvinced. "Any ideas about what to do next?"

Wyatt shrugs. "We keep searching."

Stowe sighs. "I spent hours sifting through online lists of the best Santas in the country. He was the best of the lot. Trust me."

"Then we need to find another bucket of potential candidates."

"How?"

Wyatt rubs his chin and leans back in his chair. "I have no idea. We'll figure something out, but we should report this to our bosses first."

"They aren't going to like the news," she moans.

"No, but they'll like it even less if we give up. We can come back tomorrow fresh. Have a good night, Stowe."

Under normal circumstances, Stowe would expect to get all the blame. Kriss Kringle from Decatur, Illinois, was her find. But maybe Wyatt will be true to his word and not pass the blame onto her. That would be refreshing in this town.

Not that it matters. Stowe feels like a failure. Wyatt would have had every right to do a victory dance on her head, yet he didn't, at least not to her face. What happens next is anybody's guess. Unfortunately, she'll find out soon enough.

Chapter Sixteen

REPRESENTATIVE JOHN KNUTSON

John has been in Wyatt's position before. When he joined his firm after law school as a junior associate, one of the partners handed him an important task. He didn't fail, but he sort of mailed it in and didn't exactly shine, either. John found himself standing in front of the partner's desk, much like Wyatt is now. The conversation was one-sided.

He remembers how he felt leaving that office. John was berated loud enough that the entire firm could hear what was said. He was humiliated, and it had a lasting impact. It was the last time he didn't give something one hundred percent.

It didn't mean that the tongue-lashing was warranted. It was a different time, and problems were handled differently than they are today. John isn't going to yell at Wyatt following the news of the disastrous interview. He doesn't need to. The kid feels bad enough. It's written all over his face.

"You're running out of time," John says, peering through his reading glasses at the document he's marking up. "Was Tax Evasion Santa the only candidate you've interviewed so far?"

"Yes, sir."

"I didn't expect you to nail this on the first try. When is the next one?"

Wyatt shifts his weight. "We don't have any other candidates at the moment."

The congressman removes his reading glasses and sets them on his desk. "No other candidates? That's...Wyatt, you live in Washington, right?"

"Yes, sir. I share a house with five others."

That makes sense. Young, underpaid congressional staffers fall into one of three general buckets: They have a lot of roommates, live in a dirt cheap apartment in a rough neighborhood, or sleep in the office. Whoever said the art of governing didn't include sacrifice never worked on a congressional staff for peanuts.

"Is it within walking distance to Capitol Hill?"

"Not really," Wyatt answers slowly. "I live up near Rock Creek Park."

"So, you take the Metro?"

"Most days, yes," he admits, having no idea where the congressman is going with this.

"What happens if the Metro isn't running?"

"I can take a rideshare."

"And if there are none available? What would you do if the app was down or they were on strike or something?"

"Three of my housemates have cars, and can drive me here. Or I can take buses."

The congressman nods. "And if Washington is mired in gridlock?"

"I can put on running shoes and get here on foot."

"How long would it take you? I ask because I think you've done it before."

"In decent weather, it's a two-hour walk."

"And if you run?"

"An hour and seventeen minutes at a moderate jog."

The corner of John's mouth curls. The rapid-fire questions are easy but also designed to get honest answers. The truth comes quickly. Lies take longer to formulate. It's the same technique politicians use during hearings and reporters employ in interviews.

"So, you have at least four alternative ways to get to work if the Metro stops running. And because of that, you've never once shown up late. In other words, you never put all your eggs in one basket. You have contingency plans, Wyatt. There are two or three backup plans for everything you do, yet this Kriss Kringle character was your only interview. Why?"

Wyatt hangs his head. John may not fully understand their dynamic, but he has a good idea about what's happening. It's not a unique story. But his young staffer needs to learn a hard lesson about life working in government.

"Stowe found this guy and convinced you he'd be perfect, right?" John concludes.

"Yes, but I reviewed the file and agreed with her."

"But she's leading the charge and insisted that this fellow was our guy, so you didn't bother developing a list of alternatives. You don't need to answer that," the congressman says with a dismissive wave of his hand after Wyatt doesn't respond. "Stowe is a lovely woman. I'm sure she—"

"It has nothing to do with that," Wyatt snaps.

John's eyes narrow. "Then tell me why you're taking a back seat."

"Stowe doesn't like me. I don't know why. I barely know her."

"Lots of people don't like you, Wyatt. Some of that is because of you. The rest is because of who you work for. That's never caused a problem before. Why is this different?"

"I don't know," Wyatt says, staring at his shoes again.

John knows, even if Wyatt is being truthful and doesn't. He wants Stowe to like him. Whether this is physical attraction between them or something else is irrelevant. It's causing a problem.

"I think you do. This isn't a lecture, son, but I will turn it into one if I have to. This is the United States House of Representatives. You aren't going to win any popularity contests here. I don't know why Miss Bessette doesn't like you, and I don't care. The two of you have the most important assignment for these hearings. I need you to come through."

"I will, sir."

"Good. Then my advice is to stop worrying about hurting her feelings and start doing your job. Understood?"

"Yes, Congressman."

"Good. Oh, and in case you're wondering, I guarantee Angela Pratt is having the same conversation with Miss Bessette. Neither of you needs to fall on your sword for the other. You succeed or fail as a team."

"Thank you, Congressman."

John nods and watches his young legislative staffer leave the office and close the door behind him. The congressman doesn't know the story between Wyatt and Stowe and really couldn't care less. They need to figure this out before the political circus is in full swing. There is much more at stake than trivial Capitol Hill drama. He can only hope that Wyatt and Stowe figure that out as well.

Chapter Seventeen

WYATT HUFFMAN

The house is still. With a half dozen people living here, that's a rare occurrence. Outside of the workday, there is always someone around. Not this time. Seizing the opportunity to relish the silence, Wyatt raids the refrigerator for a beer and plops down on the couch. He only gets a single swig down before his cell phone rings.

"Arrrgh."

Wyatt checks the incoming video call and is tempted not to accept. Unfortunately, his mother's wrath is the only thing on Earth he fears. This video request gets answered, or Wyatt will spend fifteen minutes tomorrow convincing her that he was busy. He opts for the safe route since his mother is a walking, talking lie detector. He got away with almost nothing as a teenager.

"Hi, Mama."

"Hello, Wyatt, dear. What's wrong?"

"What makes you think anything's wrong?"

"Because I gave birth to you, raised you, and know that tone better than anyone on this planet."

"Nothing's wrong. It was just a long day."

She shakes her head. "No, that wasn't your tired voice. That was your frustrated, stressed-out tone."

"I can't get anything past you, can I?"

"And don't you ever forget it."

Not that she ever would. Wyatt's mother was a homemaker who ran the household with an iron fist. Chores were to be done, homework finished, and shenanigans sniffed out and punished. She turned figuring out what trouble her children were up to into a sport. There was almost nothing she hadn't seen by the time Wyatt became a teenager.

"The congressman gave me a task, and it's not turning out so well."

"What task?"

"Saving Christmas," Wyatt muses.

While that's not exactly the truth, Wyatt's mother doesn't need to know the details. It would take too long to explain, and they would end up right back in the same place, regardless.

"Well, that certainly explains the stress."

"Some of it."

"There's more?"

"Congressman Knutson teamed me up with a woman who works on Angela Pratt's staff."

"Oh, a woman? Is she pretty?"

Wyatt rolls his eyes. "She's beautiful, but don't get your hopes up. She hates my guts."

"Oh, sweetie, what did you do?"

"Nothing that I know of. God's honest truth. I barely know Stowe."

"Stowe? I like that name. Maybe she doesn't hate you at all. It could be something else. Maybe she digs you!"

Wyatt ignores the 1960s lingo because his mother makes a fair point. Her rabid dislike of him may not be associated with anything he did or said. It could be something else entirely.

"It doesn't matter. Stowe scheduled the interview with Kriss Kringle. It didn't go well, and the congressman had a few choice things to say to me about it."

Bridget Huffman is a wonderful woman. She's polite, kind, and honest to a fault. She wears her emotions on her sleeve, making her a fantastic person and a lousy poker player.

"Uh, you had an interview with Santa Claus? How could that not go well?" his mom asks with a cocked head and face contorted in confusion.

"It turns out that this Santa is a tax evader, for starters."

"Ah," she says, pressing her lips together. "I'm afraid I don't understand."

"It's a long story, Mama."

"It must be. What are you going to do now?"

He'd like to close his eyes and sleep for the next two weeks, but that would only leave him hungry and unemployed. Like it or not, this is his and Stowe's assignment, and they must come through.

"Keep searching, I guess."

"With Stowe?"

"Wyatt sighs. "Yes, with Stowe."

Her face lights up. "Well, there's no shortage of Santas. They even have schools for them."

The lightbulb clicks on over Wyatt's head like he's in an old Saturday morning cartoon. He will kick himself later for not having thought of that.

"Mom, you're an absolute genius!"

"Okay, I don't know how, but I'll take that compliment! Do you want to talk to your father?"

"Another time," Wyatt says, having a reason to avoid an awkward conversation and probable lecture from his old man. "I have work to do."

"Okay," she says, using a tone that betrays her disappointment. "You know, you really need to talk to him."

"I will, just not right now. I love you, Mama. Bye!"

Wyatt disconnects the video call and retrieves the laptop from his bag. How many cheesy Christmas movies have Santa schools? Everyone knows they exist. It was an oversight but a fixable one. He needs to focus. It's time to find some schools capable of producing a great Santa.

Chapter Eighteen

STOWE BESSETTE

There are more than a few perks of having a friend whose parents are stupidly rich and generous with their daughter's allowance: the refrigerator is full, the wine cabinet is stocked, and they don't have to live in a rundown rental with five other people. Their apartment in the trendy Navy Yard neighborhood is way out of their combined salary range. Thankfully, Amanda's parents insisted that their daughter live someplace safe. Mandy was more than willing to allow her friend to have the second bedroom.

Despite having a small study to work in, Stowe takes up residence on the living room couch. She sits in an office chair all day and wants something more comfortable. The overstuffed sofa is just what the doctor ordered, and she sinks into it as she scours the Internet for anyone who specializes in training hyperrealistic Santas.

Stowe hears keys in the lock at the door, and it swings open. Mandy shuffles in, carting her work bag, a purse, a winter coat, and what looks like a shopping bag. In the morning, Mandy is one of the most put-together women on the hill. By the end of the day, she's one of the most frazzled and disheveled. Such is the life of a congressional staffer, where the only easy day was yesterday.

"I brought you a gift," Mandy says, holding up a brown paper bag with the logo from their favorite Italian restaurant down the street.

"What makes you think I didn't eat?"

"Because I knew you would be too consumed by the Great Santa Search to order something, much less cook. And you often fail to realize that a bag of salt and vinegar potato chips is not a nutritious dinner. How are you so thin eating like this?" she asks, grabbing and dangling the nearly empty bag of chips.

"Genetics. Thank you for this," Stowe says, pulling out a container of *quattro formaggi*, a delicious ricotta, mozzarella, parmigiana, and fontina cheese ravioli dish with tomato and basil.

"No problem. I figured you would need it after getting your ass chewed out by Angela."

"Ah. You heard about what happened?"

"Are you kidding, girl? Everybody knows you almost put an anti-American tax evader before the subcommittee."

Stowe puts her fork down and covers her face with a pillow. "Arrgh! In my defense, I would have found out eventually."

"Probably, except you would have no time to find a replacement. What did tall, dark, and handsome say?"

"Wyatt has brown hair."

"Oh, so you knew who I was referring to," Mandy says, holding a bottle of wine as she crashes on the couch beside her roommate. "That's progress!"

"Stop it, Mandy."

"I'm sorry, Stowe. I can't resist. What did he say?"

She shrugs. "Not much. Just that we have to keep trying."

"Wait! He didn't act like a smug middle school bully? Imagine that. Maybe he isn't such a bad guy after all."

Nobody was more surprised than Stowe was.

"That remains to be seen. I'm sure Wyatt threw me under the bus when he told Representative Knutson what happened."

"Oh, poor Stowe, she's too busy finding a proper Santa Claus to keep up on interoffice gossip."

"What do you mean?" Stowe asks as Mandy pours two glasses of wine.

"Wyatt took the blame for it. Well, as much as the congressman would let him."

Stowe studies her friend. Mandy has a history of playing games at her expense. That doesn't appear to be the case this time. She's serious.

"What? How do you know that?"

"Our staff is working with their staff, remember? We're all sharing now. They wanted to know what Angela said, and we traded information. Apparently, Wyatt left with his tail between his legs just like you did."

"Kriss Kringle was my find," Stowe says, hanging her head. "It was my fault."

"Yeah, but he made it clear to Knutson that Mister 'I Don't Want To Pay Taxes' was a great find. Well, until he wasn't. He said he owns that as much as you do."

Stowe begins to say something before stopping. That's not what she expected to hear. This city is filled with opportunists. It's the very nature of politics at this level, and everybody plays the game. That Wyatt Huffman didn't use this to his advantage is telling…and eye-opening.

Mandy sips her wine as she watches her roommate fidget. "Can I ask you a question? Wyatt seems like a decent guy, by Washington's standards, at least. Why do you hate him so much?"

"I don't hate him."

"Okay. Why do you *dislike* him so much?"

Stowe forces a smile. "Thanks for the info, Mandy. And for the late dinner. I have to get back to this."

It was a less-than-artful dodge, but it's not a topic she feels like delving into. Amanda is a roommate, colleague, and friend, but that conversation could drag on for a while, and there is work to be done. That, and she has been judged enough today. There is little doubt that Mandy wouldn't accept her reasoning.

"Fine. I'll let you off the hook, but sooner or later, you're gonna tell me, or I will handcuff you to your bed. You know that I own a pair or two."

"I remember. You gave me a spare key, just in case," Stowe laughs.

"What are you working on?"

She gestures at her open laptop. "Finding another pot of candidates. I've moved on to companies that specialize in Christmas services. This one rents professional Santas out to corporate events and such."

"Any promising candidates?"

"I mean, they all look the part, but the visual isn't the most important thing we're looking for, is it?"

"No, I imagine every answer in front of the subcommittee can't be 'ho, ho, ho.'"

"I need to find a Santa who has real Christmas magic. I'm beginning to lose faith that it's out there anymore."

"If you lose your Christmas spirit, it's hopeless for the rest of us."

Stowe's cell phone rings, and she retrieves it from the coffee table. A number comes up without an associated contact, so she has no idea who this is. She doesn't recognize the area code and would let it go to voicemail nine times out of ten. This time, she presses "accept" and connects the call.

"Hello?"

"Hey, Stowe, it's Wyatt."

"Uh, hi, Wyatt," she says as she straightens, causing Mandy to grin as she sinks deeper into the couch and watches. "How did you get my cell number?"

"Someone in your office gave it to me. I hope it's okay that I called."

"Sure, yeah, no problem. What's up?"

"I think I may have a possible solution to our Santa problem if you have a minute to talk."

"You're doing better than I am. I'm all ears."

Chapter Nineteen

REPRESENTATIVE CAMILLA GUZMAN

Every end has a beginning. For Camilla, the endgame is to use these hearings to catapult her name recognition and pave the way for an easy win in next November's election. Or so she believes. She is way behind in fundraising, and having voters recognize her name on the ballot will likely be the difference between keeping her seat and losing it. There is no shortage of candidates from both parties who would love to upset her in the primary or general election.

That's the endgame, but real change starts here with the two dozen or so people gathered outside the Capitol Building. Camilla passes groups of people every day – senior citizens from the Midwest or groups of kids on their eighth-grade field trips. Tourists arrive in busloads and filter into the Capitol Welcome Center every day. What makes this different are the signs and Santa hats.

Every protest begins this way. Someone must always be the first to arrive at the designated gathering spot. Then more come. A couple becomes a gaggle, which grows into a crowd as more and more people join. The bigger and more vocal the gathering, the more attention it gets.

Some protests turn to violence to make sure they get media traction. Camilla doubts that will be the case here. This group will sing Christmas carols at the top of their lungs. Many protesters will be decked out in full Santa costumes. Plenty more will sport Santa hats, wrap themselves in Christmas lights, and wear garland necklaces as they ring jingle bells all day. It may be the most festive rally in American history.

"I never expected you to be smiling at a protest against you," Marcia says, coming up alongside her as she pulls the tab back on the lid of her disposable coffee cup.

"How did you find me?"

"I'm your chief of staff, Congresswoman. Knowing where you are and what you're doing is my job. Which sign is your favorite? I kinda like the one that says, 'Guzman is the Grinch.'"

"Nah. It's not nasty enough."

"You're enjoying this, aren't you?"

Camilla shakes her head. "I'll enjoy it more when the crowd is a thousand times this size. What are you up to?"

"I had a meeting with Baker."

Jack Baker was one of the first men Camilla met when she arrived on Capitol Hill for her orientation. Long-serving as Ryan Hoskins's chief of staff, his only interest is to advance his boss's agenda. The speaker may have political power, but Baker greases the machine's wheels and keeps things in motion. That meeting was undoubtedly a contentious one. The best threats aren't made face-to-face. They're done through intermediaries like Jack Baker and Marcia Konstantinos. That's how Washington operates.

"Was that your idea or his?"

"His. Baker wanted to reiterate how pissed off the speaker of the House is and inform me that the consequences of this could be severe. He won't stand in your way during the hearings, but he won't be making public statements about them, either. He thinks they're reckless."

"I'll bet you a hundred dollars that he changes his mind by the start of the third day."

"You still use coupons and save your loose change. You're never willing to part with ten bucks, let alone a hundred, so you must be sure."

Camilla smiles. "Is it a bet?"

"For the sake of keeping this interesting, sure."

"The speaker has been in Congress too long. Being from a safe district, he has no reason to talk to real Americans. All of his information comes from insiders and pollsters. He doesn't know the struggles normal people are having."

Marcia nods. "Okay, but that doesn't explain how these hearings will change his mind."

"Because he will eventually see the bigger picture."

"Are you going to clue me in?" Marcia asks.

"Not until you pay me my hundred dollars."

A few more protesters arrive. One of them is holding a bottle in a brown paper bag. That's more like it. The more drunken holiday cheer, the better the b-roll footage for the evening news reports.

"You should know that several people on the staff want to put a poll in the field in our district. We have a lot of Hispanics, and many of them are Christian. They're afraid that this will adversely impact our support."

"What do you think?"

"That you may be afraid to hear the results."

Marcia should know better. Camilla wants accurate information, regardless of what it means to her or her district. She has never been the type to act like a Chinese dictator who surrounds himself with people only willing to tell him what he wants to hear. That's the road to disaster, and she steers clear of it.

"I'm not," Camilla says, resisting the urge to bite Marcia's head off. "Put two polls in the field – one before the hearings and one at the end. I want to measure the difference."

"That's not going to be cheap," Marcia cautions.

They never are. The cost of any poll is commensurate with four variables: The sample size, length, the inclusion of cell phones requiring manual and not auto-dialed attempts by law, and the polling firm used. National surveys typically have a sample of about eight hundred respondents, resulting in an approximate twenty-five-thousand-dollar invoice. Her district is small, but even a few thousand dollars hits an unknown politician's finances hard.

"We aren't going to win next year's election by out-fundraising our opponents. We'll have to outthink them. A few thousand dollars spent here and there to gain key insights won't spell our doom. Have them draft the poll questions, but I want to review and approve them before a single call is made."

"You got it."

Camilla nods at her chief of staff and heads toward the Cannon House Office Building, where a pile of messages awaits her attention. Some of them will be supporters, and others will be haters. The important ones are colleagues and donors wondering what she is up to. A smile crosses her lips as she walks. This is going to be fun.

Chapter Twenty

WYATT HUFFMAN

The plane touches down in Burlington, Vermont, the same way hundreds do worldwide every day. The tires screech when they touch the asphalt, the pilot deploys the airbrakes, and the engine thrust reversers are engaged until the speed bleeds off enough to enter a taxiway. Then, it's a short taxi to the gate, jetway deployment, crosschecking by the flight attendants, and deplaning.

Stowe and Wyatt sat in seats in different parts of the aircraft. The flight isn't full, so he assumes it's by choice. She may be more inclined to work with him than when they first were teamed together, but only slightly. He doesn't rate high enough on Stowe's list to warrant a seat beside her. Too bad because he showered today.

She waits near the gate for him, and the pair strolls toward the arrivals hall without speaking. Neither checked luggage for this short trip, so it's straight to ground transportation and rental car desks. Patrick Leahy Burlington International Airport is nowhere close to JFK or O'Hare in size. The rental car companies at BTV are conveniently located inside the terminal adjacent to the baggage carousels.

During last night's call, Wyatt and Stowe identified seven high-end Santa training schools. The one in Burlington was consistently listed as one of the best. The choice became more obvious since this area is her stomping grounds. She had heard of this academy and kicked herself for not thinking of checking this out in the first place.

When the paperwork is completed, the clerk hands Wyatt a key fob and directions to the lot. They find their vehicle, and he pops the trunk. They drop their carry-ons in, and he slams the trunk. Stowe doesn't budge. She is lost in thought, staring at the driver's seat. When she finally turns to face Wyatt, he holds the fob in front of her.

"You're letting me drive?"

"This is your back yard, isn't it? Why wouldn't I?"

She accepts the black piece of plastic and stares at it in her hand. "You strike me as the kinda guy who likes to be in control."

Wyatt scoffs. "What led you to that conclusion?"

Stowe doesn't say anything at first. "You don't think that men are better drivers than women?"

"Montana takes its state fair very seriously," Wyatt says with a laugh. "When I was growing up, they held tractor-driving contests for the kids. My brother laid down the challenge and bet chores for a week. He went first, and I went second. We were both motivated to win.

"Time isn't the only element. The competition is about precision. He finished fast but knocked over a bunch of hay bales and cones in the process. I didn't and smoked him. Then, my sister got behind the wheel and put us both to shame. She ended up winning the blue ribbon that day. From then on, I stopped making assumptions about what women could and could not do well."

"I can't believe you just admitted to losing to a girl," Stowe says.

"You've never met my sister," Wyatt moans. "We're wasting time. You can drive, or I can drive. I don't care, but one of us has to get behind the wheel so we can get moving."

Stowe spins and climbs behind the wheel as Wyatt gets comfortable on the passenger side. She fires the sedan up and pulls out. The corner of Wyatt's mouth curls as he watches her try to stifle the smile that keeps creeping back onto her face.

"Do you come to Burlington often?"

"It's the closest city to where my grandparents live. I spent a lot of time here before I moved to Washington."

"It's beautiful countryside."

"That's high praise coming from someone from Montana. Wait until you get into the mountains during the fall. You've never been to New England before?"

Wyatt stares out his window. "I've never had a reason to. I don't get to travel much unless you count going back and forth between Washington and Great Falls."

"And yet you have a passport," Stowe says, causing Wyatt to turn his head to look at her. "I saw you hand it to the TSA before we entered the security checkpoint."

"Oh, so you were watching me?"

She rolls her eyes. "Don't flatter yourself, Huffman."

"I got the passport just in case the congressman ever wanted to take me on one of his overseas trips. Since that hasn't happened, I use it as identification on domestic flights instead of worrying about the TSA not accepting my driver's license. It also makes me feel better about the hundred and thirty bucks I paid for it."

"That's very practical. Only, it costs closer to one forty-two," Stowe says. "You forgot to price in the passport photos."

"Fair enough."

"I do the same thing, by the way," she says, smirking.

"I'm amazed. We actually have something in common other than loving Christmas."

Stowe scowls as she keeps her eyes on the road. Wyatt isn't going to press his luck. That is the longest non-work-related conversation he has managed to hold with her. If there are other similarities, he doubts she will ever let him find them.

Chapter Twenty-One

STOWE BESSETTE

Stowe steers the car into the parking lot. She and Wyatt haven't said anything to each other since leaving the airport. He seems content to enjoy the scenery, which is fine by her. There is too much talk already in the world, and nothing about their relationship warrants a frivolous "get to know you" conversation. They need to finish this assignment and deliver results. Their bosses are counting on it.

The North Pole South Santa Academy is on the outskirts of Burlington in a large log cabin plucked straight from a Hallmark Christmas movie. Holiday decorations are everywhere, with garland, twinkle lights, wreaths, and bows adorning the front of the structure. Most of it looks permanent, although the wreaths look like they're made from freshly cut pine boughs.

Wyatt and Stowe walk through the main entrance into a small lobby area. A sign at the counter reads, "Back in a Jiff!" Four or five jolly men are eating cookies and drinking milk in a small dining room off the reception area. Something tells Stowe she won't find any healthy snacks here. The men sport a natural white beard and round belly befitting an old St. Nick. They wear white shirts, red suspenders and pants, and black boots. The shirts have the academy logo on them.

Three of the men smile at her and stand up from the table. If this is the reception committee, it's one hell of a first impression. They are right out of Central Casting for any Christmas movie.

"You may want to move three feet to your left," Wyatt whispers into her ear.

"Why?"

"You're about to make those Santas' day."

Wyatt looks up. Stowe studies him and follows his gaze to a spot above her head. A sprig of oval-shaped mossy-green leaves with round white berries dangles from a wood beam.

"God, I hate mistletoe," Stowe complains, taking Wyatt's advice.

The move has the desired effect. The men frown and return to their snack time.

"Seriously? How does the woman who loves Christmas and listened to carols during the flight up here hate mistletoe?"

"How did you know that?"

"It was a guess. Answer the question."

Stowe moans. "Bobby Sinclair."

"Bobby...?"

"Sinclair. He was a guy I knew in high school."

"He had a crush on you?"

"Does a toddler like sugar?"

"Okay, and Bobby made you hate mistletoe because…?"

Stowe sighs. This isn't the kind of conversation she expects with Wyatt Huffman. He has no need to know her business…or her history. Unfortunately, she's the one who opened the door, so she might as well finish the story.

"My grandparents raised me, and Nana loves hanging it all over the house. She gets twisted pleasure in making their guests kiss every chance they get. I mean, mistletoe is everywhere. There's almost no hiding from it. You have to map routes through the house like you're traversing a minefield just to get to the kitchen to make hot cocoa. I was good at avoiding it growing up, but one day, I had some friends over and wasn't paying attention."

"And Bobby Sinclair took advantage."

Stowe touches her nose and points at Wyatt.

"Was it that bad?"

"He was okay but skeevy. When we returned from Christmas break, he made it a point to tell everyone in school what happened. I was traumatized the entire winter. So, now I ignore the mistletoe rule unless I'm at home. Nana insists that the tradition be followed."

"And you listen to her?"

Stowe looks at him and grins. "I may not have met your sister, but you *definitely* haven't met Nana. She's a force of nature."

Wyatt nods. "She sounds like a remarkable woman."

Stowe glances over at him, thinking maybe he's being sarcastic. He isn't. He meant what he said. That's another thing she didn't expect.

A young blonde woman wearing pigtails and dressed like an elf steps into the room. Not the ones from *Lord of the Rings*. She's clad in a green dress with a serrated hemline that comes down to her mid-thigh. Her stockings are red, white, and green, and she's wearing black boots and a black belt. Her hat looks like Santa's, only it's the same color green as her dress and has a jingle bell at the end.

"I'm sorry for your wait. Welcome to the North Pole South Santa Academy. My name is Arnarra, and I'm the chief elf. Can I help you?"

"This is a beautiful space," Wyatt observes, looking around.

"It's Christmas all year here," Arnarra says, gesturing around the lobby.

"You're open year-round?" Stowe asks, not knowing that despite having lived near here for most of her life.

"Oh, we have to be. There is too much demand for the academy to be seasonal. Each initial course is a resident six-week immersive experience. Santas-in-Training come here from all over the world to become an expert on everything about the holiday. We are currently offering a refresher course this weekend for our graduates. Some of our best Santas are here now."

"Impressive," Stowe says.

"We take our Santa training very seriously."

If Arnarra the elf is any sign, that is a true statement. Stowe would need to guzzle a case of Red Bull to reach this woman's hyperenergetic state. She cannot be just playing her part. Her enthusiasm and bubbly persona are too natural to be an act. There is a job for everyone, and Arnarra clearly found hers.

"That's great to hear. I'm Stowe Bessette, and this is Wyatt Huffman. We work for the U.S. Congress and hope you can help with a problem."

"Well, I can certainly try. What kind of help do you need?"

Stowe smiles. "We want to talk to your three best Santas."

Chapter Twenty-Two

REPRESENTATIVE JOHN KNUTSON

The meeting has already convened by the time John and Angela arrive. It's good to see their combined staff collaborating like this. Maybe that's a strong word. At least they are chattier than they were a couple of days ago. It's a start, especially in a town where the political divide is measured in hundreds of miles.

"All right, folks. Where are we?"

"The basic research on the people testifying before the committee is done," one of Angela's staffers says. "No major red flags. All of them are experts in their fields."

"We have developed a list of questions based on their likely testimony. We weren't sure how the two of you wanted to divide them up."

"Leave it with us," John says to his staffer. "We'll figure it out."

"We need to talk tactics," Cameron interjects. "Each subcommittee member will only be allocated five minutes for questions. We know that Guzman and Blackburn are building an alliance that will only toss softballs. We also know the fence-sitters won't ask anything of substance. The hard questions will need to come from you and whomever you bring to our side."

"We have three allies so far," Angela says, resulting in a few stifled groans.

"That's it?" her chief of staff asks. "I thought we were making more progress than that."

"Welcome to politics."

"Even when Christmas is at stake?"

Angela leans forward and folds her hands on the table. "Nobody wants to cross Guzman. Not when the speaker and House majority leader weren't willing to intercede."

"Likewise with Blackburn," John adds. "He holds a lot of sway in the party and can command a lot of votes for pet projects. I think most subcommittee members think this isn't going anywhere anyway. They won't make a spectacle of it and risk offending him."

"This is insanity," one of Angela's staffers groans. "It's Christmas, for crying out loud!"

"Which is why we're fighting when nobody else will."

"I think they want us to fight," John concludes, adding to Angela's assurance.

"What do you mean, Congressman?" the woman asks.

"Well, it's something Angela and I have been mulling over. None of this makes sense. Guzman saw one Santa make a scene at a California shopping mall. It made headlines and went viral because incidents like that are exceedingly rare. It's not like there's a plague of misbehaving Santas infesting American malls. Why blow this one isolated incident out of proportion?"

"Guzman hates Christmas," Cameron grumbles.

"No, we think it's more than that," Angela interjects. "Camilla *wants* the controversy. The bigger it becomes, the closer she gets to her objective."

"Which is?"

John looks at Angela, who shrugs. "We don't know yet."

"You could be wrong," Cam argues.

"Yes, I could. But look at the people selected to testify. Half of them are divisive, and the other half will be discussing topics that will be. The selection of those individuals isn't an accident – it's meant to cause an outcry."

"So far, it's working," Angela's social media staffer interjects. "Social media interest is growing. So is mainstream reporting. I saw more Santas protesting at the Capitol this morning than I did in last year's 5K Santa Run. It's a spectacle made for cable news and viral trending."

"Are you suggesting we change our approach?" Angela asks. "Go easy on the questions?"

"It's worth considering," John admits. "We could save the thunder for when jolly old Saint Nick testifies and use him to dismantle previous arguments."

"Only Stowe and Wyatt haven't found a suitable one yet. They are up in Vermont doing interviews at one of the best Santa academies in the country and haven't checked in."

"I share the congresswoman's concerns," Cam says, leaning forward, folding his hands, and planting his elbows on the table. "It's putting our eggs in one basket. If they don't come through...."

"I agree," John says, turning to Angela and getting a nod. "It's a risk, but one we should consider. I'm not saying we won't challenge the testimonies, but maybe the better tactic isn't to go nuclear. The best defense is a good offense. Santa himself can do the heavy lifting."

The combined staff doesn't say anything. It's a mixed bag of opinions from the looks on their faces. No side has a monopoly on agreeing or disagreeing with the approach. That's a good thing. For once, nobody in this room is thinking along party lines.

"We need our Santa," Angela concludes.

"Agreed. Cam, get in touch with Wyatt and Stowe and find out where they are."

He nods. "Will do. Whoever they find will need to be one hell of a Santa Claus to pull this off."

Chapter Twenty-Three

CAMILLA GUZMAN

The Committee on Commerce and Manufactures was established on December 14, 1795. The growing demands of a new nation required Congress to exercise its constitutional authority to regulate commerce with foreign nations and among the states. The Committee on Energy and Commerce, as it is now known, is the oldest standing legislative committee in the U.S. House of Representatives.

There are sexier committee assignments like Ways and Means and Judiciary, but this one has its benefits. While not the most prestigious, Energy and Commerce has the most wide-ranging jurisdiction of any congressional committee. That means it can have an impact on the American people. Camilla was handed the assignment after her election and was tapped to chair a small and largely irrelevant subcommittee as a reward for supporting fellow House candidates.

The Subcommittee on Cultural Commerce is charged with making recommendations to the full committee on how to best regulate products and services that have a cultural impact on the United States. Much of their work in this Congress surrounds the entertainment industry, social media, and professional sports. Now they're branching out.

As with all committees in Congress, the members caucus with their party to strategize. Attendance is restricted, so Camilla has never attended the other party's strategy meeting until now. Not that they are all present. Aymos Blackburn invited her to help sway three of their more impressionable members and build support on his side of the aisle. Representatives Shelby Donaldson, Rod Bishop, and Faye Blanchard are not her biggest fans.

"This is a joke, right? Tell me it is," Donaldson says.

"I assure you, Shelby, it isn't."

"Aymos, I came here thinking you would explain how you planned to embarrass Congresswoman Guzman and her party. That's clearly not the case since she's sitting here with us."

"No, this isn't a political game," Blackburn declares. "I was proud to co-sponsor her bill, and I'm serious about these hearings. I need you to take them seriously, too."

"Banning Santa Claus in public places is something you expected us to take seriously?" Bishop asks.

"Absolutely."

"Not a chance."

Aymos lets out a heavy sigh. "Then, Rod, I'm afraid we're already off on the wrong foot."

"Apparently."

"How is this constitutional, Aymos?" Faye Blanchard asks. "Assuming this legislation gets enacted by both chambers—"

"Not likely," Donaldson mutters, interrupting her.

"And gets signed by the president," she continues, "what are the odds that it isn't struck down by the Supreme Court?"

Blackburn smiles. "I can only hope we get that far to find out."

"Aymos," Bishop says, taking up the argument, "we've known each other for a long time. Politics aside, why are you signing on to this at Christmas?"

"Well, let me see," he says in his most sarcastic voice, "maybe because nobody would pay attention if we did it in May."

It's a valid point. Christmas in July might be something people throw around as a joke, but nobody is thinking much about the holiday with six months to go. Camilla was amused at the comment. The three members of the committee she and Aymos are trying to enlist aren't.

"Is that what this is about? Getting attention?"

"This is about righting a wrong, Shelby," Camilla chimes in after Aymos looks at her. "Aymos and I agree on the goal of this legislation, even if it is for different reasons."

"You have a problem with capitalism. That's your reason."

"In general, yes. I don't deny that. Specifically, I don't think families should be guilted into buying thousands of dollars in gifts they can't afford just because of a date on the calendar."

"You could make the same argument about Valentine's Day," Blanchard says.

"Yes, I could, but no other holiday is more egregious in its commercialism than Christmas."

"And Santa is the cause of that?" Bishop says with a sneer.

"He's the symbol of it. If you come into the hearings with an open mind, it may be enlightening."

"I understand her agenda, Aymos," Congresswoman Blanchard says, "but this is more extreme than anything I would have expected from you."

Aymos leans deeper into his high-backed chair and steeples his fingers in front of his mouth. He is a renowned storyteller adept at using historical examples to prove points. Not only are they hard to refute factually, but they are entertaining to listen to. It makes him extremely difficult to argue with. Guzman has found that out the hard way once or twice during her time in Congress.

"When the three wise men arrived at the manger, they didn't come with an Xbox or iPhone. There were no Barbie Dreamhouses, Teddy Ruxpins, Transformers, or Tickle Me Elmos. They came with gold, frankincense, and myrrh."

"Each of those gifts had value," Donaldson points out.

"All physical things have a modicum of value. Their special meaning made these particular gifts endure the rigors of history. Gold honored the King of the Jews; the frankincense recognized Jesus as a divine being and Son of God; and the myrrh means that Jesus was also human and mortal."

"What's your point, Aymos?" Rod Bishop asks impatiently.

"Gift-giving shouldn't be about the value of a present, but its meaning. Jesus was a simple carpenter. He would hate how commercialized Christmas has become in his name."

Camilla doesn't know the three other representatives in this room well. Will that argument appeal to them? Other than loosely sharing Aymos's party ideology, they could be pious devotees to God or absolute heathens. Her co-sponsor doesn't mute his preaching or religiously centered language for any audience, so their reaction to that argument could fall anywhere between two extremes.

"So, you want to ban Santa because God wants you to?"

Aymos may be a man of faith, but he has a mean streak that is often conveyed by a glare that could melt ice. He didn't appreciate the tone or the incorrect insinuation of a divine motive, especially from a colleague in his own party. At least the comment answers her previous question.

"I want America to return to what's important: Family, faith, the flag, and friends. Not commercial interests or the bottom lines of corporations and retailers."

"I don't like where this is going," Donaldson says, standing. "I got elected to Congress to combat government overreach into every aspect of American lives. Even if your goals are altruistic, that's what you're proposing."

"Something I'm sure you will point out during the hearings, Shelby," Camilla says in a last-ditch effort to get him to stay.

He shakes his head. "I've heard enough. I can't support this. We'll see you in the hearings."

Aymos's three colleagues file out of the room without another word. He doesn't try to stop them. He only sits at the table with a content, almost amused look. The man is the epitome of calmness.

"That went well," Camilla mumbles.

"It went as I expected," Aymos admits. "Were the members of your caucus any more receptive?"

"That's a fair point. They weren't. This is going to be an uphill climb."

Aymos shrugs. "The steeper the climb, the better the view from the top. They will come around."

"I wish I had your optimism," Camilla moans. "I already have Speaker Hoskins gunning for me. I used every ounce of leverage I had to keep him from pulling the plug. I'm trying to keep a brave face in front of the staff, but...."

"You don't want to spend too much time in his crosshairs. I understand. May I suggest a change to the hearing schedule?"

"Sure. What do you have in mind?"

Congressman Blackburn leans forward over the table. "The only way this gets done is through public pressure. Our colleagues are too short-sighted to see past their next fundraiser, much less the next election. We need to use some shock and awe to get people to nudge them into our corner."

Camilla cocks her head and then slowly nods. "You think we should move our keynote speaker to the head of the line. Bring out the big guns early to ratchet up the pressure."

He nods. Now, it's the congresswoman's turn to sink back into her chair. The change in tactic could work to their advantage. It will certainly capture the attention they are looking for. She smiles, knowing that despite being from opposing parties, there is a lot she could learn from Aymos Blackburn.

Chapter Twenty-Four

WYATT HUFFMAN

Arnarra is pleased to fulfill their interview request once Stowe shares the details surrounding their visit. The chief elf hefts a four-inch-thick leather-bound ledger that looks a hundred years old onto the reception counter. Opening the tome, she turns to the page with the most recent entries and identifies the Santas staying at the academy. It looks like almost a hundred candidates. She reviews the list and picks the top three.

Apparently, all classes here are conducted by people dressed as elves. Each is almost as bubbly and outgoing as her, even the men. She dispatches an elf-in-training to ask each of the three Santas to come to the reception area one at a time for an interview.

He scurries off, and Arnarra invites Stowe and Wyatt to the small dining area the Santas were hoovering cookies and milk in when they arrived. They open their laptops and get situated while Arnarra brings them hot cocoa and candy canes. She also sets a plate of Christmas cookies on the table for the Santas and leaves the pair alone to decide how to approach the interviews. They agree to conduct it similarly to Tax Evasion Santa, except for asking questions about background and legal troubles earlier in the process.

The first Santa enters, decked out in full costume. It's easy to see why Arnarra selected him. There is no doubt he's popular with the kids. His "ho, ho, ho" is perfect. His cheeks are rosy, his white beard is real, and he brings jolly to a whole new level. They learn his real name is Brian, and he lives in Ashland, Virginia.

"How long have you been playing Santa?" Stowe asks.

"Oh, I graduated from here seven years ago. It was right after I retired from my job. I come back every other year to refine my craft. You can never stop learning about Santa and Christmas."

"Why do you like being Santa?"

"It makes people happy. That makes me happy."

"What do you do for work, Brian?" Wyatt asks.

"Outside of building toys for all the good little girls and boys?"

"Yes, outside of that."

"I'm retired. Most of us here are."

That makes sense. Santa is older, and the work is seasonal – two things tailor-made for retirees. A side hustle as St. Nick would be hard for a working professional to swing.

"What did you do before retirement?"

"I worked on Wall Street, believe it or not."

"Stockbroker?"

"Investment banker," Brian says, correcting Wyatt.

"You were never involved in any illegal financial dealings, were you?" Stowe asks.

It's a legitimate question and one that needs to be asked. It was the way she phrased it that captured Wyatt's attention. Her tone almost made it sound like a joke, even if the intent was serious. She is very good at this.

"Of course not," Brian says with a patented Santa laugh. "With so many financial regulations in place…the risk of breaking the law and getting caught wasn't worth the reward. I already had enough stress in my life. I needed my weekly meetings to manage that."

"Meetings? Like, with a psychologist?"

"Alcoholics Anonymous. I'm two years sober."

"Congratulations," Wyatt says. "You said you drank to manage work stress, but you retired seven years ago."

Brian shifts his considerable weight in the chair. "Yes, I did. I've had a couple of relapses since then."

"A couple of relapses?" Stowe asks. "As in two?"

"Thirteen. But the last one has stuck so far. It's amazing how getting caught driving drunk will change your life."

Stowe closes her eyes as Wyatt recovers and leans forward. "Thank you, Brian, and congratulations on your sobriety. I'm happy to hear you're getting your life in order. We have a few more interviews and will get back to you with our decision."

They shake hands, and Brian leaves. Wyatt collapses into his chair. He was perfect in every other way. Unfortunately, putting him in front of Congress will only serve to end his sobriety. The first thing anyone needs after testifying is a stiff drink.

The second Santa, Louis, files in and answers their questions as Sauced Santa did. All the answers are spot-on but sound very robotic and rehearsed. He doesn't have the charisma, and Wyatt is beginning to doubt if the man has an ounce of true Christmas spirit.

"Why do you like playing Santa? Give us the honest answer, not the one they teach you to say."

"The honest answer? The money is fantastic. I mean, who else gets paid this much to sit on your butt and take some pictures?"

"It's not for the joy it brings you or the happiness you bring to children?"

"You asked for the real answer, not my public answer. Most of the guys here would agree with me. I couldn't care less about the kids. I don't like them."

"You don't like children…?"

"Miss, try sitting in a chair for four hours listening to them scream in your ear about whatever ridiculous toy they want or how you didn't bring them something last year. I've gone deaf in my right ear from the entitled brats. Then you get the real beauties who pee or puke on you. And then there's the smell. It's horrible. Do parents even bathe their kids these days?"

Wyatt wouldn't know. He doesn't have children, and much to his father's chagrin, neither do his siblings. Stowe is in the same boat. Neither would have the first clue how easy or hard it is to get a kid into a bathtub. Of course, they wouldn't be that rude about it. Stowe asks a few more perfunctory questions, and they thank Louis for his time.

"I think Tax Evasion Santa and Jaded Santa would get along perfectly," Wyatt says after the man leaves.

Stowe smiles and shakes her head at Wyatt as Santa number three is brought in. He's by far the most promising, even beyond the first. Christopher worked as a high-school teacher, loves kids, is happily married, and lives a quiet life in Alabama.

"What do you do for fun, Chris?"

"I like going to Alabama football games."

"Go, Bama," Wyatt says, causing the big man to smile.

"Roll Tide!"

"Sounds like fun," Stowe says.

"It is. Being around men and women that age makes me feel young and vigorous."

"I bet."

That's a fair answer. Wyatt and Stowe spend the next ten minutes peppering Christopher with more questions. He has a good philosophy and an excellent repertoire of Christmas knowledge. Best of all, he's cool under pressure and willing to face the fire on a national stage.

Stowe looks at Wyatt, who nods. "We think you'd be perfect for this, Chris. Are you available to come to Washington next week?"

"Next week? Oh, I don't know," Chris says, stroking his beard. "I have a court date coming up that I can't miss."

"Court date? You said you were never arrested."

His panicked eyes dart between them. Wyatt knows he didn't mean to divulge that.

"No, you asked if I was ever convicted of any crimes. I haven't been, and I won't be this time either. It's just some minor legal trouble. Much ado about nothing," Chris says with a dismissive wave.

Wyatt leans forward, gripping the edge of the table to brace himself. "What were you arrested for?"

"Uh, indecent exposure, public intoxication, trespassing, and resisting arrest. I had too much fun at one of the Bama games this year."

Stowe closes her eyes. "You ran out on the field."

Chris laughs, although not in the jolly ho, ho, ho. "Wearing nothing but underwear, sneakers, and a Santa hat. Not one of my finer moments."

"Why the indecent exposure charge?" Wyatt asks.

"My boxers were riding up on me around the thirty-yard line, so I pulled them off before security tackled me."

"Okay, thank you, Chris. We'll be in touch."

Chris knows that was a deal-breaker. He grimaces as he shakes their hands and departs the room, much less merry than he was walking in.

"He could still work."

Stowe looks at Wyatt like he has three heads. "That game was in the SEC, which was likely nationally televised. You know the footage is on YouTube. Guzman won't be able to contain her excitement playing it for the subcommittee."

Wyatt shrugs and smiles. "I was kidding, but maybe Guzman and Blackburn will forget to request the television to play the footage. How do you know about the SEC? You watch college football?"

"We need to talk to more candidates," Stowe says. "Those can't be the best three. And, of course, I watch college football. I watch all kinds of sports."

Wyatt blinks a couple of times in disbelief. He files that nugget away for another time.

"All right. I'll get Chief Elf Arnarra."

Stowe's phone rings, and she checks the caller's name on the screen. "It's not a good time, Nana. Can I—"

Wyatt hears her stop stone cold and listen.

"He what? Oh, my God! Is he okay? No, I'll be right there. No, I'm coming, Nana. I'm already in Burlington. I'll be there in an hour."

Stowe ends the call and slams the screen down on her laptop before yanking the power cable out of the wall.

"What's wrong?"

"I'm sorry, Wyatt, I have to go."

There is no further explanation as Stowe rushes out of the room, almost knocking over Arnarra, who's carrying another plate of cookies for them. Wyatt apologizes to the head elf, thanks her for her time, and heads after Stowe, having no idea what's wrong.

Chapter Twenty-Five

STOWE BESSETTE

Her laptop case catches the jamb as Stowe rushes out the front door, knocking her off-balance and almost sending her tumbling to the ground. She recovers and hurries to their rental car, fumbling with the handle until she finally yanks it to open the door.

Stowe slings her purse and laptop into the back seat, starts the engine, and stomps on the accelerator. The sedan lurches forward before gaining momentum. She lowers her eyes to check the gas gauge and confirm it will be enough to get her home. When her gaze returns to the view out the windshield, she slams on the brakes, sending the car skidding on the gravel driveway. She stops only a foot or two from Wyatt, who's standing in her path.

"You moron!" Stowe screams after rolling her window down and poking her head out. "I could have killed you! What the hell are you doing?"

"Going with you," Wyatt says, standing upright after bracing himself for an imminent collision with her hood.

"No, you're not. Take a rideshare back to the airport. I'll meet you back in Washington."

"Then you're going to have to run me over because that's not going to happen. I'm going with you."

Stowe unbuckles her seatbelt and launches herself out of the driver's seat. She stomps over to him with a mix of purpose and anger in her eyes.

"This has nothing to do with you or this assignment."

"Something happened, Stowe," Wyatt says, his voice soothing and concerned.

"It's my PopPop. He fell and...."

She's barely holding it together. The war against her tears is a lost cause, and they begin streaming down her cheeks.

"Okay. I'll drive you there. Let's go."

"No, I'll drive myself!"

Wyatt gently grabs her arms and looks her in the eyes. "Stowe, you almost made me a hood ornament, and you're not even out of the driveway. You're too distraught to think clearly, much less drive. It won't do your grandparents any good if you wrap the car around a tree. You navigate. I'll drive. At least I'll know you got there safely. Then I can head back to the airport."

The offer is sweet and sincere. Stowe wants to protest and go alone, but Wyatt is determined. Not wanting to waste more time arguing, she relents and walks around the front of the car to the passenger side. Wyatt is already behind the wheel, adjusting the seat when she reaches the door.

"All right. Where to?" Wyatt asks as he buckles his seatbelt.

"Pick up Interstate 89 and follow it east until you reach State Route 101," Stowe says in a near-whisper.

"Easy enough."

Wyatt guides the car onto the road and presses harder on the gas. He keeps an eye for icy spots on the asphalt. He's a good driver and keenly aware of the hazards of driving on northern roads in late November. The cars up here may be good in snow, but a Zamboni is the only vehicle ever devised that works well on ice.

Stowe is fighting tears as she stares out the window. "You don't have to do this."

"I know. I'm not doing it out of obligation."

"Then why are you?"

Wyatt sighs. "Maybe someday you'll realize I'm not the soulless, heartless man you think I am."

"I don't think of you that way."

Stowe feels him glance at her but doesn't press for an explanation.

"Was it a serious fall?"

"Nana said it wasn't."

"But?"

"She usually undersells these things so that I won't worry. PopPop has been falling a lot lately."

"And you think the lack of balance and coordination could be something more serious. Have the doctors done any tests?"

Stowe shakes her head. "He won't let them. He's a Green Mountain Man. His motto is 'Stubborn, Obstinate, Impossible."

"I understand. I'm from Montana. My grandfather was the same way."

Stowe was hoping for silence during this car ride. Now, she finds the conversation soothing. And she's curious.

"What was he like?"

"My grandfather? Tough as nails, but the most honorable man you'd ever meet. He was married to my grandmother for fifty-eight years. He got away with stuff that most married couples can't."

"Like what?"

"One of my earliest memories was him working the smoker and the grill behind the house. He had a lit Marlboro in one hand and a spatula in the other. Well, my grandmother wasn't having any of that. She came out of the kitchen spittin' about how he was taking years off his life and not caring about the carcinogens the grandkids were sucking in. Keep in mind, we were sitting eight feet away from a charcoal grill and a meat smoker."

"What did he do?"

"Nothing. My grandfather stood there stoically like a British admiral on the quarterdeck. He waited and waited for her tirade to flame out. When it finally did, he looked at her, took a long drag on his cigarette, and calmly barked, 'This is why nobody likes you.'"

Stowe laughs. She has a hundred similar stories.

"Oh, my God, that sounds just like my PopPop."

"It was a different generation."

"Are your grandparents still alive?"

"No. They've both passed on."

Stowe lowers her eyes. She knows death is inevitable but doesn't want to think about it. Her parents are nothing more than faded memories now. Her grandparents have been her whole world for most of her life, and she can't bear to lose them, too. Not for a long time.

"I'm sorry."

"No need to apologize. My grandfather wouldn't abide it. He had no regrets in his life. Except maybe marrying my grandmother."

"Was he serious about that?"

"I hope not. My grandparents loved sparring about things like that. They would make sarcastic comments for the fun of getting a rise out of each other. My grandfather always professed that any marriage requires three rings."

"Three? The engagement ring, the wedding ring, and…?"

Wyatt turns to look at Stowe. "The suffering."

Another smile creeps across Stowe's face. "He sounds like quite a character. What's your father like?"

Wyatt grimaces. "Different. Very different."

He goes quiet, and Stowe knows she may have struck a nerve. She decides not to press for details, partly to avoid forcing him to talk about it and partly because she's getting nervous. Talking to Wyatt is beginning to feel natural to her. It's too natural, and that's starting to scare her. She can't do this again. Not yet.

Chapter Twenty-Six

WYATT HUFFMAN

Stowe unbuckles her seatbelt, opens the door, and charges toward the front door before Wyatt even brings the car to a complete stop. He understands the urgency. He would do the same thing if it were his mother. His father? Probably not so much.

He kills the engine and moves around the vehicle to close Stowe's still-open door before admiring the cabin. This isn't the shack in the woods he half-expected to find. It's a majestic wood structure with a steeply angled peak to the roof and lots of windows. He can see the appeal of living in this part of the country.

Wyatt climbs the stairs and quietly enters the house. Stowe is already at her grandfather's side by the roaring fireplace in the rustic living room. Her grandmother is watching from the entrance to the kitchen and hasn't seen Wyatt yet.

"Oh, I'm fine, just a little sore," her grandfather argues. "You don't need to fuss."

"This time. If you keep falling, you're going to really hurt yourself!"

Wyatt looks up at the ceiling. Stowe wasn't kidding. Mistletoe is hung in strategic locations everywhere. He sidesteps to ensure he isn't positioned under one of them. He doesn't want to be the cause of another Bobby Sinclair fiasco.

"It's gonna take more than a little tumble to keep me down. Who's your friend?"

Her grandfather nods in Wyatt's direction. Stowe looks at him, and her grandmother is startled by his presence.

"Oh, my! Well, hello there," she gushes.

"Good afternoon, ma'am, sir."

"Ma'am and sir?" her grandfather turns and asks Stowe with a raised eyebrow.

"He's from Montana."

"Ah, that explains it. I thought maybe he was military."

"Stowe didn't mention she was bringing a handsome young man home," Nana says, rushing to his side.

"Don't let it go to your head," Stowe warns with a grin. "Nana thinks everyone is handsome."

"Stowe Elizabeth Bessette! Behave yourself. I'm Dorothy, and that's my klutzy husband, Walter."

"I'm Wyatt. It's a pleasure to meet you both. Stowe speaks very highly of you. In her defense, she didn't bring me here. I drove her home to ensure she got here safely."

"That's very chivalrous of you," Dorothy says, in a tone that says she's genuinely impressed at the gesture.

Wyatt smiles and nods. "Stowe, I left your suitcase in the kitchen. I'm going to head back to the airport."

"Nonsense! You will do no such thing. You drove our Stowe down here, so the least we can do is feed you a nice dinner and have you spend the night."

"Nana, we don't have—"

"We have three guestrooms in this house, Stowe," her grandmother scolds. "There's plenty of space."

There is no doubt that Dorothy runs the household. She's a sweet and kind soul, but there is no way Wyatt would ever want to end up on her bad side. He is tired and hungry, but Stowe's pleading eyes and general uneasiness at the idea is reason enough to not stick around.

"I appreciate the offer, ma'am, but I don't want to intrude on family time. I need to get back to Washington."

"You aren't intruding. You're our guest."

"And it's Friday night. There are no flights to Washington out of Burlington until tomorrow, anyway," her grandfather announces from his chair. "Do yourself a favor, son, and surrender now. It'll save a whole lot of heartache later. Trust me."

Those are sound words of wisdom from a man with decades of experience. All Wyatt can do is nod.

"Well, I'm going to start supper and fix up the guestroom. Now, go out and get your things from the car, and let's get you settled in before we eat."

"Thank you, ma'am."

"I'll join you," Stowe decrees. "I'll be right back, PopPop."

"Take your time. I'm not going anywhere. Your grandmother won't let me. She's got me chained to this chair like I'm an invalid," he mutters under his breath.

"I heard that!" Dorothy announces from the kitchen.

Stowe struggles into her coat as they close the front door behind them and crunch on the near-frozen gravel to the rental car.

"Your grandparents are amazing."

"Yes, they are."

Wyatt stops and faces her, looking back at the majestic cabin. "It wasn't my intention to get invited to stay. If you want me to go, say the word. You can blame it on me. Say I wasn't comfortable or something."

Stowe glances down the driveway. "It's okay. Neither Nana nor PopPop would ever believe a polite cowboy ran away without my encouragement. They would make my life miserable for months. Besides, there really isn't any reason for you *not* to stay. There's nothing for us to do until tomorrow anyway."

"You're sure?"

"Yeah," she says, offering a weak smile. "But thank you for offering."

Stowe turns and walks to the door as Wyatt retrieves his carry-on from the trunk. He isn't sure what he got himself into, but he knows the meal will be amazing, the guestroom comfortable, and reality will return tomorrow when the congressman learns they are no closer to finding their Santa than they were before coming to Vermont.

Chapter Twenty-Seven

REPRESENTATIVE JOHN KNUTSON

People run for national office for different reasons. Most start with an urge to bring change to Washington – to do good things while faithfully representing their constituents back home. But one of the unalienable truths in life is that power corrupts. So, for many, that mindset changes over time. Whether it's the insatiable thirst for personal or campaign riches or the lust for power and control depends on the politician.

John is old school and still believes he is here for his constituents. He's unwavering in the belief that he's their elected representative and was sent here to be their voice. It's hard to find allies who share that mindset, even within his own party. That's why he likes Angela Pratt. While they may disagree on the issues, she has always acted in the best interest of those who elected her, regardless of the circumstances.

And that's the catch. Representing constituents' wants and needs sometimes contradicts the party's political objectives. Regardless of whether the leadership is Democrat or Republican, they only care about the great game and the ultimate prize – control. That leads to power, money, and prestige. If you stand in the way of that goal, it's at your peril. There are a lot of ways party leaders can hurt you.

The subcommittee hearings on legislation banning public depictions of Santa Claus start in three days. There is much work to be done, and that's why John is still in the office on a Friday night. The staff has long gone home, leaving him free to blast country music and focus on question preparation. When the House minority leader and whip walk through his office door, those concerns over the "ways party leaders can hurt you" become more immediate.

"Hi, John," the minority leader shouts over a tune by Jason Aldeen as he enters the office, his political capo in tow close behind.

Spencer Durant and Gregory Guillomi are practically clones. They were elected to Congress in the same year, rose through the party ranks together, are ideological mirror images, and are often attached at the hip. If they get the House back in the next election, there is little doubt that Spencer will become the new speaker and Gregory will take his place as the floor majority leader. As a result, when they speak, people listen. John pauses the music as the two men sit.

"What brings you guys to the Longworth Building?" John asks, knowing their formal offices are in the Capitol and their personal ones are in the Rayburn House Office Building.

"You do. How's the preparation for your subcommittee hearings going?"

John gestures at the papers scattered on his desk. "As good as can be expected."

"Is the game plan to fight this tooth and nail all the way?"

"Given the slate of people testifying, it seems like the best choice of action."

The minority leader cocks his head and presses his lips together. "Yeah, we don't want you to do that."

"Excuse me?"

"Call off the dogs, John," the minority whip decrees. "Vote against advancing the bill, but don't fight it during the hearings."

John fidgets in his chair. "I don't understand."

"Sure you do," Spencer says, leaning forward. "The next election is going to be a dogfight. We'll need all the help we can get to win back the House."

"And you think that not challenging testimony belittling Santa Claus will help how?"

"Never interrupt your enemy when they're making a mistake," Gregory blurts out. "Attacking Christmas at Christmas is a foolish move they'll pay for at the polls. We need to let them make that unforced error."

"They aren't attacking Christmas. They're going after Santa Claus."

"People won't draw that distinction," Durant clarifies. "This is a wedge issue handed to us on a golden platter."

Wedge issues. As if there aren't enough of those today. If there is one thing politicians and the media are good at, it's dividing people. The two key components of the political process have fostered a perfect symbiotic relationship. Politicians create the divide, relying on a willing media to widen it for ratings and clicks. Rinse and repeat. Nothing is off the table, including Christmas.

"Even if some members of their party are against it also?"

"That's the other thing we wanted to talk to you about," Spencer says smugly. "You need to quit working with Angela Pratt."

"Why?"

John clasps his hands on his desk to prevent them from balling into fists.

"It is being viewed in certain circles as…."

"Disloyal."

Now Gregory is finishing Durant's sentences. How cute.

"So, instead of showing a bipartisan, unified front against this madness, you want me to ignore what's happening because it's politically damaging to the opposition?"

"Precisely."

That's the game. It's no longer about governing. Everything is predicated on winning. It's the only thing that matters, even if it's the people who suffer in the end. The divisiveness all but guarantees they won't vote for the other party. As districts become safely homogenous in their support for one party or another, the game's intensity and number of players grow. Why pay attention to the people if there's no chance of losing an election? That's the biggest problem in today's Congress.

"And if I say no?"

The two men look at each other, but it's the minority whip who takes the lead. He's the one who levels the threats in this relationship. "Don't say no, John."

"Of all people, Gregory, I wouldn't think you would remotely care about this."

"He doesn't," Durant confirms. "His heart is smaller than the Grinch's before it grew three sizes. But this is politics. Do things our way, and when we win next year, you'll become chair of the Energy and Commerce Committee. Not just the subcommittee, the whole shebang."

"That's the carrot," the minority whip says. "Here's the stick: Several bills coming through the House will directly affect your district in next year's session. You'll need our unwavering support to do what's best for your constituents. So, as you Montanans like to say, this is horse-trading. You don't want to be on the wrong side of us."

With nothing more to say, the two men stand in unison. Both have grins that John would like nothing more than to slap off. They are leaving the decision to him, not that there is much choice in the matter, at least from their perspectives.

"We look forward to your cooperation. Have a good night, John."

The minority leader and whip depart with the same arrogance they strolled in with. The boom has been lowered. Now it's a matter of figuring out what to do next – risk his career by defying his party over a bill that will likely never see the House floor, or risk alienating his constituents and allies by refusing to fight? He knows what most of his peers would do. Unfortunately, the decision isn't as easy for him. He has never been one to go along with the crowd.

Chapter Twenty-Eight

STOWE BESSETTE

Stowe is dressed in the most comfortable clothes she has in her closet. It's approaching winter in Vermont, meaning comfortable jeans, heavy wool socks, and a plaid wool shirt over a white tank top. She would take this look over her Capitol Hill wardrobe any day.

She comes down the stairs, taking care not to slide in her socks on the hardwood treads. Stowe is frustrated enough. She doesn't need to lose traction and land herself in a hospital like PopPop did, especially with Wyatt here.

"Good morning, Nana," Stowe mutters, heading straight for the coffee pot to pour herself a cup of heaven.

"Rough night?"

"Two steps forward, three steps back. I knew finding a good Santa would be difficult. I didn't think it would turn out to be completely impossible."

"A Santa?"

"It's a long story. It would be a little easier if I had Sleeping Beauty to help," Stowe says, nodding at the stairs and the bedrooms on the upper floor.

"Who?"

"Wyatt. His door is closed, so he must still be sleeping."

Nana rewards her granddaughter with the look she uses when she's about to impart some wisdom. She seizes Stowe's arm and drags her to the window. Wyatt is outside, wielding an ax without a jacket on. He's no rookie at the task – splitting wood is something he's clearly done before.

"That boy doesn't have an off switch," Nana leans in and says. "He's been out there since the sun came up. I'm surprised you didn't hear him."

"My bedroom is on the other side of the house. Why is he splitting firewood?"

"That's what I asked him. He said since PopPop has a busted wing, he didn't want me carrying heavy logs into the house. He's been splitting them into smaller pieces so I can easily carry them. Isn't he sweet?"

Stowe wants to say no, but it is very sweet. And considerate. Neither of those attributes would she have attributed to Wyatt a few days ago.

"Yeah, I guess," she says with a shrug.

"Oh, Stowe, he's a good man. Maybe you should consider—"

"You know why I won't."

"Honey, that's in the past."

"Not that far in the past, and Wyatt isn't in my future, so can you please drop it?"

Nana frowns but does as requested. She knows she can only push so hard without upsetting Stowe. As a result, she likes to walk right up to that line without crossing it.

"Okay. Breakfast will be ready in a few minutes."

Stowe grabs another mug from the cupboard and pours a second cup of coffee. She carries both to the door, dons the winter coat hanging on a peg, and ventures out into the cold to bring it to Wyatt.

He doesn't notice her immediately. The man has incredible focus and excellent stamina. She's getting tired just watching him. Wyatt stops chopping when he sees her standing there with the coffee.

"Good morning."

"Good morning. I thought you could use this," Stowe says, handing him the steaming cup of java. "I assume you like it black."

"Like my soul," he quips.

"You're out here in the freezing cold splitting wood for my grandparents. I don't think your soul is black. Maybe charcoal-gray."

"That's an improvement. I'll take it," Wyatt says, sipping the brew and moaning. "Oh, my God. This is *good* coffee."

"Nana missed her calling. She'd be rich if she ever opened a coffee shop."

"I believe it. I know I'd be a regular."

Stowe takes a sip of her own before drawing closer to him. The freshly split wood in a pile beside him is only a fraction of his labor. Most of the cord of wood stacked against the barn has already been halved or quartered.

"Why are you doing this, Wyatt?"

"What do you mean?"

"You met my grandparents yesterday. I mean, this is really nice, and I appreciate it, but you don't have to do this."

"Ah, the typical Washington mindset. You think I have some ulterior motive."

He's right. That thought crossed her mind. It wouldn't be the first time it's happened, even if Wyatt is an unlikely candidate for Stowe's attention.

"I don't want you to think you can impress me by being nice to my grandparents."

Wyatt laughs and shakes his head. "I gave up trying to impress you after you ran into me and then proceeded to berate me after the press conference."

"Uh, you ran into me and didn't apologize."

"That's some great revisionist history, but okay."

"So, why are you out here splitting wood?"

"Stowe, people take care of each other where I'm from. I may not live in Montana anymore, but that will always be a part of my DNA. Your grandparents have been very kind to me. This is the least I can do to repay that."

They work in Washington, D.C. There are so many lies told in that city on a given day that politicians, staff, and bureaucrats become true artists in their deceit. Wyatt could be one of those excellent liars, but nothing on his face signals deception. And it makes sense.

"Okay. Well, come in and have breakfast. It's almost ready."

"All right."

Wyatt begins stacking the small pile he just split as Stowe watches. "I researched the other schools on your list last night and contacted them first thing this morning. I didn't have any luck."

"None?"

"The best Santa candidates are either booked for the holidays or want nothing to do with testifying," Stowe informs him. "The rest of them…they make the ones we met yesterday look like rock stars."

"We need to find another pond to fish in."

"Agreed."

Stowe enters the cabin first, immediately sliding to the left. Nana mines the chokepoints like doors and hallways with mistletoe like an army defending its front line. Stowe begins removing her boots without paying any mind to it.

"Ahem," Nana says, moving her eyes to the ceiling and pointing.

Stowe looks up and sighs deeply. The mistletoe was moved, and now she's standing directly under it.

"Seriously, Nana?" Stowe asks in an exacerbated voice. "You're incorrigible!"

"I didn't make up the tradition. I only embrace it. Now, go on."

Wyatt holds his hands out defensively. "I appreciate the tradition, ma'am, but your granddaughter and I work together. I don't think that's a good idea."

"Oh, one harmless little kiss won't hurt anything. Christmas spirit demands it."

"Not this time, Nana," Stowe argues after glancing at Wyatt.

"Give up now, Stowe," her grandfather announces from the breakfast table, having just sat down to scan the news. "You'll never win. And I'm wounded, so do it for me."

"Are you trying to guilt me into this, PopPop?"

He puts his newspaper down and takes off his reading glasses. "I would never. Just know my injury won't spare me the constant complaints if you break tradition. You know how it is."

Stowe is resolved to get this over quickly. The longer she delays, the more persistent Nana will become. Rules are rules. This cannot be a peck on the lips. It must be an actual kiss, although it doesn't need to be a long one.

"Keep your tongue in your mouth, cowboy."

Wyatt looks as awkward about this as she feels. She moves closer, and he gently places his hands on her sides. She leans into him and closes her eyes. Their lips meet. The kiss is soft and not sloppy. Instead of pulling away as she planned, Stowe leans in and kisses him a little harder. Her body begins to tingle. Then she realizes what she's doing.

Stowe pulls away abruptly, and Wyatt removes his hands from her sides. She stares at him for a moment. There isn't any satisfaction or gloating. He almost looks concerned by her reaction. Not so much with Nana. Her hands are clasped in front of her, and she wears a look of pure joy on her face.

"See? That wasn't so bad, now was it? Now, let's have breakfast."

Stowe looks at Wyatt before turning away. "I've lost my appetite. I'll be upstairs, packing."

She storms up the stairs, fighting for traction as her wool socks slide on the floor. She makes it to her room, closes the door, and leans against it. She stares hard at the ceiling, trying to make sense of her emotions.

"No, no, no, no," she whispers. "What have I done?"

Chapter Twenty-Nine

REPRESENTATIVE CAMILLA GUZMAN

The autumn temperatures in Washington are pretty moderate until the cold Canadian winds whistle down the Potomac and Anacostia Rivers. The frigid gift from America's neighbor to the north has made an early appearance this year. Like the Washingtonians and tourists spending an evening on ice, Camilla is bundled up to defend against the cold.

Multiple neighborhoods in the district have public ice skating rinks. Camilla prefers to meander around this one, and not just because it's only a stone's throw from her office. It's the idea of skating amid works of art and magnificent sculptures in a lush garden. The ice rink at the Sculpture Garden opens in late November and lasts until early March. It's a recent addition to the attractions on the National Mall, located between the National Gallery of Arts' West Building and the Museum of Natural History.

Camilla is from the California coast and rarely straps blades on her feet to glide over a frozen pool of water. She just likes the vibe here. The cozy rink and string of lights glowing like candles create a romantic yet family-friendly environment. And there are plenty of couples and young families to attest to that.

The relaxed atmosphere gives her time and space to think. Camilla's thoughts dwell on her cantankerous party leadership, the support of Aymos Blackburn, and nascent opposition forming on the subcommittee. Most of all, she contemplates the consequences of introducing legislation that attacks one of America's most iconic figures.

Camilla sips her hot cocoa and leans against the railing as skaters whiz by. The media reporting on her bill and the scheduled hearings in the subcommittee have been mixed. Most agree with her assertion that the over-commercialization of the holiday is a detriment. Detractors aren't so kind, managing to get "Grinch Guzman" trending on social media sites.

That normally wouldn't bother her. Negative publicity can be just as useful as praise so long as it is spun and channeled correctly. Unfortunately, her political message washing machine can't keep up with the laundry. The more her detractors talk about this, the more supporters she will need to parrot her message. Otherwise, she will be buried under an avalanche of misinformation that she and her staff have no hope of correcting.

Yes, this is about growing her profile. Even though Aymos hasn't directly confronted Camilla on that suspicion, he's been in politics long enough to realize a cry for attention when he sees one. But it is more than that. It is about the need for change.

Camilla looks at the families gathered around the rink. This is what Christmas should be about. It is about creating memories, not opening expensive gifts. America needs to be reminded of that. Since they aren't likely to come to that conclusion independently, she and the committee must spell it out for them. If legislation is required to promote positive change, so be it. That's what she believes the government is for.

Her husband agrees. Raul has always been her biggest supporter and was the one who encouraged her to run for office even when she thought she could never win. He has always said he fell in love with her because of her mind and wanted to see her working in a place where she could use it. Husbands are not built any better than that.

The kids are older and don't need her around as much as they did growing up. She took the plunge, and sure enough, won the seat. Now Raul manages the household while she's a continent away doing the people's business. He would be disappointed if she weren't willing to pick this fight.

Camilla pushes off the railing and tosses her empty cup into a trash receptacle. Many pundits inside the Beltway are calling these hearings a distraction. Regardless of their ideological perspective, they say it's a clever way to distract Americans from more pressing issues like the Mexican border, uncontrolled spending, or a myriad of social and environmental issues.

They may have a point, but that doesn't make this any less important. Santa Claus *was* real, but he has only been romanticized to his current status over the past century. It's time to reverse that trend, starting with opening statements on Monday morning.

Camilla weaves through the crowd as she makes her way back to Constitution Avenue. There is an undeniable added benefit. The current situation is going to change. Despite the press conferences and news reports with her picture, the people here still have no idea who she is. Not one person. She wonders if it will still be true this time next week.

Chapter Thirty

WYATT HUFFMAN

Stowe's grandparents don't seem to be concerned about her storming off. Wyatt doesn't think it's indifference – they clearly love their granddaughter and have her best interests at heart. It's more like they've seen this before and are giving her space.

Breakfast commences with a peppering of questions about Wyatt, his family, his life growing up in Montana, and how he came to work with Stowe. After fifteen minutes, she still hadn't come downstairs. Now, he's beginning to think he caused irreparable harm to their personal and professional relationship.

"Do you think Stowe is okay? I didn't mean to upset her."

"Oh, she'll be fine. It was just a little kiss."

Wyatt sets his fork down. "She said she had a bad experience with mistletoe…something about Bobby Sinclair."

Dorothy stops and stares at Walter, who looks at Wyatt with surprised eyes. "She told you about Bobby?"

"Only that he was sketchy and kissed her under one of these mistletoe sprigs back when they were in high school. She says it traumatized her."

Her grandmother frowns. "Did she tell you the rest of the story?"

"No. I didn't realize there was more."

People who have been married as long as Walter and Dorothy have don't need words to communicate. A look speaks volumes. The one they share is enough for Wyatt to know there is much more behind the tale of the sketchy, hormone-addled Bobby Sinclair.

"It's not our story to tell. But…we know Stowe can be difficult and very distant."

"Calling her an ice queen is a better description," Walter says, getting smacked in the head with a dish rag.

"Behave yourself!" she scolds, turning to Wyatt. "Just know she is a bright, lovely woman with a big heart. It's just a little damaged right now."

"No, it was ripped out and stomped on," Walter says, forking some scrambled eggs into his mouth before noticing the glare from his wife. "What? It's the truth."

Stowe has shared precious few details with Wyatt about her personal life. Most of their conversations have been restricted to professional discussions. Even what she has shared is sterile, including the Bobby story. Now, he knows there is likely a reason behind that.

"Stowe and I are just colleagues working on an assignment. Nothing is going on between us."

"I know that, dear," her grandmother says, placing her hand on Wyatt's forearm. "I also know that you both enjoyed that kiss more than either of you will admit."

"Dorothy, leave the poor man alone! This is awkward enough for him."

"I just call it like I see it," she says, her tone a couple of octaves higher.

Walter slides his chair out and stands. "Well, I'm going to get some wood for the fire."

"Not with that arm, you're not!"

"That's why I'm bringing Wyatt along to be a pack mule. If he doesn't mind."

"Not at all, sir."

The pair treks outside, not bothering to don coats to complete the task. It's not that the temperatures have dramatically risen. It's more that they are both used to cold late-autumn air.

"Thanks for the rescue, but now I feel a talk coming."

Walter laughs. "You're welcome, and is it that obvious?"

"Not really, but my grandfather used to find reasons to get me to tag along with him so we could talk in private. I recognize the signal."

"Ah. I don't want you to get the wrong idea about Stowe. My wife isn't wrong when she says she's a wonderful young woman. My son, her father, was killed along with her mother when Stowe was young. She's sensitive to people and has trust and abandonment issues. What happened last year…well, she's still hurting, and that brings out her testy side."

"I've noticed."

"Don't take it personally, son. It gets worse the closer she comes to letting people in. I have a feeling you bring it out of her more than most."

"Why's that?"

Walter has more to say and momentarily stares at the ground. When he makes eye contact with Wyatt, he presses his lips together and frowns.

"It's the way life works sometimes."

It's a cryptic, almost armchair philosophical response. Wyatt decides not to press for details. He doesn't want to put Walter in a position where his granddaughter could get angry with him for divulging too much. If she ever wants Wyatt to know, as unlikely as that is, it will be up to her.

"What is this assignment the two of you are on? I don't remember asking."

"We need to find Santa Claus."

Walter wears a quizzical look on his face as Wyatt begins grabbing an armful of wood. "And that brought you to Burlington?"

"They have a Santa school there."

"Ah, yes, the North Pole South Santa Academy. I had forgotten about that place. Did you find a good Santa there?"

"Not really. We found Sauced Santa, Jaded Santa, and Streaker Santa. They all play the part, but their backgrounds disqualify them."

"I'm looking forward to hearing the full of that story someday. Why don't you go to the source?"

"What do you mean?"

Walter grins. "Everybody knows Santa lives at the North Pole, son. Just drop in on him."

"I don't think we can get a flight up there. Canada or Finland is the closest we could get before—"

Wyatt freezes like he was just hit in the head with an icicle.

"What's wrong?"

"Walter, you're an absolute genius."

"Be sure to let my wife know. She thinks I'm as dumb as a tree stump."

Wyatt and Walter walk back to the cabin, the former loaded up with an armful of wood. Stowe is dressed in casual clothes and is downstairs with her grandmother. She gives Wyatt an apprehensive look and clenches her jaw before speaking.

"There's an afternoon flight back to Wash—"

"We're not going to D.C. I know where we can find Santa Claus."

"My idea," Walter proudly announces as Wyatt deposits the wood in a large copper kettle beside the fireplace.

Stowe crosses her arms. "Where?"

"Someplace much colder and more Christmasy than the nation's capital."

Chapter Thirty-One

REPRESENTATIVE JOHN KNUTSON

It almost feels to John like he never left the office. After the visit from the party leadership, he made his way home and engaged in an epic fit of tossing and turning. Sleep didn't come, and what little did was consistently interrupted by lingering thoughts of the hearings. He decided to quit the fight and returned to the Longworth Building before the first hint of daybreak peeked over the horizon.

Congress isn't in session this weekend, but that doesn't mean all work stops. A few colleagues are around, and staffers still traverse the corridors of the building. He isn't surprised when he hears a knock on the door jamb and sees Cam arrive in jeans and a fleece quarter-zip.

"I didn't expect to see you in the office, Congressman."

"It was a long night."

"A long night doing what?"

The congressman eyes his chief of staff. "Soul searching."

Unlike some members of Congress, John is informal with his chief of staff – even more so when they have the office to themselves. He wants his right-hand man to feel comfortable speaking openly and honestly.

"Are you having second thoughts about working with Angela Pratt?"

"No, nothing like that. Durant and Guillomi dropped in last night for a visit."

"Uh, oh," Cam says, wincing. "What did the minority leader and whip want?"

"Oh, you know, to patronize me before leveling the usual threats."

John explains the conversation he had with Spencer and Gregory. He replayed the encounter so often in his head while lying awake in bed that he easily recites specific details of the conversation from memory. Cam listens intently before scoffing once the congressman finishes.

"Okay, let me get this straight. The minority leader and whip want you to sit on your hands while your colleagues drag the iconic symbol of merriment and joy through the mud?"

"Pretty much."

Cam shakes his head. "What are you going to do?"

John rubs his chin. That is the question. Being a Montanan, the easy answer is telling the leadership to kick rocks. Unfortunately, politics doesn't work that way. They have leverage, and that means they can apply pressure. Anyone who resists those tactics had better have a game plan, or someone else will occupy their seat in the next Congress.

"You know, I always wanted to be a congressman. I remember being in high school and staying up late to watch election returns one cold November night. I swore that if I was elected, I would be different."

"You are."

"Am I? If that were true, why am I considering taking a knee and bowing to their demands?"

"Because you're smart enough to know what crossing the leader means. You could always find a happy medium."

John grins. "And now you know what kept me awake last night. There isn't one. It's all or nothing. I either fight this because I believe it's the right thing to do, or I face the political consequences."

That's the math, and it really is that simple. Cam shrugs. "You can't make a difference for our district if you're not here."

"That's true, but if I succumb to their threats, I'm not making a difference while I *am* here. Have you heard from Wyatt?"

"Not a peep."

"It's not like him not to report in."

"Before you ask, I spoke to Amanda Derringer over in Angela's office. She's Stowe Bessette's roommate and best friend. She hasn't heard anything, either."

"What the hell are they doing?"

The words no sooner escape John's lips than the telltale chime of Cam's phone erupts from his hip pocket. He stands and fishes it out before checking the screen.

"It's Wyatt," Cam says, wiggling his cell phone as he holds it up.

"Is he Beetlejuice? Did I say his name too many times?"

"Wyatt," Cam barks into the microphone. "It's about time you called. You're on speaker. The congressman is here."

"Apologies for not calling sooner."

"You'd better have good news," John warns.

"Yes and no, sir. We didn't find a suitable Santa in Burlington."

John sighs deeply. "You're telling me that there wasn't one good candidate in the best Santa school in the country?"

"No, there were three excellent candidates, and they would be great if we ignore that they're collectively kid-hating, drunken streakers."

"What...? You know, never mind. I don't think I want to know."

"I assume you have a new plan," Cam interjects.

"That's the good news. We do, but I'm going to need you to approve the expense. Stowe and I are going to Finland."

"I hope that's some remote town in northern Maine."

"No, sir, it's the country in Scandinavia."

It was meant to be a rhetorical question, but Wyatt seems locked in on this course of action and isn't kidding around.

"All right, I'll ask the question my chief of staff won't...are you crazy?"

"You need an authentic Santa, Congressman. Without getting into the specifics, that's the best place to find one."

"Is Miss Bessette on board with this?" Cam asks.

"She is. She's talking to the congresswoman right now."

A unified front. That's an interesting development. The way that Angela portrayed their relationship, he didn't think they would agree on the chemical composition of water. This must be a compelling plan.

"You're taking a big risk, Wyatt. We need it to pay off."

"I know. We'll know as soon as we get there. Our flight is boarding. I'll contact you once we reach Rovaniemi."

The call ends, and his chief of staff pockets the device. The congressman smirks. He asked for approval of the expense after he made the travel arrangements. That's the political equivalent of "it's better to beg for forgiveness than ask for permission." Well done.

"Finland," John mumbles. "That sounds like a Hail Mary."

"I can assign more people to the task of finding a Santa. They can work the U.S. while Wyatt heads to Lapland and tries to learn Finnish."

John rubs his chin. He's sure there are plenty of English speakers there. He also sees the logic in Wyatt's thoughts. But another angle also needs to be explored – the delay could help him with the problem that's keeping him awake at night.

"No. Let's wait it out and see what happens."

Chapter Thirty-Two

STOWE BESSETTE

On the way to the airport, there is nothing said about the kiss. In fact, there isn't much said between Stowe and Wyatt at all. She is too embarrassed to open a discussion. Luckily, Wyatt doesn't bring it up, either, for whatever reason. At least he isn't gloating over it.

What little conversation they have before walking down the jetway for the first leg of their journey is all business. They are seated on opposite sides of the Airbus, more in a happy accident than an executed strategy. It gives Stowe the time and distance to think. She knows the awkward conversation they need to have cannot be ignored in perpetuity.

The trip's second leg is a little more intimate despite the larger plane they board in Boston. Stowe and Wyatt are assigned seats together, with him at the window and her in the middle. Fortunately, the girl in the aisle seat is a petite, mousy little thing. There is nothing worse than being crushed on a flight between two hulking men who hog the armrests.

About five hours and two movies into the journey, Stowe removes her headphones. Wyatt is resting next to her with his eyes closed. She gazes at him for a little too long.

"I'm sorry about what happened at your grandparents' house," he says, not moving.

"You're awake?"

"I'm just resting," he says, opening his eyes.

"How did you know I removed my headphones if your eyes were closed?"

"Your arm brushed my shoulder. It was an educated guess."

Stowe lowers her eyes and stares at her lap. The conversation is inevitable now. "You have no reason to apologize for what happened. You had no choice."

"There are always choices. I could have said I have herpes or am gay. I could have made any excuse."

Stowe allows herself to smile. "Nana would have seen right through that. Rules are rules, especially regarding Christmas traditions in the Bessette house."

"Rules are meant to be broken."

"Not those," she says, grimacing. "Nana would have been deeply offended."

Wyatt presses his lips together. Despite Stowe giving him a pass, he's still struggling to absolve himself of responsibility.

"Still, you told me about Bobby, and I shouldn't have done it."

The sound of his name still stings. She knows Wyatt can sense her tense up. He probably thinks it's because of what happened under the mistletoe. He's wrong, but she *really* doesn't want to have that conversation right now.

"Forget it. It's over. Let's focus on our task."

Work has been her haven for a while. It keeps her mind occupied. Since Wyatt is a fellow staffer, it's also a convenient refuge to guard against the awkwardness of overly personal conversations. She turns her head and studies his reaction.

She gets another jolt. Wyatt's eyes are sympathetic and compassionate. It's enough to want to make her talk about it. It's not something she is ready for. Not with him.

"Okay."

"What's our backup plan if Finnish Santa doesn't work out?" Stowe asks, changing the subject.

"I think we're about out of options. We're absolutely running out of time."

"We need to come up with something. I refuse to—"

A loud bang interrupts the low drone of the engines, and the cabin begins to shudder. Stowe grabs onto Wyatt with one hand and the opposite armrest with the other. A cacophony of sharp screeches pierces the noise as concerned passengers look around in bewilderment before turning to gaze out the windows.

Wyatt cocks his head to look out toward the wing. Their seats are in the forward part of the cabin, a few rows up from the leading edge of the wings.

"Well, that's not good."

The noise subsides, but the panic in the passengers' voices doesn't. Their reaction starkly contrasts Wyatt's dry delivery of what must be bad news.

"What is it?"

Wyatt sits back and looks at her without a hint of alarm.

"Our left engine is on fire."

"What!"

Stowe practically climbs over him to get a look for herself. The overhead address system dings to get everyone's attention.

"Good afternoon from the flight deck, ladies and gentlemen. This is your captain. As you may have noticed, the aircraft is experiencing a mechanical issue with the left engine," the pilot says in an even voice. "Let me first assure you that we are perfectly safe. This plane can fly with only one engine, so you aren't in danger. However, airline policy is to land the plane at the nearest airfield."

Stowe doubts that it's just airline policy. She works for Congress. There is likely a law, or at a minimum, Federal Aviation Administration rules about that. Just because a plane can fly with an engine out doesn't mean it's a good practice.

"As a result, we will be diverting to Keflavik, Iceland. It should only be about forty minutes of flight time. As a safety consideration, beverage service will be suspended, and the seatbelt light will be lit for the duration of the flight. Keflavik Airport has already been informed of our arrival. We will work on arrangements to get you to Helsinki and have details for you after we land. We apologize for the inconvenience. I will let you know when we are on approach. Until then, please remain calm and enjoy the remainder of the flight."

Remain calm. There is no chance of that happening. Even if Stowe were comfortable flying, which she isn't, there is no way to relax knowing that one of their engines just disintegrated over the middle of the Atlantic Ocean.

"Crap."

Wyatt closes his eyes. He's not at all bothered by the news. In fact, he almost looks content.

"How can you remain so calm?"

"I don't try to control the things I can't."

It's a great personal philosophy that Stowe doesn't subscribe to. She has always suffered from anxiety, likely stemming from losing her parents at such an early age. Recent life events have only added to the angst. As much as she wishes she could take things in stride, her fears overcome her when the unexpected happens.

Stowe stiffens in her chair and grips Wyatt's arm even tighter. Her hand is like a vise as she desperately tries to rein in her emotions.

"This will put us behind schedule, assuming we don't explode and die in the next twenty minutes!"

"We're not going to explode. We'll be fine."

"With a diversion, we'll have even less time to spare."

"They will book us on the next flight. We'll get there, Stowe, one way or another. When we do, we make the time we have count."

He doesn't belittle her or say she's being irrational, although there's no doubt in her mind that he's thinking it. He remains perfectly calm, and it's what she needs. The anxiety releases its iron grip on her, allowing her to breathe easier. His calm relaxes her. It's a weird feeling that she's never experienced.

Stowe removes her hand from Wyatt's arm, and he makes space so she can have the armrest. It's airplane etiquette, but also considerate. She dons her headphones and sets the in-flight entertainment to a music channel playing Christmas carols. She leans her head back and closes her eyes, just as Wyatt is doing. There is no way she will sleep, but it does help her to relax. His calming influence is helping her more than the music.

Chapter Thirty-Three

WYATT HUFFMAN

The games begin moments after the wheels touch down on the asphalt runway and the plane taxies to a gate. Keflavik is a small airport, and their airline does not have a robust presence here. Maybe three or four employees are trying to deal with a couple of hundred upset passengers looking to book new flights to Helsinki.

Stowe remained calm for the remainder of the flight. That was then. Now, she's in fight mode. Wyatt left her to wait in line so he could walk around and stretch his legs. Keflavik International isn't Caribbean island airport small, but it's not far from it. Plaques on the wall explain that it was built from an old World War II base and developed into an important stop-over between Europe and the U.S. The new terminal opened in 1987, and a fivefold passenger increase has fueled continuous development.

Twenty-eight airlines call Keflavik home, but few flights are going to Helsinki. Certainly not enough to accommodate a planeload of unexpected passengers. They couldn't pay him enough to be working the airline's service desk right now. Stowe is already talking to a representative when he arrives back at her side.

"I'm sorry. We're trying to get a replacement plane in, but it won't be here until sometime tomorrow, at the earliest."

"What about a flight on another airline?" Stowe asks, polite but with a frustrated edge to her voice.

"Icelandair has a flight tomorrow, but it's already booked, and the standby list is already twenty people deep."

"Just one flight?"

The representative grimaces. "Unfortunately. The airport is experiencing a reduced schedule due to the eruption."

"Eruption?"

"We have volcanoes here," the woman says with a bright smile and a prideful look. "Lots of volcanoes."

That's one of the few things Wyatt does know about the island. There is a large concentration of active volcanoes due to Iceland's location on a hotspot over the divergent tectonic plate boundary known as the mid-Atlantic Ridge. The island has thirty active volcanic systems, of which thirteen have erupted since Iceland was settled. That was written on one of the wall plaques.

"There's nothing you can do?" Stowe pleads. "We *really* need to get to Finland."

"I'm sorry," the woman says, staring down at her computer screen. "The best we can do is get you to Berlin or London, and you may be able to connect from there. I should warn you, though, that a weather system is affecting most of northern Europe. Air travel around much of the continent is dicey."

"Which means we may get stranded somewhere else," Wyatt says, speaking for the first time.

"Unfortunately, yes. The airline can pay for your accommodations in Iceland. I can get you booked on the plane out here when it arrives. You can fill out this form to be reimbursed for your expenses."

"Thank you," Stowe says, accepting the paperwork.

Wyatt does the same, but neither is in a rush to fill it out. They drag their carry-ons into the departures area. Stowe stops and looks around. She almost looks like she's going to burst into tears.

"Now what?"

Wyatt looks around. "We find a place to stay for the night."

"Where? Do you know anything about Iceland?"

"Only that the people here seem really nice. Let's ask him," Wyatt says, pointing.

He immediately sets off for a booth near the door leading to the passenger drop-off area. Unlike most major airports, the departures and arrivals are on ground level. There is nothing fancy about the design of Keflavik International. The man greets him as Wyatt walks up to him.

"Hi. We're stuck here. Where is the best place to stay that's close by?"

"You were on the flight that was diverted?" the man asks, getting a nod. "Well, there aren't many places to stay near the airport, but there are plenty of hotels in Reykjavik. It's a forty-minute bus ride from here to the depot in the city. A little longer if you catch the one that stops at the Blue Lagoon."

"The what?"

The man smiles and hands Wyatt a glossy tri-fold brochure. The image of steam rising off a large pool of milky water graces the front. Pictures of the locker room, massage area, pool bar, restaurant, café, and lounge area are on the inside. Ten seconds later, Wyatt is sold.

"Oh, hell yeah."

"You have to be kidding me," Stowe moans, staring angrily at her travel companion. "We don't have time for this!"

"Unless you plan on swimming to Finland, we're stuck here, Stowe. We might as well enjoy it a little."

She looks around as if searching for any alternative. Wyatt is partly surprised that she hasn't looked up Santa schools in Iceland. Or, maybe she has and didn't find any. Either way, a trip to the Blue Lagoon isn't high on her to-do list.

"C'mon! Where's your sense of adventure?"

"This doesn't look like much of an adventure."

"We're on an island nation near the Arctic Circle that has active volcanoes and a population that believes in elves. I'm betting we can find one, starting with what looks like the world's largest outdoor hot tub."

"You need to stop reading brochures," Stowe says, snatching it from him.

Wyatt has tried being patient but is at the end of his rope. Stowe is not a spouse, fiancee, or girlfriend. She's a colleague who is in no position to tell him what to do. He doesn't report to her. If there were any other travel alternatives, he would consider one. But this isn't Walter Mitty. He's not going to fly in a helicopter out to a passing steamer that happens to be traveling to Finland. The plane arriving tomorrow would get him there faster, anyway.

"Suit yourself. I'm going. I'll call you when the airline gets back to us with our new flight arrangements. Where do I catch the bus?"

"It's right over there," the man says, mildly amused.

"Wyatt, wait!" Stowe shouts when he is almost outside. He stops as she catches up. "Okay. I'll go."

Part of him wants to rub this in. A bigger part forces him to keep his mouth shut. Wyatt wants Stowe to go. If anyone could use some fun and relaxation, it's her.

Chapter Thirty-Four

STOWE BESSETTE

The Blue Lagoon is on the Reykjanes Peninsula, about fourteen miles from the airport. It's renowned for its barren landscapes and cone-shaped volcanoes, not that Stowe can see anything from her window seat on the bus. It's late afternoon and already growing darker by the minute.

She is still a little resentful. The choice was hers, but she didn't want to be by herself. Iceland is English-speaking, but it's still a foreign country. Wyatt may not be her first choice of companion right now, but he's at least a familiar face.

Stowe uses the light on her phone to read through the brochure she snatched from him. The Blue Lagoon is one of Iceland's most popular attractions. The warm milky-blue water starkly contrasts with the surrounding black lava fields dusted with gray moss. Stowe thought it was a natural spring but she was wrong.

Iceland has a long history of utilizing geothermal energy for heating. Boiling water heated by magma is used to heat fresh water. Then, the plant pumps it into radiators installed in homes. After the heat transfer, the mineral-rich groundwater is released into the nearby lava field. Lava is porous, but the water is rich with silica that separates as it cools. The silica formed a muddy layer in the lava that stopped the water from seeping through. Thus, the lagoon.

The bus stops, and more than half of it empties. Stowe and Wyatt are lucky that the tickets aren't sold out, and they each purchase a package that includes a towel, robe, flip-flops, locker space, and lagoon time.

"Oh, I so want to stay at the hotel here," Wyatt says, looking around.

"Good luck getting that expense approved. Neither of us can afford to stay here unless you have a trust fund you didn't tell me about. I'm not made of money."

"I know, but a guy can dream."

Stowe checks her phone and frowns. There are no messages from the airline.

"We can stay for a few hours and then get a hotel in Reykjavik until they rebook our flight."

"I don't have a swimsuit," Stowe protests. It wasn't high on the list of items to bring on a December trip to Vermont.

"Neither do I. We can jump in naked," Wyatt counters, earning a glare. "Or we can buy one."

He points at a small boutique. Stowe grimaces. She didn't see it there but should have known they would sell swimsuits in case one was forgotten or this stop was unplanned.

After making purchases, they head to separate locker rooms, which are huge and offer a high degree of privacy. Stowe showers, changes into her swimsuit, and wraps herself in the terry robe. She stops and converses with a pair of women who have been here before. The insights into the Blue Lagoon and how she will feel after the experience have her looking forward to this, at least to some degree.

Stowe emerges from the locker room and descends the stairs. Wyatt is already down here talking with a local.

"This place has changed a lot since I first started coming here. I remember the days when you stored your suitcase in a shed out front, and there was no indoor access to the lagoon."

"What did you do in the winter when it's freezing outside?"

The man laughs. "It was a mad dash across that deck. It would have made for great YouTube videos because it was icy. The cold air was a rite of passage to enjoy the lagoon. It was a lot of fun. This place is much more tourist-friendly now."

The two men shake hands and say goodbyes after Wyatt sees Stowe standing in her robe and introduces her. Walking around in a bathrobe in a public place would be more unnerving if everyone weren't dressed the same way. Not that it does much to put her at ease.

"What's all the goop in your hair?"

Stowe reaches up and touches the mop on her head that she tied up after giving it a good coating. "Conditioner. They have vats of it in the locker room. A woman upstairs warned me to use lots of it and avoid getting my hair wet because the results aren't pretty. My hair is unmanageable enough."

Wyatt smiles. "What do you say? Time to go in?"

He strips off his robe, causing Stowe to avert her eyes to stop staring. He's in really good shape. It's a body sculpted from a childhood of working on a ranch.

Her heart begins pounding. Stowe closes her eyes and does the same. There are no beaches in her area of Vermont. She's a mountain girl. Her idea of fun was skis and snowsuits, not swimwear and sun tan lotion. She just isn't comfortable wearing a bikini, especially one with as little material as this has.

Wyatt stares at her as she hangs her robe. It is not ogling or leering. Just watching. She feels his eyes on her and begins to blush. She doesn't have the biggest boobs, but they still feel like they're about to fall out of her top.

"I know. I look ridiculous. They didn't have a big selection in the boutique."

"You're being hard on yourself, Stowe. You look absolutely stunning."

Something being "heart-warming" is more than a metaphor. Stowe immediately warms up after the compliment. Wyatt isn't acting like a dog. His eyes aren't rolling over her body, judging every flaw. His words are sincere, and his eyes are locked onto hers, not her chest spilling out of her bikini top. He's a gentleman. Stowe didn't realize those still exist.

"Shall we?"

Wyatt gestures her forward, and Stowe leads them to the ramp that descends into the warm lagoon water. She isn't tall, but the lagoon isn't deep. They walk into the chilly December air, where the darkening sky meets the charcoal lava containing the illuminated milky water. It's an enchanting view, like something out of a fantasy novel.

The water's temperature is perfect. The cold air on Stowe's face and the mineral-rich warm water against her body are exhilarating. This place is heaven.

"My God, this feels good," Wyatt moans.

"Wait until I tell Mandy about this place. She's going to die."

"There are worse places to get diverted to. I can see why Iceland has become such a popular tourist destination."

They walk toward the back of the lagoon. A station is set up for people to apply a silica mud mask. Wyatt goes first, smearing it over his face.

"How do I look?"

Stowe can't help but giggle. "It's an improvement."

"Shut up," he says with a smile. "Your turn."

Normally, she would never think about doing this in front of another person. But Wyatt is a cowboy from Montana and had no reservations about it, so why should she? Stowe starts the application, but she's missing whole parts of her face. She really needs a mirror.

"Allow me," Wyatt says, dipping his fingers in the silica and gently applying it to her forehead and cheeks.

Stowe closes her eyes. Her heart thunders as she feels his fingers caress her face. She's paralyzed by the feeling. Part of her wants to pull away and do it herself. The other part is enjoying it too much.

"There. At least you'll have good skin when you meet Santa."

"Thank you," she says in a near-whisper.

"I was thinking about a 'plan B' on the way here. We could—"

"You know, I don't really want to talk about work right now. It feels like that's all I ever do. I'm glad you talked me into coming here, Wyatt. I am. Now I want to enjoy the moment."

"Okay, sold," Wyatt says with a hint of excitement. "What do you want to talk about?"

Stowe smiles. She feared he would shut down and not want to talk. She's starting to trust Wyatt, if only a little. But it's something. What happened nine months ago was devastating and has consumed her life since. Now, she's bathing in a fountain of youth two thousand miles away with a guy she barely knows but is becoming more familiar with each passing minute. Despite their circumstances, feeling at ease with a man is something she hasn't felt in a long time.

"What was it like growing up in Montana?"

Chapter Thirty-Five

REPRESENTATIVE CAMILLA GUZMAN

Camilla may despise Santa Claus and the commercialization of the holiday, but that won't absolve her from having to do some Christmas shopping. Someday, that may change. She hopes to be an agent of that change. Until then, her family will want to open gifts purchased in the nation's capital less than a month from now.

She isn't the only one out on this blustery Saturday evening. Holiday parties are in full swing, and tired parents are getting a jump on the shopping for their children. There isn't much revelry. Nobody is singing Christmas carols as they stroll down the sidewalk. The only jolly person in sight is Santa ringing a bell to solicit Salvation Army donations. Even he is getting weary, considering how many people are ignoring him.

A woman stops and digs for some cash while two men pass by without even a glance. That's the way of things in the modern era. Or maybe it has always been that way. She likely only makes a fraction of the salary the two men do, yet she's generous, and they…aren't. Maybe they gave at the office. That's the excuse du jour. Everyone knows it's a lie.

"Thinking about stealing the cauldron? Or are you imagining what this street will look like with Santa not standing there?"

Camilla looks to her left to see Marcia standing there. "They can still solicit donations. It'd be more interesting if they dressed up as Dickens characters. How did you find me?"

"I'm your chief of staff. I always know where you are. I have a sense for those things."

"No, seriously."

Marcia grins. "I put a GPS tracker in your purse."

"What?" Camilla asks, glancing at her pocketbook as a reflex.

"I have an update on Angela Pratt's search for Santa if you're interested."

Marcia is a godsend. Most members of Congress lean heavily on their chief of staff to run the office and assist in performing their duties. They provide guidance, advice, and, in this case, information. Nothing gets done without the men and women working on staff behind the scenes.

"Do I dare ask how you got that inside information?"

"I have a mole in her office," she nonchalantly says, causing Camilla to grimace. "It's a staffer thing."

"It's betrayal."

"You don't have to be elected to office to play politics, Congresswoman. It turns out that some of her staff members are more loyal to the party than she is."

Camilla finds the thought of that unnerving. It's great when it works in her favor, but turnabout is fair play. She can't stomach the idea that one of her staff could sell her out if they don't agree with her decisions. That's likely to happen at some point in this town. Maybe it already has.

"What's the news?"

"Their search for a Santa Claus to testify isn't going well. The two legislative aides assigned to the task saw their plane get diverted to Iceland due to mechanical issues. They're stuck there."

"Did you arrange that?"

"I can make magic happen, Camilla, but causing engine failure over an ocean is outside my skill set. I'm chalking it up to divine intervention."

"Aymos Blackburn would wholeheartedly agree with you. Where were they going?"

"Finland."

That's not what Camilla expected to hear. She offers Marcia a confused look.

"Finland? I thought their wanting Santa to testify was a joke. Are you telling me they're serious enough to send aides over to Europe to scour Scandinavia?"

"I don't think that was the original plan. They searched for one in Vermont first."

"And?"

"They struck out. Apparently, none of the candidates interviewed were suitable. That's why they were heading to Finland."

Camilla smiles. "Their desperation only proves my point."

Thousands of men don the red costume and play Santa every year. Maybe tens of thousands. Some of them go to schools and learn to do it professionally. It says a lot if they can't find a suitable candidate in this country.

"You know, they're going to find one eventually."

"I know. The question is, will the Santa they find speak English? We need to know who it is as soon as possible."

Marcia stares at her boss. "Background check?"

"Oh, yeah. I want to know what their Kriss Kringle eats for breakfast in the morning. No detail is unimportant."

"You know, it won't be a good look if you destroy Santa in front of a dozen cameras."

"I'm not destroying Santa, because there *is* no Santa. I want to expose whoever they call to testify as the fraud he is."

"I'll let you know as soon as they find someone," Marcia says, nodding.

"Are both staffers from Angela's office?"

"No. Congresswoman Pratt teamed up with John Knutson of Montana. They each dedicated one person to the cause."

These hearings are turning into a bipartisan love-fest. The thought of Camilla and Aymos Blackburn working together on any initiative was unfathomable a month ago. The ideological chasm between the two political parties requires an airplane to cross. Now, new battle lines are being drawn, and politics is indeed making strange bedfellows.

"Good. Knutson won't be a threat. His party is playing politics. They think these hearings will be an embarrassment they can use in November. I'm betting they leveled all manner of threats against him to keep him quiet. Same with the others."

"For the same reason Speaker Hoskins and the majority leader tried to convince you to cancel them."

"Pretty much."

"Are they right? I mean, can this be used against us?"

"Not if we play our cards right. Aymos asked me to change the appearance order," Camilla says, digging into her coat and producing a tri-folded piece of paper.

She hands it to Marcia, who unfolds and scans it. Her eyes grow wide in surprise. The first change is seismic.

"You're bringing your queen out early."

Camilla scowls. She hates chess analogies. They're lazy. Why people insist on using them when only a small fraction of people even play the game escapes her. Despite the annoyance at the line, Marcia's point is valid.

"And setting the narrative for these hearings in the process. This is no longer just about getting attention, Marcia. The leadership of both parties is clearing the runway for us. We might as well have the impact we want."

"This is a good start. I'll let you know when I hear more," Camilla's chief of staff confirms. "Enjoy your shopping. Make sure you get me something nice. Preferably from a high-end store."

"Considering you Lojacked me, your gift won't be much of a surprise."

"I'm a congressional chief of staff. You know I hate surprises more than you do."

Marcia smiles and heads back down the sidewalk. No politician likes surprises, so their staff doesn't, by extension. Predictability is the key to controlling the narrative and crafting the message. It's what both sides count on. That's what makes political ambushes so devastating. If she is going to succeed in these hearings and stay out of the leadership's crosshairs, she will need to spring some surprises of her own.

Chapter Thirty-Six

REPRESENTATIVE JOHN KNUTSON

Something is to be said for moments of peace and quiet, especially in this town. Sunday mornings are almost sacred to John, and not because of going to church. It's a time for him to unplug, relax, and think without the distraction of staff, colleagues, reporters, and politics in general.

He's been coming to this small bistro in Alexandria since his first term. It's a metro ride from his Washington apartment, but he eagerly awaits the weekly sojourn when Congress is in session. The waitstaff is friendly, and the prices are reasonable for the metro D.C. area. It's not just the place's food or atmosphere that enchants him, however pleasant both are. The comfortable routine of coming here is most appreciated.

John is cutting into a piece of his cinnamon and powdered sugar-covered French toast when a purse slams down on the table. He glances up to see Angela glaring at him from the other side.

"Good morning to you, too."

"Cut the crap, John. What game are you playing?"

"Have a seat, Angela," John offers, gesturing at the empty chair. "Let's do what we pledged to and act like adults instead of the petulant children we work with."

Congress has steadily devolved from a place where serious people engage in debate to where they engage in petty sniping in front of the cameras. Collaboration and consensus-building have long morphed into blind hatred. Some of that is generated due to ideological, policy, cultural, or geographical differences. Some can be attributed to personality conflicts. Much of the animosity is manufactured by the political parties for public consumption. If you label the other side the "enemy," you can't be seen consorting with them.

Angela reluctantly pulls out the chair and eases herself into it. She doesn't move it closer to the table. She's not here for coffee, much less breakfast.

"I can see you're pissed."

"What gave it away? John, why are my people telling me that you're sitting out the questioning during the hearing? More importantly, why am I hearing it from them instead of you?"

John closes his eyes and squelches a sigh. Leaks are inevitable in Washington, as annoying as they are. He counts on his staff to be discreet and conduct the office's business with a degree of confidentiality. Unfortunately, nobody in the legislative branch suffers from a lack of ambition. Advancing agendas is not an activity limited to elected representatives. It's just disappointing that his staff engages in that.

"Leadership invaded my office on Friday. They strolled in with the subtlety of an armored tank division and decreed that nobody from our party was to jump into the fray during the subcommittee hearings."

"Or else?"

"They came with threats about the consequences, as well."

John considers Angela a friend, but they are still on opposite sides of the aisle. While he is willing to work with her on policy issues they agree on, it doesn't mean she's entitled to know about how his party conducts its business. Not that it would be much of a mystery to her. He's sure her party is no different.

"And you agreed to their demands," she concludes.

"No. But I didn't disagree with them, either. They were clear about what would happen. I didn't say anything to you because I haven't decided what to do."

Angela's eyes narrow. "Yes, you have. You may not have uttered the words, but the regret is tattooed on your face."

John puts his fork down. He fancies himself an excellent poker player because he has none of the usual tells. That's a game. This is reality. In truth, the decision is tormenting him, and he's likely wearing that like a Halloween mask. Still, it's annoying that Angela recognized it so easily.

"You need to understand that—"

"Don't! Just don't," Angela says, holding up a hand. "Don't talk to me about re-election."

"It's unavoidable."

Angela looks around the room and frowns as she locks her eyes on John. She must know he's right. Campaign finance is a politician's lifeblood. Those who have it increase their chances of victory. Those who don't, lose. It's another tool in the leadership's box to keep their party members toeing the line. It doesn't mean she has to like it.

"Do you remember when we first began talking? Practically nobody was back then. Our two parties were at each other's throats. We longed for a day that our colleagues would be more concerned about governing than re-election. Then we promised that we wouldn't become them."

"I'm not becoming them."

"Yes, you are. Please don't tell me that you're too blind to see it. If you let Durant and Guillomi cow you into silence like the bullies they are, then you've already become what you swore you wouldn't."

Pot, meet kettle. It's easy to say from her side of the table. She isn't being leaned on by her leadership. The picture would look much different if she were.

"Would you be eager to go against your party?"

"No, but I would charge through fire to uphold my principles. That's what Guzman did. Rumor has it that she leveled all manner of threats against the speaker and majority leader to hold these hearings. As misguided as her bill is, Camilla believes in it. That means she'll fight for it. What will you fight for?"

"This is the big leagues, Angela. I have to choose which pitches to swing at which not to. I want to defend Christmas, but leadership wants to use these ridiculous hearings as a springboard to take back the House next November. Why would I defy them if the bill won't even make it through the full committee?"

"Because that's not guaranteed in this political climate. Power is all the leadership of either party thinks about. McCormack spends more time thinking about keeping his power than he does representing his district. In the meantime, what kind of damage could be done to the country if we let them drag Christmas unchallenged through the mud?"

This is why they are friends – the woman knows how to make a compelling argument. She reminds him of his wife that way. But by arguing her perspective, she may be missing the others.

"What if they're right? Have you stopped to think about that? What if Guzman is embarrassing herself? The American people are fickle. They like their mythology. Honest Abe, Washington chopping down the cherry tree…what if this backfires for her?"

Angela presses her hands together in front of her mouth. "I know Camilla. We may not universally agree on everything, but she's shrewd. Every bill that comes out of the House alienates half the country. She's already done the math and knows the risk of attacking Christmas. If Camilla is willing to take things this far, it's because she has a plan. We need to thwart it. Or are you leaving that task to me?"

She gets up and slides the chair back under the table. John is about to answer when she beats him to the punch.

"Don't answer that. You've already made your decision. I'll see you tomorrow."

Angela picks up her purse and leaves the bistro. There goes his peaceful morning of reflection and relaxation before the circus starts tomorrow. That dream vanished, along with his appetite.

John pays the bill and leaves. He should head back to Capitol Hill, but Angela's words weigh heavy on him. It shows that you don't need insults to tear at someone's soul. The African-American Heritage Park is nearby, and he elects to take a walk. He needs time to think.

Chapter Thirty-Seven

WYATT HUFFMAN

Reykjavik is Europe's northernmost capital city and is home to two thirds of Iceland's 350,000 people. Stowe and Wyatt were up early, mostly because the time difference has scrambled their internal clocks. They found a nice breakfast place open, ate a wonderful meal, and then ventured out on the streets.

The city's compact size makes exploring surprisingly easy. Reykjavik's attractions are close to one another, and Wyatt and Stowe both like to walk. The only downside is that it's dark. Really dark. Such is life this far north as they get close to the winter solstice. Fortunately, Wyatt feels safer here than he does in D.C.

They walk up the hill to the city's most iconic sight. Hallgrímskirja is a Lutheran church that took forty years to build and is inspired by the Chrysler and Empire State Buildings. The sparse interior has an enormous pipe organ and an observation deck at the top of its tower, with a fantastic 360-degree view of Reykjavik coming to life under the purple morning sky.

Stowe and Wyatt leave the church and head to the part of Reykjavik that's as close as you get to a downtown area. Laugavegur is the city's main shopping street. There are shops, bars, and restaurants, and Wyatt steps into a Nordic-themed store to play with plastic axes and Viking helmets.

They spill back on the street and continue their walk, the conversation returning to work. It's unavoidable, despite this trip doing everything possible to derail them from their assigned task. Only their talk isn't about Santa or the subcommittee hearings. It's more philosophical.

"Our country has never been more divided!" Stowe argues.

"Tell that to the people who lived in the 1860s."

"Wyatt, the Civil War was a fight over one core issue – slavery. We're divided by...well, everything."

"Thanks to partisan media, polarizing social media, and deeply rooted cultural, historical, and regional divides hardly unique to America. Our two-party electoral system collapses social and political debates into a singular battle line. It makes our differences look like objects in the passenger side mirror – larger than they may actually be."

Stowe laughs. "Clever line. Maybe you should run for Congress."

"Not a chance."

Stowe gets quiet because she's never heard such a fervent denial before. Most of the staff on Capitol Hill have political aspirations of their own. Everyone dreams about having the big office one day. Someone rarely admits to not wanting the power that comes with that.

"I know you're not married. Have you ever been in a serious relationship?"

The change of subject throws Wyatt off for a moment. "Once. Jessie Stills. She was my high-school sweetheart. We dated until our junior year of college."

"What happened? If you don't mind me asking."

"No, I don't mind. The simple answer is we grew apart. Trivial things became more important to Jessie."

"Like?"

"I don't know…views on the economy, racial justice, climate change, law enforcement…stuff like that. She questioned whether I had core American values. That began to cut deep. I actually embraced our political differences. The different perspectives on life kept things interesting. She began to think needing to have similar views was non-negotiable."

"Most people wouldn't call that trivial."

"I would. I didn't care what Jessie thought about those things."

"Why not?"

He swallows hard. "Because I loved her."

Wyatt refuses to look at Stowe, even though he can feel her eyes on him. He doesn't want her to see the pain. It's been years, but the thought of ending his relationship with Jessie still hurts. The pain has diminished over time, but the thoughts about what could have been still linger. It's why he hasn't been in a serious relationship since.

"That started your junior year?"

Wyatt shakes his head. "No, it began earlier. We called it quits junior year."

"So, how did you make it work for as long as you did?"

"Humor. And common interests. We had a long history together, growing up on nearby ranches. We both loved riding horses and never once talked about politics until college."

"You ignored the problem," Stowe concludes.

"It never came up in high school," Wyatt says, shrugging. "When our arguments started in college, I employed 'strategic topic avoidance.' It worked until it wasn't enough. She began criticizing and belittling my views, and I, of course, reciprocated. She saw it as a challenge to change my mind. It didn't turn out well."

"How serious was your relationship with Jessie?"

Wyatt turns to Stowe and forces a smile. "I was going to marry her."

Stowe gets quiet again. The words may have struck a nerve, but Wyatt isn't going to press for details. He's curious, but the mistletoe kiss was already a misstep. He doesn't want to make another by prying into her life. She'll tell him if and when she wants to.

"I guess that's a cautionary tale. Bleeding-heart liberals and staunch conservatives can't have a meaningful relationship today."

"I don't agree with that. It's about personal values, not political ones. If you value your spouse and are committed to your vows, you should be able to agree to disagree. Ask Carville and Matalin."

Democratic commentator and campaign strategist James Carville and his wife Mary Matalin, a Republican consultant, managed to sustain a happy marriage for over three decades, two children, and two successful and diametrically opposed political careers. They never talked about politics at home. They have a lot of other things in common, and as is apparent to anyone paying attention, love and respect for one another that surpasses all else.

"They were married in the 1990s when the political world was still somewhat sane. It's unrealistic today," Stowe says, waving a dismissive hand.

"Contempt in any relationship is overcome with fondness and admiration. That fosters mutual appreciation and respect. I want to find someone who adds happiness to my life, makes my world a better place, and makes me a better person. Political differences are trivial if you love someone and cannot imagine life without him or her." Wyatt turns and smiles at Stowe. "In short, love conquers all."

"I never pegged you as a romantic," she confesses.

"You've never had a reason to."

Stowe is about to respond when her phone chimes. She opens the lock screen and reads the text message from the airline. The deep moan means it isn't good news.

"We're booked on a flight for Helsinki tomorrow morning."

"Then we have the rest of the day. We should go on a tour. See the geysers and waterfalls or something."

He expects Stowe to protest. She'll want to return to the hotel and get on the phone with the airline to plead for an earlier flight. Or even go there in person. She may be warming up a little, but this trip is all business for her.

"That sounds nice," she says as a smile creeps across her lips. "But I have a better idea."

Chapter Thirty-Eight

STOWE BESSETTE

Spelunking has always been a fascinating adventure for Stowe. First of all, she loves the word. Spell-un-king. It's fun to say. As she is from mountainous Vermont, the very idea of exploring dark, underground passageways has a romantic appeal. After reading through the brochures that Wyatt collected, she knew a road trip to the southern part of the peninsula was in order if time permitted.

Raufarhólshellir is a stunning lava tunnel a half hour south of Reykjavik. Colloquially known as the Lava Tunnel, it has ice stalagmites and cave walls coated in gorgeous hues of red. It's awe-inspiring, and she figured Wyatt wouldn't protest.

That's why she opted to forgo the standard hour-long tour and chose the three-plus-hour Lava Falls Adventure for a journey to the cave's bottom. Erik introduces himself as their tour guide and explains that much of the journey through the cave is a breeze after the recent renovations. A footbridge and stairs were added so guests don't have to worry about their footing.

The group is fairly small. Wyatt and Stowe spend much of the time talking to a young couple from Sweden as they admire the beautiful cave under the thoughtful installation of artificial lighting strategically placed to accentuate the beauty of the wall formations and the ice stalagmites.

"Do they have caves in Vermont?" Wyatt asks, staring at the cave's ceiling thirty meters over their heads.

"Nothing like this."

Up ahead, tour guide Erik explains how much of the cave remains pristine, untouched by humans or animals. Bats, even if they were native to Iceland, couldn't thrive in the cavern due to the lack of echo. He highlights how the cave's mouth has been a filming location for movies and has hosted everything from concerts to weddings.

That was the cue. The tour guide moves off with a half dozen people, but Johan hangs back and reaches into his pocket before dropping to a knee. At first, Stowe thought he wasn't feeling well. He's been a little off since the tour started. Now, she knows why.

"Hanna," he says, "I will never know what I did to deserve you. Every long road led me to your arms. The others who broke my heart were like northern stars guiding me to you. You are my North, my South, my East and West. You are the sun in my morning and the moon in my night. Because of you, I find a reason to smile. I would be forever honored if you let me be the reason for yours. Will you marry me?"

"Oh, my God! Yes!" she shrieks.

It's the answer Johan wanted. He rushes to slide the diamond on her finger, but his aim is off. The edge of the ring catches the tip of her middle finger, and the twisting motion causes him to lose his grip. He goes to catch it and fumbles, the last attempt giving it enough momentum that it careens off to his left.

The ring hits the edge of the footbridge and skitters onto a rock a couple of feet below the platform. It bounces twice before coming to a rest at the far edge, only a couple of inches from tumbling off the lava rock and being lost forever.

Distraught, Johan and Hanna move to the railing and stare. Stowe, Wyatt, and the people in the back half of the tour join them. What was a beautiful moment and a cause for celebration has become a certified nightmare. Tears stream down Hanna's face. Even Johan looks like he's about to lose it.

The ring is too far to reach from the bridge. Johan tries, but it's futile. It stopped more than six feet away from the edge. Johan hangs his head.

"Stowe, hold my legs," Wyatt says, peeling off his jacket and climbing over the black metal railing.

"What are you doing? You could get hurt! I can't—"

"I trust you, Stowe. You can do it. Hold my legs."

"I'll help," Johan says.

Three people hold Wyatt's ankles as he reaches down and plants his hands on the rocks nearest the footbridge. He slowly walks them out, avoiding the icy stalagmites as he extends into a pushup position. His back is at a thirty-degree downward slope when he reaches full extension. The ring is breathtakingly close. He stretches for it with his left arm, balancing his weight with his right. It's about a foot out of his reach.

"Can I move my feet closer to the edge?" he calls back.

"They're at the edge now," Johan says. "There's no more room."

"Damn it."

The heavy footfalls on the bridge cause Stowe to turn and see Erik stomping over to them. He's fuming.

"What the hell do you think you're doing! You can't—"

"No, no, no, it's not what it looks like," Stowe says, gently pressing her hands against his chest to stop him. "This isn't a lost cell phone or something. Let me show you what's happening."

Her words are soothing enough to calm him. She escorts Erik over to the edge and methodically explains what happened. The tour guide can see the ring precariously sitting right at the edge of the rock, just beyond Wyatt. It only settles him down for a moment. He understands the urgency, but they are all in his care. If something happens, it's on him.

Another tour member pulls Erik aside and tries to reason with him as Stowe turns her attention back to Wyatt. It still won't be enough, even if he gains another inch or two. The ring is out of reach. They are at an impasse. She needs to do something.

"Wyatt, can you support my weight?" Stowe asks, sliding out of her jacket.

"Uh…yeah, I think so. Why?"

"Hold his ankles tight," she commands as she steps on the metal cable and swings a leg over the railing.

This looked like a good idea ten seconds ago. Now that Stowe is hanging on to the wrong side of the railing with icy stalagmites below her, she isn't so sure. Icelanders are a no-nonsense and daring people. But this is stupid, even by their standards.

"I am so getting fired for this," the tour guide says, now with the program as he clamps his hands onto Wyatt's ankles.

"Keep your legs straight," Stowe says as she squats and gently lowers herself onto his calves.

Wyatt grunts but remains rock solid. She's actually impressed.

"Are you okay?"

"Just ducky. Is this a bad time to say you shouldn't have had that dessert last night?"

Stowe smiles and relaxes. "That depends on whether you want to leave this cave alive."

He snickers as she begins inching forward. The hard part is balance. Simone Biles would find this easy. Stowe didn't exactly excel in gymnastics. She carefully slides herself down to his shoulders, squeezing her legs and steadying herself with her arms as she moves. Stowe stops when she's seated just below the base of his neck.

"Duck your head. I'm going to lean over your shoulders and see if I can reach it."

"Not to be a nudge, please hurry."

Wyatt's arms have to be on fire. Stowe locks her ankles under his chest and bends forward at the waist without hesitating. She steadies herself with her left hand on the rock as she awkwardly reaches with her right. They don't gain much length, but it's enough to cover the remaining distance. She carefully tries to pick the diamond engagement ring up. One misstep and it will never be seen again.

"Got it!" she screeches, sitting upright to the delight of the tour watching from the footbridge. "I'm going to slide back. How are you doing?"

"Did I mention I *hate* planks?" Wyatt gasps.

"You're so good at them. I could stay here for hours and enjoy the view."

"I'd much rather you didn't."

Now comes the hard part: getting back. Keeping a firm grasp on the ring, she slowly shimmies backward. Stowe squeezes even harder with her legs for balance and uses her arms to nudge her across Wyatt's back and legs inch by inch. When she reaches his knees, she can feel them begin to sag in fatigue. She leans back and reaches for the footbridge.

Johan and Hanna grab her. Two other men lean over the railing and hook their hands under her armpits, pulling her off Wyatt. Once her feet are on the edge, they hold her steady as she swings her legs over one at a time and is safely on the footbridge. Then it's Wyatt's turn.

"All right, Wyatt. Time to feel the burn."

He grunts as he begins walking his arms under him. The tour guide and several others slowly pull on his legs until they can grab onto his belt. She has to give Wyatt credit. The man is strong. He twists and rolls onto his butt and uses the cables to climb to his feet. He climbs over the railing as the rest of the tour applauds and cheers.

"Mission accomplished," he breathes as he stretches his arms. "That hurt."

Stowe holds the ring between her index finger and thumb. "Do you want the honors? You did most of the work."

"Nope. You had the guts to climb on me to retrieve it. Please," Wyatt says, gesturing at Johan.

She carefully hands the ring to the most grateful man on the island. "Here you go, butterfingers."

Johan beams as Hanna holds her left hand out. The cameras that have recorded much of the rescue are still out as he starts to put the diamond on her finger.

"No, no, no," Wyatt protests. "I didn't do all that work for you to half-ass this. Do this right, or don't do it at all. Start over."

Johan is in no position to argue and does as instructed, this time with a death grip on the ring. Stowe clamps onto Wyatt's arm and rests her head against his shoulder as Johan takes a knee and repeats the eloquent proposal word for word, just like his first attempt.

He extends his arm. "Will you marry me?"

"Think about it, Hanna," Stowe warns. "He'll be dropping stuff for the rest of your lives."

"Yes! I will *absolutely* marry you!"

Wyatt is ready to play goalie as Johan carefully slides the diamond on her finger and stands. Take-Two was a complete success. They kiss to the applause of the entire tour. Even their relieved guide is ecstatic. He'll have a new story to tell. It will likely come with a stern warning to prospective suitors to be careful with precious jewelry and never try what he just witnessed.

"At least he sized it right," Wyatt whispers, earning him a playful slap to the chest.

The rest of the tour proceeds without incident. The guide needs to rush them to compensate for the time spent during the ring rescue. It doesn't matter. It is the perfect ending. The group emerges from the cave two hours later, and more congratulations to the couple are offered. People exchange email addresses so the videos can be circulated. Unintentionally, the ring rescue was a memorable moment they will all cherish.

"Thank you so much," Johan says with his fiancee hanging on his arm. "Both of you. I mean it. You saved the day. I don't know how to repay you."

"I do," Wyatt says. "Live long, happy lives and tell the story of the lost ring and two crazy Americans to your kids and grandkids until they can recite it from memory."

"Count on it!" Hanna says. "You two make the cutest couple!"

"Oh, we're not together," Stowe says, waving her hands side-to-side in a scissor motion.

"We're just colleagues," Wyatt adds.

Johan glances at his fiancee to catch her reaction. "You wouldn't know it. It takes a lot of trust to do what the two of you did for us. That's rare."

They exchange hugs and handshakes, and Stowe and Wyatt watch the happy Swedes head back to their car.

"You're a good man, Wyatt Huffman."

"You're not so bad yourself. We make a good team…at least when it…it comes to…."

"I know what you mean," Stowe says, beaming. "You're off the hook. Come on, let's catch our bus back to Reykjavik. I'm starving, and tomorrow could be a long day."

Stowe takes a deep breath of the fresh air. She thought this diversion was going to be a disaster. Instead, it's turning into something…magical. That should scare her. Instead, she looks forward to what the rest of this journey will bring.

Chapter Thirty-Nine

REPRESENTATIVE CAMILLA GUZMAN

Formal hearings are conducted to gather information from witnesses for use in congressional committee activities. In this case, it's to develop proposed legislation in a public policy matter. Most Americans pay no attention to the happenings in Congress's various subcommittees. Important confirmations to the Supreme Court or major federal agencies get the most attention.

While still true, the media presence in the room shows that the tide is beginning to turn. There are no judiciary hearings this week. There are no intelligence committee meetings or testimony from key cabinet members. Camilla scheduled it for this week because she knew they would be the only game in town.

That only drives some of the interest from the Washington media elites. The rest comes from the American people. Her press conference was a spark that followed a trail to this powder keg. It's why she got her wish to use the Commerce and Energy Committee room in the Rayburn House Office Building. It has the needed capacity for the media and spectators.

Camilla gavels the subcommittee into session. "The hearing will come to order. I want to extend my thanks to all of the witnesses who will testify before this subcommittee in the coming days. This hearing will address House Resolution 6204, a bill seeking to abolish depictions of Santa Claus in public places. The legislation was introduced by me and the honorable representative from Alabama, Mr. Blackburn.

"I have no doubt that the representatives in this room questioned my sanity when I proposed that legislation. It's unconventional thinking to question the holiday's norms and founding mythologies. But not discussing them ignores a fundamental truth: Christmas is a drag on many Americans.

"This is not an assault on a beloved holiday, or as some pundits have commented, an attack on Christianity. It's legislation designed to help America celebrate it again. For decades, we have suffered from 'Christmas creep.' It's the phenomenon of the Christmas retailing season that starts earlier and earlier each year.

"Many of us remember when a store's holiday decorations were hung in December. Then, the selling season invaded November, complete with Christmas music filling our ears even before we cooked our Thanksgiving turkeys. Now, children prepare to trick or treat while malls play 'Jingle Bells.' Many stores begin rolling out their holiday displays right after Labor Day. At this rate, my grandchildren may witness Rudolph the Red-Nosed Reindeer competing with the Easter Bunny.

"What drives the need to begin Christmas celebrations months before the holiday? Just follow the money. Consumers tell pollsters they plan to spend an average of a thousand dollars on Christmas gifts this year. More than one third say their gift-buying will top $1,500. In some states, one fifth of people go into debt to pay for Christmas gifts and festivities.

"Ladies and gentlemen, that's insanity. American consumers will spend more than one trillion dollars for Christmas this year. We are the world's biggest holiday spenders, even factoring in the seven percent of the population that will not spend anything on principle or for religious reasons. It might be forgiven, except exchanging gifts comes with another hassle.

"Sixty-two percent of Americans expect to get an unwanted gift. That's one hundred fifty-four *million* people who will be re-gifting an item or standing in a return line at a retailer. They can add that to the fifteen hours the average American spends shopping, standing at registers, and traveling to see relatives.

"Christmas should be about family, not gifts we can't afford. Santa Claus may not be the cause of these issues, but he embodies them. He is a constant reminder that a cherished holiday has become nothing more than a retailer's grift intent on extracting dollars from your wallets and purses and time away from your friends and family. I yield to the ranking minority member, Mr. Blackburn."

Camilla didn't expect applause. Unless it's a successful confirmation, that would be uncharacteristic in any committee or subcommittee hearing. She didn't say anything unexpected outside of her brazen attempt to portray the joy of Christmas as an undue burden on the American public. For some, it undoubtedly is. But that's a choice, or so some would argue. Unfortunately, it's not an easy one these days.

"Thank you, Madam Chairwoman. I ask for unanimous consent to put my full statement in the record."

"Without objection, the opening statement of all subcommittee members will be made a part of the record."

The request is a formality. There are no objections. Everybody wants their words on the record.

"Saint Nicholas was a real man, born in what is now Turkey, and widely known at that time for his generosity. If you'll pardon the pun, the Santa Claus of the North Pole is the polar opposite. He's a tone-deaf autocrat who delivers toys to the children of well-off parents while ignoring the most needy."

A wave of grumbling ripples through the room. It's precisely the reaction Aymos wanted. Calling Santa an autocrat was meant to be provocative. Now, he has everyone's attention.

"I have been accused by some in the media of hating Christmas. Nothing could be further from the truth. I want to preserve it by dispelling the mythology that makes us believe Santa is omniscient. You all know the story: He sees us when we're sleeping. He knows when we're awake. He knows if you've been bad or good. Worst of all, Santa keeps a record.

"We have bastardized a kind, gracious saint by turning him into a judge looking to dole rewards and punishments based on behavior, not morality. It should make my fellow Christians shudder. Santa has become a false idol, and this is what we eagerly teach our children to celebrate."

Camilla suppresses a grin. Her ally has gone into preacher mode. Aymos Blackburn made a name for himself in Alabama with fiery sermons the famous Massachusetts pastor John Edwards would be proud of. He brought that same spirit and passion to the halls of Congress. They are on full display today.

"Nobody questions the harm in teaching children about Santa's monitoring practices and the consequent rewards and punishments. After all, this system of control impels believers to exhibit good behavior by placing bribery at the heart of morality. That is not Christian.

"Jesus Christ preaches that following his word is the path to eternal heaven. He is the ultimate judge of our time on Earth. There is no room for a Santa Claus that punishes misbehavior while imposing a hollow system of incentives that ensures that everyone fails at goodness. Unless you think society is a better place today.

"It may be forgiven if Santa were a benefit to society. Imagine a world where he recalibrates his miraculous toy-producing capacity to feed the hungry or provide medicines to the sick. The modern Santa won't do that. His mythology exists to reward the children of the rich while the poorest among us struggle to put food on the table, much less afford the expensive gifts St. Nick is incapable of delivering.

"For Christians, it is time to return to the roots of our faith – our love and trust in Jesus Christ. For those of other faiths, the secularization of Christmas should be about time with family, acts of kindness and charity, and a feeling of hope and joy as we prepare for a new year. I hold today that Santa Claus is a despicable false idol. I sincerely hope that this subcommittee refers this legislation to the full Energy and Commerce Committee for further consideration. It's time to retire the Santa Claus myth. I yield to the chair."

"And we're off and running," Camilla mumbles under her breath as she leans forward and prepares to announce their first witness.

Chapter Forty

WYATT HUFFMAN

The hits just keep on coming. The airline customer service representative in Keflavik wasn't lying about the weather. There are delayed flights up and down the departures board once they reach Helsinki. The storm gripping Europe is causing havoc with air travel.

Wyatt and Stowe stare at the board in disbelief. Even the short flight to Rovaniemi has been pushed back more than four hours. That's assuming it takes off at all. If the weather doesn't improve and their travel luck doesn't change, nothing will stop a further delay or a cancellation.

"Now what?" Stowe asks.

"We wait."

"We should consider catching a train or renting a car," she argues.

"That may cause a different set of problems. Let's talk about it over a drink," Wyatt says, grabbing her hand and pulling her toward the domestic gates. Surprisingly, she doesn't yank it away. He lets go of her once she joins him.

Transferring at Helsinki Airport is easier than he expected. The airport has two terminals, but both are under the same roof. There is no need to wait for a bus, tram, or monorail to ride from one terminal to another as travelers endure at many major airports. It's nice having everything in one place.

That doesn't mean the journey between gates isn't an assault on the senses. Aromas, ranging from pungent perfume to freshly baked bread, emanate from the restaurants, shops, and cafés lining the wide corridor.

They stop at an Irish-themed bar with only a few patrons in the fenced-off seating area. It's not what he expected to see in the capital of Finland, but Irish pub culture is almost universal. At least, it is in America.

"Would you like something?" Wyatt asks, steering his rolling carry-on under the table.

"I'll take a beer," Stowe says, sitting.

"A beer? Aren't you afraid that will go right to your hips?"

She smirks. "Aren't you afraid that the alcohol will kill your one functioning brain cell?"

"Ouch. Solid burn. I'll be right back."

Wyatt returns with a pair of stouts. This wasn't meant to be a test, but it turned into one. Stowe didn't say which kind of beer she wanted, and he half expected her to object to his selection. Instead, she thanks him and takes a long sip. Where is the woman who ran into him and then proceeded to berate him? Times have changed.

"You know, this isn't a date. You should pay half."

"I'm just starting to like you. Don't ruin it," Stowe warns with a wink.

They laugh and commence with the people-watching. This isn't the world's busiest airport, but observing the characters passing by is entertaining. Other than staring at their phones and consuming the news, there isn't much else to do.

"Wyatt, are you beginning to think this was a bad idea?"

"Which part? Counting on St. Nick to kill Guzman's bill? Or risking our jobs to travel over a thousand miles to find a Santa who likely couldn't care less about American politics?"

"Hearing it is more depressing than thinking it. Both."

Wyatt takes a long sip and places the glass down, pressing his lips together. "I know the odds are against us, but I feel good about this."

"Why?"

"Two words: Christmas spirit."

Stowe shifts in her chair. "Okay, you need to explain that."

"I know a woman who loves Christmas as much as you do understands the concept."

"I binge-watch Hallmark Christmas movies, so yeah, I'm familiar with the term. I mean in this context."

"If a child mails a letter to Santa in the U.S., the postal service sends it to one of a dozen locations where volunteers respond. Another group has a special address, and the letters are processed in Anchorage, Alaska. Finland has something similar in Rovaniemi, where we're going. It's Santa's official post office, and they get over twenty million letters a year."

"Okay...."

"Santa's Village is on the Arctic Circle and sees hundreds of thousands of visitors yearly. In 1985, Rovaniemi was declared the official hometown of Santa Claus, and he keeps an office there. If we can't find our guy in Rovaniemi, we never will."

Stowe nods slowly before cocking her head. "You know that sounds crazy, right?"

"Yeah, I was already told."

"You know that our bosses aren't talking at the moment."

Wyatt frowns. "I heard not long after the congressman told me I'm nuts. I checked in with the office before we left Iceland."

"Do you agree with Knutson's tactic?"

It's a loaded question with no correct answer: Agreement is a betrayal of their mission. Disagreement equates to disloyalty to the man he pledged to serve. But Stowe has taken things this far. She deserves an honest answer.

"I wasn't elected to Congress. I'm also a legislative aide, not a strategist. There are political forces at work I don't pretend to understand. But, no, I don't agree with it. It takes courage to go against the party. Courage is what we all need to stop this insanity, the congressman included."

Stowe looks down as she uses her fingers to turn her glass on the table. "Were you given any instructions?"

"Find Santa Claus and get him to Washington. The congressman didn't care if I had to kidnap him and hijack his sleigh to do it."

"Then why isn't Knutson participating in the questioning?" Stowe asks, challenging the instructions.

Wyatt shrugs. "He didn't elaborate. All he did was raise the stakes for us."

Something is bothering Stowe. Wyatt may not know her well or for very long, but she wears her emotions on her sleeve. She's troubled, and it's something more than worrying that they will fail.

"I was…." She hangs her head.

"What's wrong, Stowe?"

"I should have told you sooner. Marcia Konstantinos ordered me to return to Washington."

"What?"

"She said that Congresswoman Pratt's decision was crystal clear. She wants me back in D.C. I'm supposed to book a flight from here and return to the office tomorrow."

Wyatt stares at his half-finished beer. "Then why are you still here?"

"I think…." Stowe starts before stopping and forcing a smile. "The lava cave."

"What about it?"

"Most people wouldn't have lifted a finger to help Johan and Hanna. You didn't need to jump in and help them. Someone would have found a way to retrieve Johan's ring, and he could have slipped it on Hanna's finger later. That wasn't good enough for you. They were upset, and you didn't want what happened to spoil the proposal. You weren't about to quit even when you couldn't reach it. Then you found a way to retrieve it."

"Actually, *you* did."

Stowe leans back. "That's why I'm still here. You're strong and determined. I know you can do this alone, but I think the odds are better if we work as a team. We've proven that."

Nothing about this assignment is going as expected. Wyatt would have eagerly escorted her to the gate if he felt like he did after their meeting in the coffee shop. A lot has changed since then. A lot.

"Stowe, I don't want you to go, but I also don't want you to sacrifice your job. That's what staying could mean."

"I know," she says in a near-whisper before looking him in the eyes. "But you said it. It takes courage to save Christmas. I'm all in. I only need to know your intentions."

It takes three milliseconds to decide. "I'm seeing this through until the end. It's not about politics or doing what the congressman wants. This is about Christmas. If that means delivering Santa to Washington, then that's what I'm going to do."

Chapter Forty-One

REPRESENTATIVE JOHN KNUTSON

"These studies *do* suggest that parents' lies may have a detrimental effect on a child's behavior. A recent MIT study conducted on six- and seven-year-olds found that when authority figures omit the truth, children become suspicious of anything that authority figure says in the future. Another experiment conducted by researchers at the University of California, San Diego, found that when children in that age range are lied to, they're more likely to cheat and then lie in return."

Dr. Amelia Slitheen is an accomplished psychologist, professor, and lead researcher at the New England University School of Behavioral Science. The first ten minutes of her statement have been rock-solid. Her testimony is well-reasoned and supported by research. The doctor's portrayal of the facts is even and steady. She's a confident woman.

"The Santa myth is such an involved and long-lasting lie that vulnerable relationships between parents and children will be adversely affected. If parents can convincingly lie about Santa Claus over such a long period, what else can they lie about?

"Without wading too deep into the water of attachment theory, kids develop their ideas of themselves and the world based on their bond with parents or guardians. They ask the questions: Am I safe? Is the world around me safe? Are people trustworthy? They look to the people they trust for love, support, honesty…and answers.

"Parents may not know everything but should never intentionally mislead or lie to a child. I am a Christian. My husband and I teach our children about God, Jesus, and the Holy Spirit. Although the Trinity isn't seen in physical form, we explain that they are real and around us all the time. If I also tell them that Santa Claus is real, how will they feel about God when they learn the truth about Santa? It's a breach of trust. I don't want to find out how that would affect my kids' moral compass. It's not worth the mental gymnastics required to convince them that an obese geriatric man sneaks into every single person's house in one night to deliver presents. Thank you for your attention."

John rubs his chin. Amelia was well-prepared for this hearing. The religious overtones have Aymos's fingerprints all over it. Guzman and Blackburn will have coordinated with allies like Representatives Salib and Bass to pose leading questions to bolster her testimony. With the restrictions that Durant imposed on members of his party, that means only Angela Pratt and maybe one or two others will stand against her.

They are outnumbered, and the lion's share of the media coverage will be about Dr. Slitheen's opening salvo of protecting children. It's brilliant.

"That concludes the witness's testimony," Guzman announces. "We will now allow each member of the subcommittee five minutes for questioning. Please respect that time, as we have additional testimony to hear today. We will begin with the gentlewoman from North Carolina."

"I have no questions," Faye Blanchard says. "I yield my time back to the chair."

"Very well," Guzman says, taking a note. "The gentleman from Ohio."

Every committee and subcommittee handles questioning according to the rules adopted at the beginning of the congressional session. Sometimes, the order is by seniority in the House; other times, it's longevity on the committee. Either way, questioning almost always alternates between the two parties.

"Thank you for your testimony, Doctor," Representative Edward Bass announces. "Tell me. At what age do most children stop believing in Santa Claus?"

"Between seven and ten years old," the doctor says, "and that variance is attributed to factors such as region and peer group. Additionally, kids with older siblings or relatives who might explain that Santa isn't real may stop believing much earlier."

"I see. So, some of their most formative years?"

"From a cognitive standpoint, absolutely."

"Don't they know, on some level, that Santa doesn't come down the chimney with presents? Especially if they live in the city or a house that doesn't have one?"

"Parents usually craft excuses to get around this when the question arises. On the whole, children believe what they're told during their development. To kids, Santa is as flesh and blood as you and I unless a parent blatantly says he isn't real."

Bass makes a show of sitting up and folding his hands in front of him for the cameras. "Dr. Slitheen, you mentioned early in your opening remarks that parents using Santa to control behavior is problematic. I don't see how that's the case. Can you explain what studies are showing?"

John fights the urge to roll his eyes. He expected softball questions, but that one was just short of grabbing a pair of pom-poms and leading an anti-Santa cheer.

"Parents use many tools to mold a child's behavior," Dr Slitheen advises. "Using the threat of Santa Claus delivering coal for being naughty is potentially not the best parenting method. Instead of fostering good behavior on moral grounds, children are being taught that a mythical being decides whether presents are delivered or not."

"And you maintain that this is problematic?"

"Having studied the issue for years now, it is my opinion that parents coercing their children to believe in Santa is a form of child abuse that should be immediately halted."

"I yield my time to the chair," Congressman Bass says as a grumble ripples through the room.

John stares at the press corps in the back of the room and the photographers huddled in front of the witness table. The media are getting their wish. That line will be played in countless news promos and be the headline for every article covering this hearing for the rest of today's news cycle.

"The gentleman from Montana has five minutes."

"Thank you. I…"

John lets his voice trail off. This is a quandary. He was planning on doing as instructed. The consequences of going against the party leadership are too severe for him. But he can't bring himself to do it. This testimony needs to be challenged. He needs to draw a line in the sand.

"You know, when my children were in preschool, they usually took pictures with Santa. That was perfectly fine with me. If my kids hadn't wanted to participate, neither my wife nor I would have forced the issue. As they got older, they asked more questions. I believe it's because their critical thinking skills began to sharpen. When they asked me directly about his existence, I answered honestly. In your opinion, what is the harm in that?"

"It's about trust, Congressman. What we teach our kids about the dangers of life is not physically seen. We ask them to take our word for it because we don't want them to learn the hard way. That's hot, don't touch it. Put on your jacket, or you'll catch a cold. Wash your hands so the germs don't make you sick. Parents are their children's safe space. If children learn they can't trust those who love them most, then who can they trust?"

"And yet, most of the people here managed to survive that trauma. Doctor, what are the *benefits* of believing in Santa?"

"I'm afraid I don't understand the question."

"Yes, you do. Dr. Slitheen, your testimony was well-researched and comprehensive. Only it focused on one side of the coin without examining the other. Are there studies that show the benefits of believing in Santa?"

Dr. Slitheen fidgets in her chair as John pulls a stack of papers closer to him. Her eyes nervously dart between John and Camilla Guzman. She hopes the chair will shut down or challenge the questioning. That's not going to happen. One of the perils of congressional testimony is that nobody will save you when you start drowning. Welcome to the deep end of the pool.

"I'm afraid that research is sparse."

"Why is that?"

"I can't say."

"Fair enough. I find that interesting, but 'sparse' means there is at least some research," John says, tapping the papers with his fingers. "What do the studies that were conducted indicate?"

"That there are benefits of having a vivid imagination. Believing in impossible beings like Santa Claus or flying reindeer exercises a child's counterfactual reasoning skills."

"I see. You don't agree with the findings?"

"As a child psychologist, I believe the harms outweigh the benefits. You're setting your child up for inevitable disappointment when they realize the truth about Santa. Everyone remembers that moment they realized that Santa Claus wasn't real. Notable authors have labeled it the 'JFK effect' — people remember where they were and what they were doing when they heard the sad news."

"Because Christmas isn't as magical for children without Santa."

"Your time is up, Congressman," Guzman announces.

Guzman needed to wrap this up. They are advancing an agenda and don't want anything heard that could refute that. Too bad. Questions are a means to understanding truth. If the American people are asked to take sides, they should have all the information.

"Point of order," John interjects before she can announce the next questioner. "If I may appeal to the chair, one of my colleagues has already yielded her time. I assume others will, as well."

"And I may reallocate that time as I see fit. We have a lot to get through today, Mr. Knutson."

"Of course. I'm asking that you indulge me on this critical issue for another minute or two. I don't believe we are in jeopardy of having this hearing run over its allotted time, and I think we owe it to the American people to delve into this important issue properly. Millions will likely see this testimony."

The media presence does more than cover the hearings and increase exposure. It reduces the number of games played and hampers the success of the ones that are. Guzman doesn't want to give him more time. But she has created circumstances where failing to do so will make it look like she's hiding something.

"The chair grants the gentleman from Montana three extra minutes."

"Thank you. Doctor, you are a very accomplished woman and leader in your field. Are you married?"

"Yes, I am."

"Do you have children?"

"Yes, Congressman, I do."

"Are they happy?"

Amelia cocks her head slightly after hearing the question. She knows she's being set up. Everyone in the room knows it. Her challenge is parrying the question when it's finally posed without looking like she's avoiding it. That's the game.

"Yes."

"Are you satisfied with your life and career path?"

"Very much so."

"Did you have a happy childhood?"

"Yes. My parents were amazing."

"Did you believe in Santa Claus?"

Amelia Slitheen stares at John from her position at the witness table. Cameras click away as she remains stone-faced. The reason for the pause is obvious enough. She walked into that question.

"Congressman, I was brought here to testify as a highly regarded child psychologist. I separate my professional opinion from my personal experiences to remove bias. I don't see how that's important."

"I am not a school-trained psychologist, Dr. Slitheen. But I understand that pushing the border between possible and impossible is at the core of all scientific discoveries and inventions, from bifocals to the cotton gin to the airplane. Studies won't show that perhaps the greatest benefit to children's cognitive development arises from discovering that Santa Claus isn't a real physical being, because those studies aren't being conducted."

"That's a vast overstatement."

"That cannot be disproven by the existing research, can it?"

"No."

"The singular point in time when their child demands and learns the truth is often preceded by a protracted period during which children become increasingly unsure about Santa's existence. Is that true?"

"Yes, that is usually the case."

"And toward the end of this period, children search for evidence to confirm their suspicions. Some children try to stay awake. Others look at the roof to see if the snow was disturbed by Santa's sleigh. You conducted that same analysis, and it contributed to your cognitive development. Did you believe in Santa Claus as a child, Dr. Slitheen?"

"Yes, I did."

"Thank you, Doctor. I appreciate your testimony today. I hope every child grows to be as happy and well-adjusted as you are. I yield the balance of my time to the chair."

Chapter Forty-Two

STOWE BESSETTE

Transportation in and around Rovaniemi is pretty easy. They opted for a rideshare to bring them from the city to the hotel. The trip went quickly because the driver was chatty and extremely proud of his city.

He delivered a monologue explaining that ninety percent of the city was destroyed in October 1944 during the Second World War. It was naturally rebuilt, and many of those post-war buildings have been renovated and transformed to modern uses. The Arctic Sky Hotel is one of those places.

Wyatt and Stowe bid their farewell to the driver and enter the lobby. There is nothing about it that could be considered sterile or boring. The large fireplace is immaculate, and the décor plentiful and appropriate. There is everything from snowshoes on the walls to large plush polar bears seated on the overstuffed purple chairs and sofas in the lounge.

Stowe isn't used to traveling, at least outside the United States. She's feeling the effects of it. Her body is weary, and her mind is tired despite having pent-up nervous energy. That sofa looks really comfortable.

"Welcome to the Arctic Sky Hotel," a pleasant young woman greets them as Wyatt takes the lead at the counter.

"Thank you. We have a reservation for two rooms under Wyatt Huffman."

She types on a computer and looks at her counterpart, who leans over to view the screen. "Yes, Mr. Huffman. Two rooms with queen beds and, uh…I'm sorry, we have a small problem."

"What kind of problem?"

"One of your rooms suffered a burst pipe and is unusable. It only happened a couple of hours ago. We tried calling several times but couldn't reach you."

Wyatt pulls out his phone and checks it. There are three dozen missed calls and more than a dozen messages. Like Stowe, he planned on going through them once he got settled in the room.

"Okay, is there another available?"

"I'm sorry, the hotel is completely booked."

Stowe studies her face. It's not the canned response hotel employees are trained to say. The young woman has genuine remorse about the situation and feels bad that there is nothing she can do. She's also looking at Wyatt like he's Mr. March on the latest fireman calendar.

"Okay, I understand. What about other hotels?"

"I took the liberty of checking others in the area. The weeks before Christmas are a popular time of the year in Lapland, as you might imagine. There are no vacancies. I'm so sorry. I'm happy to check again for you."

Wyatt turns to Stowe. "Take the room here. I can find a place to stay."

It's sweet of him to offer, not that she's come to expect less.

"Where? Where are you going to stay?"

"I can find a last-minute online rental, or maybe there's a cancellation somewhere. Don't worry about me."

Stowe grimaces. "I have to. You'd sleep outside without telling me, and I'd walk out to find you hypothermic in a block of ice on the sidewalk. How big are your rooms here?"

"They're pretty large," the receptionist says.

"Do you have cots?"

"Yes, ma'am, we do."

"We'll take the room," Stowe says, turning to Wyatt. "Add this to the rest of the Christmas movie clichés that this trip has become. You had better not snore."

"I could say the same."

Stowe laughs. "I don't snore."

Wyatt tries to suppress a grin. "Oh, the passengers on the flight from Iceland would say otherwise."

"I wasn't snoring!"

"Keep believing that," Wyatt argues as the two women behind the counter desperately try to hide their smiles.

"Your room is 402. Take the elevator up to the fourth floor. I'm very sorry for the inconvenience. We are going to work on getting you a hotel credit. Please enjoy your stay with us."

"Thank you," Wyatt says, flashing a smile that causes one of the girls to blush and bat her eyelashes at him.

Stowe rolls her eyes as they head to the elevator. The thought of sharing a room with Wyatt Huffman before this trip was unthinkable. Now, she leaped at the opportunity to share a room with him. She doesn't know what's happening, but it scares her to think her heart is suddenly in the driver's seat.

Chapter Forty-Three

REPRESENTATIVE CAMILLA GUZMAN

The hearing was the lead story on the network news broadcasts. Most local stations covered it, many including field interviews to gauge the response from citizens and leaders. Social media has erupted into a maelstrom of accusations, threats, and memes. In other words, it was a typical day of chaos for the nation's keyboard warriors.

Camilla sits on the sofa and pushes the power button on the remote. Unless the Women's World Cup or the Olympics is on, the television in her office is tuned into cable news. The coverage has been extensive, or so the report from her media analyst highlighted. While there are plenty of other stories to cover globally, most have zeroed in on this as a huge national interest story.

"Miranda Skatt, the director of the Bridings Institute of Child Welfare, is joining us in-studio tonight to discuss today's testimony. Thank you for agreeing to speak with us, Miranda."

"Thank you for having me, Colin."

"You watched the hearing in the Cultural Commerce Subcommittee today. You know, I have to be honest: I thought this would be a joke. Instead, the witnesses made some valid points worthy of consideration, especially Dr. Slitheen."

"I agree. I have long advocated that teaching children about these myths damages their mental health," Miranda says.

"No, you haven't!" Camilla shouts at the television. "That's why *you* weren't invited to testify!"

"Dr. Slitheen had a well-articulated argument for something I professed for years. More needs to be done to protect children," Miranda finishes.

"What about the counterarguments made by Representative Knutson? He was one of the few that attempted to challenge the assertions. Do you agree with his points?"

"I understand he has a job to do, but he's a politician. On what wall did he hang a doctorate in child psychology? I've been doing this my entire adult life. I can tell you his implications were wrong, and I thought his line of questioning was inappropriate."

"At least you got with the program now, Miranda," Camilla mutters. "Fraud."

"Not everybody can be a trailblazer," Aymos announces from the threshold. "Your staff is gone, so I let myself in. I hope you don't mind. Catching up on current events?"

Camilla mutes the television. "You're working late."

"I want to keep the momentum going. Tomorrow's questioning will be crucial, especially if John Knutson enters the fray again."

"I thought you said that your party silenced him."

Aymos shrugs and takes a seat on the sofa opposite Camilla. "That's what I was told."

"By Spencer?"

"No," Aymos says with a chuckle. "The minority leader isn't speaking to me right now."

Camilla doesn't know where her colleague got his information, but it doesn't matter. His joining in on this bill is enough to show that he's committed. That doesn't mean someone can't or won't use leverage to get him to betray her. This is Washington. That happens every day here.

"Does that worry you?"

"There is no chance of me being challenged in a primary, much less losing my seat in the general election. Not in my district. I'm not going anywhere, so Durant and Guillomi have little to threaten me with."

"They could find another way."

"Not those two. They're blunt objects and just as sharp. They only use one tactic because it's all they know. They won't be a problem."

"And Knutson?"

"His district isn't as safe, and they *will* find someone to primary him. He committed political suicide today. May God have mercy on his soul."

Camilla isn't sure he cares whether God takes mercy or not. Blackburn and Knutson might be in the same political party, but that's where their solidarity ends. Frankly, she doesn't care. There are more pressing concerns to address.

"You were right to move Dr. Slitheen to the front of the line. Her testimony is all anyone is talking about. How did you know?"

Aymos leans back into the sofa. "The same way you knew the media would cover the hearings in the first place. Intuition. It's the same intuition that tells me things are going to get harder from here."

"Why do you say that?"

"Because you're getting your wish," he says, pointing at the television. "You wanted these hearings to raise your profile."

"That's not—"

Aymos holds his hands up. "It's not meant to be an accusation, but don't deny it. We both know that's the reason, and that secret is safe with me. There isn't a single politician in this town who hasn't used a tragedy, crisis, or social issue to get where they are."

There is no arguing that point. It's an ethos for both parties. Whenever a crisis erupts when the other party is in charge, it must be exploited. The converse is also true. Sometimes, the wagons must be circled and defended.

Only this issue transcends party politics. It has elements of ideologies on both sides of the aisle and aims to keep children safe. That's a hard point to argue against.

Camilla leans forward. "You wouldn't have defied your party and co-sponsored this bill if you thought this was a publicity stunt. So, why did you?"

"Because it's the right thing to do. It was a stunt when you started, but I think you began to believe in the possibilities. Your opening statement was fire – the perfect secular argument against Santa Claus. You didn't mail it in. There was power behind those words because you *believed* them."

"How can you know that?"

"I'm a preacher, Camilla. I've been one my entire adult life. I know when someone stands up and believes what they say. Just remember your convictions when the artillery begins landing on your position."

It's not every day a preacher from Alabama uses a war analogy. To her knowledge, Aymos never served in the military. That means he's trying to make a point.

"Do you think it will be that bad?"

"No, it will probably be worse. You're making a lot of people angry. Angry people have big mouths, and there is nothing the media loves to do more than put them on television to fan the flames."

"Even at Christmas?"

"Especially at Christmas. This rollercoaster just pulled out of the station. The ride we paid for starts tomorrow."

Chapter Forty-Four

WYATT HUFFMAN

After a quick dinner at the restaurant, Wyatt and Stowe set out for a walk around downtown Rovaniemi. It isn't large, and there isn't much to see at this time of night. Lordi's Square has a huge Christmas tree, winter events for young children, and booths selling crafts. Unfortunately, everyone went home for the evening. Even the pubs and coffeehouses are calling it a night.

Stowe and Wyatt are almost alone as they admire the beautiful Christmas lights and the little cottage with a nativity scene. This isn't how he imagined things. A nice, almost romantic stroll with Stowe was unthinkable this time last week. Talking to her back then was painful. Now, it's almost effortless.

"What are your parents like?" Stowe asks, kicking a clump of snow.

"Old."

"No, really. I want to know."

"Okay. Mama is a saint. She's the family's matriarch, making her the peacemaker, diplomat, and enforcer of house rules. My father is a hardboiled rancher who does what my mother says and expects his children to carry on the family legacy at the ranch."

"And none of you did?"

Wyatt smiles. "Two of us did. My older brother and sister are both married and work at the ranch. I'm the black sheep."

"Ah. Your father doesn't approve of your career choice?"

"Approve? No. He'd rather have seen me dealing drugs for a Mexican cartel instead of working in Washington."

"That sounds rough."

"It's manageable, but it makes trips home more dramatic than they should be. It will be easier when my father gets what he really wants."

"You out of Washington?"

"Grandkids," Wyatt says with a smile.

They keep walking despite there being not much to see. The temperatures are around what it is in Montana this time of year, without the biting wind blowing down from Canada. It feels refreshing, and Stowe doesn't look like she's in a rush to return to the hotel's fireplace in the lobby.

"Go ahead and ask."

"Ask what?"

"About my parents," Stowe says, kicking at another clump of snow. "Ask what happened."

Wyatt takes a deep breath before responding. "I didn't think you would want to talk about that."

"It's about time I do."

"Okay, but I'm not going to ask you directly. Let me try a lead-in. How did you get the name 'Stowe?'"

She smiles. "You're very stubborn. And clever."

"Two character traits my father despises in me."

"My parents met skiing on Mount Stowe. At least, that's how I remember my father telling the story. Mom would call it a 'collision course with destiny.' They were both going down the hill, as fate would have it. He was the better skier, so she didn't see him come up alongside her. She zigged, he zagged, and they collided and became an avalanche of intertwined arms and legs tumbling down the hill."

"Oof. Sounds painful."

"As Mom would say, love often is. She ended up on top of him when they stopped sliding down the slope. They locked eyes, and she didn't think twice. She kissed him right there on the snow."

"Gutsy. She's lucky he didn't have a girlfriend."

"Oh, he did. Her name was Brenda, and she was very unhappy when she made it down the hill to find them sucking face."

Wyatt lets out a belly laugh. "That's epic."

"So was their love story. Brenda was quickly out of the picture...that day, in fact. My parents got married six months later. I came a year after that. They named me Stowe to commemorate their chance meeting on the mountain."

"I thought maybe that's where you were conceived."

"It may have been," Stowe admits. "They loved skiing."

Stowe swipes a tear out of her eye. He knows this must be painful for her and gives her time to find the words. Or end the story. Some things are too painful to relive. Instead, she takes a deep breath and lets it out.

"My parents died when I was nine," she says in a solemn whisper. "They were out late one night with friends, and the roads were icy. Dad lost control of the car going around a corner, and...they were killed instantly. When the police found them, they were still holding hands.

"I remember seeing the red and blue flashing lights outside my grandparents' cabin. I remember Nana coming into my bedroom in tears. She sat on the edge of my bed and told me that Mommy and Daddy were in heaven. I couldn't grasp that. I couldn't understand the concept of never seeing them again. I remember it all like it was yesterday."

"I can't imagine going through that. Especially at that age."

"Yeah," she says, still struggling with her tears. "Enough of the sad talk. Let's do something fun."

"Uh, look around, Stowe. Everything is closed."

She stops to face him. "Improvise. I don't talk about my parents with anybody. I don't think Mandy even knows the story. Find something that will take my mind off being sad."

Wyatt looks around and focuses on the far horizon. "All right. I have an idea."

Chapter Forty-Five

REPRESENTATIVE JOHN KNUTSON

Cam expected the congressman to get another office visit. He was certain that challenging the testimony at the hearing would cause the minority whip to kick down the door. The messages taken by the staff from Durant and Guillomi were clear enough. They're angry, and John is the focus of that rage.

"Anything?" he asks when his chief of staff pokes his head into the office.

"Nothing. Not a word."

John packs up his things to head back to his apartment. He can work from there and maybe spare the tongue-lashing until tomorrow. After saying goodbye to the staff, the congressman opts for the long route to his car. The air is crisp and cold, and he could use the exercise and time to clear his mind.

He exits the Longworth Building and takes a long breath of cold air. The air is different, but the temperature of it reminds him of home. Very few other things about this city do.

Two men wearing wool overcoats are waiting for him outside the building. He should be surprised to see them, but he isn't. The only curiosity is how long they have been there. Someone tipped them off. Neither would wait in the cold for two minutes to pick their mothers up from the bus stop.

"Spencer, Gregory…to what do I owe the pleasure?"

"I think you know the answer to that," Guillomi crows.

"You disobeyed my directives," the minority leader piles on.

John frowns. They aren't mincing words, so he won't either.

"Your directives are stupid."

"John, you've been here long enough to know how this works. You shouldn't need a refresher class."

"And you've been in leadership long enough to know when the selected course of action is about to blow up in your face. That's why you stuck your head in the sand. You aren't on the subcommittee. It allows you to easily shift the blame if pressed about why we didn't fight. You have plausible deniability. You could even make up a story that you told me to, and I refused."

"I wouldn't do that," Spencer barks.

"You would. It's politics."

"These hearings make Guzman look petty. It makes her party look like Scrooges."

"And I think remaining silent makes us look weak. It makes us appear impotent. Our supporters want fighters who stand up for their principles. Instead, millions are watching highlights of our party doing nothing. Nobody from our side of the aisle was engaged. They just sat there and listened in silent consent to the utter vomit being spewed."

"How colorful," Gregory moans.

"Are you really lecturing us about the mood of the party? We know far more than you do."

"All evidence to the contrary, Spencer."

He nods. "We came here to give you one last chance. I see you don't want it, and that's too bad. We told you that actions have consequences. For you, it will be your seat. For the rest of us, it will be failing to regain control of the House next November."

The two men begin to walk away triumphantly. All that's missing is the celebratory high five. That offends his Montanan sensibilities. He's done being intimidated by these clowns. He doesn't care if they're in his party. They don't reflect his values, at least on this issue.

"Nah, it's not going to be like that, Spencer. You're not going to hang your ineptitude on me."

"Excuse me?"

"Not this time. Americans have a short attention span, gentlemen. I know you understand that concept because I've heard you say it. If we fail in the next election, these hearings will have nothing to do with it – except the lingering perception we leave with our constituents that there is no point in electing us because we don't fight when we get here. Why should we convince them we're not too busy keeping our jobs rather than actually doing them when it's true?"

"That's not how the American people will see it when we're done," the minority leader says, stomping over.

"I know you believe that, Spencer. But you're forgetting something."

"What's that?"

"Aymos Blackburn co-sponsored Guzman's bill. He stood beside her at the press conference and had no problems asking questions during today's hearings. Just for the side you say is embarrassing itself."

"We can deal with Aymos."

"Can you? Because I don't think Blackburn gives a damn about what you have to say. Unless you think you can primary him next year. *That* would be entertaining."

"You have some nerve!" Guillomi shouts, rushing over to back up his buddy.

"I know you two are dinosaurs that see everything through a partisan lens. It must be terrifying for you to deal with an issue with bipartisan support. It's not how your brains are wired."

The two men look at each other, causing John to smile. They know he's right, not that they will ever have the guts to admit it.

"I'm full steam ahead, gentlemen. Get on board the train or get off the tracks. Either way, do what you want at the end of this. I'm done with your threats. I'm here to fight for my constituents. If you expect anything less, maybe you clowns should try to replace me next fall. But it will be their choice, and I will always work for them, not you."

This time, it's John who turns and walks away. He expects a barrage of threats to chase him down the sidewalk, but none come. He wants to hazard a glance back but refuses to give them the satisfaction. The damage is done. If he just ended his political career, he might as well go out with a bang. It's time to take the gloves off.

Chapter Forty-Six

STOWE BESSETTE

The rideshare pulls up to the front of the building, and the pair climbs out of the back. Wyatt thanks the driver and offers a wave before the man shifts the car into drive, pulls it around the loop, and heads toward the main road. It's quiet and peaceful up here but also a little unnerving.

"Where are we?" Stowe says, looking around the trees at the top of the hill.

Wyatt points to a sign and reads, "Welcome to Own-a...Ow-na-sh...Ounasvaara!"

Stowe is fairly certain he didn't say it right on the third attempt, either. "Seriously?"

Ounasvaara is a year-round family ski resort south of Rovaniemi. It features ten downhill slopes with five lifts and several cross-country tracks during the winter. Summer tobogganing and downhill biking are available when no snow is on the ground.

"Uh, Wyatt, this place is closed."

"Nothing escapes your powers of observation, Captain Obvious," Wyatt says in a tone more playful than condescending.

"And it's dark."

"We'll let the stars guide our way."

"Please tell me you don't use that line on other girls."

Wyatt grins and leads her around the side of the building. It's not completely dark. There is artificial lighting around the lodge, and the moonlight reflects off the blanket of snow covering the ground. They walk to the top of the slope and peer at the glittering lights of Rovaniemi and the surrounding villages below.

"This is more like it. Are we allowed to be here?"

Wyatt shrugs. "Probably not, but it's Finland. The police won't come up this mountain unless we vandalize the place."

"That's encouraging. Do you plan on killing me and hiding my body somewhere up here?"

"That may have been tempting a week ago, but no."

"Then what are we doing here?"

"I'll show you."

Wyatt walks to the chairlift and sits. He's content to admire the beautiful view of the city on the other side of the river. Stowe sits next to him on the cold wooden bench. They savor the quiet stillness for several minutes. It is very peaceful...and relaxing.

"You know, as nice as this is, making me feel nostalgic for home isn't getting my mind off things."

"I didn't expect it to. I've never been here before. I wanted to enjoy the moment."

It's easy to forget to slow down and appreciate the small things – the smell of a flower, the feel of a pet curled in your lap, or, in this case, a scenic view. Washington is a city constantly in motion. It's also a long way away from the mountains in Vermont. Stowe had almost forgotten how to take time to appreciate the world around her. If she's learned anything from this trip, it's that.

"Okay, it's time to go."

"Where?"

Wyatt points down the slope. There are lights near the bottom, but the hill is dark and foreboding. Nighttime skiing is a thing, but it's always under the glow of artificial lighting. The accidents that would occur hurtling down the hill on laminated wood and metal planks would be nasty. Even though there are no other people on this slope, there are plenty of trees to run into.

"I'm not skiing in the dark."

"Good, because I ride horses. I've never been skiing."

Wyatt walks over to a shed twenty feet away and grabs a two-man toboggan leaning against the door. He inspects it, and once satisfied, walks back over to Stowe with a Cheshire Cat smile.

"You're nuts, Wyatt! Do you even know where this trail goes?"

"Of course. To the bottom of the hill."

"You're crazy!"

"I'd prefer to think of it as adventurous. You're named after a mountain in Vermont," Wyatt says, sitting down in the toboggan and sliding to the rear. "You're the crazy one if you let a guy from Montana sled down this mountain by himself."

"How will we get back to the city?" Stowe argues.

"We'll figure that out at the bottom. Coming?"

Stowe sits in front of Wyatt. They use their arms to push against the snow until it gets steep enough to give the toboggan momentum. It is darker down the slope, but there is enough light from the moonlit snow to show them the way. It's pretty much a straight shot, so not much steering is required.

They careen down the hill, picking up speed. Stowe lets out a couple of laughs in nervous excitement and hears Wyatt doing the same behind her. They catch a small mogul and plow through the air before landing and regaining speed.

Stowe closes her eyes. She savors the feeling of the icy wind on her face, flakes of wet snow brushing her skin, and the warmth of Wyatt's chest on her back and arms around her. It's…perfect. And over too soon.

The four hundred meters to the bottom are covered quickly. Wyatt turns the toboggan sharply when they reach the bottom of the hill. The edge catches the snow and flips, halting their momentum and dumping them off. They tumble through the snow, and Stowe ends up on Wyatt's chest when they finally come to a rest.

Stowe stares down at Wyatt. Memories of the story her parents told her growing up race through her mind. Her mother always said she didn't think about what she was doing. She was caught up in the moment. Stowe finally understands how.

She moves her face to Wyatt's. She closes her eyes, and their lips touch, soft at first, then harder and more urgent. Her heart beats faster, warming her as she feels Wyatt gently place his hands on her back.

Reality is cruel. When their lips part, doubt takes over. Wyatt is a colleague who works for the other party. This could never work out. They're different people with different ideals. What is she doing?

Stowe pushes herself off him, sitting in the snow. Now embarrassment has moved in. He had reason to kiss her under the mistletoe at her grandparents' cabin. She has no such excuse here. Now, Wyatt will make it something it isn't – something it can't be.

"Did I succeed?" he asks, sitting up and brushing snow off his sleeves.

"In what?"

"Taking your mind off things. I think we got some good speed on that hill. We even caught some air."

"Yeah, you succeeded," she says with a chuckle. "We should figure out how to get back. Any ideas?"

Wyatt stands and helps Stowe to her feet. He pulls off a glove and retrieves his phone. There is good cellular service here, and he maps a route back to the hotel using an app. It's not as far as she thought.

"Are you up for a walk?"

She smiles. "Lead the way."

He's going out of his way to not make this awkward. In fact, if anything, it's comfortable. Stowe loops her arm around his. She'd like nothing more right now than a long walk with Wyatt. That should scare her. Right now, it doesn't.

Chapter Forty-Seven

WYATT HUFFMAN

The walk back to the hotel was nice. Wyatt avoided anything that would remind Stowe of the kiss at the bottom of the hill. She got weird about it, and he didn't want to make things even more awkward. It might be easier if they weren't sharing a room with him lying in a cot ten feet away from her. Despite being exhausted, neither of them can sleep. The room is dark and silent, but he can sense her movements and hear her breathing.

"I apologize, Wyatt," Stowe says, likely sensing he can't sleep either. "I shouldn't have kissed you."

So much for his idea of avoidance. Stowe will try to dismiss what happened. That's getting harder and harder, for him at least. They shared their second kiss, and it was even better than the first. That's hard to forget.

"You were caught up in the moment."

"I know, and that's why I'm sorry. I shouldn't lead you on like that."

"Apology accepted," Wyatt says, granting her wish to end the conversation and return some balance to their work relationship. "It was a nice kiss. Let's leave it at that and call it even after what happened under the mistletoe."

"You had no choice. I was being impulsive."

"No, I was wrong to do it. I explained that. I never should have. Not after what you told me about Bobby Sinclair."

Stowe sighs. "You don't know the whole story."

"There's more?"

"I thought maybe Nana had clued you in."

Wyatt thinks back to the breakfast table and the looks Dorothy and Walter shared when he mentioned Bobby Sinclair. Her grandmother definitely wanted to tell the story. Wyatt is glad she didn't.

"Nana alluded to it but said it was your story to tell."

"I'm surprised you never asked me."

Wyatt shifts on the cot. "It's none of my business."

"Maybe, but you told me about Jessie. It's only fair that you know my backstory."

"I told you because I wanted you to know. There is no quid pro quo, Stowe. I'm not entitled to an explanation of your private life."

A long moment passes. Wyatt thinks that's the end of the conversation and closes his eyes, trying to clear his mind to allow sleep to come.

"Bobby was my fiancé."

Now his eyes are wide open.

"Okay, I didn't see that coming. You had said you were traumatized all winter by the kiss."

"I was. Then spring came. And then summer. One day, I went swimming in a nearby lake. I was in my bikini, which was kind of revealing…and far too skimpy for Nana's tastes, so I didn't tell her I bought it. Some boys from another school were there…. It started off with compliments. The kind a young girl wants to hear. I was flattered but not interested in any of them. I went into the water, and, well, they joined me and started getting aggressive. They began grabbing me and trying to pull my top off. And my bottom."

Wyatt winces. That explains a few things in Iceland. He thought that maybe Stowe was uncomfortable about her body despite having no reason to be. Now he knows her apprehension to taking off that robe runs much deeper than that.

"That's why you were so uncomfortable at the Blue Lagoon."

"It was the first time I've worn a bikini since that day at the lake."

"You haven't been to a beach or pool since you were a teenager?"

"No, I have – and I only wore one-piece swimsuits. Anyway, it got worse. I tried to escape the water, but they were blocking the way. The other girls on the shore just watched. But then, who entered the water but Bobby Sinclair. I thought he was going to join in the fun. He didn't say anything. He saw me in tears…then proceeded to kick the crap out of all three of them in the shallow water."

Wyatt sits up in bed. "The same Bobby Sinclair?"

"Nobody was more surprised than I was. He was my knight in shining armor that day. It was like he stepped straight out of a romance novel. All three guys had to go to the hospital by the time he was done with them. Then, he walked me back to my car and drove me home.

"By the next day, I was smitten. Two days later, we were a couple. We went to the same college and dated all four years. I was convinced he was going to ask me to marry him. It took him two years after we graduated, but he finally did. It was the happiest day of my life. Then I took the job Congresswoman Pratt offered."

Wyatt turns on his side and supports his head with his hand. "He didn't like the idea of you being in Washington?"

"No, not at all. I understand why, but I felt I needed it to grow. It was a great opportunity, and I wanted the experience, even for only a couple of years. Then, I would work out of the district office. I even asked him to come down with me."

"And he refused."

"Yeah. Bobby had no desire to leave Vermont. He said that absence makes the heart grow fonder. We were in love. A little time apart wasn't going to ruin that. So, I moved in with Mandy and went home to see him as much as possible."

"Did he ever visit you?"

"Not once," Stowe admits, the long pause betraying her attempt to hide the hurt. "One time, I thought I would surprise him. I came home early one Saturday without telling him. I walked up to the bedroom and…let's just say, I was the surprised one. It turns out Bobby started having affairs with multiple women starting right after I left. I never knew a thing. I never even suspected."

"I'm sorry, Stowe. Is that why you were so hostile to me?"

She sighs deeply. "You remind me of Bobby. At least, the man I thought he was. He was strong, and confident, and courteous…it ended up being an act. I thought you were putting one on, too."

"What changed?"

"Do you remember what happened when we got out of the water at the lagoon?"

"We ate dinner."

She laughs. Wyatt wasn't trying to be funny. That's what happened next. There's no reason to think it's hilarious.

"Before that," Stowe says once the laughter subsides. "See, you don't even remember. That's how I knew you weren't like Bobby."

"Okay, I'm lost."

"You got my robe for me as we stepped out of the water."

"It's not a big thing, Stowe. I thought you would be cold."

"No, you *knew* I was uncomfortable in that bikini. You didn't know why, but you got the robe so I wouldn't feel exposed in front of all those people. That's why we're sharing a room, Wyatt. People can fake being nice, but their true colors eventually show. That was my initial thought when you were splitting wood for PopPop. The more time I've spent with you, the more I learned how wrong my assumptions were."

Wyatt doesn't know what to say. He didn't think twice about fetching her robe – it was a natural reflex. He assumed any man would do the same thing. Apparently, that's a wrong assumption.

"Thank you for sharing the story."

"I think I needed to. Good night, Wyatt."

"Good night."

He hears the mattress springs groan as she turns over. Everybody has baggage. Everyone has a past, and that past often dictates the present and even the future. There was good cause for Stowe's anger and bitterness, even if it was misdirected. He wouldn't have acted differently in her position because he didn't when it happened to him. Jessie may not have cheated on him, but she did hurt him. That pain has lingered…until now.

Wyatt closes his eyes. He's getting a feeling he hasn't felt in a long time. It was recognizable only one other time in his life, sitting atop a horse in a meadow with a beautiful blonde next to him. He can try to deny it, but it's there. He's beginning to fall for this woman.

Chapter Forty-Eight

REPRESENTATIVE CAMILLA GUZMAN

Like most protests, this one started small with the announcement of her legislation. Since then, Camilla has watched it grow. Now, the gathering of people outside the Capitol numbers in the thousands.

The costumes have even gotten better. While there are still plenty of Santa hats, there are also full Santa costumes, elves, and even a few reindeer. Mrs. Claus has become a popular addition. Even the signs are getting wittier.

"Admiring your handiwork?" Harlan McCormack asks, coming up alongside her.

Camilla doesn't turn to acknowledge him. "As a matter of fact, I am. Are you here to issue more orders for me to ignore, or are you planning to get on the bandwagon?"

"Bandwagon? It must be a small parade. I notice there aren't too many people here supporting your position."

She looked that term up once out of curiosity. "Bandwagon" comes from mid-nineteenth-century American English and is a large wagon used to carry the band in a circus procession. It's pretty straightforward, and that's not why she looked it up. The term was used by Theodore Roosevelt in his writings discussing celebrations of successful political campaigns. Being on the bandwagon was coopted to mean "attaching oneself to something that looks likely to succeed" in the modern vernacular.

"I didn't expect to see my supporters. They're the silent majority."

"Yeah, sure they are," Harlan says after scoffing. "You know, there are five times this number in Lafayette Park assembling right now. The size doubles every hour. They plan a march to the Capitol later today, singing Christmas carols and everything."

"Really? True Christmas spirit? That's amazing!"

"No, it isn't. It's a bad look for the party. It's going to be bad for you."

Camilla shakes her head. "I disagree on both counts."

She turns to walk toward the Capitol. McCormack matches her turn and gait as she walks.

"Okay. Out with it. I know this isn't a social call."

"Why would you say that?"

"Because the house majority leader has better things to do than track me down outside my office in thirty-degree temperatures. What do you want, Harlan?"

Politics is a dance. Sometimes it's a waltz, and sometimes it has the energy of a jive. Rarely does anyone cut to the chase here until that last note plays. Camilla doesn't have the patience for that. If he has something to say, he should just come out with it.

"It was a bad idea to antagonize Speaker Hoskins like you did."

"Are you saying he's holding a grudge?"

Harlan chuckles. "As only a Southerner from Mississippi can. You may think you have won, but trust me, you didn't. It's not if he comes for his pound of flesh. It's when."

"Noted."

"I would think that might bother a first-term congresswoman," Harlan says, studying her reaction. "You have no war chest to fund your next campaign. You have no major donors or political action committees backing you. After this stunt, I'll be surprised if we don't have to hold a raffle among the prospective candidates to select who runs against you in the primary."

The corner of her lip curls. "All true."

"So, why do it?"

"Tell me, Harlan, would any of that be different had I not introduced this legislation? You didn't even know my name until last week."

"I most certainly did," the majority leader protests.

"Don't lie. You're not as good at it as the whip is. You may fool your constituents back home, Harlan. But, to anyone more than a casual observer, cellophane is less transparent than you are."

Harlan McCormack is, in reality, an exceptional liar. As much as Americans want to believe their representatives are angelic, they aren't. The higher in the ranks they climb, the more likely it is they took the shady and underhanded path to get there.

"Then you know why I'm here."

"Of course. You want to make a deal. I cancel the remaining hearings…call it the flu or some family emergency. In return, you…?"

"Ensure your re-election next November."

The promise of all promises. "I'm sure the voters will have something to say about that."

"You needed a platform, Camilla. You found one with this. Kudos, but I have a better one."

"Which is?"

"The Foreign Affairs Committee."

Camilla stops walking.

"We have a vacancy opening, and I want you to fill it. Breckenridge is stepping down in January. Keep that between us. It won't be public until after the holidays. In addition, you'll keep your seat on Energy and Commerce and continue as chair of the Cultural Commerce Subcommittee."

Foreign Affairs is one of the highest-profile committees in the House. It may not have the impact of Judiciary or the prestige of Ways and Means, but it is a powerful committee that will be hearing testimony on countless upcoming foreign issues. It's not a position doled out to assuage a temperamental member. They badly want her to cease and desist.

"It must be painful for you to make that offer."

Harlan looks around as he weighs the words in his head, pouting as his head rocks back and forth. "It's not the approach I would have opted for, but Speaker Hoskins insisted."

Camilla smiles. "Good day, Leader McCormack."

"Do we have a deal?" he asks, calling after her after she continues her walk.

"You'll find out later this morning."

Camilla isn't stupid. She knows when something is too good to be true. They tipped their hand. Something is going on, and she needs to find out what before she makes any decisions. She pulls out her phone to call Marcia. If anyone can find out, it's her.

Chapter Forty-Nine

REPRESENTATIVE JOHN KNUTSON

The day in Washington starts much like it does in every other city. Working men and women wake up, shower, dress, grab breakfast and coffee, and head for their door. There is no data to back up the assertion, but John has long believed most of the staff on Capitol Hill arrive at precisely the same time. It certainly feels that way.

The corridors are filled with new arrivals. Most wear wool overcoats and carry laptops and files because they haven't reached their offices. Others are on coffee runs. John has been here for a while. He's been pacing his office, trying to muster the nerve before squaring off against an angry lioness.

"Here goes nothing," he mumbles as he rounds the corner into Angela Pratt's office.

He breezes past her receptionist and staffers. Most of them have no time to react to his sudden presence in their office. Her chief of staff recovers in time to set off on an intercept course.

"She doesn't want to see you, sir!" he barks, reaching her office door at the same time John does.

"I don't care," John says as he pushes past him and barges into Angela's office.

The congresswoman sets down her reading glasses and stands as her right-hand man charges past John. He puts a hand on his chest to hold him back, not that it would have a prayer of stopping the burly Montanan.

"I'm sorry, congresswoman. I tried to stop him," her chief of staff informs her, standing between John and Angela like a cop holding back a riot.

"Is this how it's going to be now, Congressman Knutson? Complete disrespect for me and my office staff?"

"The name's John. And if it comes to that, yes."

"What do you want?"

John stares at her chief of staff. "Privacy."

The forcefulness of the comment causes the man to scowl. He looks like he's about to take a swing. It'd be a career-ending move. Politicians may be insufferable, but responsibility for dealing with that comes with the job description.

"It's okay. Leave us."

The chief of staff glares at John as he leaves the office. He closes the door a little harder than is normally appropriate. He won't be getting a Christmas card from this office.

"That guy needs some spiked eggnog."

"You're the one I'm beginning to think has had too much holiday cheer this early in the morning. You have guts storming in here."

"You need to hear this."

"I don't need to hear anything from you. Do you think your watered-down questions yesterday accomplished anything?"

"They managed to piss off Durant and Guillomi."

Angela crosses her arms. "That's your party's fault for electing those clowns to leadership positions."

"I couldn't agree more."

"John, I'm very busy," she says, returning to the stacks of files on her desk. "Someone needs to carry the water in these hearings. Just tell me what you want."

"To apologize."

Her head snaps up. He knew that would get her attention. A politician apologizing for anything is as rare as seeing the tooth fairy riding a unicorn at the World Rodeo Championship.

"Angela, we have our differences, but I have always valued your friendship. You're always straight with me. You could have run to the media and told a reporter what you told me on Sunday. You didn't. You said it to my face. You have no idea how much I value that."

John hands her the manila file folder he's carrying. She takes it and retrieves her reading glasses from the desk.

"What's this?"

"The line of questioning for today's witnesses."

"I have my own questions. I don't need these," Angela argues.

"I know. These are mine. I want to make sure we aren't asking the same ones."

Angela puts on her glasses and scans the paper. She starts to say something and stops. It happens again. And then again. Two minutes later, she finishes digesting the list and pulls her reading glasses off her face.

"I thought you were sitting this out."

"I was. Then a fiery woman from Vermont interrupted my breakfast and set me straight," Johns says with a smile.

"That was two days ago."

"I'm a man. We're known to be a little slow."

Angela laughs. She doesn't argue the point.

"You're willing to cross Spencer and Gregory?"

"I already have. The Wonder Twins ambushed me leaving Capitol Hill yesterday. Since I told them to kick rocks, I might as well go all the way with it."

"You didn't actually say that," Angela concludes.

"No, I didn't. I called Durant and Guillomi dinosaurs…and clowns. I'm pretty sure I also called them clowns."

Angela winces. "That's even worse. It could be the end of your political career."

Normally, John would agree with her. Members of both parties know the perils of tangling with leadership. There are a few legislators who can get away with it. They are in a class all their own. John is not one of them.

"There may be a way to save it."

"How?"

John stretches his arms out. "Christmas is the time for miracles. Let's start creating one today."

Chapter Fifty

STOWE BESSETTE

Santa Claus Village, located in Rovaniemi, is the official hometown of St. Nicholas. Or so it is claimed. The Finnish claim Santa Claus has made this part of Lapland his home for centuries. The village is a magical place straddling the Arctic Circle and has become a family destination where children and adults can meet Santa every day of the year.

Stowe feels like she's stepped into the pages of a storybook. This place is filled with joy and wonder. She feels like she's reliving her childhood and is undoubtedly not the only one. The Santa Claus Village's mission is to "spread Christmas love and cheer, amplify the well-being of children and the kindness of elders." It's succeeding.

The village features plenty of souvenir shops, cafes, and restaurants, and Santa's Main Post Office, where kids can send letters to Santa and parents can mail cards home with a special Santa postmark. There is also the Arctic Circle Husky Park and the Elf's Farmyard Petting Zoo, where children build memories while their parents unleash their inner child.

"This place is straight out of a postcard," Stowe marvels.

"No kidding, right? We need to take a picture standing on the painted Arctic Circle line."

"Absolutely. We should go see Santa first before the line gets too long. Then we can enjoy this place. Come on."

Stowe takes Wyatt's hand and leads him to the entrance to Santa's office. Visitors have been afforded the opportunity to meet Santa Claus and his elves here for over thirty years. Unlike seeing a mall Santa, there is no entry fee. This village makes its money in other ways. Since he's a jolly man who enjoys meeting and chatting with people of all ages, it would be awkward to charge a fee to see him.

"Here goes nothing," Wyatt says as he opens the door.

The office is nothing like you would see in corporate America. There are no cubicles or harsh fluorescent lights overhead. The space is right out of Dickens, with wood walls and furniture bathed in the warm glow of soft white bulbs. Aromas of sawdust and fresh-baked sugar cookies waft into their nostrils. The sights and smells are the physical manifestation of everything Stowe loves about Christmas.

An elf standing behind a counter near the door looks like a movie star, with golden blonde hair and rainbow eyes. She isn't perky or obnoxious, but that doesn't detract from her warm, inviting nature. This elf is Santa's administrative assistant, and she plays the part well.

"Santa is free," the elf says with a brilliant smile. "You can go on in. He's waiting for you."

Stowe and Wyatt slowly creep to the opening in the wall that separates the office from the entrance. She takes a deep breath. Meeting Santa is a unique experience at any age. They are here on a mission, but that only partially explains her nervousness.

"Come in…don't be shy," Santa announces in a baritone voice from his seat on a thick wooden bench.

The Santa sitting comfortably on a cushion is not what she expected. He has a red jacket on, but not the bright red with the snow-white trim she is accustomed to in most depictions. His pants are green, and his boots are brown, not polished black. He isn't wearing a hat, and if he has a big belt buckle, it is covered under a white apron draped over his chest.

He has white hair, but it's not pure white. And his beard is long and wavy but not nearly as curly as often seen. The thick hair reaches almost down to his stomach. Despite the similarities, there is a sharp contrast with the American depiction of St. Nick. That makes him perfect. Then again, she's thought that before.

"Hello, Santa," Wyatt croaks.

Stowe can't say anything. She's caught up in reliving her childhood and is speechless.

"Hello. Please, have a seat next to me."

Stowe is a little starstruck as she slowly sits on the bench next to Santa. She imagines this is like when she was a child meeting him for the first time at a ski lodge. Stowe was too young to remember the moment, but Nana shows her the picture almost every Christmas. This one will stick with her for a long time.

"Ah, you both love Christmas."

"How can you tell?" Stowe asks, almost whispering.

"I have been doing this for a very long time. You are here without children, yet you have the same look of awe they do when they visit."

They're busted, and there is no point in disputing Santa's observation.

"We actually came to see you because we have a request."

"You're too old for a pony," Santa says, causing Stowe's mouth to hang open before he turns to Wyatt. "And the real fire truck you wanted won't fit in my sled."

"How did…?" Wyatt begins to ask before letting his voice trail off.

Stowe recovers first. "No, that's not what we're asking for…this time. Santa, we're from Washington, D.C. We could use your help with a problem."

The jingle bells on the entrance to the office ring, and they hear a group of kids come in with their parents. The kids sound full of wonder and excitement. She knows the feeling.

"I see. This sounds like a longer conversation, and I don't want to keep the children waiting."

"I promise it will only take a few minutes," Stowe eagerly argues.

Santa lets out a chuckle. It's not the deep belly laugh "ho-ho-ho" they are used to hearing. It sounds more…realistic.

"A few minutes of children having access to candy canes will make for a long day for those parents. Please come back to see me later tonight. We can talk about your problem over nice cups of hot cocoa. My elves make the best you have ever tasted."

"Okay. We will. Thank you, Santa."

"You're welcome, Stowe. Make sure you and Wyatt have fun while you're here."

The elf hands each of them a candy cane when they leave. She isn't as bubbly and sugar-addled as Arnarra was at the Santa Academy in Vermont. But somehow, that makes her feel more authentic.

Wyatt is practically jumping out of his skin. She's never seen him so electrified and animated. If his smile gets any wider, he's going to break his face.

"Why are you so giddy?"

"Because we met Santa Claus, and he invited us to have hot cocoa later."

"Seriously?"

"Okay, little Miss Christmas. Don't tell me you didn't dream about meeting Santa when you were a kid, much less want to have hot chocolate with him…I bet that's going to taste amazing."

Stowe takes his hands in hers and looks into his eyes. "Wyatt…I know it's hard, given the magic of this place, but we have to remember that he's not *really* Santa."

"Of course not," he says, grinning. "How old were you when you wanted a pony, Stowe?"

"That's not," she says, pausing before conceding the point. "Five. I was five."

"That's the same age I sent a letter to Santa wanting a fire truck. Not a toy. A real one."

"That doesn't mean anything."

"No, it doesn't," Wyatt admits. "Wait until it dawns on you."

"What does?"

Wyatt grins. It's the kind of look someone has when trying not to smile and failing miserably.

"Santa used our names when we left."

"I heard him. So? I'm sure he calls everyone…." Her eyes light up when she makes the connection. "Oh, my God! We never told him our names!"

Chapter Fifty-One

REPRESENTATIVE CAMILLA GUZMAN

On paper, he's the perfect man to testify about how Santa became a commercial symbol. Mitchell Abernathy did his doctoral thesis on Coca-Cola and received his degree in 1992. Since then, he has spent over forty years researching the brand and is considered the world's foremost expert on Coca-Cola's marketing prowess. The downside is that he is as dry as unbuttered toast and looks like Waldorf from *The Muppet Show*.

"Santa Claus had come into focus as the jolly soul we recognize today by the 1920s," Mitchell slowly says in a heavy Southern drawl. "Artists would still occasionally tweak the color of his robes or add a few pounds to his midsection. He was rarely depicted as American poet Clement Clarke Moore described in 'A Visit from St. Nicholas' as a 'little old driver, so lively and quick.' Coca-Cola relied on these images, which had prevailed for a century, to recreate Santa.

"In the early 1930s, executives turned the D'Arcy Agency to design a new Santa for their holiday campaign. Haddon H. Sundblom redrew Santa Claus as a plump, cheerful man with snow-white hair and dressed him in red and white. These colors were already associated with Santa but also matched Coca-Cola's signature hues. It is Sundblom's Santa who decorates your greeting cards and home décor. We all owe that to Coca-Cola wanting to increase its winter sales.

"Haddon's illustrations of Santa appeared regularly in *The Saturday Evening Post*. It was also featured in mainstays of the time, such as the *Ladies Home Journal*, *National Geographic*, and *The New Yorker*. Back then, it was hard to imagine a holiday season without Coca-Cola adverts. Today, there are commercials with a cute family of polar bears and penguins enjoying bottles of their product. But Coca-Cola will always be known for the cultural impact of bringing us the modern Santa Claus."

Dr. Abernathy concludes his opening monologue to Camilla's relief. She quickly instructs the first questioner to begin his five-minute examination. Representative Edward Bass clears his throat before speaking.

"Thank you for your testimony today, Dr. Abernathy," Bass says. "Given all of the imagery we see of Santa is based on this almost century-old campaign, is it fair to say that Coca-Cola invented Santa Claus?"

"Maybe not the legend, but the American Santa Claus took shape largely due to the repetition of these advertisements. So, yes, from that perspective, they did."

"Did Haddon Sundblom use a model for his depictions?"

"Of course. In the campaign's early days, a retired salesman named Lou Prentiss was the basis for the images. When Lou passed away, Sundblom used himself as a model and often painted while looking into a mirror."

"So, in many respects, the icon of Christmas is really a self-portrait of the main figure in Coca-Cola's marketing team. Have there been many changes since then?"

"No. People are sensitive to this marketing. For example, they sent letters to The Coca-Cola Company when even subtle changes were made. Sundblom painted via a mirror, and one year, Santa's belt was backward. It didn't go unnoticed. Another time, he appeared without a wedding band, causing a flood of inquiries about what happened to Mrs. Claus."

There are a few chuckles in the room, likely from men wondering what Santa would be like if he were a bachelor. That has all kinds of marketing potential for dating sites and divorce attorneys.

"So not only is Santa Claus linked to the commercialization of the holiday, but the man we know today was born from it. It's time to relegate this myth to the dustbin of history. Thank you, Dr. Abernathy. I yield to the Chair."

Camilla smiles. Bass did his job connecting the dots. It's nice to know that some of her allies can be counted on to come through when needed. She now gets to see how effectively the naysayers can deconstruct the testimony.

"The gentleman from Montana has five minutes," she announces.

"Thank you, Madam Chairwoman, and thank you for your testimony, Dr. Abernathy. Has your research only focused on Coca-Cola?"

"Most of it, yes."

"But you're familiar with other advertising."

"Of course."

"Do you know Kim Kardashian?"

Abernathy smiles. "Not personally, but if you're offering to make an introduction…."

There is another chuckle in the room, and even Knutson smiles. It is a rare bit of humor from a man whose opening statement could make paint dry faster.

"I'll tell you what, sir, if I ever get the opportunity, I will pass along an invite," he says, getting yet another amused laugh from the observers. "Do you know how she became a celebrity?"

Dr. Abernathy leans forward to speak into the microphone. "Not specifically. I know Kim worked closely with several stars when she was young."

"And then?"

The doctor looks at the members of the committee and grimaces. "A sex tape got released."

"Yes, it did. Shortly after that, Kim landed a reality show, and the rest, as they say, is history."

"Point of order," Representative Bass bellows from the far side of the dais. "Is this questioning relevant? We're here to discuss Coca-Cola's marketing of Santa Claus, not the secret lives of celebrities."

"Mr. Knutson, I ask you to stay on topic," Camilla admonishes.

"If it pleases the Chair, Kim Kardashian is famous for being famous. She is a cultural icon who was created by a well-oiled marketing machine. I'm wondering if you'll be introducing legislation to ban public depictions of her."

The comment causes the observers in the room to erupt in laughter. They needed the release and would have seized any joke, good or bad, to get one. Camilla has to bang her gavel several times to regain control.

"Is that necessary, Mr. Knutson?"

"Are you talking about legislation to ban Santa or Kim Kardashian? I mean, we can create a provision to allow her to walk outside if she's wearing a bag over her head—"

"I understand the gentleman from Montana is trying to make a mockery of these proceedings," she interrupts. "If you don't ask pertinent questions, I will force you to yield your time."

It's not an idle threat. Members of Congress pine to be on the best committees for visibility. They want to chair others for the power it offers. She gets to set the agenda and run the meeting. While there are rules providing time to hear both sides of an argument, the chair also has the power to restrict the antics that usually ensue.

"Mr. Abernathy, despite how my colleagues portray it, did Coca-Cola invent Santa Claus?"

"As I testified, it's not that simple—"

"A yes or no answer will suffice, sir."

"The answer is, of course, no. Various illustrated depictions of Saint Nick have existed for centuries."

"So, Coca-Cola didn't create Santa Claus. They hired Haddon Sundblom to illustrate a more modern depiction so they could show images of Santa holding a bottle of Coke to market their brand."

"Sundblom reshaped his appearance, which has directly and undeniably led to his commercialization," Dr. Abernathy concludes.

"Do you think we should ban all things that have been commercialized by corporations and marketers? The polar bears are depicted by Coca-Cola as cute and cuddly, when in reality, they're deadly animals. That shapes public perception. Should depictions of polar bears be banned in the name of public safety because of Coca-Cola's marketing?"

"No."

"I see. Then maybe this government shouldn't be banning icons just because some company wants to use them as a shill for their products. Kim Kardashian will be relieved. I yield to the Chair."

Camilla leans back in her chair. She always considered Knutson to be rather dull and dimwitted. It's a trap that's easy to fall into. His questions woke the audience, and the quips about Kim Kardashian will be replayed on the news and social media. He scored points in this round. That's something she will need to deal with later.

Chapter Fifty-Two

WYATT HUFFMAN

Wyatt and Stowe get their pictures straddling the imaginary line that denotes the Arctic Circle. They take pictures of each other and gratefully accept an offer from a pair of German tourists to have some shots taken together. Wyatt has to pinch himself. The Arctic Circle is the southernmost latitude at which the sun will not rise during the winter solstice, and he's standing on it. The converse is true during the summer solstice when the sun never sets. For someone who doesn't travel the world, he's amazed to be here.

After checking out the rest of what Santa's Village has to offer, Wyatt orders a rideshare. He didn't tell Stowe where they were going, He wanted to keep it a surprise. She reluctantly agreed, and they made the short journey down the road to one of Lapland's countless reindeer farms.

They are greeted warmly and ushered into a room where they are given warm clothing and gloves. They meet the rest of the tour outside, where a dozen red sleighs are ready to be pulled by an equal number of reindeer. The guides explain that the safari lasts an hour, and they may take all the pictures they want. There will be another opportunity deeper in the forest when the reindeer get a well-deserved break.

"You know, they had reindeer sleigh rides at Santa's Village," Stowe observes as Wyatt positions the blanket in their chariot.

"This is more…nicer."

"More nicer?" she asks with a laugh. "You were going to say romantic, weren't you?"

"Traditional. I was going to say traditional."

"No, you weren't."

Wyatt doesn't argue. He'd be lying, and Stowe has already switched her focus to petting their reindeer. The guide said that is a taste of the old traditional way of traveling in Lapland. Wyatt pulls out his phone and snaps a couple of pictures of her. She looks content.

"Do you want one of the two of you?" one of their guides asks.

"Sure, that would be great!"

Stowe hands her the camera, and the woman snaps away, mumbling about how great they look. Even their reindeer is hamming it up. For most of the shots, she's looking straight at the camera as Stowe and Wyatt stand behind her antlers. Clearly, this amazing creature is a veteran of these rides and a pro at pleasing tourists.

"Thank you so much," Stowe says, flipping through the dozen or so pictures on her phone.

"You're welcome! You two make such a nice couple."

Stowe doesn't correct her. Wyatt is about to but stops. He considers silence a form of consent and isn't about to give her second thoughts. He doesn't know what this is, but it's become more than colleagues.

They sit comfortably in the reindeer-drawn sleigh, enjoying the snow-covered forests and untouched wilderness. The crunch of the reindeer's hooves on the snow and the rustle of overhead branches in the wind are nature's music. Nobody is speaking. The quiet, comfortable reindeer sleigh ride almost matches the relaxation he feels riding a horse through the Montana countryside. His mind is free from the stress of their assignment. He is caught up in the moment.

Wyatt has his arm draped around Stowe, more for comfort than an attempt to be closer. But it works, regardless. She was right – he was going to say romantic. And it is. The rides at Santa's Village were geared more toward children. These cater to couples as well as families. He wanted the experience of a sleigh ride away from the hustle and bustle of one of Lapland's greatest attractions.

Stowe is nestled next to him in the sleigh under an unnecessary blanket. The thick, cold weather suits they are wearing are already toasty warm. She leans her head on his shoulder. The wool blanket isn't for warmth – it's for ambiance. They are at the Arctic Circle, being pulled in a red sleigh by a reindeer. It's a perfect moment he could never have expected when they left Washington.

The hour-long ride is too short. Five hours would have been too short. The reindeer herders have prepared coffee and warm cinnamon buns on a campfire in the middle of an enclosure that blocks the chilly arctic air. They gather everyone to share stories of reindeer husbandry in Lapland. That there are more reindeer than people living in Lapland is one of the many facts that Wyatt didn't know.

With the questions answered, everyone is left to chat around the fire. The people are pleasant and engaging. Stories are swapped, and discussions ensue about home and what brought them to Lapland. People slowly filter out of the cabin as they finish their coffee. Wyatt is in no rush to go anywhere. Stowe is studying her souvenir. They are content with their surroundings…and maybe even each other.

"This may come in handy someday," Stowe says, holding her reindeer driving license between her index and middle fingers.

"I'm going to show mine the next time a cop pulls me over for speeding just to see what happens."

"Thank you for taking me here, Wyatt. It was…magical."

"I'm glad you enjoyed it. So did I."

She claps her hands. "So, you're basically an Arctic cruise director. We still have time to kill before seeing Santa. What's next on the agenda?"

Wyatt checks his watch. She's right. It's still too early to drop in on St. Nick.

"We need some education. It's almost time for school."

Considering the look on her face, Stowe has no idea what he's talking about. That's part of the fun. She may have snatched his brochures in Iceland but not in Rovaniemi. He only hopes this next adventure lives up to its billing. It might not be as romantic as a wintry sleigh ride, but it will be entertaining.

Chapter Fifty-Three

REPRESENTATIVE JOHN KNUTSON

The afternoon session kicks off with Dr. Herbert Slinkard, a renowned economist, and apparent holiday hater. He has authored countless articles about the impacts of the Christmas shopping season on the culture. John actually found himself agreeing with several of Slinkard's arguments. The shopping season is too long and does suck the spirit out of the holiday. Unfortunately, he laced the commentary in his papers with a lot of anti-Christmas sentiment. Clearly, the economist resents the holiday, and that defiles an otherwise reasoned argument.

The opening statement was chock full of data to support his complaints. It also didn't have any soul or appeal. People in the room are fidgety and restless. The media looks bored. He has noticed that the testimony isn't capturing anyone's attention, and so has Guzman.

John's questions were short and to the point. Angela wanted to tackle this economic argument, and he was more than willing to let her take the lead on the questioning. She only needs to wait for one of Guzman's staunchest allies to go first.

"The Chair recognizes the gentleman from Illinois."

Ali Salib is a three-term congressman from a district encompassing part of Chicago and one of its suburbs. He is Muslim but doesn't appear to hate Christmas at all. He does resent the outsized role he believes it occupies in the culture, and many of his questions during these hearings thus far illustrate that.

"Thank you, Madam Chairwoman, and thank you for joining us today, Dr. Slinkard. Every year, I notice that the Christmas shopping season begins earlier and earlier. When I was younger, I rarely saw decorations or holiday promotions at the beginning of November because it was Thanksgiving season. However, we routinely see Christmas commercials starting in October, and store shelves are filled with holiday items as early as September. What is your perception of this trend, Doctor?"

"Simply put, Christmas in today's society is a marketing ploy for greedy corporations to take consumers' money. In 2016, the total expected holiday sales exceeded a trillion dollars, and that number has risen every year since. By expanding the holiday shopping season, retailers have more time to manipulate what used to be a wholesome day for families to celebrate into something materialistic and superficial. Unfortunately, the trend will not reverse anytime. In a recent survey, just over half of U.S. consumers started their holiday shopping in October last year. This share was forty-five percent the previous year. That's a more than five percent increase, and the growth is accelerating."

John can't argue with that. Spending on Christmas is out of control. That is one of the reasons people are so miserable. With the cost of everything rising and wages stagnant, who wants to go into credit card debt because of the pressure to buy Christmas gifts? No wonder there is no joy in the season anymore.

"Dr. Slinkard, you have authored several papers on the impacts of economics on society. In your expert opinion, what effect does this focus on holiday sales beginning in September or October have on our culture?"

"The over-marketing of Christmas takes away from the joy of the holiday. There was once a general festivity of shopping around the holidays. With the start of the season moving closer and closer to the summer, it is no longer something special that people look forward to for a limited time each year."

"I see. As a Muslim, I have always considered Christmas a Christian religious celebration. It now seems to be a blanket term for the holiday season, including New Year's."

"I am not religious," Dr. Slinkard says, "but commercialization has secularized the holiday. Many people no longer associate Christmas with a day of religious observance, making the celebration seem more superficial. That demonstrates how pervasive the commercialism that infects American society has become. The facts bear that out. Nine out of ten Americans celebrate Christmas, but thirty-two percent say it's less about religion and more of a cultural holiday. That percentage is also rising."

Salib nods and mugs for the cameras. This is his face time with the American people, and he is making the most of it. He has more interest in the media at the back of the room than the man testifying.

"Very interesting. How have retailers and companies handled this?"

"Some retail companies no longer use the term 'Christmas.' Over the past decade, you are more likely to hear 'Happy Holidays' or 'Season's Greetings' to appeal to a wider range of consumers. These marketing strategies aim to maximize profits by gaining money in any way possible. Commercialism is taking away from the positive experiences associated with the holiday. It's no longer about giving a thoughtful or personal gift but purchasing the biggest and most expensive. Corporations have made the holiday more about money than celebration. Unless America changes its money-driven culture, Christmas will continue to become more superficial."

"Thank you, Doctor. I yield the balance of my time," Representative Salib says.

Guzman turns to Angela. "The Chair recognizes the gentlewoman from Vermont for five minutes."

John watches her stare intently at Slinkard before sitting a little straighter in her chair. "Doctor, how much do Americans spend on Valentine's Day?"

He looks around and then appeals to Guzman. She can't save him from the questioning.

"I'm not sure I understand the question."

"Yes, you do. You're Ivy League educated and speak perfect English. How much do Americans spend on Valentine's Day annually?"

The economist makes a show of flipping pages in the binder of data he brought with him. John leans back and rubs his chin. He is trying to run out the clock on Angela. It's a tactic that he was likely briefed on by Guzman and Blackburn. It's not uncommon. Five minutes isn't enough time to get through questions when the witness isn't concise or manages to stall.

"Dr. Slinkard, you are an economist. You devour more data in a day than most Americans do in a year. You know the numbers off the top of your head. There is no need for theater."

He leans back in his chair. "Americans are planning to spend $23.9 billion on Valentine's Day this year, according to the National Retail Federation and Prosper Insights & Analytics."

"Thank you. Is that up from the previous year?"

"Yes, it will be an increase of about two billion and change. It's the second-highest year on record in terms of inflation-adjusted dollars spent."

"What about Mother's Day? What is the spend, on average?"

"Mother's Day spending is expected to total $31.7 billion next year, up thirteen percent. Eighty-four percent of U.S. adults are expected to celebrate Mother's Day."

"I'm sorry, I'm not as strong with math as you are. What does that average per person?"

"Just shy of two hundred and fifty dollars a person."

Angela nods. "It's good that people are eager to find memorable ways to honor the important women in their lives. Do companies market during these holidays?"

"Of course."

"Do you believe this marketing debases the spirit of these holidays?"

Slinkard is not a man who likes being challenged. He shifts in his chair and glares at Angela, who isn't remotely intimidated by the mousy economist. He bites his lip before leaning forward.

"No, but the marketing doesn't start as early."

"Of course not. You don't see Valentine's Day stuff until the week before the holiday…and by holiday, I mean New Year's, a full month and a half earlier," Angela says, earning snickers from the observers in the room. "What happens if someone doesn't have the money for chocolates or flowers?"

"Uh, they don't spend it."

"Wait, can they do that without government intervention? Is it true that consumer behavior has the biggest impact on business behavior?"

"I would say that government regulation also plays a sizable role, but yes."

"So, if nobody shopped for Christmas items until, let's say, Black Friday, would stores continue to roll out displays in September?"

"I think the trend would eventually reverse given that behavior."

"And if Americans decided to make homemade gifts or cap the value of those exchanged, would that ease the financial pressure of the holidays?"

"Probably."

Angela removes her reading glasses and leans forward. "Does any of that have anything to do with Santa Claus being present in shopping malls?"

"No, but he is an icon of this commercialization. Perhaps *the* icon."

"So, you're stating that, as a renowned economist, there is a direct correlation between shoppers seeing Santa and opening their wallets and purses. That must be very powerful imagery to compel someone to shop just because they saw a fat bearded man dressed in a red suit. Do you have a study or evidence in that binder to corroborate that argument?"

Angela points at the massive volume for effect. A couple of cameras in the room pan over and zoom in on it. Even Dr. Slinkard looks at it nervously.

"No, I don't believe I do. But it—"

"So, you just made an emotional and psychological argument, not an economic one?"

"I'm sorry, Ms. Pratt, your time has expired," Camilla announces, sparing the economist the humiliation of answering.

"That's fine. I don't need to hear an answer. We all know what Dr. Slinkard was going to say."

John glances at his watch. There is one more witness for the day. They are putting up a good fight but are still behind on points. They need to throw a haymaker and go for the knockout in the final round on Thursday. It's the only thing that will move the needle. He can only hope that Wyatt is making some progress. Everything rides on finding the perfect Santa Claus.

Chapter Fifty-Four

STOWE BESSETTE

Deep underneath the Arctic Circle lies Santa's secret cavern, where it's Christmas all year round. At least, that's how this place markets itself. It's a tourist trap voted as the top Christmas destination in the world. Stowe isn't completely sold, but it does exude Christmas spirit.

The selling point of this place is that it's indoors. Finnish winters are rough for anyone hailing from warmer climates. The temperatures don't bother Stowe, who is used to harsh New England winters. Wyatt's Montana roots equally prepare him for the cold.

The pair walks around, visiting the Ice Gallery, watching an amusing elf show on the main stage, and grabbing a quick bite before waiting in line for the attraction Wyatt brought her here to see.

Her cell phone rings, and she searches her coat pocket for it.

"You get service in here?" Wyatt asks.

"I don't think we're as far underground as they want us to think. It's Mandy. I should take this. Do you mind?"

"Not at all. I can hold our spot in line."

Stowe answers and asks Mandy to hold on as she moves away. It's not that the call is sensitive. With all the over-stimulated children running around, it's just loud. She finds a quiet place and holds the phone to her ear.

"Sorry about that. It's a little crazy here."

"So I've noticed," Mandy says. "I see from your profile that you were in a forest with a real cutie pie. The reindeer was a love, too."

"Stop it, Mandy."

"Stop what? I wasn't the one on what had to be an ultra-romantic sleigh ride with one of Washington's most eligible bachelors."

"It wasn't that big of a deal."

"Not a…wait, hold on! Not a big deal? Stowe, I've never seen you look so happy."

"Nothing's happened," she snaps. "And nothing is going to. Wyatt plays for the other team."

"Oh, the hell he does!" Mandy shrieks.

Stowe closes her eyes and kicks herself for walking into that one. "Not *that* other team. I mean politically."

"So?"

"So, it could never work."

"Says who?" Mandy argues. "Deny it all you want, but you have the glow."

Stowe frowns. "I have no idea what you're talking about. What glow?"

"The one of a woman who has fallen in love with an amazing man," Mandy practically sings into the phone.

There is no arguing with her. This was supposed to be a work call, not a synopsis of her private life.

"And you know this from practical experience?"

Mandy sighs heavily. "Love is love, Stowe. I know it when I see it."

Wyatt gestures her over. "You're crazy. How are the hearings?"

"Ugly. You need to find Santa."

"We're working on it. Anything else?"

"Yeah, have you kissed him yet?"

Stowe rolls her eyes. "I have to go. Elf School is starting."

"Elf School?"

"It's a long story."

"I can't wait to hear it. Stowe, do yourself a favor. Follow your heart. You owe yourself that. Tell me you kissed him? You did, didn't you?"

"I have to go," Stowe says, ending the call.

She slides under the ropes and joins Wyatt as the line begins to move. Kids are jumping around them, nervous and excited at the same time.

"What's up?" he asks. "That looked tense."

"It's nothing I can't handle."

After a brief introduction by one of the elves, Wyatt and Stowe file into the classroom with around forty other adults and kids. It isn't a traditional setup with rows of desks, sterile walls, and a teacher's desk with an apple. Instead, it looks like an old study filled with dusty wooden artifacts and Christmas décor.

There are couches, cushions, and chairs for everyone to select from. Stowe and Wyatt sit on a couch where, for the next half hour, they are taught lessons by wise professor elves. The presentation is interactive, and the kids in the room are mesmerized. They learn important elf secrets and skills, such as peeking through the windows. The best is the instruction on the importance of kindness.

The whole thing is silly but fun. It is geared toward children and their parents, but Stowe still enjoys the feeling it brings out. Wyatt looks a little less impressed. She thinks he may have wanted to go to actually learn something.

"What did you think?"

"I'm filled with Kiiber Oober Toober magic!" Stowe screeches like one of their seemingly methamphetamine-addled elf instructors.

Wyatt chuckles and shakes his head. "You're killing me."

"Aw, c'mon, it was cute. The kids in there were on cloud nine. And the lessons they taught are important ones."

"Maybe we should arrange a congressional field trip. Politicians could use a refresher in Kiiber Oober Toober."

"And they'll even get some swag to put on their office wall."

Stowe holds up the diploma. They both received one, along with small elf hats. Wyatt's barely fits on his head.

"Do you think those elves overdose on sugar before class?"

"I'd need to. What do you think of this place in general?" Stowe asks, taking a last look around before they head for the exit.

Wyatt joins her in taking in their surroundings. "I think it's a great place to bring young kids. I know I would have loved it when I was little."

"But?"

"I don't know. It's missing the magic that Santa's Village has. It's cool, and I'm glad we came, but it feels more like a Christmas production than actual Christmas here."

"Agreed." Stowe positions her elf hat on her head and looks at him with her sexiest eyes. "How do I look?"

"Dreamy."

She can actually feel herself blush before removing the hat. "What time is it?"

"About the time to head back for cocoa with Santa."

"What if he turns us down? What are we going to do?"

"Grovel. Plead. Anything we need to do for him to say yes. He's the Santa we were looking for. It's up to us to convince him of how important this is."

Stowe is hoping it's as easy as it sounds. They are gambling everything on this. Santa is kind and generous, but this isn't like asking for a new bike for Christmas. Having him travel across an ocean to talk to a group of politicians is a big ask. She can't help but feel nervous about the outcome.

Chapter Fifty-Five

REPRESENTATIVE CAMILLA GUZMAN

It's already been a long morning. Most subcommittee hearings don't monopolize time like this one has. Four days of testimony is a lot to ask of the members, even if the schedule doesn't fill all the working hours. Despite public perception, the men and women elected to Congress have a lot on their plates.

Camilla didn't initially intend to have three economic testimonies in a row. It just worked out that way. She knows there is a danger of people's eyes rolling into their heads. It's not the most exciting thing they will hear this week, but it is necessary to understand.

Akari Ishikawa is one of the few people without a Ph.D. whom she will call before the subcommittee. That is, unless John Knutson and Angela Pratt are insane enough to call Santa Claus on Thursday. Camilla doubts he has a college degree unless the jolly fat man took online courses. She's half surprised some university hasn't tried cashing in on that gem.

Ishikawa is a retail expert popular in media circles and is often called upon by the national media to explain trends and impacts on that sector. What she lacks in doctoral credentials, she makes up for in knowledge and reputation for having her fingers on the pulse of American purchasing habits. She's also an attractive woman, and the cameras love her.

"Thank you for your testimony this morning," Camilla says after the rest of the committee asks their questions. "I know we are running long this morning, and everyone is eager to get to lunch, but I do have a few questions for you if you don't mind."

"I don't mind at all," Akari sweetly says from her seat at the table.

"There have been countless questions about the so-called 'War on Christmas.' It is alleged that corporate actions secularizing the holiday are helping destroy the magic of the season. What do shoppers think about that? What are their thoughts about how they are greeted in stores?"

"From my research, the percentage that actively thinks there is a coordinated assault on the holiday is relatively small. Most customers shrug and go about their business. When asked specifically to choose between 'Merry Christmas' and non-religious greetings, sixty percent of Americans say they prefer that stores and businesses greet customers by saying 'Merry Christmas.' Only one in four prefers Happy Holidays or Season's Greetings."

"Do those numbers change depending on age?"

"Yes, ma'am, they do. Younger shoppers tend to prefer more secular and inclusive greetings."

"It seems like our youth is losing the Christmas spirit," Camilla muses. "What about when it comes to Christmas displays in public?"

"Americans overwhelmingly support allowing public Christmas displays. More than eight in ten say Christmas symbols such as nativity scenes and Christmas trees should be allowed on government property. Only eleven percent disagree with that sentiment, but there is an important caveat. Most respondents believe symbols of other faiths and holiday traditions should be included."

"Meaning Hanukkah, Kwanzaa, and other symbols?"

"Yes, Congresswoman, that's correct."

Camilla plots her next question. She has a point she needs to drive home. She wants the people in this room and the audience watching on television to think about something over their lunch breaks.

"What about Santa Claus?"

Akari shifts slightly in her chair. "There is no study I know of that asks about him directly. Mine did not."

"So, we're to assume depictions of him are okay. Or, he is not viewed as controversial enough to even ask the question. Interesting. Tell me, Ms. Ishikawa, what do they say about commercializing Christmas?"

"Respondents say it's a concern. Fifty-two percent are bothered, at least to some extent, by the commercialization of Christmas."

"And this study was wide-ranging?"

"Yes, it was extensive. It covered over a hundred thousand people covering the lower forty-eight states."

"So, half the country is concerned about the commercialization of their favorite holiday, and yet that's what's happened with many facets of the holiday, correct?"

"It began long ago and has only accelerated today."

"Can you cite an example, Ms. Ishikara?"

"Certainly. Christmas ornaments are one. F.W. Woolworth brought glass ornaments from Germany to the mass market in the U.S. in 1880. His variety store in Lancaster, Pennsylvania, bought twenty-five dollars' worth of hand-blown glass bulbs, and they sold within two days. Ten years later, more than 200,000 glass ornaments were imported. The rest, as they say, is history. What was once a German cottage industry grew into a global market for Christmas decorations, including lights and other items, estimated to be worth over six billion U.S. dollars in 2022."

"What about Christmas trees?"

"The tradition had a humble beginning. The first documented appearance of a Christmas tree in the United States traces back to 1747. This original Christmas tree was fashioned from a wooden triangle and adorned with evergreen branches in

Bethlehem, Pennsylvania. Now, approximately twenty-five to thirty million real Christmas trees are sold in the U.S. every year."

"At what cost?"

"1.33 billion dollars in 2023. That number is expected to rise to 1.64 billion by 2028."

Camilla can feel the reaction in the room. It's expensive to purchase a tree that will only be in the house for a month. Most people don't think of the collective cost.

"So, the American people are spending billions on Christmas, and we haven't even gotten to shopping for gifts yet?" Camilla asks incredulously.

"That's correct. We also haven't discussed corporate expenditures for parties, personal outlays for food for family gatherings, travel costs…the list goes on."

"No wonder everyone is stressed out. How do businesses take advantage of this?"

Akari takes a sip of water and nods at the question. "The most obvious answer is Black Friday. As you know, it stemmed from the tradition of department store parades sponsored around Thanksgiving designed to kick off the holiday shopping season. If you can get people onto the streets, you can get them into the stores. The term appeared in the mid-1960s but didn't catch on until about two decades later.

"Then came Cyber Monday and Small Business Saturday. The former was devised by a division of the National Retail Federation in 2005. The latter was a promotion sponsored by American Express, which even registered the trademark for the term."

"All designed to separate Americans from their money in the name of Christmas spirit," Camilla concludes.

"Yes, but those are obvious ploys. The most devious of them all is the shopping mall Santa."

That comment gets everyone's attention.

"How so?"

"Shopping mall Santas are probably older than you think. The first appeared at a Philadelphia store in 1841 with a life-size Santa Claus model that drew children to it."

"Here we go with Pennsylvania starting things again."

There are some snickers around the room. Even the lone representative on the subcommittee representing the Philadelphia area cracks a smile.

"Indeed, that does seem to be the case. This spawned a trend in which store owners offered opportunities to see a real live Santa. In 1862, R.H. Macy of Macy's in New York City was the first to feature an in-store Santa for children to visit. By the 1890s, the Salvation Army had begun sending "Santas" into the New York City streets to solicit donations. Now, you see them everywhere."

"But why Santa? Why choose him?"

"Simple. This commercial version of Christmas was largely secular. By stripping away the religious nature of the holiday in this imagery, he could be used to shill for products and push for sales. You can't exactly have Baby Jesus do that."

They would if they could. Camilla smirks, almost picturing what that advertising would look like. If Coca-Cola created Santa, could Huggies diapers pull off the same thing with Baby Jesus? Probably not. It would be controversial, generating a lot of heat and a likely boycott.

"So, this was the start of Christmas without Christ."

"Correct. Store displays rarely, if ever, include images of Jesus. The commercial aspects of the holiday are not closely tied to Christmas theology."

"And this is intentional?"

"Very much so. The idea was to create a holiday season that all Americans, Christians and non-Christians, could experience. It was sold as an opportunity to share joy. In reality, it was created so more people would spend more money."

"Ms. Ishikara, would you support banning public depictions of Santa? As an expert in retail business, do you think he should be removed from stores?"

"I believe you should go much further than that. The behavior of retailers and businesses must be reined in for the nation's fiscal health. Spending during the holidays has reached epidemic proportions. Credit card debt is ballooning. Consumers are struggling, and it's because of all this pressure. Removing Santa from the equation is a good start. Black Friday, Cyber Monday…anything designed to exploit spending during the holiday should also be banned. Maybe that can be the next bill."

The next bill. Aymos and Camilla haven't thought much past getting this one advanced. Even if it passes through this subcommittee, it will be a hard sell in the full Commerce & Energy committee. It will be dead on arrival on the House floor. But it's an incremental step, and Rome wasn't built in a day.

"Thank you, Ms. Ishikawa. We appreciate your insights. These hearings are adjourned until this afternoon."

She slams the gavel down. There is little chatter among the members of the subcommittee. Most of them beeline for the door. Camilla is content to sit in her seat and watch the room. They are making progress. Very good progress.

Chapter Fifty-Six

WYATT HUFFMAN

Santa's office is much the same as they left it earlier. There's no reason it wouldn't be. It probably hasn't changed much since Santa's Village was constructed. The legend of Santa has spanned centuries. His office must remain as timeless as he is.

This time, the elf isn't there to greet them. They turn the corner to find Santa standing as he waits for them. In a feat of impeccable timing, the elf comes from a back room with a tray carrying three hot cocoas, all topped with whipped cream and a candy cane stirrer. The rainbow-eyed elf distributes the mugs before retreating from the office.

"Stowe and Wyatt. I apologize for making you come back," Santa says, sitting with his mug of cocoa.

"We understand, Santa. How were the children?"

"Precious, as always. After all these years, seeing their smile still warms my heart and puts a smile on my face. Now, what did you want to talk with me about?"

"We work for representatives in the United States Congress. One of its members introduced legislation to ban public depictions of you."

Santa nods in understanding. "That's unfortunate."

"It is. Our bosses are trying to stop it, but the subcommittee has had people testify all week about how you are bad for children and for the celebration of Christmas."

"I see."

"Santa, Christmas was once a profoundly important season of Christian worship. Then, it became a time of charity. As it became more secularized, it turned into a festival of shopping. Now we fear it's being used as a political weapon."

"You know, I have avoided politics my whole life. There is little to be gained by my involvement."

"Even with Christmas at stake?"

"People are going to believe what they believe. I spread joy during the holidays. It is up to the individual whether they embrace it. I'm not sure how I can help you."

"I know this is a big ask, but we want you to come to Washington with us and testify before the subcommittee."

"Testify? Is this a trial?"

"No, you've broken no laws. We would like you to…give your opinion."

"Santa, you are the best spokesman for Christmas there is," Wyatt adds.

"I'm not sure what I would say," Santa says, stroking his beard. "What am I supposed to testify to?"

"The spirit of Christmas and your role in it."

Santa places his mug down. "You know, Christmas is the second-most important holy day of the Christian year. Only Easter is more important. What is lost is that both holidays were historically preceded by a season of preparation. For Easter, it is Lent. For Christmas, it is Advent. Christian tradition uses these four weeks of Advent to train adherents to ready their hearts for the birth of Christ. It is meant to be a lengthy, quiet period of reflection. Now, it has been replaced by the Christmas shopping season."

Stowe nods. "Christmas music is piped into stores as early as September, Santa. We're inundated by advertising intended to trigger our desire to give. But it's not out of charity or generosity. Retailers want to sell bigger and more expensive stuff to be given as presents. Nobody disputes that, but we don't think you are to blame for it."

"I understand. I will have to think about it."

"We are under significant time pressure, Santa," Wyatt says. "We would need you to testify the day after tomorrow."

"Which means we would need to leave *tomorrow*," Stowe adds, highlighting the urgency.

Santa strokes his beard. "Return first thing tomorrow morning. I will check with the elves this evening and let you know then."

Wyatt wants to argue but doesn't. Stowe's face contorts as she fights similar feelings. You can't bully Santa Claus. The world doesn't work that way.

"Have you seen the Northern Lights yet?" Santa asks, changing the subject.

"No, not yet. We were only in the center of town last night."

"Ah, yes, too much light. It would be best to go to the Lapish countryside to see them. There is increased solar activity this evening. The show will be spectacular tonight. They make your Christmas wishes come true."

"I don't think we've made any."

Santa laughs and cocks his head. "Haven't you?"

Wyatt doesn't know what he means. Well, he does, but he isn't ready to admit it to himself. Stowe glances up at him. She must be thinking the same thing.

They say their goodbyes and step back into the arctic air. The sun has long since disappeared beneath the horizon. The warm glow of artificial lights leads the way as they head to the main courtyard area. Families are still posing for pictures while standing on one of the globe's most infamous invisible lines.

"Well, that was a little disappointing," Stowe moans once they are out of earshot of the office.

"I'll take a maybe over a no. I'm optimistic."

"Tomorrow will tell the tale. What should we do until then?"

"We do as Santa says and watch Mother Nature's most impressive light show."

"It wasn't an order, Wyatt."

He offers her a disapproving smirk. "No, but I won't risk landing on his naughty list this close to Christmas. I'm also not going to tempt fate. Besides, I want to see them. I've never witnessed the aurora this far north."

"All right, all right, I'm sold," Stowe says, holding her hands up in surrender. "How will we get there?"

Wyatt gestures around them. "It's Lapland. I'm betting there's a tour or two...hundred."

Chapter Fifty-Seven

REPRESENTATIVE JOHN KNUTSON

Guzman adjourns the hearings for the day, and everyone scatters. Some members return to their offices to catch up on work and return phone calls. Others flock to the media assembled outside the committee room to provide their insights to thirsty reporters. John is doing neither.

He's not ready to head back to the office. It's been a long day, and he isn't relishing the prospect of it becoming longer. That will be what happens the moment he walks through the door. Cameron will greet him with a stack of pink memos of calls to return. Staffers will swarm him, asking for guidance on everything from problems in the district to fundraising challenges.

It never ceases to amaze him how little legislating actually happens in Washington. Most of his job entails talking to donors, the media, and his staff. No wonder members of Congress don't write bills anymore. That responsibility was delegated to special interest groups long ago. They don't have the time, nor do the people who work for them.

John walks down the corridor to an empty committee room. It's quiet, like much of the rest of Capitol Hill. It's the last session before Christmas, and the Santa hearing is the only game in town. Nobody would want to compete for attention with that.

He crashes into a chair, relishing the silence. After a few cleansing breaths, he pulls out his cell phone and checks the news. As usual, the media is foaming at the mouth. These hearings are *the* Christmas story of Christmas stories, at least from within the Beltway. It has all the drama they are looking for to dominate the holiday news cycle.

The protests are getting even bigger and more widespread. At least the most vocal people are on their side. It's about the only thing going their way. The testimony sure isn't. And that's becoming a problem.

John opens an article about the most recent poll on the matter. Support for Santa is waning. Guzman is making her points, and the media spin is taking its toll. They are strangling Christmas spirit right before his eyes. Of all the pressure he's facing, that's what's weighing on him most.

The door opens, and Angela walks in. "I thought I saw you walk in here. Are you okay?"

"Never better." The words are positive. The tone was anything but.

"I can leave you be if you'd rather be alone."

"No, it's okay. Have a seat. You have your choice," John says, gesturing around the room.

Angela selects a seat only a couple away from his. "What are you doing in here?"

"Hiding."

"From the media?"

"From everyone. My chief of staff is likely pacing in my office with a long list of things for me to do when I return."

"Ah. You know, I need to thank you." Angela says, staring at her lap.

"For what?"

"Fighting alongside me. I couldn't do this without you, but I can't help but think I guilted you into it."

"Oh, you did," John says with a broad smile. "But you were right to, and I'm glad you did."

He means every word. Angela shouldn't have had to do that. He should have been willing to do the right thing from the onset. Some things are more important than selling out to keep a congressional seat. Christmas is one of them.

"Stowe checked in with the office while we were in the hearing. Have you heard from Wyatt?"

"No," John says, subconsciously looking at the phone he's holding. "But I haven't checked my messages. What did she say?"

"They made their pitch to Santa. She sounds encouraged. They'll have his decision tomorrow."

"Does he have to check with Mrs. Claus or something?"

"She didn't say. Santa won't say no, will he?"

"I hope not," John says, straightening in the chair. "I mean, I don't see how. He's the protector of all things Christmas. How could he take a pass on this?"

It sounds good, but he's keenly aware that a hundred things could go wrong. Everything from a passport issue to Finnish labor laws to an ornery Mrs. Claus could derail the whole thing.

"John, you know he isn't really Santa, right? He isn't even American."

"Neither was the real Santa."

Angela lets out a sharp laugh. "Touché. They're cutting this close."

"Too close. We aren't going to have much time to prep Santa. I'm going to have to have Cam take a vote count of the committee members. We need to know where we stand. It will clue us in how to prepare Santa for the questions."

"Good call. Let me know if anyone on my side of the aisle gives Cameron a hard time. Marcia Konstantinos may have instructed their side not to answer that question."

Politics is like war without the death toll. One of the basic tenets is not letting your enemy know your weaknesses. Members are not obligated to disclose how they intend to vote to anyone. When they do, it's often to get something in return. Favors rank only below campaign contributions in the political sphere.

"Don't you wish we could always do this?"

"Do what?"

"Work together on issues we agree on without worrying about parties or ideology? I had almost forgotten what that was like."

That wasn't always the case. Politicians on different sides of the aisle used to be mortal enemies in the political arena and best friends outside it. Working with the other party on shared goals was once a cherished endeavor. That dynamic has changed, and not for the better.

"I think that's part of why America is so caught up in this. Christmas isn't subject to ideology. No party has a monopoly over it."

"Maybe. We've all become so linear in our thinking. There is no crossover anymore. No working together. It's all about creating a divide and telling everyone to get on one side or the other. Can people even co-exist in that environment?"

"I have hope," Angela muses. "Wyatt and Stowe have spent a week together and haven't killed each other."

"Yeah, but don't think for a second I wasn't concerned about that before they went to Vermont."

He was anxious about their ability to work together. John even expressed it to Cam, who pledged to keep close tabs on them. Having the staff collaborate over the phone or in a conference room is one thing. Assigning two members to travel the country and the world together is another. Wyatt is not a pushover. He doubts Stowe is either. If they lock horns over some obscure political issue, one or both will likely land in prison.

"I think they have more in common than they think they do."

"I hope so. We need Wyatt and Stowe to come through in the worst possible way. I think Santa's testimony may be the only thing that saves this for us."

Angela is about to answer when John's phone vibrates in his hand. He stares at the caller ID. Cam is wondering where he is.

"Break time is over."

"Go get 'em," Angela says, standing. "I'll talk to you tomorrow. I need to call my husband anyway."

"Issues?"

"No. I could use a pep talk, and he's good at them. Our political process has decayed to the point where I've spent two days defending Santa Claus. It's taking a mental toll on me. Have a good night, John."

"You too, Angela."

John decides to head out as well. Cam will hunt him down anyway. He might as well get back to work without having his chief of staff drag him back to the office.

Chapter Fifty-Eight

STOWE BESSETTE

Stowe has already resolved to come back to Finland someday. She loves Lapland, and there is so much she won't be able to do. There is snowmobiling, downhill sledding, dog sledding, and cross-country skiing. That will all be saved for another trip. Seeing the northern lights tonight will be the icing on the cake for this adventure.

After being picked up at Santa's Village, Wyatt and Stowe headed north out of Rovaniemi, away from the light pollution. Their bus pulls onto a road around a secluded lake. They stop at a large cabin and are treated to a delicious Lappish BBQ with about fifty other people on the tour. At the end, they drink delicious blueberry tea before heading out to the edge of the lake to spend the evening awaiting the northern lights to begin their dance high above the Finnish countryside.

Stowe wasn't sure if she would need the additional winter clothing they offered. She's used to the cold and has a resistance to it. Thinking it's better to be safe than sorry, she and Wyatt donned their white and blue snowsuits and thick gloves.

The northern lights are an atmospheric phenomenon widely regarded as the Holy Grail of skywatching. They are beautiful dancing waves of light that have captivated people for millennia. Unfortunately, this spectacular light show is elusive and can only be seen at the highest latitudes. Most of the world will never witness the raw, natural beauty in person.

"Have you ever seen the northern lights?" Stowe asks as she and Wyatt patiently wait along the shoreline.

"Once. My father took me to Canada after I did a project on them for a science class in middle school. I was obsessed with them and still remember much of the report."

Stowe smiles. "Tell me."

"Okay, here it goes. 'Aurora' comes from the Latin word for 'sunrise,' and 'borealis' means 'to the north.' Energized particles from the sun slam into Earth's upper atmosphere at speeds up to forty-five million miles per hour and hit Earth's magnetic field. The particles are redirected toward the poles, and that dramatic process gives us this cinematic phenomenon."

"I'm impressed. Most adults I know can't give me a synopsis of the last book they read."

Wyatt clasps his hands. "I was expecting you to accuse me of mansplaining that to you."

"Stop it!" Stowe exclaims, slapping him on the chest. "I asked the question. I guess Santa didn't need to work too hard to talk you into this."

"No, he didn't. Besides, I really like being outside."

"Does this remind you of Montana?"

He looks around. "Actually, it looks more like Vermont without the mountains."

Stowe surveys the shoreline. He has a point. It does have that look and feel.

The oohs and ahhs around them compel her eyes to scan the horizon. A faint arch of green light appears in the sky before fading thirty seconds later. Then, subsequent ones grow more intense, last longer, and have red and yellow hues to accent the green. The lights dance across the sky quickly.

"Oh, wow, will you look at that," Stowe whispers.

It really is a truly spectacular phenomenon to see in real life. The experience goes beyond the images she's seen. The radiant shimmering of colors lights up the starry night sky. The lights she once saw in person were nowhere near this impressive. It's absolutely breathtaking.

"What do you think?" she asks Wyatt, her voice low.

"It looked as if someone had brushed glowing green paint across the sky and then set it on fire. It's the most enchanting thing I've ever seen."

The lights fade, and the darkness of the inky Finnish night returns.

"Enchanting?"

"Yeah, it ranks just above seeing you in that snowsuit."

"Shut up," she says with a laugh.

She feels herself getting carried away. Her heart is racing. It's the perfect night with an amazing man. Someone who is beginning to feel familiar…and comfortable. She looks up at Wyatt, who returns her stare.

The sky erupts in another wave of dancing green hues, not that she's paying attention. Without thinking, Stowe moves her head closer to his, unsure he's up for this. He is. He leans down to meet her, and their lips touch. It's soft and tenuous at first. He wraps his arms around her, and she reciprocates. They press their bodies into each other as the kiss grows harder and more sensual. And then it's over too soon.

She should feel jittery. Uncertainty is what she expects to creep in. Neither happens. Instead, she rests her head on his and continues watching Mother Nature's greatest show with his arm around her. The night sky isn't the only magical thing about this evening.

Chapter Fifty-Nine

REPRESENTATIVE JOHN KNUTSON

John wanted to avoid the protest for this precise reason. Unfortunately, people in Santa hats are everywhere around Capitol Hill. After catching up on work, he wanted to get out of the office and clear his head. There was almost no way he could leave the grounds without running into at least some of them.

Most legislators are unknown to the general public outside of a few prominent congress members. Bureaucrats and reporters may know all the players, but John Q. Public wouldn't know their representatives if they stood behind them in line for coffee. Reality television stars get more attention than the men and women who make policies that affect their everyday lives.

John was once cloaked in that anonymity. No longer. The throngs of Santa hat-clad protesters keep calling him the man trying to save Christmas. It may be an inaccurate title, but he likes the sound of it. It helps reaffirm that fighting is the right approach, even if it costs him dearly.

Pictures with them are a cost of doing business. Unfortunately, five more people wait for their turn every time one short photo shoot finishes. Thirty seconds for a snapshot with a pair of twenty-somethings has turned into ten minutes with a waiting crowd still to go.

Cameron finally shows up to rescue him. When he explains that he has important business to discuss with John ahead of tomorrow's hearings, the disappointed crowd enthusiastically cheers him on as they walk toward Upper Senate Park and Union Station beyond it.

"Your walks aren't as quiet as they used to be," his chief of staff says with a smirk. He won't let John forget this rescue mission for a while.

"No kidding. What's up?"

"I'm going to preface this news with the obligatory warning that you aren't going to want to hear it."

John glances at Cam. "It's become apparent that I get that disclaimer almost daily now."

"And, usually, with good reason. You really aren't going to like this."

"Is it about the hearings?"

"Indirectly," Cam says, inhaling a cleansing breath of cool air. "It's about the staff."

"What about them?"

He sighs. "One of them is feeding information to Marcia Konstantinos."

John is about to say something before growing quiet. Congress leaks like a sieve. Most of the damaging information released to the media, the FBI, or other politicians comes from disgruntled staff members. John has always treated his people with respect and offered them a chance to share their opinions when they disagreed with his position. It doesn't appear those tactics made a difference in this case.

"Do you know who?"

"It's Jacqui."

John stops walking. "Cam, are you telling me that one of my constituent affairs staffers is selling me out?"

That one hurts. Jacqui is part of the team that takes calls from residents in John's district who are having trouble with local or state officials, have been somehow wronged, or need the congressman to advocate for an issue. Constituent affairs staff are among the most trusted people in the office. He *needs* to be able to trust them.

"I didn't want to believe it either, but yes. That's what I'm telling you."

"How sure are you of this?"

Cam bobs his head back and forth on his shoulders as if weighing the percentages.

"It ranks in certainty between death and the likelihood that Congress will try to raise taxes next year."

"So, one hundred percent. Got it. What information was Jacqui giving Marcia?"

"Updates on Wyatt, and by extension, Stowe Bessette. She has provided Grinch Guzman all the details on their search for Santa Claus…should I be concerned that those words don't sound weird coming out of my mouth anymore?"

"Focus, Cam. How did you find out about Jacqui?"

"I'd love to say I waterboarded her until she talked, but I can tell you don't appreciate my sense of humor right now. Angela Pratt had a similar problem. Text messages were exchanged between Jacqui and a guy on her staff. He got busted and confirmed the two of them were coordinating their communications. They both think we're on the wrong side of this issue."

This issue didn't split along the usual partisan divide. Instead, it has split parties and now even staffs.

"Where is Jacqui now?"

"I don't know. I'm not MI-6. I didn't order someone to follow her around."

John shakes his head. "It doesn't matter. The damage is already done."

"You want me to let it go?"

"Hell no. I want you to head back to the office and pack all of Jacqui's crap in a cardboard box. Hand it to her when she shows up tomorrow morning with instructions to never return. I don't ever want to see her face in my office."

"What about Wyatt?"

"Is he selling me out, too?"

Cameron stuffs his hands deeper into his pockets. "No, but he is failing his mission miserably. He seems more interested in playtime with Stowe Bessette than finding a suitable Santa to testify."

"I'm not firing him for that if that's what you think."

"No, I'm not suggesting you do…at least, not yet. But Wyatt's running out of time. The odds of their success are decreasing exponentially with every passing hour. Even if they leave tonight, it will be cutting it close. Helsinki to Washinton isn't exactly a popular airline route."

"I'm aware. Are you concerned that we don't have a backup plan?"

Cam exhales deeply this time. John can almost tell what he's thinking by the cadence and depth of his breaths.

"Wyatt is being reckless by putting all their effort into landing this one Santa Claus. I'm more concerned that Guzman will try to leverage their failure. That's why she's so concerned about what Wyatt and Stowe are doing. Marcia isn't stupid. She isn't asking for advance copies of the questions you plan on asking because she knows they won't hurt Guzman. She wants updates because she knows Santa Claus can."

"It's the last day of the hearing…our last chance to leave a lasting impression on the subcommittee and the public."

"What are you going to do?"

"Finish my walk and try to avoid taking more pictures. I have a lot to think about. Thank you, Cam."

John stares up at the night sky. This is a big risk. His political future may rest on Wyatt's success or failure. It's not a position he wanted to find himself in. The hard part will come if Wyatt fails. His life will be impossible in the office, and the young man will likely make more mistakes trying to atone for the failure. John hopes it won't come to that, even if it means needing a Christmas miracle.

Chapter Sixty

REPRESENTATIVE CAMILLA GUZMAN

Some members of the House have an excellent work ethic. Camilla considers herself one of them. Tonight, the time is dedicated to reviewing the questions for the upcoming subcommittee testimony. At least, that was the plan.

She keeps getting sidetracked. While she prides herself on her ability to focus, the media coverage of her and the hearings is too irresistible. She finds herself tumbling down the media rabbit hole, clicking on article after article. It's a mixed bag, both in opinion and description of the testimony. Not only is there a variance in the opinions presented as facts, but sixty percent of the confirmable information is reported incorrectly. That's typical for the modern media.

A knock on the door interrupts her. Marcia is standing there, still dressed in her work clothes. Not that her wardrobe has been comprised of many casual options.

"Good, you're still here," Marcia says, bouncing into the office and collapsing into a chair in front of Camilla's desk.

"Yeah, I am. The question is, why are you? I thought you had dinner plans."

"Drinks, actually. I met with one of our sources and got some intelligence on Knutson's and Pratt's Great Santa Search."

Camilla considers herself to be one of the harder-working members of Congress. For as many hours as she puts in representing her district, her chief of staff outpaces her easily. Marcia is not only brilliant but well-connected. She knows the game and how to play it. Sometimes, that means doing things most people would consider conniving or unsavory.

"Ah, their Hail Mary. Did they find one?"

"Not yet," Marcia says gleefully. "They're in Finland trying to convince a Santa Claus there to testify."

"That's a long way for them to travel. Will he?"

Marcia shrugs. "That's anyone's guess."

Camilla removes her reading glasses and sets them on the desk. "If they find a Santa Claus in Finland, it'll be harder for us to conduct a background check on him."

"No, it will be impossible to do one. At least, not in the timeframe we would need it completed."

Camilla taps her nails on her desk. The odds of their success are long, but they aren't zero. She needs to put her thumb on the scale and rig this in their favor.

"What are the odds that Santa has a passport?"

"I wouldn't know, but he'll need one to enter the country."

"Mmhmm. Who do you know at CBP?"

Employing over sixty thousand people, U.S. Customs and Border Protection is one of the world's largest law enforcement organizations. They are charged with facilitating lawful international travel and trade while identifying and denying entry to prospective terrorists. The organization takes a comprehensive approach to border management and control by combining customs, immigration, and border security into one mutually supportive activity.

"Camilla, are you asking me to use my relationships with government bureaucrats to deny Santa Claus entry into the United States?"

"It's not as bad as it sounds," the congresswoman says, knowing it probably does sound that bad. "First, he's not really Santa. Second, a delay might be sufficient. They're up against the clock."

"Okay. I'll see what I can do," Camilla's chief of staff says, straightening and smoothing her jacket.

"Marcia, there's one more thing. What do we do if the Santa they're trying to get doesn't come?"

"I'm not sure what you mean."

Camilla leans back in her chair and interlaces her fingers. "Thursday's testimony is reserved for Santa. If Knutson and Pratt can't find one...."

"What stops us from inserting one in their place? That's deliciously devious."

"How good is your contact giving us this information?"

"Excellent. I'm practically getting firsthand knowledge."

The congresswoman knows better than to ask any more questions. Marcia has her methods, and Camilla can't maintain plausible deniability if she presses her chief of staff for details. Part of this job is knowing what questions not to ask.

"Do you have the information on the Santas they interviewed and took a pass on?"

"I do. But why not pick someone we want?"

"Optics," Camilla says. "I don't want it to look like we brought in the worst possible depiction. However...."

"If we choose someone they interviewed, it's plausible that we didn't know the backstory about why he was disqualified."

Camilla taps her nose and points at Marcia.

"I'll see what I can do. Congresswoman, for what it's worth, if you keep thinking like that, you will have your seat for a long time."

That's the plan. Camilla is risking a lot with this tactic. The majority of the American people are against her. She embarrassed the speaker of the House and the majority leader. She is working closely with a member of the opposing party. None of those guarantee re-election in this polarized political environment. But there are upsides.

"One step at a time, Marcia. One step at a time. But thank you."

Camilla slides her reading glasses to her face and returns to the online articles. The inaccurate depictions of Grinch Guzman are waiting. It doesn't matter. If she pulls this off, nothing they write will.

Chapter Sixty-One

WYATT HUFFMAN

It's early. Santa Claus's Village is only just beginning to show signs of life. Only one other family came through the entrance with Stowe and Wyatt, and they turned right and headed toward the Christmas House.

Stowe and Wyatt cross the Village Square. Nobody is taking pictures next to the lit pedestals demarking the Arctic Circle. The freshly fallen snow has already been cleared from the line in what is likely a daily ritual here.

Wyatt opens the door to Santa's Main Office. It's eerily quiet inside. Maybe it's nerves or the gravity of the moment. The only sound Wyatt hears is his own heart thundering in his chest.

The rainbow-eyed elf is there to greet them. She moves a whisp of blonde hair out of her face and offers a knowing smile. Wyatt and Stowe return it as she gestures them into Santa's office.

Santa is already seated on his wooden bench. Wyatt gives the man credit. That must wreak havoc on his back.

"Stowe, Wyatt! How were the lights? Did you enjoy them?"

They look at each other and smile.

"Very much, Santa."

"That's good to hear," the jolly man chuckles. "Come, sit with me before my young guests arrive."

"Did you have a chance to think about our request, Santa?" Wyatt asks as he and Stowe sit on opposite sides of Santa.

"I did."

"And?" Stowe presses.

He looks around his office. "I have seen and heard a lot. I spend every day here – well, almost every day – listening to precious children tell me their heart's desires. You know, it isn't always about toys. Some of their requests…well, they touch my heart.

"I have dedicated my life to giving. Doing so has brought me great joy. I never thought I would see a time when the act of spreading that joy would come under attack."

"We didn't either, Santa," Stowe says, giving Wyatt an optimistic look. "But it is, and that's why we need you to help us."

"I would like nothing more."

Wyatt feels a surge of excitement. Santa's words are music to his ears.

"Then you'll come to Washington with us?" Stowe asks, ready to jump out of her skin.

"I'm afraid not, my dear."

Wyatt's mouth goes dry. The rumbling of his heart ceases, even feeling like it skips beats. He heard the words clearly. Only they aren't the ones he was anticipating.

"Why not, Santa?" It was meant to be a question. Wyatt almost made it sound like an accusation.

"The easy answer is that I'm needed here."

"You could find a replacement," Stowe says, placing a hand on Santa's knee. "It'd only be for a day or two."

"This isn't a suburban shopping mall. There are no shift changes or multiple Santas in my village. I *am* Santa Claus, and people come here from great distances to see me. But, as I said, that is the easy answer, not the full one."

"What do you mean?"

Santa gives Wyatt a mournful look. "I cannot make people believe in me. I cannot make them believe in the spirit and magic of Christmas. It's something they must find on their own."

"But you can help them find it."

"They will never find what they do not seek."

"But Santa, they want to ban public images of you," Stowe pleads.

"Can they ban me from people's hearts?"

They would if they could. That's what Wyatt wants to say but doesn't. It's manipulative, and he doesn't want to offend Santa Claus.

"No," Wyatt and Stowe answer simultaneously.

"That is what matters most."

"I understand, Santa," Wyatt says, "but this will make people stop believing even more. Christmas is something many people still look forward to."

"People are trying to take that joy away from us."

"I cannot fix that. I spread holiday cheer and encourage generosity and charity. I bring joy to children. But belief in me is voluntary, Stowe. I can't force others to feel my passion for Christmas. I show them the path through my actions. I do not force them to walk it themselves."

"But we need you to be that inspiration," she continues.

"And I will be. I always will be so long as I live in people's hearts and minds. They don't need to see me in public to carry my spirit with them. We were all endowed with free will. We must be willing to accept the decisions people make when exercising it."

Wyatt has never even thought about arguing with Santa Claus. As a child, he was larger than life. Even as an adult, the thought of sparring with St. Nick feels inappropriate. But that's not the reason he is at a loss for words. Santa is right. The challenge of having individual freedom is respecting that others do as well. Who would have thought that Santa Claus was a philosopher?

"Is there any way to change your mind, Santa? This is our Christmas wish."

"I think we both know that isn't true, Stowe. It's not yours either, Wyatt."

They look at each other. There's truth to that, despite neither of them wanting to admit it.

"Santa," the rainbow-eyed elf says from the entrance to the office. "The first group of children has arrived."

He nods, and she disappears into the front of the office. Wyatt doesn't even know where she came from. She wasn't there when they arrived. All he knows is their time with Santa is done. There will be no further negotiation or pleading.

"You are both very special to me. I hope you come to understand and respect my decision."

"We do," Wyatt croaks. "Thank you, Santa. Have a very Merry Christmas."

"And to the two of you, as well."

Stowe and Wyatt leave the office with a fraction of the energy they entered with. That's not how either of them expected this meeting to go. They were more concerned about getting Santa packed and making the necessary travel arrangements and accommodations in Washington. Instead of joy, they are feeling very different emotions. For Wyatt, it's frustration and disappointment. When he sees Stowe's hands balled into fists, he knows the emotion welling inside her is decidedly different.

Chapter Sixty-Two

STOWE BESSETTE

Life is a rollercoaster. It is a ride with ups and downs, loops and turns. Along the way, everyone experiences the highest of highs and lowest of lows. Stowe has felt both in less than fifteen minutes.

She went into this morning's meeting with Santa optimistic. It wasn't even cautious optimism. How could Santa say no? Why wouldn't a jolly old elf want to defend his name against a bunch of crusty politicians seeking to suck the joy out of the season? He could take a couple of days to do that. At least, that was her reasoning. Unfortunately, it's not to be.

Stowe tilts her head back and stares deep into the dark Lapland sky. The sun is still hours away from peeking over the horizon for its brief stay. She turns to see Wyatt's nauseated face in the pale light outside the office.

"Well, that didn't go as planned."

It was a statement of fact. Indisputable. Undeniable. It was also matter-of-fact. Maybe that's what triggers her anger.

"That's all you have to say?" Stowe asks, snapping at him.

"I don't know—"

"This was your idea, Wyatt!"

Wyatt recoils in surprise. "Yeah, but he was the best candidate we've found."

"Yeah, he is. But he still said no! So, what good is it?"

She's seeing red. Santa could have disappeared up a chimney right in front of them. He could have had Rudolph, with her glowing nose, standing next to him in that office. None of it would have mattered if he wasn't willing to come with them. They need a Santa to testify. How close he is to the real thing is a secondary consideration.

"Stowe—"

"Don't! Don't try to justify it!"

"Wait, do you think this is my fault?"

"If not yours, then whose? Who should I be blaming? You said you would convince him."

"I tried."

"You should have tried harder."

Wyatt pulls off his knit cap and runs his hand through his hair. He's speechless, as he should be. There is no defense for that.

"We have nothing to show for any of this," she says, her voice low and troubled.

"Look, Stowe, maybe we can—"

"Can what? This was our only option! Maybe we would have one if you weren't so busy trying to play kissy face with me."

Stowe doesn't know if she meant to disparage their budding relationship. She's so upset that she isn't thinking clearly. She feels the need to lash out at someone, and he happens to be standing closest.

"What?"

"You heard me."

"Is that what you think I was doing?"

Opportunity cost. It's an economic term representing the potential benefits an individual misses out on when choosing one alternative over another. Because these opportunity costs are unseen, they're often easily overlooked. Stowe certainly overlooked them. That's the problem right now.

"What else could it have been, Wyatt? Instead of doing our jobs, we were soaking in thermal spas, exploring caves, and going for sleigh rides. Were you trying to distract me? Did you want us to fail?"

"How could you even ask that?"

"Because I think it's the truth. You never cared about finding a Santa to testify. That's why you let me do the work in the beginning. Then I agreed to…. You know what? It's my fault. I can't believe I let myself get caught up in that…in you. Of all the stupid mistakes I've made…."

Sticks and stones may break your bones, but words can never hurt you. Every child in America is taught those words or something similar. It's a lie. Words can hurt. They can cut deep into your soul. They can break bonds and destroy trust. Worst of all, once uttered, they can never be taken back.

"Is that what it was?" Wyatt asks softly. "A mistake?"

"What else would you call it?"

He starts to speak but stays quiet. Stowe doesn't know what to expect. Maybe she wants him to say she means something to him. Maybe that he's even falling in love with her. Instead, she's rewarded with silence. As irrational as her feelings are, his silence answers the question.

"I thought so," Stowe says, turning and walking away.

"Where are you going?"

Stowe stops and turns. "Back to Washington. I need to start salvaging what's left of my career. Find your own way home."

She bounds off, only looking back after passing through the square and reaching the Santa Claus Gift House. Wyatt is still standing there, alone. It's exactly how she feels.

Chapter Sixty-Three

WYATT HUFFMAN

Stowe is gone. Wyatt followed her to the parking area and watched her drive away in the rideshare, presumably back to the hotel to pack her things. He thought about chasing her, but she made her feelings crystal clear. Whatever he thought they may have had didn't exist.

There is no point in Wyatt's rushing back to the Arctic Sky. Checkout isn't until noon, and he wants to ensure Stowe isn't there when he arrives. It isn't a bitterness thing. Well, maybe a little. He's hurt, and the last thing he wants is an awkward encounter with her in the lobby.

Needing to kill some time, Wyatt heads to Santa Claus's Main Post Office. A part of Finland's official postal service network, this is St. Nick's official post office. The merry elves working here exude Christmas spirit and apparently speak several languages. A wide range of delightful Christmas products, stamps, postcards, gift items, and souvenirs is available to purchase. It isn't busy this early, but some families are already toiling away, filling out postcards to send home to friends and relatives.

Wyatt sits at a table in the corner and reads the instructions on the table tent. Cards, letters, and parcels sent from here are stamped with a genuine postmark that can't be found elsewhere. It conveys greetings from Lapland, the Arctic Circle, and Santa Claus himself and is delivered around Christmas, no matter what time of year they are mailed.

He would fill out a postcard but isn't in the mood. Instead, he retrieves his cell phone to check the flight options to Washington. There are a few, and he will take a later one. Stowe won't want to share the same aluminum cylindrical tube as him at thirty thousand feet, even if they are seated at opposite ends of the aircraft.

The caller ID pops up, and Wyatt closes his eyes. His mother is almost the last person he wants to talk to right now, but he needs to take the call in case it's important. It's an eight- or nine-hour difference to Montana. He checks his watch as he answers.

"It's late there. Is everything okay?"

"It's fine. I had the urge to call and check up on you. How's Finland?"

Wyatt smiles. That woman has a sixth sense when something is bothering him. It's always been that way.

"Beautiful."

"Are you almost done there?"

"Yeah, I am. I'll be flying back to the States tonight."

"With your new ladyfriend?" his mother asks, her voice an octave or two higher.

"No, Stowe is already heading to the airport to catch an earlier flight."

His mother sighs. "Uh, oh. What happened?"

Bridget Huffman is a gossip. When you're the wife of a rancher in Montana, there isn't much else to do. It's not that she will spread the news around town, but she will want every gory detail about what happened on this trip. The romance stuff. She couldn't care less about politics.

"It just didn't work out."

"I don't believe that, Wyatt. You gave me the impression that she really liked you, and you're not a quitter."

Wyatt grimaces. "That's what I thought, too."

"I'm so sorry. That can be hard. I know you had a thing for her."

"It's okay. I'll get over it."

That's Wyatt's way of telling his mother he doesn't want to talk about something. Sometimes it works. This isn't going to be one of those times.

"Like you got over Jessie?"

"You're hitting below the belt, Mama. Keep the gloves up."

"Well, someone needs to tell it to you like it is. Jessie was your childhood sweetheart, Wyatt. I know that can be tough to get over."

"It's not about her," Wyatt says, staring at the adorable family walking through the door. "Is Dad with you?"

"No, he went up to bed. He's going to have a long day tomorrow. Why?"

It was a mere passing thought as he walked here from Santa Claus's office. He dismissed it as being hurt. Now, the more he thinks about it, the more worthy it is of consideration.

"I'm thinking about coming home."

"Of course, it's Christmas. We'll see you in another week."

"No, I mean permanently. This assignment I was on…well, it was important, and I dropped the ball."

"The congressman isn't going to fire you, Wyatt."

"No, but his chief of staff might. It doesn't matter. I may resign. I don't think this is for me."

Wyatt hears his mother stop moving. "And you don't want me to tell your father."

"No, not yet. I can't stomach him saying, 'I told you so' right now."

"He won't do that."

He frowns. "Seriously, Mom? Rethink that."

Bill Huffman has been ridiculing Wyatt about his career path since the day he chose his major in college. Not only would his father say the words, he'd have them engraved on a plaque and hang it in the living room of their house. It's not that he's vindictive by nature. It's that he enjoys being right more than anyone in the entire state of Montana.

"Okay, I won't say anything. Are you sure that's what you want?"

Wyatt tightens his jaw. "I don't think life cares what I want right now."

"It may seem that way, but…regrets are powerful, Wyatt. I would love for you to be closer to home, but it needs to be for a good reason. I don't want you living your life wondering what could have been."

"I understand. Thank you, Mama. I'll call you when I get back."

"Travel safe."

Wyatt disconnects the call and pockets the phone. He can make his flight arrangements later. Right now, he needs to think about what he really wants. It'll be okay so long as Stowe Bessette doesn't keep popping into his mind.

Chapter Sixty-Four

REPRESENTATIVE JOHN KNUTSON

John slams the receiver back into its cradle. Being in Congress has its fair share of frustration, and that's far from the first time he's done it. At the other end of the room, Cam hangs up as well. He listened in on the whole conversation with Wyatt from the other phone in the office.

His chief of staff sits on the arm of the sofa as John leans back in his chair and exhales deeply. That was not the news he was hoping for. Now, he needs to consider the implications. None of them look pleasant.

"Well, that was a kick in the balls."

"I give you credit for keeping your cool, Congressman," Cam says. "I wouldn't have if our roles were reversed."

"What did you want me to do, scream at him?"

"For starters, yeah."

John would be lying if he said he didn't want to. He had a lot to lose and relied on Wyatt to come through. His young staffer didn't. Part of that is his fault.

"It was a tough assignment. We knew that when we handed it to him."

Cam stands and moves to the chair across the desk from the congressman. He's about to get serious. The relaxed posture and informality of sitting on the sofa arm are replaced with a professional demeanor.

Wyatt is well-liked in the office. Cameron is tough on him, but they could almost call each other friends. Right now, he's an office manager. Politics is a "what have you done for me lately" business. The coming conversation isn't personal and probably not easy, but it is necessary.

"Congressman, he was tasked to find a suitable Santa. Instead, you paid for him to go to the Arctic Circle in Finland like he was searching for the actual Santa, which, of course, is preposterous. He got diverted to Iceland and claimed he had it handled. It took Santa time to decide, but he said he had it handled. He clearly didn't have anything handled."

"Wyatt is reliable. By your own admission, he's maybe one of the best staffers in this office," John argues.

"And yet, he failed. Miserably."

"That's never happened before."

"No, it hasn't," Cam says, rubbing his hands on his pants. "Maybe he was distracted. Let's be honest – Miss Bessette is a beautiful woman. Maybe Wyatt was too busy chasing her to do his job."

John would like to discount that but can't. Stowe Bessette would distract him if he were twenty years younger and single.

"We'll deal with Wyatt when he returns."

"As you wish. What do you want to do about the testimony? Guzman is expecting Santa Claus. By extension, so is half the country."

"We cancel the request and let Guzman hold her vote."

"The last count I had was a tie. Not having Santa there will likely tip the scales in their favor."

Vote counting on a twenty-two-member subcommittee is much easier than counting the four hundred and thirty-five representatives in the whole body. They can be relatively certain that the numbers are accurate. The fence-sitters will make the difference, and Cam is likely right.

"And then there are the political implications," he continues. "If the leadership withholds funding, it may cost you your seat."

Durant and Guillomi play hardball, and they don't make idle threats. They are going to come after John, that's for certain. It's also a problem for another day.

"There's nothing we can do about that now. Wyatt didn't have a backup plan – for some odd reason. He was our only hope short of scouring the streets of Washington and praying for a miracle."

Cam cocks his head, amused at the prospect. "I could try."

"Don't waste your time."

"Do you want to tell Angela Pratt, or do you want me to?"

"I'll do it. Thank you, Cam."

John's chief of staff nods and leaves, pulling the door closed behind. The congressman takes a deep breath and picks up the phone, half surprised it's still working. He presses the speed dial button, and the call is picked up on the second ring.

"I take it you heard the news," she says, not bothering to say hello.

"Unfortunately. Wyatt just called. He's checking out of the hotel now."

"Stowe is already boarding her flight home."

So much for her being a distraction. That or things didn't go well. Not that it matters. It was a work trip, not an episode of *The Bachelor*.

"They aren't coming back together?"

"Apparently not. If you have any bright ideas, I'm all ears because I'm fresh out."

John grimaces. "Not really. My chief of staff is willing to scour the city looking for a replacement."

"Well, a few thousand Santas are protesting around Capitol Hill. Maybe we can steal one of them."

"And watch whoever we find get destroyed in front of a national audience because he can't name all the reindeer? I don't think so."

He has a greater appreciation for what Wyatt was up against. Santa not only had to look the part, he had to *be* the part. Christmas knowledge is as important as having an authentic beard. Being able to answer the hard questions launched at him is not something just any Santa impersonator would be up for.

"John, I don't have to tell you that the media is going to eat us alive. They're hyping this up nonstop. My media specialist informed me that networks are discussing carrying this hearing live. Cable news absolutely will. We're going to get crucified."

"I know. We bet the mortgage on a roll of the dice and came up craps. We have to live with the consequences of that, like it or not."

Everything has a price in this town. To get ahead, you have to take a chance and hope it pays off. If it doesn't, you learn the hard way why so many people don't take the risk. In this profession, image is everything, and all your hard-earned work can be undone with one misstep. They just made theirs.

"I'm going to talk to Stowe in the morning when she arrives. I want to know what happened."

"Ditto. I'll talk to Wyatt, and we'll compare notes before the hearing. In the meantime, I need to think about what to say to the press."

"I'll come up with some talking points as well. Maybe one of us will have an epiphany."

"Angela…I'm sorry this didn't work out."

"Me, too. Have a good night, John."

John leans back in his chair and rubs his temples. He gambled and lost. Tomorrow, he begins to pay the debt.

Chapter Sixty-Five

REPRESENTATIVE CAMILLA GUZMAN

4-1=3. It's simple math, and so is counting votes. So long as there are no fence-sitters, the arithmetic is easy for a seven-year-old. Usually, votes in Congress break along party lines, so a crystal ball isn't needed to determine how the math will turn out. This is different.

Camilla came over to the Commerce and Energy Committee Hearing Room to think. Her office felt stuffy, and she needed to get out. She looks around the desolate space. Tomorrow is a big day. The room will be filled with observers and packed full of reporters. It is her moment…if she can seize it.

There was an expected two-to-one advantage coming into the hearings. Again, simple math. With the opposition sitting this out to play politics, Camilla knew the vote would go her way. Representatives like Knutson and Pratt are a hard no, but others will want to check which direction the political winds are blowing. There is no reason not to abstain. Thus, she will have double the number of ayes than nays.

Then, the math changed when Knutson got involved. He didn't sit this one out after all. Angela Pratt was eager for his support and got it. Camilla is still irritated by the betrayal of a woman in her party.

The dynamic duo has made waves at these hearings, and the simple math isn't so simple anymore. The margin is tightening. Aymos walks into the committee room chamber. Now, she's about to find out how tight it is.

Blackburn sits where the witness would and leans back in the chair. The suspense is killing her. After ten seconds of him not speaking, she leans forward.

"This can't be good."

"We're tied," he mumbles.

"What?"

"You heard me. We're all knotted up at eight apiece. Five members haven't decided – two are from your party."

Camilla shakes her head. So much for their two-to-one margin. She knew it had tightened but didn't expect to lose so much support.

"What happened?"

"Politics. It's Christmas. Knutson and Pratt are raising good points. They don't like that they could be perceived as anti-Santa Claus a couple of weeks before NORAD tracks his global deliveries."

That's the downside of the protests. Camilla wanted them to be big and attract attention. Sometimes, getting your wish is the worst thing that can happen. They have the attention they want, but the sight of protestors singing carols around the Capitol has generated a lot of sympathy. It is causing people who despise holiday stress to rediscover the season's joy.

"I wish they expressed that level of interest to ensure my Christmas gifts get to California on time. Can you bring anyone over from your side?"

"Maybe. What about you?"

"I won't get any help from the party leadership, and I don't have a lot of chips to trade."

"You need to do something. A tie is a loss in this place," Aymos concludes.

"I know. It's time to play our trump card."

Camilla picks up her phone and dials her chief of staff. The call is picked up on the second ring.

"Hey, boss."

"Hi, Marcia, I'm here with Aymos Blackburn and have you on speaker. Is our man ready?"

"Yes, ma'am. He's ready and raring to go."

"And?"

"He'll be perfect for what we need him to do. Are you certain you want to do this? It could backfire."

Politicians preoccupy themselves with measuring risks. Every action or comment comes with them. Some are acceptable. Some aren't. The key is making the correct call when an opportunity presents itself. Careers are made and destroyed that way.

"We have no option. The curtain goes up tomorrow morning. Thanks, Marcia."

"All right, you've piqued my curiosity," Aymos says as Camilla disconnects the call and sets her phone down.

"Knutson and Pratt sent a pair of staffers to find a Santa to testify before the subcommittee. They insisted on calling him as a witness on Thursday."

"I know, but they're talking about rescinding that request."

Camilla smiles. "They already did because they couldn't find a suitable one in the U.S. and had to go to Finland. Which tells you everything you need to know about the people we have playing Santa Claus here. Anyway, they opened the door, so we'll walk through it. We aren't going to fail where they did. They want the people to hear from Santa…and now they will."

Chapter Sixty-Six

STOWE BESSETTE

Stowe wheels her carry-on into the bedroom and drops her purse on the dresser. It was a decently long flight home, made worse by the circumstances. She's emotional, and that made the time crossing back over the Atlantic grind to a halt.

Mandy is nowhere to be found. She's likely still on Capitol Hill, helping the staff plan for tomorrow and whatever the day brings. It's too bad. She could really use someone to talk to right now.

Her iPad chimes, and she sees a video request from Nana. She swears that the woman has ESP or something. She looks like hell, but refusing the video call will only lead to more questions.

"Hi, Nana," Stowe says, holding the iPad up as she brushes the hair out of her face.

"I'm sorry to bother you, dear. I can call another time if you're busy."

"No, it's okay, Nana. I'm always happy to hear from you. I'm sorry I haven't had the chance to call more."

"It's okay, Sweetie. Are you back in the country?"

"Yeah, I just got back. How's PopPop's shoulder?"

"On the mend, but he's as stubborn as ever. I swear, that man is going to be the death of me. He refuses to take it easy."

Her grandfather is a typical Vermont mountain man. He's fiercely independent and doesn't like people doing things for him. Stowe isn't shocked that he's doing more than he should. She's more surprised he took it easy at all.

"That sounds about right."

"Oh, Stowe, you sound like you've run out of Christmas spirit. What's wrong? Is it your job?"

"No," she says before realizing that lying to her grandmother never works in her favor. "Well, yes…it's a lot of things. We didn't find a Santa in time for tomorrow's hearing. Our one prospect in Finland refused to come. We bet everything that we could convince him…. Anyway, I got really angry and blamed Wyatt. I said some horrible things to him before we left."

"Was it Wyatt's fault?"

"No, of course not! He was amazing, and the Santa there was perfect. Wyatt did everything right."

The words ring in her head. It's what she should have said back in Finland. Why did she lash out at him? It was stupid.

"Then maybe you should tell him that. It's not too late."

Stowe sighs, wishing that were true. "It really is."

"Have you talked to him since?"

"No. We went our separate ways. We weren't even on the same flight home."

"He's home now, right? Give him a call."

"I don't know if he is yet, Nana. Not that it matters. I doubt he ever wants to speak to me again."

She can't say she would blame him. They spent a week working through their trust issues, only to have her undo the progress in the span of a few minutes.

"I'm willing to bet Wyatt feels just as bad as you do. He'll talk to you, but you'll need to make the first move."

"Why?"

"He respects you, Stowe. And your privacy," Nana says before leaning closer to the camera. "Did you tell him about Bobby?"

"Wyatt knows the story. I told him in Finland."

"I thought so. Then he's going to give you space because he thinks that's what you want. You really like Wyatt, don't you?"

Stowe averts her eyes from the camera. How can she say yes when she's having difficulty admitting it to herself? Yes, she does like him. A lot. But there are so many obstacles. She can't allow her heart to get torn to pieces. Not after it just started to heal.

"After Bobby, I swore I never wanted to feel that way again."

"Honey, walling off your heart to prevent it from breaking again is no way to go through life. And Wyatt Huffman is not Bobby Sinclair."

"How can you know that, Nana? Did you know that Bobby was going to cheat on me?"

Her grandmother frowns. "Of course not, honey. But Bobby always viewed you as a prize instead of a partner. That's why he reacted badly when you wanted to go to Washington. Everything was about him and his needs. He never cared about yours."

"I know. Wyatt is easy to…."

"Talk to?"

Stowe nods. "I let him in. Further than I should have. I'm not ready for that."

"Most people aren't ready for love when it arrives."

Hearing that word sends a shiver up her spine. "It's not love!"

"Do you mean that, or are you just trying to protect yourself from getting hurt? I think Wyatt has fallen in love with you if that changes anything. I saw the beginnings of it when he was here."

"How do you know that? And don't say 'a grandmother knows.'"

Nana smiles. "It's how he looked at you, Stowe. That's the key. He had a twinkle in his eyes after you kissed him in the kitchen. He was trying to hide it, but he felt something. Did you kiss him again?"

The memories flood back. In the snow at the bottom of a dark hill…under the dancing green sky of the aurora borealis. Two magical moments. Both impulsive and unexpected. Much like the entire journey has been.

"Yes. Twice, actually."

"And what did *you* feel? Set aside your misgivings about political nonsense and fear over what happened with Bobby. What did you *feel?*"

Tears roll down Stowe's cheeks. She fights to wipe them away, but more follow in their tracks. She swore she would never again cry over a man. But that's not why she is. It's a feeling of personal loss. She's missing the one emotion she felt in those moments.

"Happiness."

Nana smirks and gives her a knowing nod. "Then you owe it to yourself to see if he feels the same. I'm betting he does."

Stowe shakes her head. "It may not matter. We could be out of a job tomorrow."

"Those things have a way of working themselves out."

"How? Why?"

"It's almost Christmas."

Those aren't simple words of reassurance. Nana absolutely *believes* in the power of the holiday. She fervently believes in Christmas magic, miracles, and the world of possibilities the season brings. Stowe wishes she could believe with her.

"I need to go and find PopPop and tie him to his chair before he does something stupid," her grandmother announces. "You take care, Stowe. We'll see you in a few days."

"Bye, Nana."

Stowe closes the cover on her iPad and collapses back on the bed. She grabs a throw pillow and clutches it against her chest. The tears are coming, and there is little chance of beating them back this time.

Chapter Sixty-Seven

WYATT HUFFMAN

Wyatt is back in his suit. For a while there, he felt normal. His father only wears a jacket and tie for weddings and funerals. He can't comprehend why any man would want to wear one all day. Wyatt is constantly at odds with his old man, but that is one thing they agree on. While his chosen career demands this attire, he's never felt particularly comfortable in it.

He did wear a Christmas tie today to mark the occasion. It was a gag gift given to him years ago and not something he was overly excited to wear until now. It hits all the traditional marks – green, red, and is ugly sweater loud. It may be his last day working on the congressman's staff, so he might as well go out in style.

Knutson wasn't overly hostile during their brief conversation. He wasn't friendly, either. It was a little like talking to his father after receiving a poor grade in high school. The tone was more of disappointment than anger.

That anger will be reserved for the chief of staff. Cameron Alcott runs the office with an iron fist. If he hands out an assignment, it had better get done. Wyatt failed. The mission was critical for these hearings, and Wyatt didn't come through. He also never arranged a backup plan. The congressman may be forgiving, but Cam is likely going to be the one who tells him to pack his things when this is over.

A half hour before the hearing is scheduled to start in the Rayburn House Office Building, Wyatt takes the long stroll over there. He feels like the condemned walking to the gallows. He can only wait for the rope to tighten around his neck. A woman leans on the wall beside him outside the Commerce and Energy Committee Room.

"It looks like you had a nice trip."

"I'm sorry. Do I know you?"

"I'm Amanda Derringer. Stowe's roommate."

"Mandy. Of course. It's nice to finally meet you. Stowe spoke very highly of you."

"She ought to," Mandy says with a grin. "I pay most of the rent. She also speaks highly of you. Present tense."

Wyatt hangs his head. "I doubt that."

"I know what happened right before you left Finland. I promise you, her anger had nothing to do with you."

Wyatt really doesn't want to talk about this. Stowe didn't mince words. She let him know *exactly* how she felt.

"I appreciate what you're trying to do, Mandy. But you weren't there. Trust me. Her anger had everything to do with me."

Mandy is about to argue her point when something catches Wyatt's attention.

"Who is that? Is that…? It can't be."

Mandy turns briefly to check out the man with the oversized belly stuffed into a traditional Santa suit. She shakes her head.

"Guzman had moles on our staffs. She must have learned about Streaker Santa, and that's why he's here. She's going to humiliate him in front of a national audience."

"Wonderful," Wyatt moans.

"Wyatt, you and Stowe did your best. It was a tough thing to pull off."

"I appreciate it, but I doubt many others think it was. I suppose it could be worse. Tax Evasion or Jaded Santa would be more devastating. There are three hundred and fifty million Americans, Mandy. There are thousands of Santa impersonators. By the law of large numbers, one of them should have worked. Instead, I dragged Stowe to Finland."

She was ultimately right. Wyatt gambled and lost. After the horrid interviews at the North Pole South Santa Academy, they could have scoured the country for others. They may have been the best school, but that doesn't mean they had all the best Santas. The best college hoops players in the country don't always play for the eventual national champion.

"You didn't drug her, Wyatt. I've known Stowe for a while. She wouldn't have gone along unless she wanted to. If you had more time, you might have convinced Santa to come to D.C."

"Thanks. It's a moot point now. That was my fault. Stowe is going to pay the price for it right alongside me. It's not fair that I put her in that position."

"She would disagree."

"No, she wouldn't. She made that abundantly clear before we left."

Mandy nods over Wyatt's shoulder. "Don't be so sure you're reading this right. You should ask her yourself."

Wyatt turns to see Stowe walking toward him dressed in a blue blazer, white blouse, and knee-length skirt. She has a decorative scarf around her neck that almost matches his tie. Her hair falls gracefully over her shoulders instead of being up in a bun or ponytail. Her makeup is flawless. Stowe is amazing even on her worst day. Today, she looks…breathtaking. Not that it matters. She stops beside them and stares at Wyatt.

"Can we talk?"

He presses his lips together. "Sure."

She looks at Mandy, who's wearing a devilish smirk. "In private."

"Excuse us, please."

Stowe leads him down the corridor and ducks into one of the empty committee rooms. She closes the door and nervously folds her hands in front of her. Wyatt never expressed interest in the women he works with for this reason. The awkwardness is suffocating.

"Did you see Streaker Santa?"

"Yeah. Mandy explained the situation."

"This is going to be a disaster. Guzman and Blackburn will destroy that poor man during his testimony to prove a point."

"It's too late for us to stop it now."

Stowe lowers her eyes. "Your boss told Congresswoman Pratt that you tried to take the blame for our failure."

"It's completely my fault."

"I missed the part where you tied me up and held a gun to my head."

Wyatt can't understand why Stowe is doing this. She accused him in Finland of causing their failure. Now that he's falling on his sword so she can keep her job, she's arguing with him using some serious revisionist history.

"You warned me that we were betting everything on this one Santa. You wanted to find a way to Rovaniemi after we were diverted to Iceland. I convinced you to stay in Reykjavik. We lost a lot of time. We shouldn't have gone at all."

Stowe slowly walks toward him. "We weren't going to get to Finland any faster, not with the storm and all the rebookings. As for Finland, we were looking for the perfect Santa and found him. You couldn't have known he would say no."

"I could have had backup plans. You pleaded for us to come up with one."

Stowe hangs her head. She recognizes her words. She also wasn't wrong, as it turns out. A less-than-perfect Santa is still better than none at all.

"I owe you an apology, Wyatt."

"You don't owe me anything. I owe you—"

"Yes, I do. My behavior before we left Rovaniemi was atrocious. I shouldn't have called you a distraction or blamed you for not having a Plan B. You didn't deserve it, and I'm sorry."

"No, I deserved it."

"You didn't. At all. I was angry at the situation and took it out on you. I was…."

Stowe stops speaking and shakes her head as she stares at the ground. The tears are already forming when she lifts her head and looks Wyatt in the eyes.

"It felt like we were living in a Hallmark movie. The lagoon, the cave, our trek down the ski slope, the sleigh ride…the search for Santa Claus…it was all so perfect, and I was expecting the happy ending that came along with it."

"So was I, but we didn't get one. Now come the consequences."

"I'm sure that—"

"I'm leaving D.C., Stowe."

Stowe reflexively takes a small step backward as her mouth hangs open. "What?"

"I'm resigning my position on the staff after Congress adjourns and am going back to Montana."

"Why?"

"I've come to realize that my father is right. I don't really belong here. There's nothing left for me, so I'm going home to live the life I know."

"Wyatt—"

A knock on the door interrupts her. Mandy pokes her head in, her face contorted in regret.

"I'm sorry to interrupt. The hearing is starting, and I was sent to find you before I head back to the office. You're both needed in there, ASAP."

Mandy disappears back into the corridor and closes the door. Wyatt starts to take a step up the center aisle before Stowe slides in front of him.

"They can live without us for five minutes. I *really* need to tell you something."

"Not now, Stowe. Tell me later. I'm not going anywhere until the session ends. Let's get through this first."

He moves around her, leaving her standing in the middle of the chamber. He feels bad, but a congressional hearing isn't going to wait for them to hash out their litany of problems. Whatever she has to say, it can wait. The music is about to play, and he needs to stand there behind the congressman and face it.

Chapter Sixty-Eight

REPRESENTATIVE CAMILLA GUZMAN

The press pool in the back of the committee room is huge. It's easily triple the size of the one at the beginning of the week. Camilla can't remember ever seeing this many reporters at a subcommittee hearing. She guesses that's what happens when the country learns that Santa Claus will testify. That announcement captured the media's attention and, by extension, the nation's.

The man Marcia selected is perfect. He looks the part, for sure. He's about as close a facsimile to St. Nick as Sundblom drew for his Coca-Cola advertisements. That will make what happens next so much more delicious. Getting the man who assaulted the teenager at the mall in California wouldn't be a more fitting end to these hearings.

Camilla waits for the other members of the subcommittee to get settled before she calls the meeting to order. Red lights pop up on the cameras in the back of the room. There isn't an empty chair available. Everyone is dialed in and paying rapt attention to her. It's just the way she wanted it.

"This is the last day of our scheduled hearings on the proposed legislation to ban public depictions of Santa Claus. We have heard from child psychologists, economists, historians, and marketers, and we thank them all for the insights they provided during their testimonies.

"The esteemed members of this subcommittee thought it prudent to hear from Santa Claus himself. I agreed to this because, after all, this legislation directly affects his…shall we call it notoriety? To that end, I have agreed to end this hearing with testimony from St. Nicholas himself."

A ripple of excitement travels through the room. Politics isn't always about making decisions and voting on bills. Often, it's theater. It's a show that elected leaders put on for the masses. Camilla is sitting center-stage in their latest production, which will surely be a crowd-pleaser.

"Did the gentleman from Montana and the gentlewoman from Vermont secure Santa Claus to testify?"

Camilla knows the answer. She was informed that their Santa wasn't coming. The inquiry is meant to be embarrassing. Knutson and Pratt had their fun during the hearings. Now, it's time for payback.

"As the Chair was previously informed, we were unable to bring Santa here so close to his Christmas Eve duties."

"That's unfortunate, Mr. Knutson. I think we owe it to the American people to have this discussion with him. That's why I talked him into it."

The reaction is one of surprise. Or, it is for everyone in the room except Angela Pratt and John Knutson. They have a far different response to the news.

"You mean you got an imposter to testify at these proceedings and advance your agenda!"

"Ms. Pratt, you're out of order," Camilla says, smacking the gavel down. "I am doing no such thing, and the Chair resents the implication that I am. This was *your* idea."

"The Chair knows it was our intent to—"

"Bring the actual Santa Claus before us? Is that what you would like us to believe?"

There are chuckles in the room. While everyone here might be willing to indulge in this fiction, it doesn't mean they aren't acutely aware of what Santa Claus is – a real-life man who has been turned into a fictional character.

"Well, I'm sorry, but we all know that's impossible," Camilla says, gesturing around the room. "This is the best we can do. The Chair calls to testify the jolliest of elves...Kriss Kringle."

Camilla leans back and grins. All the cameras swing in the direction of the doors. This is going to be epic. Santa will be there in all his red and white glory. He is the perfect representation and will prove why the mythology behind him must be destroyed. It almost feels like it's Christmas morning. Everyone will be in awe. Then comes the fun part.

The double doors leading into the hearing room slowly swing open. The audience has the expected reaction. Only the tables are turned this time. It's Camilla whose jaw hangs open. The man standing there is not who she expected to see.

Chapter Sixty-Nine

REPRESENTATIVE JOHN KNUTSON

This is not who John expected to see when the doors opened. He briefly saw the man Wyatt called "Streaker Santa" when he came to the Rayburn Building for the hearing. Cameras click as the man waits at the threshold. Mouths hang open as everyone in the room is entranced by the man's appearance. Instead of a fat man in the traditional red suit, this Santa is a spectacle to behold.

The man is exactly how Wyatt described his Finland Santa. His hat is longer and deeper red than the typical depiction. He's wearing a long red coat with white trim and narrow, decorative piping adorning the sleeves. Santa isn't wearing a belt, or at least one that is apparent. He has on green pants tucked into worn brown boots. It's a very Scandinavian look.

The beard and the hair are authentic enough. They are snow-white and wavy, more than curly. The beard easily reaches down to his navel. Most captivating of all is his aura. He exudes Christmas. This isn't a man dressing a part. He feels like the real deal.

Santa Claus effortlessly glides across the floor to the table in front of the committee. He takes a seat and rests his hands in front of him. He doesn't bother adjusting his microphone or pouring a glass of water. There are no nerves or obvious tics indicating stress. The man is perfectly at ease.

"That's him," Wyatt whispers into John's ear after coming up behind him.

"Who?"

"The Santa from Finland. That's him."

Guzman is at a complete loss for words. As Chair, it is her responsibility to announce the witness. Caught up in the moment, she has abdicated that responsibility. John sees an opportunity to take the reins.

"Thank you for joining us today, Santa."

"It's my distinct honor to be here, Congressman Knutson."

"This is not Santa!" Camilla finally barks.

John and Angela share a knowing look. That was an unforced error. She clearly didn't mean to say it like that. She came across as in denial of something everyone is seeing for themselves. Everyone in the room is mesmerized, and now she looks like a fool.

"I beg your pardon?"

Camilla tries to recover. "This is not the Santa meant to testify today!"

Santa closes his eyes and nods. "Yes, you arranged for Christopher to testify. I met him in the corridor before entering. He's a good man filled to the brim with knowledge and Christmas spirit. He also likes beer, football games, and, shall I say, a degree of public nudity."

The audience laughs as John leans forward in to his microphone. "Things I'm sure you were eager to point out during his testimony."

Guzman ignores the comment. "Sir, you claim you are Santa, but how are we—"

"I go by many names in many regions. Here, I am Santa Claus, St. Nick, or Kriss Kringle. In Greece, I am Agios Vasilios. In Italy, Babbo Natale, which translates to Daddy Christmas. I am Christkindl, Sinterklaas, Svyatoy Nikolay, San Nikolas, Weihnachtsmann, and Pere Noel."

"All right," Guszman says, holding up a hand. "May I just call you Santa?"

Santa graciously nods. "Of course."

John leans back. Camilla is looking for a way to impeach his testimony. This is an attempt to voir dire Santa Clause to determine his eligibility to testify. It's almost unheard of in a subcommittee session, but she's the chair. She can do as she pleases until someone objects.

"If I may, you don't look like Santa."

"Madam Chairwoman, Jesus Christ was a Jew living in the Middle East. Why is he depicted as a white man in most imagery? Can we agree that people see what they want to see and that the depictions of me can be whatever they choose?"

Heads nod in agreement around the room.

"No, Santa, I mean dressed like that."

"I'm aware I may not appear as you are accustomed to seeing me. I don't have Coca-Cola's excellent marketing team working for me."

"So, the testimony we heard…if you are familiar with it, is true?"

"I am familiar with it, and it is true. I appreciate the makeover. However, the illustrator perhaps went a little overboard on making me…more portly than I'm comfortable with."

Even the reporters and cameramen get caught up in the laughter. They are enjoying this. Not only is Santa magical and engaging, but he's also funny. Camilla is losing this battle badly.

"Tell me, Santa, how did you get the name Kriss Kringle?"

"Ah, of course. Kriss Kringle is a debased form of the German word *Christkindlein*, which translates to 'Christ child.' I'm unsure how a reference to Jesus became a name for me, but it began being used widely in 1849. Here in America, it caught on with the original version of *Miracle on 34th Street*, which featured a Santa character with that name."

John looks back at Wyatt, who is amused. What looked like it could be a complete disaster has turned into something else completely. Stowe is whispering into Angela's ear. She nods at John. The games are about to begin.

"You know your Christmas lore. I'll grant you that. It also means nothing."

"It means everything, Madam Chairwoman. We have a lot in common."

"How's that, Mr. Kringle?" she asks, a tinge of condescension in her voice.

"We only work one day a year, keep naughty lists, and hand out gifts to those we deem worthy. The big difference is that I make people happy when I work."

The people in the gallery erupt in a fit of laughter. That quote is meme-worthy and may be used on social media every holiday season. It will definitely be used when Congress isn't in session. It's that good.

Camilla looks like she just ate some week-old gas station sushi. There is no chance she can disqualify his testimony now. The people want to hear what he has to say. Any attempt to squash it will look childish and likely impact her reputation. The eyes of the nation are watching.

"Thank you for the explanation, Santa. Would you like to make an opening statement?"

Chapter Seventy

WYATT HUFFMAN

Stowe finishes her conversation and retakes her post along the back wall. She turns her head and stares at him with a look of disbelief. All he can do is shrug. Maybe she thinks he somehow arranged this behind her back. He would hope she knew better by now. He's just as bewildered at Santa's sudden arrival as she is.

They never shared the hearing details during their time in Santa's office. There was no discussion of a location or start time with the rainbow-eyed elf. They never got that far because they never needed to. Santa made his decision, and that was that. How he managed to get to Washington and find this hearing is a complete mystery.

But he's here and is sitting in front of the subcommittee. Santa doesn't look like he understands what Camilla means by an opening statement. He's a toymaker, not a lawyer or bureaucrat. Wyatt is hoping that either his boss or Angela will run interference. Santa shouldn't be forced to explain who he is or why he's important to millions of children. Fortunately, none of that is necessary.

"Point of order," Edward Bass of Ohio bellows. "This is a mockery of the political process. Is this body really about to let Santa Claus testify as if he's real?"

"He's sitting before this committee, willing to answer questions. He looks real enough to me," Angela counters.

"Sure he is," Bass sneers before turning to their witness. "What did you do, Santa? Park your sleigh next to the Smithsonian? Are the reindeer eating the grass on the National Mall following your transonic flight from the North Pole?"

"No, sir, I don't believe they are. They prefer carrots."

Another ripple of laughter spreads across the room.

"Then how did you get here, *Santa*?" Congressman Bass demands.

"Finnair Flight 1331 to Reagan National with a connection at London's Heathrow."

The ripple turns into an eruption of laughter. Even members of the subcommittee can't help but chuckle. Reporters and cameramen are beaming, likely thrilled at the prospects of this testimony. People will tune into this hearing in massive numbers when the word spreads.

"Oh, so Santa Claus carries a passport now," Bass says, undeterred. "That's good to know."

Wyatt doesn't know much about Edward Bass. He's a member of the other party but has a reputation as being a moderate. He does know that the man despises everything about Christmas and made that clear during these hearings.

"I do an astonishing amount of international travel, Congressman," Santa admits. "That coming and going became problematic in the modern age, so Canada granted me citizenship and a world-at-large passport granting me full legal autonomy to avoid dealing with border control and immigration customs."

"Is that so?"

"It is. The Canadian government even hosted an official ceremony in 2013 to ensure my generous travel benefits."

"But you said you flew in from Finland. Is that correct?"

Santa smiles. "Canada isn't the only nation that wants to call Santa Claus a citizen. The nation of Finland declared that I live within the proximity of its borders and don't require documents to prove it."

"Yes, I'm sure that's the case."

"You are still bitter with me, aren't you, Eddie?"

"The name is *Congressman* Bass."

"Apologies," Santa says, nodding in deference. "You went by Eddie in the letter you sent me when you were seven. I remember it well because you didn't ask me for toys. All you wanted for Christmas that year was for your father to tell your mother that she was pretty and that he loved her. You were frightened by their arguments and wanted me to tell you that you'd be okay."

A series of sympathetic moans echoes around the room. It's the most touching thing anyone has heard in this building in a long time. While unintentional, Santa Claus just humanized one of his biggest detractors. Everyone feels for seven-year-old Eddie right now.

The impact on Congressman Bass is equally profound. Considering the look on his face, he may have never told that story to anyone. Nobody is more stunned than he is.

"How…? How could you know that?"

"I am more than a man who lives with elves and has flying reindeer living in my barn. I am Santa Claus," he says, spreading his arms wide. "And you addressed the letter to me."

Bass stares at his hands. Even from his spot along the wall, Wyatt can see them trembling. The congressman starts to speak before stopping. He finally looks at Santa.

"My Christmas wish wasn't granted. My parents got divorced."

"I know," Santa says, a tone of remorse evident in his voice. "And you were heartbroken because of it. In a fit of anger directed at your mother, your father blatantly told you before Christmas that I didn't exist. You came to resent me because of that. In fact, you resented everything for a long time. But in the end, you succeeded in turning that pain into great strength. You became a loving husband and a wonderful father to your two daughters, Ava and Liana. Your father may never have told your mother that she was pretty and he loved her, but you tell your wife that every day. You turned out okay, Eddie. You turned out okay."

Bass leans back and swipes a tear from his eye. The room is dead silent. Everyone is looking on in awe.

"I, uh...I withdraw my objection."

Wyatt glances at Stowe, who is staring at him wide-eyed. They've both experienced this in Finland. Santa knew their names. He knew Wyatt's Christmas wish. None of this should surprise them, but it has.

Chapter Seventy-One

REPRESENTATIVE JOHN KNUTSON

Silence blankets the room. Even Guzman is stunned into silence. Politicians are naturally egotistical, and having twenty-two of them in a room can cause all kinds of fun and games. Sometimes, hearings are boring. When you add cameras and public attention, they can get decidedly animated.

Not today. At least, not yet. Everyone is processing what they just heard. This Santa Claus is a throwback to the magical figure John envisioned as a child. The people in the room must be thinking the same thing. They are under a spell when Ali Salib leans forward to break it.

"If it pleases the Chair," he says, adjusting his microphone. "I have a question to ask. Santa, what would you say to my telling you, '*As-salamu alaikum*?'"

Santa smiles and nods. "*Wa 'alaykumu as-salam.*"

Nobody expected that, least of all Representative Salib. Plenty of politicians on this subcommittee fancy themselves cultured individuals. He doubts that any of them know the proper response to that Arabic greeting.

"Are you not a Christian, Santa?"

"I am. However, should I not be appreciative that you wished me peace? Should I be offended because you and I are not of the same faith? Or, perhaps, it is better to appreciate that we can bridge our differences and still wish each other well?"

John studies Salib's face. That answer derailed his line of questioning. He undoubtedly aimed to make a religious argument, but that has been thwarted. At least, it has so far.

"What about Happy Hanukkah?"

"I believe it's entirely appropriate to wish people of the Jewish faith 'Happy Hanukkah.' I think Christians should also understand that it's not the functional equivalent of 'Merry Christmas,' at least in terms of the importance of the holiday. Hanukkah is not in the Torah. It celebrates the re-sanctifying of the ancient Temple in Jerusalem by Jewish warriors. According to legend, there was enough sanctified oil to burn for one day, but it burned for eight. That's why the holiday lasts eight days and includes candle-lightings."

John leans back. He has countless Jewish friends and associates, and he didn't even know that. No Santa plucked off the streets of Washington by Cameron or procured from a well-regarded training academy in Burlington would be expected to possess that knowledge. Yet a Santa Claus from the remote Lapland region of Finland is answering these questions without hesitation.

"All right, Santa. Besides Christmas, are there other holidays you like?"

"Easter, of course, but one of my favorites is Holi, the Hindu festival of colors. Holi marks the arrival of spring and celebrates the triumph of good over evil. Participants throw colored water and powders over one another. After everyone bathes and dons clean white clothes at its conclusion, they visit friends and relatives. It's a great holiday."

The answer delights the audience as well as John's colleagues. It's inclusive, which is always a bell ringer in modern Washington. It also sounds fun. America likes to steal the best holidays, St. Patrick's Day and Cinco de Mayo included. They should consider borrowing this one. It would be a party.

Ali runs out of steam. He looks at Aymos Blackburn, who looks eager to take the floor. Meeting decorum has gone out the window. Nobody is asking the Chair for permission anymore. So long as the questioning doesn't get out of hand or turn into a shouting match, Guzman looks content to let things play out as they are.

"Santa, is Christmas a Christian holiday?" Congressman Blackburn asks.

"Its origin was meant to celebrate the birth of Jesus Christ. The date was picked to coincide with pagan gatherings celebrating the winter solstice. But it is now embraced by many non-followers as well."

"Why is that?"

"Because Christmas may be a religious holiday, but it is viewed by many as an occasion to spread peace and joy. That desire is, and should be, universal, not restricted to just adherents of Christianity."

"You go by the name St. Nicholas. You don't believe that this secularization jeopardizes the true meaning of Christmas?"

Santa smiles. John swears he can see a twinkle in the man's eyes.

"You are a devout man of faith, Congressman. It's been that way since you were a boy. You preach the word of God to all those who will listen. I understand your perspective. You want the holiday to be a strictly Christian observance because that's the meaning you assign to it."

"Yes, that's correct."

"You must also acknowledge that traditions often break free from their roots. You have been a government member for some time, but I don't believe you have ever called for the renaming of Saturday or Wednesday because you no longer worship Saturn or Wōden, the Roman and Norse gods who gave the days their names."

"That's not the issue here, Santa."

"Isn't it? You agreed to this proposed legislation that would ban depictions of me in public, did you not?"

Blackburn nods. "I am a co-sponsor, yes."

"You believe you are representing disgruntled Christians and seeking common cause with colleagues who despise the thought of Christmas becoming little more than a shopping burden."

He nods. "I did because we both agree you damage Christmas more than promote it. I don't like the materialism associated with the holiday. I like your taking the place of Jesus Christ even less."

"Am I? Or am I honoring him?"

"Making Christmas about you instead of him is taking away. You are a false idol."

"Nobody idolizes an aging, overweight man living in one of the most isolated places on Earth. Nobody prays to Santa Claus, Congressman. I am not asked to forgive sins. If anything, I'm a myth, not an idol to be worshiped."

"Fine. If you're a myth, Santa, you're a damaging one."

The groans from behind are almost deafening. Santa has transformed, at least to the people watching the proceedings in this room, from a caricature to a real being. He isn't the fixture seen in stores or the man created by Coca-Cola to sell bottles of soda pop. He has become as real as they are.

"Myths are not lies, Aymos," Santa says, his soothing words simmering down the anger from the people gathered behind him. "The world relies on myths to convey truths that are otherwise inexpressible. My dropping presents down chimneys and delivering presents to the world's children has neither the depth nor factual reality of the story of the Nativity. But little Christian children cannot comprehend their Savior being a baby born to a virgin given as a gift to all humankind.

"Here is what children do understand — the joy and wonder of something magical happening that they can feel but not see. They understand the delight of laying out cookies for me on Christmas Eve. It's the same anticipation others in the world experience during Advent.

"They understand the joy and wonder of Christmas morning, even if they don't fully realize why. Christian parents will teach their children its meaning. For non-believers, it affirms that we are all just trying to lead good lives in a sometimes cruel and perplexing world. With Christmas comes renewed hope for peace on Earth and goodwill to all. Perhaps that is the greatest gift of the holiday."

Chapter Seventy-Two

STOWE BESSETTE

This is unbelievable. Stowe didn't want to get out of bed this morning. If it hadn't been for Mandy pounding on her door, she may not have. It was the closest thing to depression she had ever felt. And it wasn't all because Santa declined their offer.

Regrets are a powerful thing. They are also a waste of time to dwell on. The best way to avoid their nagging power is to avoid creating the circumstances that lead to them. Take the vacation of your dreams. Don't make the decision you know is wrong. Spend the time with your parents before they are gone.

She regretted her words to Wyatt before she got in the car to leave Santa Claus's Village. The anger she felt allowed her to deal with it. When that dissipated on the flight high over the Atlantic Ocean, regret took its place. She needed to talk to him, but it had to wait until this hearing was over.

It could have been torture. Streaker Santa would have been a laughingstock. They would have humiliated him for sport, destroying someone who is likely a good man with a fun side. Instead, their Santa showed up, validating Wyatt's intuition and making the feeling of regret that much stronger.

The truth is, even if he hadn't – if it had been Streaker Santa instead – she would still feel this way. The feelings for Wyatt were easily dismissed when he was next to her. It wasn't until she was alone again that she realized how much she missed him.

Stowe watches as Aymos sits motionless in his chair. Santa is waiting for a follow-up question that isn't coming. The preacher from Alabama is one of the staunchest voices on this committee. He is never at a loss for words, proving there is a first time for everything.

The congressman lowers his eyes for several seconds before training them back to Saint Nick and smiling. "Beautifully said, Santa. Thank you. I have nothing further."

He turns to Guzman and nods before leaning back in his chair.

"Madam Chairwoman, if I may have the opportunity for questions. I'd like it now," Congresswoman Wang says, straightening in her seat as she speaks in to the microphone.

"The Chair recognizes the gentlewoman from Nevada."

Felicia Wang is on the anti-Santa bandwagon. Stowe isn't quite sure why. She's a moderate insofar as partisan politics is concerned. Wang doesn't have an agenda to promote. In her limited interactions with Felicia, she found her to be a sober, attentive representative for her district.

"Santa, if I hear you right, you must think I'm a terrible parent. I don't believe in you. I have taught my young children not to believe in you."

"Who am I to judge you, Felicia? Whether you are a good parent depends on multiple factors, none of which involves believing in me. Your children are well-behaved. They are respectful. They are polite and generous to those around them. You have raised them to be all those things. You and your husband love your kids and do your best. In my opinion, you are not horrible parents. You are excellent ones."

"How can you possibly know that?"

Wang is incredulous. Welcome to the club. There is a lot of disbelief in this room. The jolly old elf sitting at a table before the subcommittee and the nation shrugs. It's the first demonstrative action he's taken since he sat down.

He smiles. "Because Santa knows."

"You are judging me, Santa. That's what you do. You keep a list. Naughty or nice…good or bad…asleep or awake. You do know, and then you punish. The good kids get presents. The naughty ones get coal. That's how it works, doesn't it?"

"It rarely happens, I assure you. Have you checked the price of coal recently? Your renewable, green energy initiatives have made it very expensive."

Laughter erupts in the room. Stowe doesn't think Santa could possibly know how effective that line is in this room. It's one of those things.

"The rest of that is true," Wang argues.

"No, it isn't. That is a part of the myth created around me. I know who is naughty and who is nice, and presents are delivered accordingly. Tell me, Felicia, have you ever heard of anyone who has actually received coal? Ask the people in this room. The real beauty of Christmas morning is that everyone gets a present. Even the naughty ones. Even the ones who do not believe in me."

"Even the poor kids?"

"During what other times of the year are there toy drives? When is charity more present? What other holiday causes people to open their hearts and help the less fortunate? Christmas is for everyone, not just the most well-off."

Representative Wang stares down at her hands. Her questions aren't antagonistic. If anything, Stowe senses that they're personal.

"I remember when I first learned you weren't real. I was eight years old. Someone at school learned the truth and told me. I yelled and screamed that it wasn't true and went home and asked my parents. They sat me down and broke the news to me.

"I was so upset. How do you reconcile that, Santa? How can you be okay knowing that all these children you claim to love will have their hearts broken?"

"My job gives me great joy, Felicia. But there is a hard part of it. All the children I meet eventually grow up. It's easy to see that passage as a positive progression. The ways of childhood must be replaced by the ways of adulthood. But viewing it that way treats children as miniature, imperfect adults. They are not. They have their own wisdom and special ways of perceiving the world.

"Eventually, their little brains develop, and they begin to ask questions about the world around them. Why would Santa come to my house and not theirs? If there is no Santa, how do my parents hide all those presents? Sooner or later, they begin to search for the truth.

"Some ask the question. Others climb into the attic in search of an unwrapped Tonka truck or doll. When they learn the truth, they are satisfied with figuring it out. That is balanced with mourning the loss of the magic and realizing they have outgrown their favorite childhood fantasy."

"Why indulge them in the fantasy of you in the first place?" Wang asks.

"Because fantasy is a normal and healthy part of child development. Think of your children, Felicia. Think about the tea parties with your daughter in her pink bedroom with the unicorn and tiger stuffed animals. Think about the living room castles you make from couch cushions with your son and the kitchen utensils used as armor and weapons."

"Wh–what about them?" The observation has shaken her. He must be spot-on again.

"Children spend much of their playtime pretending. They are constantly exposed to television and books where animals talk, people can fly, and objects magically appear out of thin air. Is a flying reindeer more fantastical than a talking mouse or a singing snowman? Unfortunately, this magical thinking decreases between the ages of seven and nine. Children grow up, and that is one of the things lost in the passage from childhood to adulthood. It's something most adults pine for."

"I don't know what you mean," Wang confesses.

"Yes, you do. Adults need magic in their lives, too. It's the source of our superstitions. It's why we have Superman, Wonder Woman, and Iron Man. It creates an audience for Stephen King and *Lord of the Rings*. Everything fantastical that we appreciate and the imagination that gave birth to it all started with belief in Santa Claus."

Felicia leans back. Stowe watches her intently. This woman invested the most emotion in her questioning and seems satisfied. This was personal, and she took Santa's answers to heart. No agenda. No preconceived notions. She nods.

"I yield to the Chair."

Chapter Seventy-Three

REPRESENTATIVE CAMILLA GUZMAN

Camilla has heard enough. This guy is killing them. She thought she would be well-prepared for anyone Knutson and Pratt managed to dig up. Even though they had apparently failed, she brought her talking points to the hearing, just in case. Her allies did the same. None of them are landing. Not one.

It's time to shift gears. The cameras are rolling, and the world is paying attention. Camilla needs to discredit this Santa and do it now.

"Parents buy gifts, Santa! We all know it. It's indisputable. Let's not pretend you circumnavigate the globe in a sleigh with flying reindeer. It's a proven fact that it's impossible."

Santa smiles and laughs. "Yes, I read that breakdown once over a couple of cups of cocoa. Would you allow me to address it?"

Camilla gestures at Santa to go ahead. This ought to be good.

"It's true that no known species of reindeer can fly. However, this doesn't completely rule out flying reindeer, which perhaps only I have ever seen. Now, I have three hundred and seventy-eight million children to deliver gifts to on Christmas Eve. Assuming an average of three and a half children per household, a high number given modern demographics, that's 91.8 million homes. Trust me, there's at least one good child in each.

"Considering time zones and east-west travel, I have thirty-one hours to complete the task. This works out to 822.6 visits per second. This is to say that for each household with good children, I have only a thousandth of a second to park, hop out of my sleigh, shimmy down the chimney, fill the stockings, distribute presents under the tree, drink milk, eat cookies, get back up the chimney and into the sleigh to move on to the next house.

"Assuming that these 91.8 million stops are evenly distributed around the Earth, which they aren't, it's a total trip of seventy-five and a half million miles. My sleigh must travel at six hundred and fifty miles per second to cover that distance. That's three thousand times the speed of sound. That's fast, considering a reindeer can run, tops, fifteen miles per hour."

Laughter erupts in the room. Camilla is about to bang her gavel but refrains for appearance's sake. The room quiets down soon enough. Santa has more to say.

"And then there is the payload. If every child gets one medium-sized LEGO set, which is a joke for most households, my sleigh will carry 321,300 tons. That would require over two hundred and fourteen thousand reindeer to pull, and the Dutch don't leave me *that* many carrots.

"This increases the payload to over 353,430 tons needing to travel at Mach three thousand," Santa concludes after another round of laughter dies down. "The heat generated would make poor Rudolph and her friends absorb 14.3 quintillion joules of energy per second. Each. They would burst into flame instantaneously while subjecting me to centrifugal forces 17,500 times greater than gravity and pinning me to the back of my sled with over four million pounds of force. Madam Chairwoman, if I delivered gifts the way you think I do, it's safe to say I wouldn't be sitting here talking to you right now."

The observers in the committee room go crazy. The laughter and applause are almost deafening. Santa's testimony is going to become a thing of legend in this town. Camilla sees John turn back to his staffer, who's smiling like he just hit the MegaMillions jackpot. He nods his approval. There is no doubt he succeeded in finding the perfect Santa. Camilla needs to find a way to undo that.

"So, you admit you don't exist?"

"What I explained is based on classical physics. I *am* Santa Claus. You need to consider quantum phenomena in my case. You may know variables such as velocity and mass, but my location at any given moment on Christmas Eve is highly imprecise. In other words, I am 'smeared out' over the Earth's surface, similar to how an electron is 'smeared out' within a certain distance from an atom's nucleus. Thus, I can literally be everywhere at any given moment."

"Do you really expect us to believe that, Santa?" Camilla challenges.

"You can look it up. Your scientists call it Heisenberg's uncertainty principle. I call it Christmas magic."

That was all these people needed to hear. Applause erupts into a standing ovation. They have been won over.

"Parents buy gifts, Santa!"

"And who compels them to do so? Are the presents they purchase for their children marked with their names or mine? Madam Chairwoman, if you deny my existence, are you open to the possibility that the true miracle of Santa Claus is that my spirit lives in so many people?"

Chapter Seventy-Four

WYATT HUFFMAN

While the subcommittee meets, it's customary for a staff member to remain close to the member in case they need something. Most are along the front wall unless the meeting is televised, in which case they hang off to the side out of frame. Wyatt missed the first three days of the hearing because he was searching for Santa. Now, he has a front-row seat to this amazing moment and is in complete awe of what he's seeing.

He knew this Santa was special. When he and Stowe first met him, they were captivated. They knew he would be great at the hearing. Neither of them thought he would be *this* great.

Guzman is learning that the hard way. She's getting noticeably frustrated in front of a national audience. If it's publicity the congresswoman wanted, she's getting it. Only Wyatt doesn't think this is the kind she was hoping for.

"That's not at issue here!" Guzman argues.

"No, it isn't," Santa says calmly. "This started when you watched a mall Santa attack a teenager in a shopping mall in front of children. It affected you deeply."

"Yes, but that only brought the deeper problem into focus – Christmas has become a commercialized mess instead of a religious celebration, and you are to blame."

"I can see why you would draw that conclusion."

Wyatt closes his eyes as people in the room grumble. Did Santa just admit he's part of the problem? That's not what anyone wanted to hear.

"Your detractors say you are doing this for publicity…that your Christmas wish was to raise your profile by dragging me through the mud," Santa continues. "They want others to believe these hearings are nothing more than a stunt."

"It's not true!"

"No, it isn't."

The audience seems to disagree. They begin grumbling, earning a warning glare from Guzman. Wyatt is with them on this one. He one hundred percent believes that's the reason she wanted these hearings.

"You were already bothered walking around the shopping mall that day," Santa continues, undeterred. "Camilla, you once loved Christmas. You had fond memories of falling snow during trips to the California mountains, where you would make snow angels with your children. You watched Christmas movies, sipped hot cocoa, and basked in the politeness and generosity that the holiday ushered in. You wanted to give them the same experiences you had as a child."

"Yes," Camilla croaks, feeling every pair of eyes in the room trained on her, awaiting confirmation. "How…how could you know that?"

"Christmas was your favorite time of the year. Then, you watched as others molded this special holiday into something for personal gain. It was commercialized for corporate profit. The celebration of Christ's birth was morphed into a cultural event. Stress replaced generosity. The pressure of buying gifts sucked the joy out of the season. Families lost their holiday cheer, making gatherings painful experiences, not joyous ones. The season no longer felt like the Christmas celebrations of the past. It became less exciting and more ordinary. The magic was gone."

Guzman looks like she's seen a ghost. Wyatt doesn't know how Santa knows what he does. But he's on target. She nervously clasps her hands as she struggles to find her words.

"Yes, Santa, that is exactly true."

"Very few of us have true control over the commercialization of Christmas. But you do, as a government representative. You decided it was time for a change. No longer were you willing to allow the hustle and bustle to ruin people's sanity. No longer did you want people to 'do Christmas' like it was something to be survived. You wanted a national change of perspective. You have begun that journey by seeking to remove me."

"Correct."

"My dearest Camilla, it wasn't the holiday and what it has become that was making you miserable. It was you. Your own mood was to blame."

Santa's voice is even and measured. It wasn't an accusation. At least, Wyatt didn't think it sounded like one. It was more a statement of fact from someone who knows. Not that he could. He wasn't there. But he doesn't come across as a man taking a shot in the dark. His words have authority behind them. It's almost creepy.

"No, Santa, that isn't true."

"It is. When I was approached in my office by Wyatt Huffman and Stowe Bessette with an offer to travel here, I initially declined. I explained to them that people have free will and that it is not in my power as Santa Claus to force them to celebrate the holiday in a certain way.

"That has not changed. The truth is that peace is available for everyone who wants it right now. If you want to experience the holiday's joy, peace, and good cheer, all that's required is for them to simply be present in the moment. When you seize the opportunity to be still, your heart rests, and your soul finds peace."

"There is too much to do over the holidays for that, Santa."

"That is a choice, Camilla, not an obligation. And that is my point. Obtaining peace doesn't require more work. It requires less. If others choose to distance Christmas from its religious origins, that is their choice. If others believe that expensive gifts are the meaning of the holiday, nothing stops them from walking that path. Those who choose to embrace the moment will realize a simple truth: Christmas is a time to celebrate and appreciate love."

Wyatt breaks his gaze on Santa to look around the committee chamber. Everyone is entranced. You could hear a pin drop in the room. There is no fidgeting, nor are there side conversations analyzing Santa's conclusion. People are doing the one thing sorely missing from modern society: They are listening.

"I have watched throughout the years as Christmas flourished from a celebration of Christ's birth to a time for everyone to spend with family, friends, and loved ones. A moment for the world to pause and be grateful for what we have and are still yet to receive. However, that must come from our hearts, not long-standing traditional practices, age, or circumstances.

"Generosity, kindness, and charity toward others cannot be imposed, nor can it be fostered by forcibly removing symbols some feel detracts from them. Christmas spirit is within us. Camilla, you were a strong and passionate girl who became an equally strong and passionate woman. You are not Grinch Guzman but a lover of the season with an intense Christmas spirit. Ask yourself if this is the best way to use it. You don't need government rules to be an instrument of powerful change. Show these people the Christmas spirit within you and inspire others, as I seek to. You have that power. We all do."

The trance slowly releases its grasp on the room. One person begins to applaud, and then another. The staccato of clapping hands reaches a crescendo as people rise from their chairs for a thunderous ovation.

Wyatt enthusiastically claps with them, pondering what Santa has done. Whether by accident or design, he provided Camilla Guzman an off-ramp. He may have changed her heart in this hearing, but not the political reality of the fallout. The media will decimate her, painting her in the most unflattering light.

Now that Santa has destroyed the Grinch Guzman narrative by highlighting the real emotion and humanity behind her actions, she will be viewed in the eyes of the public as misguided instead of despicable. He's okay with that. Santa has filled him with Christmas spirit, too.

Wyatt glances over at Stowe, who is watching him from the other side of the room. She looks…sorrowful. Maybe it's regret over the way she left things. Maybe it's something else completely. One thing has proven to be a certainty: The trip to Finland was worth every ounce of the effort.

Chapter Seventy-Five

REPRESENTATIVE JOHN KNUTSON

Whatever plan Camilla had for this hearing has completely gone to hell. The order of representatives asking questions has been completely altered. John is used to going second. Instead, he seems to have moved down whatever list Guzman has generated since Santa arrived.

"Madam Chairwoman, if I may," John says as the applause dies down and everyone retakes their seats.

Guzman nods. "The chair recognizes the gentleman from Montana for five minutes."

John isn't sure he can ask anything Santa hasn't already answered. Maybe the time for questions is over. It's time to put a bow on this.

"We have heard testimony all week on this legislation. People want you to believe that telling children about Santa betrays their trust. In reality, there is no real evidence to support that. Are any of you resentful of your parents because they lied about Santa? Probably not.

"But even so, it's a parental decision, not a governmental one. Santa may or may not be a real figure as we interpret him, with flying reindeer and a bottomless sack of toys. But he is undeniably part of the fabric of our global culture. And why not? What is the harm in people across the globe telling children about Santa and spreading the joy he exudes?

"I happen to agree that Christmas has become too commercialized. I concur with the sentiment that many have forgotten how to embrace the holiday spirit. But does banning depictions of Santa in public places do anything to correct that? Isn't it up to each and every one of us to embrace the message Santa Claus symbolizes?

"He is generous and full of joy and peace. We have witnessed that here today. These are the very traits every parent wants to instill in their children. What does it say that we want to ban a figure who brings the best out of us? Christmas may be a Christian holiday, but it represents a time of giving, family, and happiness that we can all embrace. Santa Claus stands for all of those things. He is the representation of the Christmas spirit. Thank you, Santa, for reminding us all what the holidays are really about."

It starts with one person sitting in the back. Her clapping quickly spreads. Ten seconds later, the entire chamber is applauding.

"Madam Chairwoman," Angela announces, speaking over the applause. "I move to vote on H.R. 6204 so we can enjoy the rest of this wonderful holiday with our staff before going home to our families."

"Seconded," John says.

Guzman doesn't have to accept the motion. There are other members of the subcommittee entitled to ask questions. Politicians get ornery when they don't get face time in front of the cameras. In this instance, none of them object. There is nothing more that needs to be said.

"By voice vote, those in favor?"

"Aye," a chorus of voices sings out.

"Opposed?"

Not a sound is made.

"Santa, thank you for taking the time to join us today. You are excused as a witness. We will move on to—"

"Point of order, Madam Chairwoman," Angela interrupts. "Santa journeyed a long way to testify before us today. And, as you stated at the beginning of today's hearing, the proposed legislation affects him more than anyone else in this room. Perhaps he would like to remain for the vote."

"I don't think that's appropriate," Guzman says, shaking her head.

Angela gestures toward the cameras. "I wonder if America would agree with you."

She glances at John, who nods. The comment was perfect in that it serves two purposes. First, it reminds Guzman that the country is watching. Second, it prompts everyone at home and at work to answer the question for themselves. While Americans never agree unanimously on anything, John is willing to bet that the vast majority think having Santa present for the vote is perfectly appropriate. Guzman probably realizes that, too.

"Very well. In the matter of H.R. 6204, we will move to—"

"Point of parliamentary procedure," John barks. "Would the Chair please announce the bill's full name and not just the reference number for the record?"

Guzman wanted to play games at the beginning of this hearing. She wanted to embarrass John and Angela. Now it's payback time. His question doubles as a slight because he knows how this vote will go. He wanted her to utter the name of her legislation in front of the man who enchanted everyone in this room.

The chairwoman sighs. "In the matter of H.R. 6204, legislation to ban public depictions of Santa Claus, should the bill be advanced from this subcommittee to the full Commerce and Energy committee for its consideration. By a show of hands, those in favor?"

Not a single hand is raised.

"All those opposed?"

Twenty-two representatives sit on the subcommittee, split almost equally down party lines. Most votes break that way, plus or minus a vote or two. This was never a partisan issue. It was about who still believed in the power of Christmas and who didn't.

Minds have been changed. Every single hand reaches for the sky. Even Aymos Blackburn votes against the measure.

"There are no abstentions. The bill will not be referred to the committee and is defeated."

John leans back. The eruption in the audience is breathtaking. It reminds him of the end of *Scent of a Woman* after Charlie, played by Chris O'Donnell, is excused from any responsibility to sell out his classmates. All he needed was a well-timed "Hooah" from Al Pacino and music dubbed over it to complete the image.

People are standing and shouting their approval as they clap wildly. Even the reporters and cameramen in the back have joined in. This scene will play on every television in America for the next twenty-four hours. It will pass with the news cycle, but it is one of those moments that will likely see plenty of replays.

Guzman shouts over the din, seeking permission to adjourn the subcommittee, not that anyone can hear. The subcommittee members closest to her raise their hands, and the gavel comes down. John can finally relax. It's finally over.

Chapter Seventy-Six

REPRESENTATIVE CAMILLA GUZMAN

There is no reason to stick around. Aymos has already disappeared from the committee room. Camilla can't bear to face the media and decides to hightail it back to the office, where she can collect her thoughts and figure out how to spin this disaster. She was encouraged at the prospect of the Santa who was meant to testify, and she learned the hard way why Knutson and Pratt sent their staffers to Finland.

Camilla elects to take the short tunnel that connects the two buildings. She didn't want to be ambushed outside while walking to the Cannon Building. The sprawling pedestrian tunnel system constructed under Capitol Hill was designed because of Washington's weather. Security and privacy concerns of staffers and members of Congress traversing the office buildings, Library of Congress, and Capitol were secondary. It is foremost in her mind as she needs to stay out of sight of protestors and the media.

Her office resembles a morgue when she enters. When the day began, she expected enthusiastic fanfare once the hearings concluded. It was going to be a major victory they could all celebrate before breaking for Christmas. Instead, the staff is dead quiet. Marcia is waiting near the door with a morose look on her face.

"This can't be good."

Marcia nods behind her. "Ryan Hoskins and Harlan McCormack are waiting in your outer office."

Camilla nods and removes her coat before handing it to her chief of staff. The party leadership was likely already giving her an earful. Camilla isn't going to continue the torture by making her sit in on this meeting.

"Okay. Thank you. I'll take it from here."

Camilla takes a deep breath before walking into her outer office. She knows what awaits. It's like walking into the Colosseum with a pair of lions waiting to eat you.

"Mr. Speaker, Mr. Leader, what a wonderful surprise. Please come in."

The men don't speak as they enter her office. She shuts the door behind them. Congressional staffers are nosy. It comes with the job description. Camilla doesn't need them overhearing what is about to ensue. She only hopes the two boisterous men keep their voices down.

"What brings you over to Cannon?"

"We wanted to stop by and congratulate you on the outstanding job you did, Grinch Guzman. Not only did your bill fail, but you've angered the entire country. You sealed your fate for re-election and dragged the party down with you."

"Is that what I did?" Camilla asks, cocking her head.

"Which part?"

She shrugs. "Any of it."

"I don't think you realize the damage you did."

Camilla points at the television. The media are having a field day covering it. The signs are gone. Now, it has turned into a massive Christmas block party. There are people caroling, cups of cocoa getting passed around, and even an elves versus Santas dance-off. She's willing to bet all the eggnog is properly spiked. The people are having fun. It may be the most festive protest in American history. Better yet, more people are coming to join the celebration. She should make this an annual event. Food for thought for next year.

"Yeah, the people look traumatized."

"That's not the point!" the majority leader barks. "They are celebrating your *failure.*"

"No, Harlan, it's exactly the point. That crowd doesn't care about right versus left. I guarantee healthy percentages of people from both parties are having a good time down there. For the first time in a long time, we found an issue that isn't dividing us along party lines. People want to celebrate the holiday without caring who their friends or family members are voting for in the next election. They should enjoy their time together, not demonize each other over ideological viewpoints."

"We want them focused on that," Hoskins argues.

"Then maybe *you* are part of the problem, Mr. Speaker. Maybe you're the real Grinch in this story. You and everyone else who wants to divide us, even at Christmas."

"Elections matter."

"Yes, they do, Mr. Speaker. But so does Christmas. If we fray all the ties that bind us together, what's left to govern? There will be plenty of time to drag each other through the mud before the next election. Why can't we take this time to celebrate as Americans?"

"So that's your spin?" Harlan asks, crossing his arms. "You think people will believe you did this as a stunt to heal the partisan divide at Christmas?"

Santa had a profound impact in the committee room. It was clearly felt outside it. Hatred is a plague. But joy can be equally contagious.

"Right now, I don't care what they believe. This is what matters."

Hoskins looks unimpressed by the images on the screen. Harlan won't even look at them. These two men are set in their ways. There is nothing she can say that will change their minds.

"You should have accepted our committee seat offer, Camilla."

"I know you think that matters, Harlan. It doesn't. I started this journey because I watched a mall Santa accost a teenager in front of horrified children. At that moment,

I thought we had lost all our Christmas spirit. That there was no point in celebrating the holiday if all we care about is the material side of it.

"But I was wrong. The Christmas spirit is alive and well. It was just buried under the weight of all the crap we shovel. It took these hearings and a very special visit from Santa for us all to realize what the holiday season *should* mean. You can call that spin if you'd like, Harlan. I call it a Christmas miracle. And if that's the legacy I leave here, it will be my proudest accomplishment."

There's nothing more for them to say. Camilla found her answer to the criticism coming her way. Some people will believe it. Her detractors won't. What that means come next November is anyone's guess, but that's a problem to be addressed in the new year.

"We'll talk more after the holidays," the speaker mumbles as he walks out the door.

"Gentlemen?" They stop and turn to see Camilla smile as she reaches her office threshold. "Have a very Merry Christmas."

Chapter Seventy-Seven

STOWE BESSETTE

Most of the subcommittee bolted right after the hearing adjourned. Guzman and Blackburn are nowhere to be found. Some members stuck around to explain to the media how they are champions of Christmas. The two people most responsible for the day's events aren't taking a victory lap for the reporters in the back of the room. Wyatt's boss is talking to his party's leadership. Angela Pratt is chatting with a colleague.

"How the hell did you do that?" Mandy says, arriving at Stowe's side completely winded.

"Did you run here?"

"Uh…yeah…pretty much…I need to get more exercise. How, Stowe?"

She shrugs. "I wish I knew. I thought maybe Wyatt did something behind my back, but he was as surprised as I was when Santa walked through that door."

"Well, it's blowing up everywhere. Social media is going crazy. Whole towns and neighborhoods are getting together to celebrate. You should see the party outside the Capitol. It's amazing. We should check it out."

"Maybe later."

"That Santa…he knew so much. How?"

Stowe shrugs. "Christmas magic."

Mandy frowns, but what can she say? She can't even explain it herself. Nobody can.

"What about the magic between you and Wyatt?"

"I…don't know."

"There's still time for one Christmas wish," Mandy says, in full cheerleader mode. She's still shipping the two of them.

"I already cashed that in. I don't think Santa grants multiples."

She royally screwed up in Finland. Wyatt wasn't to blame for Santa initially declining to testify. He did everything he could to succeed in their assignment, including finding *that* Santa. Nobody else could have pulled that off. She was frustrated at their failure and scared about where their relationship was heading. Santa's initial refusal offered her a convenient escape route, and she took it. It's the worst mistake she's ever made. No number of Christmas wishes will undo that.

"You never know. You should ask him," Mandy says, nodding behind Stowe.

"Miss Bessette, would you be so kind as to show me the way out of the building?"

"Of course, Santa. It would be my honor. Thank you for coming. It means a lot."

Santa signals Wyatt, who excuses himself and rushes over. Cameras snap as they walk up the center aisle. The media shout questions, but Santa is completely oblivious to them.

"You know, I almost didn't come here for this."

"What changed your mind, Santa?" Wyatt asks.

"The two of you. I haven't met two people more deserving of a Christmas wish in a long time. You have both always been on the nice list."

"That's good to know."

"Well, Wyatt, you did cut it close once or twice. There was that one time in middle school when you replaced your sister's face cream with white glue. That was very naughty."

Wyatt stops walking as Stowe starts laughing. "How could you possibly know about that?"

Santa smirks as they navigate the corridors and exit the building. He stops and looks at the overcast sky. He takes a deep breath of early December air.

"Snow is coming. That will add more merriment to the festivities."

"Not likely," Stowe says, shaking her head. "It rarely snows this early in Washington. It'll be rain."

"Be optimistic, Stowe. That is what you need to work on. Believe in yourself…and others."

Stowe looks at Wyatt. That has been her problem since she walked in on Bobby and the tramp he was with. She lost belief in herself and her faith in men. Wyatt began to restore it, but fear is a powerful emotion.

"It's time for me to go. I have many more children to greet back home."

"You know, Santa, I half expected to find a sleigh with nine reindeer parked out here."

He waves a dismissive hand. "Countries don't like it when I violate their airspace outside of Christmas Eve. Mrs. Claus worries enough about my getting shot down in a misunderstanding."

"Any last words of advice?" Wyatt asks.

"The people who love you the most are often the hardest on you, Wyatt. Talk to your father. He needs to hear from you."

Wyatt is speechless.

"And, Stowe, my dear, you were named after a grand mountain, and your heart is the same size. It's not cold and hard like the granite earth but radiates compassion and love. You shouldn't be so frightened to let others in to share its warmth."

"I wish it were that simple, Santa."

"Perhaps you overcomplicate the simple things."

Stowe lowers her head. "It's the world we live in."

Santa reaches with his gloved hand and raises her chin. He looks her in the eyes. His own are twinkling. She would swear to it under oath.

"Is it, Stowe? Or is it the excuse you use when you're too frightened to try? The real magic of Christmas is finding joy with family and friends...and each other. Your first kiss may have been under the mistletoe, but your next two weren't. The only excuse you have to not be with each other is the one you conjure in your head."

Santa touches his nose. Stowe looks at Wyatt, who returns her gaze. For a moment, they are lost in each other. There are no media or congressional staffers around them. Santa Claus isn't standing next to them. It's Blue Lagoon, the lava cave, the ski slope, the Northern Lights...it's the perfect moment.

Chapter Seventy-Eight

WYATT HUFFMAN

Wyatt stares at Stowe. His feelings are undeniable. He was crushed in Finland when she lashed out at him. They had come so far, and he didn't want it to end that way. He never wanted it to end at all. Then something dawns on him.

"You know, Santa, we never told you we kissed——"

He cuts the sentence short when he realizes that Santa is no longer standing beside him. He was so caught up gazing at Stowe that he never noticed him leave. He searches up and down the sidewalk. There's one problem – Santa is nowhere to be found. He couldn't have gone that far in ten seconds.

"Where'd he go?"

Stowe is equally confused. "And I didn't think this day could get any weirder."

Cameron Alcott walks out the door and approaches them as they begin to laugh. What else can they do? Knutson's chief of staff isn't sure what they could possibly find this funny, and Wyatt doesn't feel the need to let him in on the joke.

"There you two are. Where's Santa?"

"Uh, I think he's heading back to the North Pole," Wyatt says, cocking a thumb over his shoulder to the north.

"No, seriously."

Stowe smiles. "Seriously."

"All right, whatever. I don't know how the two of you pulled this off, but it was amazing work. Congressman Knutson and Congresswoman Pratt want to meet you both in her office immediately."

"Is there something wrong?"

Cam gives her a confused look. "Wrong? Were you hiding under a rock during that testimony? Everything is exactly right! Your bosses are over the moon about what happened. It's just…well, there's a small inconsistency."

"A small inconsistency? Speak plainly, Cam. What's the issue this time?"

"We did some digging at the start of the testimony. I thought some fact-checking would be appropriate. Santa said he was on Finnair Flight 1331 from Helsinki to Reagan National via Heathrow."

"Yeah, so?"

"The flight exists, but no jolly fat men were on it."

Stowe looks at Wyatt. "Maybe he was mistaken about——"

"He wasn't on *any* flight from Helsinki, Miss Bessette. And there's no record of him coming through passport control. Let's be honest – he's the kind of guy who draws attention. Couple that with some of the things he knew, and…."

Wyatt places a hand on his boss's shoulder. "Cam, are you admitting to us that you believe in Santa Claus?"

"Don't be preposterous, Wyatt! I'm not saying that at all. But the media are gonna go crazy when they find out. Your Santa was almost *too* real. People on social media are already going nuts over this. There's a conspiracy percolating that Santa is an alien. We need to stay ahead of the questions…after we enjoy a celebratory cup or two of eggnog."

"We'll be up in a few minutes," Wyatt says, getting a nod from Stowe.

"I'll let them know. I hope you two are prepared for what comes next."

"What do you mean?" she asks.

"Are you kidding? You will both be household names on Capitol Hill after this…maybe even in the country. You may have single-handedly rekindled Christmas magic. Everybody is going to want to hear your story."

Cam moves off, leaving the two of them outside the building. They're going to get grilled about meeting Santa. John and Angela are going to want to hear every detail. Depositions will take less time and energy.

"I don't—"

"You didn't—"

They speak at the same time and let out matching nervous laughs.

"Go ahead," Stowe offers.

"No, please, ladies first."

"All right. Here it goes. You were completely wrong."

Wyatt frowns. "About what? There are usually so many things."

"In the committee room before the hearing. You said there wasn't going to be a happy ending."

"Okay, I'll admit," Wyatt says, nodding, "I didn't think Santa would show up."

Stowe moves closer to him. "Huffman, for such an intelligent man, you're completely dense. That's not the happy ending I'm talking about."

She grabs his jacket, balls the material into her fists, and pulls herself up to kiss him. It's a risk. Stowe knows she hurt him and wouldn't blame Wyatt for pushing her away. Only he doesn't. Their lips meet, and she feels the same sensation she felt during their previous kisses. The world melts away. The kiss is slow and soft…and perfect.

They look into each other's eyes when their lips finally part. A wet blob lands on Stowe's cheek. Another lands on Wyatt's nose. They touch them and look up as snowflakes begin to fall from the heavens. Santa was right, as usual.

"*Now* we have our Hallmark movie."

"And I got my Christmas wish," Stowe adds.

"Me too."

The pair holds hands as they walk back to the Longworth Building from the Rayburn Building. Big snowflakes whirl around them. It's not heavy snow – it's more like walking through a snow globe. One last bit of Christmas magic.

"Stowe, there's just one thing we need to agree on before this goes any further. I know your family likes naming children after mountains, but if this works out and we somehow end up married, we aren't naming our daughter Ounasvaara."

Stowe giggles. He still can't pronounce the name of that ski slope in Lapland.

"Agreed," she says with a smile. "We'll save that name for our son."

A Note from the Author

I love Christmas. Sure, as a child, it was because of the presents. But it was also because it was different. The decorations would go up, and there was a palpable excitement in the air. It distinguished itself from other times of the year. It still does.

Autumn is another of my favorites for largely the same reasons. The leaves turn colors, there is a crispness to the air, and different flavors return. Yes, I actually like pumpkin spice.

But it still doesn't compare to Christmas. Like many people, I think that our Christmas spirit is waning. Too many people look at the holidays as a burden. There is a lot of stress, and that's part of what I wanted to address within this novel. I think Christmas should be special. It should be joyous. When developing the idea for this book, I started by uncovering what could suck the remaining joy from the holiday. The answer was easy – the United States Congress.

I wrote this despite strongly believing that Christmas and politics don't mix. So, I decided to mix them to see what happens. I didn't want this to be about political processes like the Michael Bennit Series. I wanted to use the government as the story's antagonist, but it couldn't be the entire story. It needed a human element. Enter the Hallmark Christmas movie.

Okay, I will publicly admit that I love them. There, I said it. During the holidays, you will find television tuned into one of two programs: football or Christmas movies. Not just the classics but the two-hour made-for-television variety on stations like Hallmark.

Yes, the plots are simple, and every movie follows a similar template, leading to a happy ending. I don't watch them expecting twists and turns. They help put me in the holiday spirit. And it's nice having them on as I write because I don't need to pay that much attention to them to follow the story.

That's the genesis of Stowe and Wyatt. If their budding relationship feels a little Hallmarky, that's why. It's intentional. I have had some romance in my novels but never truly developed one like I did here. I wanted to show how two people who didn't like each other could work together and become close. It would take more than sitting in a conference room for eight hours a day to do it. Not to mention how boring it would be to read. Enter travel and the search for Santa.

Iceland is a great country with fantastic people. I have been there multiple times, twice for New Year's Eve. If you like fireworks, that's an experience you shouldn't miss. I have soaked in the Blue Lagoon and gone spelunking in a lava tube, although not the one featured in this story. It is one of my favorite islands, and if you ever get the opportunity to visit, I strongly suggest going.

I have also been to Finland. My wife and I went there in early December one year because nothing screams "vacation" like going to the Arctic almost at the onset of winter. I actually didn't find the temperatures dissimilar to what I experience every year in New England. I'll take cold over hot and humid any day.

The trip was amazing. It was inspirational and one of the reasons I began writing this novel. I have pictures straddling the line in the main square at Santa Claus Village in Rovaniemi. My wife and I visited Santa in his office there. We did a reindeer sleigh ride, which was as magical as I described in that chapter. We also went for a dogsled ride through the forest, but that didn't make the cut for this book. Maybe the next one.

Our trip to Finland was the ultimate Christmas experience, even as adults. I can imagine what that would feel like as a child; plenty were there when we visited. I look forward to going back someday.

So, is banning public depictions of Santa Claus constitutional? I have no idea. Considering some of the laws debated in the marbled halls of Congress, it wouldn't surprise me to see them try. The federal government likes its regulations and restrictions.

The effort needed a face, and that's where Camilla Guzman and Aymos Blackburn come in. Was she a bad person? Was she only after publicity, or was she serious about banning depictions of Santa Claus? Do you believe her at the end when she said she wanted only to bring people together, or was that spin? You won't get answers from me. I'll leave that to you as the reader to decide.

This book isn't meant to be partisan. You won't find the word Republican, Democrat, liberal, or conservative in this novel. Readers may be able to glean which party each member of Congress belongs to, but that is not necessary. Not everything needs to be measured against the partisan divide. I don't want this book to be, either, so those omissions were deliberate.

On a final note, I'll answer the obvious question: Is there a sequel planned? Yes. In fact, this is shaping into a trilogy, so the story of Wyatt and Stowe will continue. The next novel touches upon their political differences, which is a somewhat personal topic. My wife and I are on different sides of the political aisle. It can absolutely work, but there has to be a foundation of mutual respect. Will it work for Wyatt and Stowe? You'll have to see in the next book, *Delivering Santa*.

Acknowledgments

Whether you celebrate Christmas as the birth of Christ or take a more secular view of the holiday, the season is meant to be spent with friends and family. My first thanks go to you for taking time out of spending time with them to spend it with me. I sincerely hope this novel brought you some holiday cheer. I wish each and every one of you peace and joy this season.

Anyone who has read my novels knows I like to change where my wife appears in the acknowledgments to keep her guessing. I moved her up with my wonderful readers in keeping with the holiday spirit. Michele, you are my rock and my greatest cheerleader. Merry Christmas, honey.

Thank you to all those who support me and follow my exploits on social media. I like to share my travels and keep it light and fun there. I hope everyone has a wonderful holiday season!

Family is important to me. Thank you to my mother, Nancy, for all her support. Merry Christmas to Krissy, Ken, Gibson, Justin, Lauren, their kids, Maureen, Jess, Carl and the entire Hoyt family, and all my cousins and extended family members. Warm holiday wishes also go to the Guidaboni family – Mary Ellen, Jay, Michelle, John, Britney, and Gabriel. Merry Christmas to Carol and Norm up in Cape Cod – I look forward to visiting you again soon!

Closer to home, I always look forward to holiday celebrations with Sandra, Jen, Jill, Simon, Logan, and Tyler. It will be full of laughs if it's anything like last year.

We are the company we keep, and I have some fantastic friends. Bill, Chris, Tony, Alex, Jenn, Steve, Amy, Billy, Meg, Aimee, the other Chris, Jess, Erienne, the Mash family…all my wishes for a fantastic holiday and many more to come.

The first novels in a series are fun to design because they open up the options for the layout. Banning Santa is no different. Dave at JD&J Design did another fantastic job of taking my vision and turning it into a reality. This isn't a political thriller, at least like many of my other novels. It includes romance and holiday elements, and we tried to capture that on the cover. I think he did an amazing job, as usual.

Mike Waitz of Sticks and Stones Editing has now edited twelve of my sixteen novels, including the re-release of the America, Inc. Saga. Writers and editors are often like cats and dogs – sometimes they get along famously, and other times they want to kill each other. Fortunately, after working with a series of editors who weren't the right fit, I finally found an excellent one. Best wishes to you and your family this holiday, Mike.

Merry Christmas, everyone!

THE CHRISTMAS MAGIC CONTINUES. . .

A dying child makes a Christmas wish that only Stowe and Wyatt can help fulfill. With the help of the president of the United States, they find themselves traveling the world in a race against time to deliver a Christmas miracle.

Delivering Santa

2024

About the Author

Mikael Carlson is the award-winning author of *The iCandidate* and the Michael Bennit Series of political dramas. He also wrote the Tierra Campos Series, Watchtower Thrillers, and the dystopian America, Inc. Saga. This is his fifth series, and *Banning Santa* is his sixteenth novel.

A retired veteran of the Rhode Island Army National Guard and United States Army, he deployed twice to support military operations during the Global War on Terror. Mikael has served in the field artillery, infantry, and in support of special operations units during his active-duty career at Fort Bragg and in the Army National Guard.

A proud U.S. Army paratrooper, he conducted over fifty airborne operations following the completion of jump school at Fort Benning in 1998 and trained with the militaries of countless foreign nations. He never jumped out of Santa's sleigh, though. That aircraft would have been a great addition to his jump log.

Academically, Mikael earned a Master of Arts in American History and graduated with a B.S. in International Business from Marist College in 1996.

He was raised in New Milford, Connecticut, lives near Danbury, and always tries to stay on the nice list.

Manufactured by Amazon.ca
Acheson, AB

14290357R00178